THE CARSWELL
COVENANT

THE CARSWELL COVENANT

Steve Fisher

ISBN: 9781533136497
ISBN 10: 1533136491
Library of Congress Control Number: 2016908302
CreateSpace Independent Publishing Platform
North Charleston, South Carolina

This is dedicated to my brother, the Reverend Doctor Glenn J. Fisher.

TABLE OF CONTENTS

Yet did not Shishak stand to the covenants he had made, but he spoiled the temple, and emptied the treasures of God, and those of the king, and carried off innumerable ten thousands of gold and silver, and left nothing at all behind him.
—Josephus, *Antiquities of the Jews*, AD 94

Egypt and Palestine (Israel), 2016

Dr. Clarence S. Fisher
1876-1941

LIST OF CHARACTERS

Egypt 1335 BC
Akhenaten—first pharaoh to worship one god
Moses—led Exodus from Egypt
Smenkhkare—pharaoh

Archaeologists (1916–1941)
Clarence Fisher—University of Pennsylvania archaeologist, b. 1876, d. 1941
Florie (Pree) Carswell—wife of Clarence Fisher, b. 1876, d. 1963
Howard Carter—discoverer of King Tut's tomb
Flinders Petrie—famous archaeologist, resided with Fisher at American School of Oriental Research, Jerusalem
Shaker Ahmad Suleiman—friend of Clarence Fisher

Zionists (1941)
Moshe Hakim—leader
Itzak Herz—bartender, American School of Oriental Research, Jerusalem
Eliyahu Czeny—tracks Clarence in Nazareth (at age nineteen)

Carswell Bible College (2001)
Lonnie Jenkins—IT guy, Dead Sea Scrolls concordance
Anna Hamed—Lonnie's girlfriend, cousin of Achmed Hamed
Dr. Alexander Feeney—professor, worked with Jenkins on Dead Sea Scrolls
Julia R. E. Carswell—professor, former president of Carswell Bible College
Mark Hamilton—president, Carswell Bible College

Archaeologists (2002)
Chris Houser—Cairo, Theban Mapping Project
Isabella Browne—Cairo, American University
Edwin Harer—Luxor, Chicago House
Donald Hughes—Luxor, Dra Abu el Naga
Zahi Hawass—Cairo, head of Egyptian antiquities
Eric Tobin—Penn Museum archivist
Caroline Dosker—Penn Museum employee in 2002 who knew Clarence Fisher as a teenager
Lucille Noble—librarian at Chicago House, Luxor

Tourists (2002)
Steve Fisher—Clarence Fisher's grandson
Glenn Fisher—Clarence Fisher's grandson
Tina Gilbert—doctoral candidate at University of Pennsylvania
Anok Badawi—guide for entire sixteen-day trip

Terrorists (2002)
Achmed Hamed—terrorist leader, cousin of Anna Hamed
Abu Ayyub al-Khawi—terrorist

Mossad (2002)
David Solot—director of research
Eliyahu Czeny—Mossad assistant director responsible for intelligence operations and analysis (at age eighty)
Bob Ebel—Mossad agent, posing as a publisher from Chicago

Penn Museum (2002)
E. Wells Newsome—director
David Carpenter—curator, Egyptian Section
Timothy Barnes—Tina Gilbert's fiancé, associate curator/ field director

Miscellaneous
Barbara Mertz—author of Amelia Peabody mysteries
Helen Mears—owner, Marsam Hotel (2002)
Nancy and Frank O'Connor—friends of Steve Fisher in Ocean City, New Jersey

Prologue

1335 BC
Thebes (Luxor), Egypt

For the eleventh time, Moses and his brother, Aaron, approached the palace originally built by Amenhotep III, the father of Pharaoh Akhenaten and grandfather of Tutankhamun, King Tut. They entered the palace through the side rear entrance, which was topped by a stone lintel with carved hieroglyphs praising the king.

Some people were there to plead for relief from the king; others just to watch the opulent proceedings. Moses and Aaron were there to once again plead for the release of their enslaved people; freedom to head east to God's Promised Land.

Located in Malkata, south of the Valley of the Kings, the palace had been abandoned by Akhenaten when he created a new city at el Amarna in order to worship one god, Aten, the sun god. Akhenaten's successor had moved the government back to Thebes and had refurbished and re-opened the palace at Malkata.

Moses and Aaron now stood in the Hall of Adoration, with its eight massive columns reaching to the ceiling. Each was topped by multicolor flaring, while the bases were painted a dark red. The walls, floor, and columns contained hieroglyphs and paintings paying tribute to the gods and to Pharaoh. The ceiling had two great wooden beams running length-wise, each supporting horizontal beams. The remaining ceiling areas were painted dark blue and contained multiple white dots, depicting the night sky. There were four rectangular window-like openings on each side of the hall, near the ceiling. There were no seats or benches; only the king could sit. Moses and Aaron faced the throne, bounded on each side by massive doors that almost reached the ceiling.

A sound was heard behind the great doors, and the courtiers took up their positions in lines before the throne. The door at the left of the throne was now flung open, and a group of young Nubian slaves entered. They were bearing small bronze censers that threw off pale bluish smoke and spread a delicious vapor throughout the great Hall of Adoration. Behind them came two men carrying large ostrich-feather fans that were mounted on the ends of gilded poles. These two ascended the platform and stationed themselves behind the throne.

The palace ceiling was thirty feet high, but this, and the rectangular openings, seemed to offer little relief from the high heat. The Akhet, the annual flooding of the Nile, was almost at its fullest, adding extreme humidity.

The king appeared; he was middle-aged and was a commanding figure. Brown-skinned and dark-haired, he had a braided, rectangular goatee but was otherwise cleanly shaven. He walked with the high priest of Egypt, who had a closely shaven head and was clothed in simple, long linen robes with no ornaments.

The king was not wearing his usual crown of Upper and Lower Egypt but rather was wearing a skullcap ornamented with a golden sun disc and a pair of ram's horns, above which rose two emblematic feathers. He wore a closely plaited white shirt that reached his ankles. Over this, he wore a short cloak that was open at the front. Around his waist was a wide belt, richly embroidered in bright colors and covered with gold ornaments, the two broad ends hanging down the front almost to the bottom of his shirt. On his neck was a heavy gold necklace composed of rows of gold beads interspersed with longer-shaped beads. The necklace rested below his chest and enclosed a gold medallion with figures of the three main gods worshiped by the people of Thebes. He carried a slender ivory staff topped by a golden gazelle.

As the king entered the room, all of the people bent forward with their arms in front of their faces, palms out. The king mounted a set of steps that led to the throne. When he was seated, everyone resumed their normal stance, but the courtiers continued with their hands in front of their faces, eyes down. A courtier who had accompanied the king stepped forward to present his favorite cat, but he waved him off. The two feather bearers moved closer and began fanning in earnest, alternating stokes from each side, directly on the king.

The king spoke in a low voice to the high priest, who then summoned one of the nobles. The noble approached the throne and bowed in the same manner as the courtiers. After the king spoke to him, he stood upright and, beginning with many words praising the king, gave a report of the terrible suffering and despair of the people in his province due to the latest plague, which took the lives of the firstborn of Egypt. Other province heads followed, all with the same sad story.

When they finished, the king sat with bent head, nervously fingering the ends of his embroidered sash. Finally, with a resigned expression on his face, he whispered a command to his high priest, who then brought forth Moses, with Aaron at his side.

Moses was thin and had flowing white hair and a full beard that reached his chest. He wore a simple white robe that reached his sandaled feet. His face was rugged, and he walked with a stoop. Moses remained confident, but Aaron was trembling slightly, despite having pleaded with Pharaoh in the past. They approached with heads bowed.

Moses and Aaron, who was the high priest of the Hebrews, now faced Pharaoh from about ten feet away. They had both pled with Pharaoh to free their people, God's chosen people—first Aaron and then Moses. Each time, they had prophesied plagues striking Egypt, Aaron threatening the first three with the snake that God had turned into a rod. Moses had threatened the other seven plagues. Pharaoh stood up and took a step forward on his platform.

For a moment, he gazed at the slight, white-bearded man before him. Then he said, "You now call yourself Moses, and you dress and look very different, but to me you will always be Akhenaten. As pharaoh, you brought shame to Egypt by establishing your city, Akhetaten, and worshiping just one of our gods, Aten, the sun god. You built statues and carvings depicting yourself in a very strange way. You have lived among the Hebrews, and you have outlived your son, Tutankhamun. I and the worthy high priests persuaded you to abandon your reign and city peacefully, and we are restoring Thebes to its original glory. You were raised as royalty when Thutmose's niece, Bithia, found you floating in a basket on the Nile. Now you have abandoned all of our gods and aligned yourself with the Hebrews and their one god, which they call Jehovah."

He paused. "Why does your God of Israel, who we know not in Egypt, bring so much sorrow, suffering, and now death, upon my people?"

Akhenaten-Moses, who was filled with great pride in his mission, stood erect and looked into the eyes of the man who held the land of Egypt in the palm of his hand. "O worthy Pharaoh Smenkhkare, you have married my daughter, Meritaten, and you were once my very dearest friend. I appreciate your peaceful actions and am grateful that you have spared my life. I have indeed found a home with the Hebrews and now worship their God, my God, whom the Hebrews call Jehovah."

Moses paused. "Our God, O Pharaoh," he said in a voice that was heard in every part of the hall, "is not a God of images and temples. He is one God, above all temples and earthly kings. The forefathers of the Hebrews came as guests into the land of Egypt, and your peoples' forefathers received them and honored them. They served well, as they serve now. But the past, O Pharaoh, has been forgotten. Instead of being friends and even citizens of Egypt, they have become its slaves. My God has sent me to tell you that He has a new land for His people, the land of his ancient promise. He has sent me to tell you that you must let us depart, so that we may be free—free to worship Him in that land, and there find peace and rest and plenty. Many times He has shown his power to you, even taking the lives of firstborn sons, including your firstborn, my grandson, to no avail. Once more, He has shown you a sign. Listen to His voice and soften your heart, O Pharaoh. Let my people go. For truly Jehovah, our God, has neither forgotten His promises to His people nor forsaken us."

As Moses finished speaking, strong rays of the morning's sun filtered through the open window above and to the right of the throne. It fell upon Moses's face; truly God had sent a sign to Pharaoh that Moses's words were true.

The king felt a great fear in his heart but showed no outward sign of concern. He paused and then said, "I have seen the power of your God and that he does indeed place his protecting hand over you. In times past, I saw that our own gods were able to produce similar miracles. But now I see that your God has power even over life and death. I see that your God is a true God and a powerful one. Egypt has been wrong to not let the Hebrews go to serve their God."

Moses's heart raced as the king raised his right hand and continued, "Now therefore, I, Smenkhkare, pharaoh of this great land of Egypt, decree that the people whom you, Akhenaten-Moses, call yours, are now free. I decree that you will gather your people together and depart from our land. Depart to that land which is to the east, the land of Canaan." He paused and looked around the great hall. "As pharaoh, I further decree that you shall have dominion over that land for one hundred years, and I shall give you a covenant stating so. May happiness and peace smile once again upon my people, the people of Egypt. And may you go with this sign of my favor; go in peace. It is so decreed."

At that, the king removed from his neck the golden medallion with the figures of the three main gods and passed it to the high priest. Reluctantly, the high priest placed it over the head of Moses, who bowed, reluctantly as well. The king then signified that the audience was at an end. As all in the hall bent low, Smenkhkare descended from the throne, departed the Hall of Adoration, and returned to his quarters.

Saturday, September 1, 2001
Suburban Philadelphia

It was a beautiful day in the northeastern United States. In the Philadelphia area, the high was forecast to be eighty-three degrees. Along the southern New Jersey coastline, my destination, the high was projected to be eighty-one degrees with low humidity. The five-day forecast showed much the same.

I awoke at 8:00 a.m. to the gradually increasing sound of my new Bose clock radio. I got out of bed, stretched, and took my high blood pressure pill. As I usually did each morning, I reminded myself that at fifty-eight, I relied on several pills that accompanied getting older, especially for someone who did little exercise. I had already had my share of things repaired: one shoulder and one knee. I thought, "This getting old crap? It's getting old!"

I moved to the bathroom sink, quickly shaved, and then put my toiletries into my tote bag. As I looked at myself in the mirror, I thought of my mother's comment that, as a six-year-old, I stood with my arms out to my side in front of a mirror, then rotated them to about a five-after-seven position and said, "Look, Mommy. A half twist." Another thought: winning the Pennsylvania state high school diving championship as a fifteen-year-old sophomore.

Next, I carefully chose and donned my boardwalk clothes: a light blue polo shirt with "OCNJ" embroidered on it, khaki Bermuda shorts, white athletic socks, and white sneakers. I was disappointed when I looked into the mirror. I had stopped coloring my hair two years earlier. It was now completely white. My face was full, and my polo shirt did little to hide my paunch. As on most mornings, I thought that I needed to lose weight, but that thought was quickly replaced with "Oh, well."

Putting the tote bag into my duffel bag, I then decided to add a sweatshirt in case it got cold at night. Gathering up my pillow, I carried the duffel bag downstairs and added them next to a paper bag containing books and magazines. The suitcase, which I had packed the night before, was there as well. From the hall closet I pulled out my ball cap that had a springboard diver embroidered on it, a tribute to my youth, and also a light jacket. I carried it all to the car and put everything but the cap in the trunk. I returned to the house to get my clock radio and beach chair, and I was surprised to find that all fit into the small car trunk.

Returning one last time, I said to my wife, Linda, "Well, I'm all set. It looks like a perfect week ahead in Ocean City."

"Okay. Please drive carefully, Steve, and say hello for me to the O'Connors. Lenore and I will be down around eleven thirty on Tuesday morning."

We kissed, and I went out to the driveway, got into my new, green, midlife-crisis Mustang convertible, fired it up, and listened proudly to the deep-throated rumble from the exhaust. I headed up the street, turned onto a road leading to US Route 202, and turned onto the four-lane highway.

Little did I know that one sentence soon to be pointed out to me in a book would change my life. Little did I know that two different groups related to the legacy of my paternal grandfather, archaeologist Dr. Clarence S. Fisher, would threaten my life. Little did I know that I, Steve Fisher, computer guy, grandfather, ordinary guy, might impact history.

PART ONE
DR. CLARENCE S. FISHER

CHAPTER 1

.

Tuesday, February 17, 1915
Western Cemetery, Giza Pyramids

In 1914, at age thirty-seven, Clarence S. Fisher was appointed curator of the Egyptian Section of the Museum of the University of Pennsylvania (Penn). He was chosen to lead archaeological expeditions to Giza, next to the Pyramids; to Memphis, south of the Pyramids; to Thebes, today's Luxor; and to Dendereh, north of Luxor.

In January 1915, he took over, from famous archaeologist George Reisner, an area west of the Pyramids called the Minor Cemetery; it held the graves of minor officials. This morning, he had been called over to tomb G 2093 because workers had uncovered the top of what appeared to be a small statue.

Fisher climbed down the rickety ladder to the bottom of the brick-lined twenty-four-foot shaft and into the offering room, which had been cleared. He then entered an adjoining room that was partially cleared. Dropping to his knees, he drew a brush from his suit coat and then loosened his tie. He bent over.

Archaeology is often boring for an expedition leader, waiting for workers to uncover something. Today was beginning to get exciting. Fisher saw what looked to be the top of a small statue. It had coloring and was quite possibly a head.

He began clearing away sand, dirt, and pieces of mud-brick debris, his brush and fingers his only tools. It was delicate, tedious work. Finally he cleared everything away from the beautiful statue, with its colors dull but otherwise intact. While of limestone, not gold, it was eleven inches high and easily the best relic found to date. Hieroglyphs on the statue, interpreted by his supervisor, indicated that this was a minor official named Mesty.

In his tent that night—since he held only a three-month concession, or permit, to dig, no structure had been built—Fisher stepped away from his drawing board and moved to a folding chair, one of two in his tent. He had just dismissed a supervisor who was helping him with learning Arabic. He sat down and opened a bottle of whiskey. His propensity for liquor was no secret among his supervisors and, thus, the workers.

He poured three fingers and took a big sip. He finally relaxed and thought about how lucky he was. Now thirty-eight, he knew that he was one of the youngest archaeologists to lead a major expedition. This one, Giza, was but a prelude to significant, large expeditions to Memphis, Dendereh, and Dra Abu el Naga, across the Nile from Luxor. An ample building, with room to house him and even large finds, was almost completed at Memphis, and a dwelling, called the Pink House, had already been been built directly across the street from Dra Abu el Naga and near the Valley of the Kings.

His thoughts turned to family back in Philadelphia. He was proud of his son, Clarence Jr., called Stanley, now six years old. That made him smile, but he frowned when he thought about his wife, Florie Carswell Fisher. He had married her partially because her father was well situated and partially because she had helped him with his stuttering at her father's school in Philadelphia.

Florie enthusiastically followed Clarence, with Stanley in tow, to Egypt in 1911, when he was on a dig with George Reisner at one of the earliest pyramids. On the voyage over, however, she got deathly seasick and complained the whole rest of her time in Egypt. Returning suddenly to Philadelphia after a scorpion was found in Stanley's crib, Florie was seasick again and stayed sickly the rest of her life. Clarence was devastated because each of his summers back home in West Philadelphia consisted of nothing but arguments, mostly about his career choice.

His thoughts then turned to the war. The expedition had started because the university had received assurances that the European war would not disrupt any work in Egypt, and he had arrived just as the British had declared its protectorate over Egypt. He was dismayed, however, when he arrived at Giza to find Australian troops, including a few kangaroos, camped out in a tent city just yards beyond his dig site.

In anguish over the negative parts of his life, Clarence filled almost the entire glass with whiskey and began just sipping and staring, staring across at his beloved drawing table—he was trained as an architect—and the single candle, its flickering flame accenting the beauty of the painted statue of Mesty, which was probably 3,500 years old. With a tan, almost orange color to his skin, Mesty was wearing a brown hat covering his braided black hair and a white wrap that went only from his waist to just above his knees. His shoulders were broad and his arms muscular. His hands encircled one-inch rods as if he was carrying something, possibly into the afterlife. Surely, this was Clarence's greatest find to date!

Intending to retire to his bed, Clarence took another sip and settled back into his chair, just for a few moments.

Suddenly, he was awakened from his deep sleep by a shuffling sound and a hot breeze against his forehead. He yelled a dull-sounding "Hey" as he struggled to get up from the uncomfortable folding chair. All he saw was an ankle and a sandal going out the canvas tent door. He looked at his drawing table. The candle had gone out, and his beloved statue was gone!

He went to his footlocker and quickly retrieved his Webley Mk VI revolver, which he had purchased in Southampton his last trip over. Breaking down the pistol to check that all six rounds were loaded, he went out the entrance, fortunately still dressed and with his boots on. He staggered for his first few steps, but he seemed to sober up quickly. He pulled back the hammer, cocking the trigger. About seventy-five feet away, he saw a man move behind one of the small lorries or carts that ran on narrow rails. These one-foot-gauge rails were easy to move, and they allowed the lorries to carry debris away from many parts of the dig.

Fisher fired a shot at the thief, but he was shocked to find that the thief returned his fire. They then each exchanged several rounds until Fisher took a few seconds to make a plan. On the next exchange, Fisher cried out as if he was hurt badly. His cry was loud, but then it faded and stopped suddenly, in midcry.

There was silence for several minutes, and then the thief figured it was safe to leave. Just as he stood up, Fisher pulled the trigger and shot him in his chest, killing him instantly.

Fisher recovered his statue and, from that point on, earned a tough reputation that would accompany him throughout Egypt.

CHAPTER 2

Thursday, August 25, 1921
Jerusalem

This was the fourth and final day that Penn archaeologist Clarence Fisher was allowed to inspect Qubbat Al-Sakhrah, the beautiful golden dome, commonly known as the Dome of the Rock, that is so visible in any skyline photo of the city of Jerusalem.

But it didn't always look that beautiful; in late 1918, Fisher agreed to assist in the reconstruction and restoration of the site so sacred to people of the Islamic faith. At that time, it was in serious disrepair, and the dome's exterior was lead, not gold.

The request for Fisher came from British general Edmund Allenby shortly after winning the Battle of Megiddo in 1918. Allenby thought Fisher could help ease tensions. Fisher had earlier advised both Allenby and T. E. Lawrence (Lawrence of Arabia) on how best to gather and lead Arabs to assist the British against the Turks, who had allied with Germany. The battle drove the Turks out of Palestine and began the dissolution of the Ottoman Empire. Allenby had requested Fisher to participate in the reconstruction because of his training as an architect, his knowledge of Islamic architecture, and his reputation as an archaeologist.

Due to the pressures the British had in governing Palestine following the war, however, Fisher was forced to delay his inspection. Finally in 1921, he was able to begin his work. Clarence had taken two days to survey both the outside and inside of the building. He made meticulous diagrams, based on many measurements and sketches of key structural elements, but he was not allowed to take photographs. He was always accompanied by an Islamic mullah.

After more work on the third day, he had asked to be taken throughout the Temple Mount, entering areas, including any tunnels, forbidden to the public. He was refused by the mullah who accompanied him. Fluid in Arabic, Fisher was able to persuade the mullah to allow him to speak with the imam later in the day. Fisher later described to the imam his architectural training, showed the documentation he had already accumulated, and stated his need to get down to the bedrock beneath the supporting structure of the dome in order to learn what needed to be strengthened. He was refused, but the imam did authorize his entrance into the Well of Souls the next day.

The Well of Souls is a small cavern under the Foundation Stone. In turn, the Foundation Stone is enclosed by the structure of the Dome of the Rock. This mosque is on the Temple Mount, a large platform that covers the ruins of Solomon's First Temple, believed to have been built in 832 BC and destroyed in 586 BC. The Temple Mount is also on the site of the Second Temple, which is believed to have been built in 516 BC and destroyed in AD 70. The Temple Mount is partially enclosed by the ruins of a great wall. The Wailing Wall is part of that wall, which surrounded the Second Temple and which was renovated and expanded by Herod the Great, the Roman king at the time of Jesus's birth.

Jewish people pray at a specific section of the Wailing Wall because it is the closest that any person of the Jewish faith should ever get to the Holy of Holies. They also pray from anywhere in the world toward the Temple Mount. The Foundation Stone is holy to them because it is said to have been the location of the Holy of Holies. The Ark of the Covenant is described in the Bible and is said to contain the tablets of the Ten Commandments. The Holy of Holies, the room that contains the Ark of the Covenant, is believed to be under the Foundation Stone.

To people of the Islamic faith, the Dome of the Rock is the third-most-sacred site. The prophet Muhammad is said to have stood on the Foundation Stone as he ascended into heaven.

To Christians, it is the site of the temple where Jesus overturned the tables of the moneychangers and, later, preached.

At 10:00 a.m., Clarence Fisher, in his light suit, tie, and brown jack-boots so typical of archaeologists working in the field, was led by the mullah into the Dome of the Rock. On Monday, he had stood in wonder at the state of disrepair. The Temple Mount, which surrounded the dome, consisted mainly of flat stones, but many were missing, and there were weeds growing between them. Other areas were just dirt. For a site so sacred to so many, the condition of the mount was appalling. Fisher had examined the octagonal structure that supported the dome and noted the many missing tiles and windows. Inside, he had found that the colors were well preserved but the rugs, though beautiful, were well worn. He had noted the sixteen supporting columns that descended into the bedrock. His unsuccessful pleading with the imam the night before was based mainly on his need to inspect these columns to determine the extent of any damage.

What he didn't say was that, as an archaeologist, he wanted to get down to the bedrock under the Dome of the Rock. He also wondered whether, if he was allowed in any tunnels, he might spot what others hadn't, secret rooms, possibly the Holy of Holies with its Ark of the Covenant, or indications of who may have removed any treasures.

He walked into the Dome of the Rock, again noting the huge rock, the Foundation Stone, at the center of the ring surrounding it. Portions of it appeared to have been chiseled out, possibly by the Crusaders, although he could discern no particular patterns, inscriptions, or artwork.

The mullah walked Clarence over to the top of the steps leading down into the Well of Souls. As he stood there looking down the steps, Clarence thought that he might possibly be the first Christian to walk down them since Saladin recaptured Jerusalem from the Crusaders in AD 1187. A chill went up his spine, and he asked the mullah to pause for a moment. He said a prayer to himself, knowing he was entering a truly sacred spot for Jews, Muslims, and Christians.

Then he and the mullah walked down the sixteen steps and into the cave. The ceiling was a maximum of ten feet high. Near the steps was a small ceiling hole that had been carved out through the Foundation Stone. It let in some natural light, and there was a single electric bulb suspended from a wire through the hole. With a notebook and pencil in one hand, Clarence took out his electric torch with the other. He looked around the cave, ignoring the smooth areas that had been either paved over or cut expertly. He made cursory glances at the altars and other Islamic fixtures and carvings. He spent much of his time looking at the floor, although much was covered by worn rugs. Instead, he looked at the portions of the cave where the rough-hewn rock met the floor and the smooth, possibly plastered, areas. He wanted to knock on various places to see if they were hollow, but the mullah stopped him after he made one solid knock on the floor near the smooth walls. He continued, making measurements and recording them in his notebook. He pretended to look for things relating to the structure. But he was looking for anything that would be a clue to an entrance into anything beyond the walls. He examined cracks, crevices, and rocks that looked like rubble, but found nothing. He even got on one knee to look under a rock that overhung some rough stones. Because he was not allowed to touch anything, his search was in vain.

Just about giving up, he gave one last try. From his Bible readings and discussions with fellow archaeologist William F. Albright, he knew that a pharaoh named Shoshenq I was believed to be the biblical Shishak. He was also familiar with the cartouche of Shoshenq I from a scarab excavated by famed archaeologist Flinders Petrie. He had recalled one of the two places that Shishak is mentioned in the Bible, 1 Kings, chapter 14, verses 25 and 26:

> 25 And it came to pass in the fifth year of King Rehoboam, that Shishak king of Egypt came up against Jerusalem:
> 26 And he took away the treasures of the house of the LORD, and the treasures of the king's house; he even took away all: and he took away all the shields of gold which Solomon had made.

Fisher had thought that it might be possible that he could find some reference to Shoshenq I in the dome or in the Well of Souls, so the night before, he had committed the cartouche of the pharaoh to memory.

Finally, he looked again near the area of the overhanging rock just to the right of the steps. He thought he saw something, just the tip of something. Like most archaeologists, he had a keen eye for spotting tiny but important things. In the grouting at the edge and near the top of a vertical rock that was maybe two feet high and six inches wide was the tip of something roughly oval. He knew that the mullah would be annoyed at him taking another look, so he bent down and tried to look like he was adjusting his knee-high boot. He put his electric torch on the floor and took out his pencil. He hoped that his body was shielding the pencil from the mullah as he reached with it.

Fortunately, the grouting was ancient and loose. Holding his breath and partially standing to cover up what he was doing, he used the pencil tip to pry out more of the grouting around the object. With his thumb and fore-finger, he gently wiggled the object free and held it between the knuckles of his first two fingers. Making a bit of a commotion about hurting his back, he gathered up his electric torch, pencil, and notebook in his left hand and reached around to his lower back in feigned pain with his right hand. He clenched the object between his knuckles. With a grimace, he stood up and nodded to the mullah that he was almost ready to leave. With that, he slipped the object, which he thought was a scarab, into his coat pocket.

He moved around the cavern one last time to impress the mullah. He then turned and said, "My work here is done. I have about all that I can get from what I've been granted access. I'm not sure, without getting more access, if I can draw up plans for how best to strengthen this struc-ture, but I'll do my best." With a slight bow, he said, "Thank you," and started up the steps.

Clarence exited the Temple Mount and returned to his motorcar. He opened the slightly creaky door and moved into the driver's seat. Only then, and after carefully looking around, did he remove the object from his pocket. He examined it in his lap, keeping it out of sight from the outside.

It was indeed a scarab, maybe a half inch long by three-eighths wide. One side was smooth and white, a characteristic of steatite, the material from which it was made; it was not an actual beetle. The other side was remarkably well preserved and may have been used as a seal. While there were some brown spots, most of it was white. The indenta-tions indeed formed a hieroglyph, and most of the indentations had been painted green. Clarence immediately believed that it was the cartouche of Shosheng I—Shishak. There were eight symbols in all, including a flow-ering reed at the left, two symbols for water, two crowns, and a sekhem scepter at the bottom. There were also two symbols that each looked like a table with three wine glasses on top.

Bumping his way back to his headquarters at Beth, Clarence was thankful to be the owner of a 1915 Morris Cowley Bullnose. It was his first motorcar, which he had purchased in the summer of 1920 from an aide to General Allenby, but he found that upkeep was very expensive. Nevertheless, it was a quicker journey than by train and donkey. It was also cooler, with the top down, especially when he could get it going as fast as twenty miles per hour.

Back at his headquarters in Beth Shan in Palestine, where he was excavating a three-hundred-foot-high mound for the University of Pennsylvania, he opened his Bible to 1 Kings and reread chapter 14, verses 25–26. He also searched through 2 Chronicles, where he found that chapter 12 also told the story of Shishak's conquest and included verse 9:

> 9 So Shishak king of Egypt came up against Jerusalem, and took away the treasures of the house of the LORD, and the treasures of the king's house.

He was sure, from earlier discussions with fellow archaeologist James Breasted, that Shoshenq I was the Egyptian pharaoh referenced in the Bible as Shishak. He knew also that Shishak conquered Jerusalem and destroyed the Second Temple, which was built by King Solomon. And he knew that the Holy of Holies, which contained the Ark of the Covenant, was in the Second Temple. His discovery of the scarab was proof that Shishak, or one of his warriors, had been inside or underneath the First Temple.

As he began to think of the implications of this, he poured himself three fingers of whiskey and sat back. If he could find Shoshenq I's tomb, he could find fabulous treasures, maybe even the Ark of the Covenant! He decided that he would mostly ignore the work at Memphis when he returned to Egypt in the fall. No, he would spend almost all of his time at Dra Abu el Naga. He knew that Penn Museum director George Gordon would want him to work all three sites, so he decided to feign illness and also argue that managing three sites was too hard for him. Even spending the winter season in both Beth Shan and Dra Abu, eight hundred miles apart, was a daunting task. He looked forward to his new assistant, Ernest

Mackay, taking charge of Beth Shan, reducing his travel and allowing him to spend more time in Dra Abu.

Yes, Clarence thought as he poured himself another drink, 1922 could be an exciting year.

CHAPTER 3

Friday, March 27, 1922
Dra Abu el Naga, near Luxor, Egypt

As darkness approached, Clarence Fisher called to his rais, the foreman of the archaeological workers from the town of Qift, to dismiss the workers. For more than twenty-five years, these Quftis had constituted the skilled workforce necessary in performing archaeological excavations. Much of Fisher's duties as the director of the expedition were concerned with workers: their payroll, housing, feeding, and general welfare. Additionally, he had to accommodate demands for reports from both the museum's director, George B. Gordon, and the director general of the Department of Antiquities of Egypt, Pierre Lacau. In 1914 all archaeologists in Egypt had come under tight control by Lacau, who insisted on strict compliance on concessions, the plot of land granted to an organization for archaeological excavation.

Once darkness had settled, Fisher walked farther up the hill at his dig site. Fisher's concession, sponsored by the University of Pennsylvania, was on the eastern slope of the hillside at the tiny Egyptian village of Dra Abu el Naga, across the Nile from Luxor. While he had already opened several tombs on the hillside dating back 3,500 years, Fisher was curious about what may lie on the other side of the hill. Could he find the tomb of Pharaoh Shoshenq? He had searched there in the nights before and after each new moon since he resumed his excavations on September 19, 1921. Fisher's concession stopped at the ridge at the top of the hill, so he wanted to avoid his silhouette being seen from the dirt road at the base of the hill.

The temperature had dropped to ninety-eight degrees from its high of 110. The workers would be released on Friday; the winter season had ended and wouldn't resume until October.

As he proceeded up the steepest part of the hillside, he reflected on how his career as an archaeologist started. Graduating from Penn in 1897 with a degree in architecture; signing on as an artist/photographer to a Penn excavation at Nippur in Samaria (modern-day Iraq) in 1898 studying the work of archaeologists there and publishing his first book, *Excavations at Nippur*, in 1905, at age twenty-eight.

Fisher subsequently worked in Egypt under the tutelage of famed archaeologist George Reisner. The dig had been funded by Harvard University. Working together, they described a new approach to excavation, later called the Reisner-Fisher method. Instead of digging a trench straight down through multiple levels of civilization, as had been the practice up to then, Fisher, based on his training as an architect, insisted that large open areas be excavated so that objects could be uncovered and documented in their architectural setting. While employed by Harvard, Fisher also worked in cemeteries to the west of the Giza Pyramids outside Cairo.

In 1914, after he impressed many as an archaeologist, despite having no formal training, Clarence Fisher was appointed curator of the Egyptian Section of the University of Pennsylvania Museum. The years 1914–1920 found him extremely busy, working at excavations in Memphis, near Cairo; Dendereh, north of Luxor; and at Beth Shan in Palestine, now Israel. And, during work stoppages due to the world war, he drove an ambulance for the Red Cross. By 1921, Fisher's energy and enthusiasm for his work peaked with his new concession at Dra Abu el Naga.

Fisher continued up the hill as night was falling, passing a more modern area, possibly a Coptic set of apartments from as early as AD 200. He stopped to catch his breath and looked back. He saw the lights of the elegant Winter Palace Hotel, almost directly across the Nile. There were lights along parts of the Corniche, the east-bank road that bordered the Nile, but most of Luxor was without electricity. Reaching the top, he quickly crossed the ridge and went to a seemingly barren area about fifty feet down from the ridge. He had seen no evidence of tombs, but he knew that the Dra Abu hillside had contained many settlements over thousands of years, with many poor living in the caves and tomb entrances, leaving behind artifacts of their occupancy as well as soot on the tomb ceilings from burning torches. An extremely detailed and determined man, Fisher had surmised that hillside occupants had discarded things over the hill from where they lived. He had already found, in his travels over the ridge, several areas where things had been dumped by modern-day occupants. This night, however, he came upon a small depression covered loosely by some rocks. The rocks looked like they had been purposely put there.

He pulled the rocks away and found that the area widened into a small horizontal opening. Crawling in only five feet, he found a vertical shaft that was about three feet by four feet. He reached in his suit coat pocket and pulled out his electric torch. Switching it on, he saw that the shaft went down only about seven feet, where there appeared to be another opening, this one small and horizontal.

Clarence was now faced with a dilemma: how to get down there without attracting any attention. A ladder would make it easy. But returning to his Pink House dwelling across the road at the bottom of the hill, carrying a ladder up the hillside and over the steep ridge, searching the tomb, and then returning seemed unlikely, due to the time remaining before daylight. He thought of using his coat and pants as a rope ladder, but he could find nothing that he could attach them to. So he decided to come back the next night.

As he started to walk away, he had a second thought. Always curious, always impetuous, he turned around, crawled in again, and using his electric torch, looked down the shaft. "I can easily get down by hanging and dropping. It's getting back up," he muttered to himself. He thought that there might be something in the horizontal shaft that he could use to stand on to get back up, but that was risky. He thought that he could drop rocks in and make a pile that he could stand on, reach the top, and pull himself out. Dropping rocks in seemed like a good idea, but if he put too many in, he could block the horizontal shaft. If he put too few in, he wouldn't be able to climb back up.

He spent the next ten minutes searching around the opening for large rocks that he could use. Finally, he had more than enough, so he had to decide which ones he could put in that would make a high, stable plat-form for his escape.

He picked up five larger rocks and dropped them in. Next, he lay on his belly facing away from the shaft, moved his legs backward over the opening, and slid slowly down. As he was in the shaft at chest level, his one hand slipped, and he dropped into the shaft and onto the rocks. Not good; despite his boots that almost reached his knees, he twisted his left ankle badly as his foot landed on the side of a rock. At least he had his electric torch.

He caught his breath and felt his ankle, then maneuvered around and crawled into the horizontal shaft, which was only three feet high. It led into a very small room, about four feet high, that seemed to be littered with broken pottery and building materials. He turned to leave, figuring that this was another one of the dead ends so often encountered by archaeol-ogists. As he started to crawl back through the horizontal shaft, his foot hit a board, and he heard an almost metallic sound. Backing out, he shined the torch into the corner where the sound originated. There he saw two twelve-inch bullet-shaped clay jars, with their mouths pointing to the wall. Each jar had a top with a ridge in it and was secured by a twisted rope running across the top and tied to small handles on each side of the jar.

"Now how do I get these out?" he muttered. Sweating profusely, he placed the jars on the floor, got on his belly, put his feet into the opening of the horizontal shaft, and backed out, pulling the jars with him.

Now he was standing in the vertical shaft. He undid his belt, with the thought of hooking the belt through the rope on each jar—one at his left, one at his right. It worked, but the shaft was not wide enough to accom-modate his new width; he had to turn in the shaft at a forty-five-degree angle. To his dismay, he found that he couldn't bend over to move the rocks to build himself the crude rock ladder. He found, however, that he could move the rocks by doing a deep knee bend. But the rocks he piled on either fell by themselves or fell when he stood on them. Desperate now, he tried for what seemed like an hour to build a rock stool.

Giving up, and exhausted and scared, he screamed, "Am I going to die here? What about my wife, what about my twelve-year-old son? Oh God, help me." He sank in despair, but only so far, for he found that the shaft wouldn't let him sink very far down.

"Okay, I've got to calm down, I've got to rest, I've got to think." In that cramped position, he actually slept for about fifteen minutes. Dreaming of the time that he had actually had a gunfight and killed someone who was trying to steal one of the objects that had been excavated at the cemetery west of the Great Pyramid, Fisher woke with a start. He reached for his electric torch but found it had dropped from his pocket to the bottom. Doing a knee bend, he felt around for it, but it had apparently rolled into the horizontal shaft.

With his senses now sharpened, he realized that he didn't need to see; he just needed to climb. At an angle, he put his right foot on the opposite wall and his weakened left foot on the side wall, both in the corner. He did the same with his elbows. The walls were dry, and his coat was dry and not damaged. He found that his feet didn't slip, but he had a hard time putting pressure on his left foot. Slowly, he inched up the shaft and, after ten minutes, was able to roll out, jars intact.

He quickly limped down the hillside, glancing again across the Nile where, at this hour, only a few lights from the Winter Palace could be seen. He reached the road, waited for a man in a white galabia who rode by on a donkey, and crossed the road. He turned left and walked the quarter mile to his Pink House, his Spartan but comfortable quarters in Dra Abu. The outside of Fisher's house was covered with pink plaster; it was clearly different from the mud-brick structures in the rest of Dra Abu. While he complained about his pay, he was satisfied with the dwelling, which had been funded by the Penn Museum due to the $500,000 bequest by Eckley Coxe, the museum president who died in 1916.

Unlocking the door, he lit a lamp and carried it into his kitchen. He hid the jars in the back of his kitchen cabinet, too exhausted to examine them. Ahead of him in the next few days was closing up his two Egypt sites for the summer, Dra Abu el Naga, near Luxor, and Memphis, near Cairo. He would then relocate to Beth Shan in Palestine for the summer. He decided to leave the jars in the cabinet and go through the contents in the morning.

He then took a long drink of water from a jug. Moving toward his bedroom, he sat down in his wicker chair, removed his shoes, felt his ankle, which had swelled somewhat, and then fell asleep in the chair, not even making it to his bed.

CHAPTER 4

Sunday, November 5, 1922
Valley of the Kings, near Luxor, Egypt

Darkness was almost upon the two archaeologists, Clarence Fisher and Howard Carter, as they approached the many rocks that now crudely covered the steps down to the tomb door. They had paid Sharif, the night guard at the entrance to the valley, to be certain that no one else could enter, and they had handsomely paid Amar, who was to guard the tomb that night, to not show up. It was early November, but the 105-degree high for the day was still lingering, causing sweat to drip out of them like moisture on a cold glass of beer. They paused outside the supply tent to catch their breath from the short climb; neither was in great shape. Their destination was a pile of rocks just thirteen feet below the floor of the valley. They stood in the welcoming shade caused by the steep slopes that surrounded the large dead-ended canyon, and they waited for complete darkness to envelop the valley like a black mask. Both wore their standard archaeologist's outfits: dark fedora and suit, white shirt, and a tie. Instead of the normal jackboots used for digging, they wore dress shoes to avoid suspicion. They had both brought two pairs of gloves, which they took out of their suit coat pockets, and a tarpaulin for use if they needed to crawl. Taking off their fedoras, coats, ties, clean white dress shirts, and pants, they carefully laid them in the tent. Underneath, they each had another shirt and pants. They knew they would have to crawl through the small opening that had been made by tomb robbers two or three thousand years before.

No word was spoken as they began removing the rocks—just enough material so that they could get down to the top of the ancient tomb entrance. Both men knew the danger they were in if they were caught clandestinely entering the tomb. Danger, because word had gotten out regarding the possible contents of the tomb. They faced expulsion from the country at a minimum, or prison. But most of all, they would lose their reputations, minor as they were, and their careers. Their futures would be destroyed.

They knew there was no rational reason to be digging. Carter's workers had begun digging on November 1, the opening day of the 1922–23 excavation season, at the spot where Fisher had indicated. In January, Fisher had discovered two sealed clay jars in the hills on the Nile side of the Valley of the Kings. Both contained documents, mostly in the demotic language. One document was unlike the others, however. It mentioned that the "boy-king's" tomb was below that of Rameses VI, and Carter had used that information to convince Lord Carnarvon, his benefactor, to fund one more season. Yesterday, November 4, the workers had dug through the coarse, packed sand near the man-made rock wall of workers' huts previously built below the tomb of Rameses VI. After more digging, they uncovered what looked like a step cut into the limestone bedrock. Further digging uncovered a rectangular cutout, then a set of stairs. By this afternoon, November 5, the workers had uncovered twelve steps, each five feet wide, that led down to the upper portions of the tomb entrance. Carter noticed that the door had been sealed, except for an area at the upper left corner. It had been refilled with rocks and then roughly plastered over, indicating that the tomb had been entered in antiquity. Carter's hopes had dropped; the tomb had been robbed! Furthermore, while he found hieroglyphic imprints in the plaster sealing the part of the door that was exposed, none indicated Tutankhamun. Discouraged, he still needed to inform Carnarvon to have him return from his five-thousand-acre estate, Highclere, in England, to witness the opening of the tomb. Carter, based on Fisher's advice, planned to send Carnarvon a telegram the next day. Following the revealing of the entrance, Carter immediately had the workers refill the stairway using rocks, not stones or sand, to await Carnarvon's arrival.

Thus, all would be known in less than three weeks when they could just watch as workers removed the rocks and rubble all the way to the full door. But curiosity was killing them, and they believed that their careful planning, and the fact that ancient robbers had already made a small entrance, would allow them the time to remove the rocks, gain entrance to the tomb, and then replace the rocks. Additionally, they were convinced that their knowledge, experience, and even their artistic abilities would allow them to cover up their entrance and avoid any detection. They had no malice in what they were doing. They were professionals, and their reputations were based on their intense curiosity about the past.

But it was easy for them to talk and plan their incursion. Now was the time to proceed or back out. They both nodded to each other to continue.

After two hours of removing many of the rocks that had been filled in that day by the workmen at Howard's insistence, they had created a narrow passage down to the door of the tomb. "Get the hand pick, tarpaulin, plaster, and some more water from the tent, Clarence. We're ready to open the upper left corner where robbers had broken in."

In two minutes, Clarence was back. Wiping off sweat with the back of his almost-destroyed first pair of gloves, Clarence said, "Howard, this is our last chance to back out. We can find out if this is the greatest find of all time when Carnarvon gets here in three weeks."

"You don't really mean that, do you? You were the one who found the clay jar at Dra Abu that told you to look below the tomb of Ramses VI, you were the one who came up with the story about the water boy finding the steps, and you were the one who begged me to hold off sending the wire to Carnarvon until tomorrow. Hell, without your bloody jars, I would not have been able to persuade Carnarvon to fund one more season! Hand me that pick, and let's see if we can get through this."

"Bloody hell," said Howard, after breaking through the poorly concealed robbers' entrance. "There's a corridor leading to another doorway about twenty-five feet away. It's filled almost to the top with rubble, mostly limestone. I think we can crawl across it to the second door; hand me the tarpaulin."

Crawling on their stomachs and keeping the tarpaulin under them was difficult; it took them a half hour to make their way across the rubble, which was possibly from the original excavation of the tomb. At this second door, they again found that robbers had made an opening in the upper left corner of the door. Unlike the first opening, which had been patched up with plaster, this opening was only filled with rocks. Carter easily forced the rocks out.

Howard Carter, soon to become one of the most famous men in the world, peered in, using his electric torch. "I'm afraid that it's small, maybe too small for a pharaoh's tomb, but it looks like there hasn't been much looting. And I see gold! Quick, come take a look! Look at all the gold. It's either a storage cache or Tutankhamun's tomb."

Both were now peering in. Through the narrow opening, they could see only a portion of the tomb. But what they saw was breathtaking. Immediately in front of them was a golden couch. It was about four feet high and seven feet long. Each leg ended with a foot in the shape of an animal's. At both right corners were the golden faces of a horned cow, and at both left corners were red curved tails. All the gold was inlaid with dark blue cow spots, possibly made of glass. "That couch alone should help in satisfying Carnarvon," said Carter. They could also see the head of another golden couch to the left and the tail of a third at the right. Under the right couch, they could make out the golden legs of a chair, but the rest of it was shrouded in black. Under the middle couch were piles of clay jars.

Carter and Fisher then squeezed through the opening and stood up in the small room, which was about twenty-five by thirteen feet and eight feet high; the walls were undecorated. Carter shined the electric torch around. "Look at this stuff; it's a treasure house! The robbers must have taken some things, but all this hasn't been touched. It may not be Tutankhamun's, but it could be the greatest find of modern times!"

To their left were the disassembled parts of several chariots—wheels and wicker baskets looking like the aftermath of a horse-and-buggy wreck. The most striking objects to their right were two elegant black-and-gold statues. Life size, they seemed to stand guard over just the right wall of the chamber,

"Wait, shine the light to your left, at the bottom of the wall in front of you," said Clarence. "There's a small opening under the table."

Carter dropped to his knees and peered in. "I knew it. There's another room. It's filled with more objects, but everything looks ransacked by robbers. We may not find much jewelry. It's another storeroom, just like this. But we won't know if this is really Tutankhamun's tomb unless we find a burial chamber."

Carter pulled his head out from the small opening into the other room and turned toward Fisher. "Look at all this stuff. Even if it isn't Tutankhamun, Carnarvon will love it. He won't be able to wait to get it back to England."

To their right, in opposite corners, were the two imposing life-size ebony figures, each more than six feet high, with solid gold sandals, head ornaments, and bracelets.

"Hand me the light," said Fisher. Using his training in architecture, he noticed where the wall to their right met the floor. It was a slightly different color than the other three walls of the room.

"Remember, my dear Howard, we are archaeologists. We have to approach this in the interest of science and education."

"Bloody hell, Fisher, Lord Carnarvon wants fame and fortune, not science. That's why he's been paying for my dream—my dream of the greatest Egyptian finds in history! This tomb is not decorated like a pharaoh's, but there appears to be plenty of gold."

"Look over here," said Fisher. "I think there must be something behind this wall. See down there? There are reeds along the whole length of the wall. But the other walls don't look like that at all. Maybe that's the burial chamber. Look closer. Look, here's where the entrance was sealed up when the builders finished. Look there, that looks like a small hole robbers probably made, about two feet in diameter."

"Well, let's break in there. Quickly now, hand me the small pick!"

"No, there's not enough time, and anything we do will be detected. Don't be a fool. We need to get out of here."

"I can't back away now," screamed Carter. "I have to see if we've found Tutankhamun's tomb. I'll make an opening in the robbers' hole just big enough for my head and peer in. You try to find something to cover it with." While Fisher found some reeds, four alabaster vases, and a small, ornate chest with beautifully painted hunting scenes, Carter began to dig through with the hand pick. "We can cover up the hole, and if it's discovered, we can say that it must have been poorly done by the robbers. Relax, Fisher."

Carter broke through even quicker than the two archaeologists expected. Lying on his belly, he peered in. "It's a narrow hallway running right and left. There's gold everywhere." He then pointed the electric torch up and then left and right along the narrow hallway, straining his neck in three directions. "It's huge! It's all gold with blue inlays! It's maybe nine feet long to my left and four to my right, and maybe nine feet high. I can't see how wide it is. It's the burial chamber, and the shrine it contains is magnificent! It looks intact, and I'm sure it's never been opened! It has to be Tutankhamun's! We've found it! It's the find of the century! We'll be famous, Clarence—the whole world will know us!"

"No, Howard, you'll be famous. Remember, we talked about this. No one can know that I found a jar or where I found it, because I did not have a concession to dig there. This is your find, and for our professional reputations, this night must be kept a secret. Now let's get that covered up and get out of here. Here, see if you can somehow patch that up, and then I'll cover it."

Fisher removed more reeds from the corner of the room near one of the two ebony-and-gold statues and placed them on the floor in front of the small opening that Howard was able to quickly fill. He then put the reeds against the opening and held them in place with a basket lid almost as big as the opening Howard had made. Finishing, he moved the painted chest against the reeds to support the lid and placed the four vases in among the reeds.

Since time was running out, and they knew that there was work to be done to cover up the damage to the door, they hastily retreated. Carter removed his shirt and made an effort to sweep to cover up any tracks they may have made. True to their plan, neither man tried to remove any of the objects. They each had some trouble climbing their way back into the small door opening. Carter struggled into the opening and then helped to pull Fisher up. They worked intently on covering their tracks at the door; they knew that they were in trouble with the time.

Three hours later, they had repaired the two doors, refilled the steps with the rocks that had originally been removed by their Egyptian workers, and hastily donned their good clothing over the clothes torn and soiled by their crawling. Then they calmly, but exhaustedly, walked down the hill as first light was just appearing. As expected, Sharif was still asleep. They exhaustedly mounted their donkeys and left the Valley of the Kings.

Back at Carter's large, three-domed house, both men rejoiced. "We did it!" said Carter, over and over. "Ah, but I should have taken just one thing as a souvenir."

"But, Howard, we're professionals. No one must know what we did here tonight." With a wry smile, Clarence reached into his suit coat pocket. "But despite being a professional, I did remove this papyrus which was inside one of the vases that I put in front of the basket lid."

CHAPTER 5

**Monday, November 6, 1922
Carter House, Valley of the Kings**

"**N**ow let's talk about your bloody papyrus," Howard Carter said angrily.

He and Clarence Fisher had both ridden the four miles back to Carter's large, three-domed house. It was the finest in Upper Egypt, thanks to Carter's benefactor, the very wealthy Lord Carnarvon. When he was in Egypt, Carnarvon spent some nights at Carter's and other nights in a suite at the Winter Palace Hotel, across the Nile in Luxor.

They had cleaned themselves up, and Fisher was wearing a shirt and pants provided by Carter. Both were the same size, around five feet six inches, both had high foreheads, usually covered by fedoras, and their noses were remarkably similar. But Fisher was somewhat slighter of build and had a similar but wider mustache than Carter, whose mustache was fuller. The best way to tell them apart was that Fisher wore round, wire-frame glasses; Carter's vision was excellent. Carter was two years older than Fisher, and he was more outspoken, arrogant even, and talked confidently, while Fisher tended to be shy, due to a slight stutter, and very humorless. Both were artistic; Carter was known more for watercolors, and Fisher for his highly accurate, detailed drawings of the structures found during his excavations.

They sat in drab wooden chairs in the dining room, under high, massive wooden beams. The dining room table contained stacks of papers and drawings. The dining room was not one of the three rooms that featured the domes that so distinguished Carter's magnificent home, called "Castle Carter" by many. His house was made of mud brick but finished with fine white sandstone. By contrast, Fisher's Pink House was plain, except for the color, much smaller, and simpler.

"Fisher, your papyrus! You were the one who insisted that we not touch anything and definitely not remove anything! We're professionals, we're scientists, we're…"

"We're grave robbers, Howard!" interrupted Fisher. "We risked our reputations, our futures, by going in there. If we hadn't found anything, if we were caught…"

Carter interrupted, "But we now know that we have probably made the most amazing find in all of history. We've seen the gold, the objects. All wondrous things! And we know that we have found Tutankhamun's burial chamber and that his shrine is intact. It's fifteen or sixteen feet long, and I don't know how high!

"No, Howard. As I said inside the tomb, you'll be famous. Yes, I found the clay jars at Dra Abu and went through all that boring material. Scroll after scroll, tightly rolled together, all written in demotic. Lists of accounts, legal transactions, marriage contracts, housing contracts—all really boring, and from the time of Ptolemy, twelve hundred years after Tutankhamun. Except for the scrap that mentioned that the tomb of the boy king was under the tomb of Rameses VI. But I found those jars outside my concession, and I lied when I reported that I found them in the corner of one of the rough apartments abandoned in antiquity. So I have that unprofessional scar, and now this."

Carter got up and started into the kitchen to order tea from a servant. While Carter was gone, Fisher reflected on the morning after his finding of the jars back in January. He had been able to get in four hours of sleep before going out to his site on the Dra Abu hillside. The workers had just uncovered a small tomb that had been abandoned as a dwelling by poor Arab villagers, possibly as recently as fifty years before. It was located near a gully, and the outer court of the tomb had been subdivided into apartments.

The morning after his find in January, he carefully removed the ropes from the two long, bullet-shaped jars. He immediately saw that the contents of both were papyri, all in the demotic language, a language that existed for a thousand years. Demotic was not picture-oriented like hieroglyphics. Its earliest usage overlapped with hieroglyphics, with early use of demotic only for legal, administrative, and commercial texts. And its usage centuries later overlapped with Coptic script, which is a combination of Greek and demotic used to this day by the Coptic Orthodox Church in Egypt. Fisher had gone to a great effort to learn demotic and Coptic due to his keen interest in Coptic Christians, who were an oppressed minority in Egypt.

Carter now returned with tea. Fisher said, "Howard, you are going to get a lot of attention. There will be pressure from reporters. Hey, you can sell the rights to one newspaper and keep the others out! But you won't keep the Egyptians out. That Frenchman, Lacau, and his henchmen in the Department of Antiquities have already started to try to keep everything for Egypt, everything. And he will be relentless. If you're not careful, Carnarvon will end up with nothing. I don't want any of this; I just want to work Palestine!"

"I guess you're right. I have to stay with this, but I agree that it will probably be horrible. I can't blame you for wanting to get out. I agree, we'll keep your involvement a secret, but I do want Carnarvon to invite you to go into the tomb when he arrives. That reminds me, I need to get off a telegram to him,"

"Good God, you can't tell him you've found Tutankhamun's tomb. Be optimistic so he'll want to come, but don't let on that you know what's really in the tomb."

Carter wrote out a note and dispatched one of his servants to ferry across the Nile and post the telegraph at the Winter Palace.

DATE: 06NOV1922
TO: LORD CARNARVON
FROM: HOWARD CARTER
    AT LAST HAVE MADE WONDERFUL DISCOVERY IN VALLEY; A MAGNIFICENT TOMB WITH SEALS INTACT; RE-COVERED SAME FOR YOUR ARRIVAL; CONGRATULATIONS.
H. CARTER.

"Now what about this papyrus that you pilfered? Where was it, and why did you take it?" Both approached the table, where Fisher had casually placed the papyrus when they returned from their overnight adventure.

Fisher responded, "I guess I just wanted a souvenir, maybe something that I could save for my son; he's thirteen now. It looked to be of no value. It was in a vase that I moved to put in front of the opening we made inside the tomb where you saw the burial shrine. Only the top of the papyrus was sticking out; I don't know how it survived, other than from the oil that was on it. I put the vase there to help hold up the basket lid and the reeds. There really didn't seem to be a reason why the papyrus was there. It looked like it had been put there at the last moment. Robbers would not have left it there, and it could not be part of documents that Tutankhamun was to take into the afterlife with him. I saw that it was hieroglyphic, which I can't read, and I thought it was of no importance."

Carter took the papyrus from Fisher and began to translate it. He frowned as he started into it and got up, went to his desk, sat down, and dipped his pen in ink. As Fisher sipped his tea, Carter started writing on a piece of paper, working slowly. He was not an expert in translating hieroglyphic, but he had worked closely with Arthur Weigall, who was often used for translations.

When he finished, he said, "Clarence, you won't believe this. Let me check it again." While Carter reviewed his translation, Fisher stood up, walked over, and read over his shoulder:

> Majesty, I am Mery-re, a scribe serving at the will of Royal Scribe Ahmose during Akhenaten's reign, and also overseer of Akhenaten's harem. I also served as a scribe under Ay during your reign. I wanted to tell you this when you were older, but now your worldly life has ended too soon. I'm an old man now, but I feel compelled to try to add this, if I can, to what goes with you to the Afterlife. Kherue was a scribe with me under Ahmose and was like a son to me. As Akhenaten got older, he longed for a son to follow him. After fathering seven daughters, Akhenaten turned to Kherue, who had fathered five boys, and compelled him to lie with your mother. Akhenaten is not your father, but Akhenaten

was grateful and treated your true father, Kherue, well. But after Akhenaten fled Egypt, leading the Khabiru out of Egypt after the plagues, your uncle Pharaoh Smenkhkare had Kherue killed by Ay and buried as Akhenaten. May Aten be with you.

"What?" cried Fisher. "That can't be correct. Look at it again!"

"Clarence, this is absolutely incredible. It is saying that it was Akhenaten who led the Hebrews out of Egypt. I guess it means that Moses was actually Pharaoh Akhenaten, and that Akhenaten was not Tutankhamun's father. Oh my God. Oh my God. This is not possible!"

"No, no...it can't be true. I excavated Mereneptah's palace seven years ago. That was where Moses pleaded with Pharaoh to 'let my people go.' It made headlines all over the world! Let me see the papyrus."

Carter handed it to him. "This papyrus certainly looks ancient, like others I have examined. Are you sure you translated it correctly?"

Carter replied, "Sure. Look at this." He moved his chair alongside Clarence and pointed to the papyrus. "This is clearly the cartouche of Akhenaten. And this, 'Khabiru,' as you know, means 'Hebrews.' This means 'leader' or 'led,' this means 'out of,' and this means 'Egypt.' Akhenaten led the Hebrews out of Egypt. And this means 'after the plague.'"

Both men sat in stunned silence for a minute.

"Well, I certainly can't have any association with this now. I made a lot of fuss over finding the palace where Moses pleaded. Now this is saying that I was off by over a century."

"Clarence, there's much more to it than that!" cried Howard. "This is even more important than the discovery of the tomb. It is saying that Moses was actually Egyptian, that he was the pharaoh who moved the capital from Thebes to Amarna and built a city there. He's the one who tried to get the Egyptians to worship one god, called Aten, the sun. He tried to ban Egyptians from worshiping multiple gods but failed. History says that Akhenaten died, but this says that Pharaoh Smenkhkare, Akhenaten's co-regent and then successor, had a scribe killed and placed in a tomb in place of Akhenaten. Incredible! Incredible."

"Howard, this could be very dangerous. During my work for the British during the world war, I consulted with Field Marshal Allenby, and..."

Carter interrupted, "You mean when you spied for the British!"

"Okay. Anyway, I knew that the British intended to make Palestine a protectorate. But I also know, directly from both Allenby and Keith-Roach, that the British would like to establish a national home for the Jewish people in Palestine. This document in the hands of the Zionists would prove that the Jews have rights to all of Palestine."

"You're right. And in the hands of the British, that would give them more cause to oppress the Arabs and move quicker to establish a Jewish state."

"And Arabs could claim the reverse: that Moses was Egyptian, and that the Jews have no right to anywhere in Arab lands," said Carter.

Carter stood and walked over to the arched window. Peering out, he could see Al Qarna and the ferry docks on the near side of the Nile. Through a shimmer almost like a mirage, he could make out the imposing Winter Palace Hotel to the right. It was a typical November day, hazy, humid, and in the upper nineties. He turned toward Fisher.

Both were silent for several minutes.

"We've got to get rid of this," said Fisher finally. "The British and Zionists would want this to prove that there must be a Jewish state. And the Arabs would interpret this to mean that Moses was Egyptian and that Palestine belongs to the Arabs alone. It could cause huge fighting between Arabs and Zionists that could go on for decades. Jerusalem has been the scene of bloody fighting for centuries. It's been destroyed, besieged, and attacked too many times to count. No one should know about this papyrus and its contents, and we should never speak about it again, to ourselves or others."

"I agree." Carter took the papyrus, picked up a candle, walked to the empty fireplace, lit the papyrus, which was hard to get started, and threw it on the hearthstone. Watching until it cooled, he carefully picked all of the remains out of the fireplace and motioned to Fisher. "Come with me."

They went into the kitchen, and Carter got a loaf of bread. He pulled off the end of the bread and made a hole in it. Tearing the charred remains of the papyrus into even smaller pieces, he placed them into the bread. "Come. This is the best way I know to dispose of something absolutely securely." They walked to the servants' huts behind the house, and Carter threw the bread into the deep latrine. "Now let's try to forget about this.

Let's go back to the house and talk about what's next. I'm dead tired, as I'm sure you are, but we should get back to our digs."

Back inside the dining room, which was lavish for Egyptian standards, Fisher said, "So you've cabled Carnarvon that you've made a great discovery of an intact tomb, and that you've covered it up?"

"Right, and I think we've covered our tracks pretty well."

"Well, there doesn't seem to be anything else to do until Carnarvon gets here from Highclere."

"Well, when he gets here, he's going to want to see into the tomb right away. I suggest that before he arrives, we have the workers pull out the rocks down the steps to the first door. Then we have them open that first door and quickly remove all the debris up to the second door, the one directly into the tomb.

"Then, Carnarvon can come in, even with Lady Evelyn, walk up to the door, and I can break through into the upper corner that we've patched. I can break through, reach in with a candle to see if it's safe, and then peer in and report what I've seen."

"That's dramatic," said Fisher, "but it will make for spectacular press!"

CHAPTER 6

Wednesday, November 29, 1922
Pink House, Valley of the Kings

28 November, Tuesday. In late afternoon Lord Carnarvon came to invite me to a new tomb they have found in the Tomb of the Kings. He says it is one of the most magnificent yet found and full of beautiful stuff. Lunch is to be served in the Valley near the Tomb.

29 November, Wednesday. Went to the Tombs of the Kings, where luncheon was served to a party of about thirty, including local officials. After luncheon two by two Lord Carnarvon and Mr. Carter took us into the tomb.

Clarence Fisher added comments describing what he saw in the first room of the tomb, most notably the two life-sized ebony statues, and then closed his journal. It was the only mention he would ever make about his involvement with the tomb of Tutankhamun.

In the twenty-three days since Howard Carter had cabled Lord Carnarvon about the find, Clarence and Carter purposely avoided each other. Only after Carnarvon personally invited him did Fisher agree to go to the tomb. He felt that it would seem strange to decline the invitation.

It was the end of the day, and Clarence got up from his easy chair, one of the few real comforts he had in his Pink House. His bedroom was serviceable, and his study included a sturdy desk, his drawing table, and well-lined bookshelves. Another room was used for storage of artifacts, but his living room had only an oil lamp, a small table, and a chair. He entered the kitchen, where he added to his glass of whiskey.

Returning to his chair, he thought back over the incredible events of November 1922. On November 1, Carter began digging at the precise spot indicated by Fisher's find in a papyrus at Dra Ab el Naga near the end of the spring season. The top of a staircase was found on November 4, and the steps were cleared down to the first door on November 5. Carter and Fisher had surreptitiously entered the tomb that night, and Carter cabled Carnarvon on November 6. The rocks blocking the steps were kept in place, awaiting Carnarvon's arrival from Highclere Castle in England.

George Edward Stanhope Molyneux Herbert, Fifth Earl of Carnarvon, arrived in Luxor with his daughter, Lady Evelyn Herbert, on November 23, settling into the Winter Palace Hotel. Work then began in earnest to excavate the tomb. By the afternoon of November 26, the passageway had been cleared to the second door. With great fanfare, Carter opened a small hole in the area where he and Fisher had entered on the fifth, first testing the air with a candle, then peering in. As he and Fisher had planned, Carter had exclaimed that he saw "wondrous things."

Clarence sat back, took another sip, and laughed out loud. "What a showman! And now he has to pretend that everything he finds is a surprise!" He closed his eyes, peacefully knowing that his and Carter's entrance into the tomb would be kept a secret. And knowing that the controversial contents of the papyrus he found in the tomb would not cause any disruption to the world.

CHAPTER 7

Tuesday, October 23, 1928
Jerusalem

Clarence Fisher walked up the short flight of steps that led from the Via Dolorosa to the hotel lobby. In his hand was an old map, folded into quarters.

"What on earth is so damn important that you had to wire me to come up from Tel Megiddo? Don't you know that I'm busy? What a goddam terrible trip; five hours to go damn eighty miles. That bloody Wadi Ara Road, even in a motorcar, is impossible; it's almost a goddam donkey trail. And even the narrow Way of the Patriarchs was impossible, with three wrecks. Bloody hell, what do you want? It can't be a problem with Stanley; you would have posted me. I'm too damn busy. I want a…"

"Clarence, calm down. And don't use such foul language with me. You know better than that," interrupted Florie Carswell Fisher, his wife of twenty-one years. Clarence sat down next to her on a settee, placing the map at his left side. "And you want a, what, a drink? You're still impossible! I come all this way, and you know how seasick I get. It's been horrible."

Florie, also known as Pree because her older sister, Lessie, couldn't pronounce her name, had made her way from Philadelphia's Broad Street Station to New York's Pennsylvania Station via the Pennsylvania Railroad. She paid a round-trip fare of $290 for second-class accommodations on the SS *Providence* of the Fabre Line. While she would not have to change ships to get to Palestine, she would have to suffer through thirteen stops all over the Mediterranean before finally landing in Haifa.

"P-Pree, huh-how did you get the m-money to ka-ka-come here?" Clarence's stuttering had suddenly rekindled in earnest, worse than it had been in almost twenty years, due to the stress of the surprise visit of his wife. She had cabled him the night before from her room at the al Hashimi Hotel on the Via Dolorosa. The old hotel, which had recently been remodeled, was on one of the blocks of the Via Dolorosa that was barely an alleyway. They were now seated in the small lobby of the hotel. Above was a high skylight, with walkways around the second floor furnished waist high with marble-arched windows above. Over the front desk, which they faced, was a sign that stated, in English only, "Absolutely no alcohol."

"At least the hotel is nice, and my room is comfortable. I can look out my window and see the Dome of the Rock, but it still looks drab as always. I thought you helped restore it?"

"I-I did, but the war interfered, and the B-British never really followed through, although, as I had su-suggested, they did strengthen it, rebuilt s-some of the foundation, and other things to make it safe. It was a wreck when I got to look at it, and every s-step I took, I was followed by a guard, so I didn't get to inspect things as I'd hoped. Also, the earthquake last July damaged some of the repairs, so-so it needs more work."

"B-but how did you get the ma-money to come here?"

"From Father. He took what may be the last of his money for me to come here so that I could…"

Clarence interrupted, "Money? I thought he was well off. Wa-what happened to it all?"

"Well, he had big profits from Carswell College, his religious books, his missions speaking around the country, and the schools in Baltimore and Philadelphia for stutterers and stammerers. He was doing so well, and was so grateful for what the Lord had given him, that he decided to put most of his money into a trust for the college. He thought that he could prosper without it. But times got tough, and he had to close the Carswell Institute for Stammerers in Baltimore earlier this year. So Broadus and Caroline have moved in with us on Frazier Street in Philadelphia. Now he's writing a book on stammerers, but that isn't going to make much money. And I don't know…"

"So-so you spent money to come here? W-why on earth…"

"Clarence, I…" Her lower lip began to tremble, and her eyes began to water. She paused, looked down, and her shoulders began to shake. She hunched forward and began to quietly sob.

Pree was a frail woman. At fifty-three, she looked more like she was almost seventy. She was often prone to illness, either real or imagined. But she was strong in business; she was the principal of the Carswell Institute on Parkside Avenue, directly across the street from Philadelphia's Fairmount Park, site of the 1876 Centennial. The institute was elegant, with its large foyer, meeting/class/dining room, piano room, and even a small gymnasium. Upstairs there were small bedrooms with a common bathroom. Students—adult male students from different parts of the country—could live there and learn and practice overcoming their stuttering or stammering. Most, including day students, improved significantly after attending. Pree served as administrator, assisted with teaching, and taught piano to students, even to children from the upscale neighborhood where the school was located.

Pree tried to compose herself, while Clarence remained silent. "I came all this long way to see you face to face. I want to somehow, somehow…" She sobbed again and leaned forward.

Unexpectedly, and to Pree, uncharacteristically, Clarence leaned to his right, reached across her shoulder, and hugged her. Pree broke down completely. She was so thin that his hands met behind her as she was sobbing. After thirty seconds, he made a decision. Reaching around her with his left hand, he removed a ring from the little finger of his right hand. He pushed her away somewhat and showed the ring to her.

"Here, take this ring. It contains a scarab that I found under the Dome of the Rock in Jerusalem. I had it mounted in sixteen-karat gold. The cartouche, of Shoshenq I, matches a portion of a stela we unearthed at Megiddo. We are calling it the Shoshenq I stela, because it tells of that pharaoh's conquests in Palestine. Shoshenq I is the pharaoh Shishak from the Old Testament. Do you remember that Shishak took away the treasures from the temple?"

Pree sobbed, "Yes. But it's not a very pretty ring."

"Look underneath. That cartouche on the scarab indicates the pharaoh Shishak. This ring is important and valuable. Please take it now…And if you don't like it, give it to your niece. Or give it to Stanley. Just, please, make sure that it's not lost, and please keep it in the family. I may need to photograph it sometime. Or, it may be important if I die suddenly."

As she put the ring in her pocket, her lips began to quiver, and she began to sob again. She leaned into him, and he held her for almost two minutes.

She released herself, sat up straight, reached into her pocket and extracted a handkerchief, blew her nose, composed herself, and sternly continued. "Clarence, you have abandoned us completely. You send no letters; you send no money. I used to be able to say that you were home summers but then went back to dig in the winter season. Now, I haven't seen you since you quit Penn in 1925. Stanley hasn't had a father since he was sixteen. Yes, you got him a scholarship to Penn, and he completed his freshman year, but now he's followed friends of his to Muskingum College in Ohio. Did you know that? Do you at least read my letters?"

She continued, barely pausing for breath. "And yes, my father paid for that too. Stanley's out there now, but I worry about him."

"Pree, you worry about everything, and I'm—"

She interrupted. "Well, don't you think I have a right to worry about money, about the future, about my, my, husband…" She began sobbing again.

"W-well, I think—"

"No, you don't think. You never think about us!" Getting angry and gathering strength, she said, "You just think about yourself, and, and your drinking. Yes, don't look at me that way. I know about your drinking. You quit Penn because of it; they covered it up nicely. They built that wing at the museum to house the columns you excavated from Egypt. At least they invited Stanley and me to the opening. Despite my shame, we both went to the grand opening because we had to maintain that we were a happy family and that you were too busy with starting at Megiddo. Paid for by John Rockefeller, was it, where was the money? And then you had to be replaced—which I read in the newspaper, with not a word from you—because of your health. Ha! I'll bet it was your drinking again! Look at that sign over there: no drinking. I'm glad we're meeting here. At another place, you'd be over grabbing a drink now."

"But—"

"But be quiet! Now what about the rumors about you liking men? Penn archaeologists are still talking about you, even though you abruptly quit. And those rumors, disgusting rumors, get back to me, including rumors that you were involved with a man named Valentine Gere at Nippur before we were married. That's disgusting! I know, you certainly…" She leaned in closer and whispered, "I know that you haven't slept with me since shortly before Clarence was born." Louder she said, "Are you a queer? God, how can I even say that? Just to think…" She paused again, looked at Clarence, but he held his tongue.

"Clarence, I came here because I wanted to see if there's any way I could repair things, to bring you closer to me and to Stanley, to make me at least a little bit happy. The trip from New York to Cherbourg was much colder than I expected, and I was seasick the whole time. I thought that maybe we could spend some days together, that you could show me around the Holy City, take me to your digs, introduce me as your wife to other people. I want to persuade you to try to make things better between us. I want to make us happy, make you happy. Maybe we could even sleep—"

"Stop right there, dammit!" Clarence interrupted. While she had been talking, he had gone from a position of defense to one of offense; anger was driving him. And, as always when he was angered, his stuttering stopped completely. "Stop, goddammit! I've let you talk long enough! Okay, yes, I've had a damn drinking problem, and yes, it's been covered up by both Penn and the University of Chicago. I've kept a very important secret known only to Carter and me. That's been weighing heavily on me. I know where a vast treasure is, but I've had to keep that secret until the political tide turns in Egypt; then I'll be rich and famous, as I so rightly deserve. These things keep me awake sometimes, and drinking helps. But I've had other health issues, too. You're always sick. Have you ever had malaria? Well, I have; it's horrible. It's why I started drinking. Yes, I feel guilty about not being with my family, but drinking helps with that too.

"But I am married to my work. I love it. I've achieved some fame, and there have been many exciting things that have happened to me. I've made important discoveries, in Egypt and here in Palestine, that relate to biblical things." He moved his hands together. "I've proved that Pharaoh Shishak, from the Bible, was at King Solomon's temple and at Megiddo.

The Bible says that he took away all of the treasures. I know where his tomb is; I'm just waiting for things to calm down after Carter's discovery. And I found a secret that can never be shared with anyone, when Carter and I went into Tutankhamun's tomb before Carter arrived. Yes, I was the second person into the tomb, not Carnarvon. Money? I've never been paid anywhere near what I should be, what other archaeologists like Petrie, Breasted, and that dolt Carter are making. Yes, my real reason for leaving Penn was to make more money. I thought Rockefeller would pay three times what he ended up paying me. I ended up taking the job because I had no other; he probably knew that. Millionaire. Ha!

"And rumors be damned! Yes, I enjoy the company of men. Always have—probably because of my shyness with women. I enjoy talking with men, drinking with men, and just being with men. Before we were married, I tended to my mentor, Valentine Gere, who was sick. He was chief architect at Nippur, and I learned so much from him as a young man! So much." He paused. "He got very sick in Baghdad, and I accompanied him to London, then to Nippur. I nursed him and I cared for him very much. But in no disgusting way.

"And I'm beginning to care for Arab boys, who have been so poor, have so little schooling. They've been orphaned—I even volunteer at the Schneller Orphanage for Arab boys here in Jerusalem. Lord knows that things are hard enough for them. And yet, the British are bringing in Jews from all over the world, calling them colonists. Most of them are nice people, but they have no right to be here. Believe me, I know, they have no right to be here!

"But hear me, hear me. I am not queer! Things that queers do disgust me as well."

"Okay, Clarence, but can't we at least—"

He rose suddenly, turned, and towered over her. "Enough of this silliness. You are foolish to have ever thought to come over here, spending money, to no possible outcome. Here, take this." He handed her the folded map. "Just take this map; it's extremely important. It's the map of Olympia that I created in college, but I've made some small but important changes. I need to have it in the States, in a safe place. Give it to Stanley and make sure he keeps it."

"But, what—"

"Just do it! It's really important, valuable, like the ring. Now, I have important work to do that I must get back to. I'm leaving! Have a safe trip home. And leave me alone!" With that, he quickly walked out, going down the three narrow steps leading from the lobby to the Via Dolorosa.

Pree was mortified, but she ran after him to the top of the short set of steps. "Damn you!" she yelled as he stepped out. She reached in her pocket and extracted the Shishak ring. She was ready to throw it down the steps after him, but then thought better of it. Instead she shrank into the nearest chair. She tried to keep her sobs to herself. After four minutes, she composed herself enough to walk up the wide steps to her hotel room. Once in, she took off her dress and lay down on the bed in her slip. She was hot, tired, exhausted, and even thought of killing herself. Finally, she let herself go, crying herself to sleep.

The next morning, she woke up after hearing the shrill sound of the Islamic call to worship, heard loudly through loudspeakers newly installed on a nearby minaret. It sounded like a loud telephone voice muffled by a sock. She fixed herself up, got dressed, and looked at herself in the mirror. She felt now like she looked: an old woman.

Putting on a confident facade, she walked downstairs and was fortunate to have a good breakfast, which, amazingly, she was able to hold down. She asked the desk clerk for the nearest Thomas Cook office. She walked there and changed her departure to the next day, nine days sooner than she had planned. She'd have to take a tramp steamer to Constantinople; she didn't care what she had to put up with. From there, she would have to wait three days to catch the SS *Bryan*, on the National Greek Line, which would stop in Cherbourg, France, on its way to New York.

Following that, Pree walked back to her hotel, where she made plans to visit some of Jerusalem's sights that afternoon.

She never saw Clarence again.

CHAPTER 8

**Monday June 30, 1941
Jerusalem, 8:30 p.m**

"So, Clarence, what do you plan to do now that your retirement is effective as of today?" asked Hilda Petrie. "Are you going back to the States?"

The three, Sir and Lady Petrie and Clarence Fisher, were the only permanent residents at the American School of Oriental Research in Jerusalem. They were in the large dining/meeting room located in the left rear wing of the magnificent stone building at Twenty-Six Saladin Road. They were sitting near the small bar. Founded in 1900, the ASOR supported the training of new archaeologists as well as research and expeditions. Fisher had a small room on the second floor, overlooking the courtyard, but he was pleased with the large room downstairs dedicated to supporting his work on his monumental *Corpus of Palestinian Pottery*.

It was 8:30 p.m., and they were finishing a dinner of shepherd's pie, with the dessert some sort of concoction with dates, and were enjoying drinks. Both men were wearing suits with dark ties on starched high-collar white shirts. Lady Hilda Petrie was dressed in a simple light blue shift, cinched at the waist. Her red hair was graying, parted in the middle and tied in a bun. At age seventy, she looked much younger than the eighteen years that separated hers and Flinders's ages. Flinders maintained his large body shape and his flowing, full, white beard, but his hairline was receding, although full. Clarence had maintained his slim shape, but his face was fuller, and his hair, which was combed back from a high forehead, and mustache were both white. He had maintained the same rimless glasses throughout his life.

"No," Fisher replied. "I'm afraid that it looks too dangerous to travel far, what with Italy invading Greece, and Germany bombing London and occupying much of Europe, including France. The government has deported all of the Germans from my beloved Schneller Orphanage, and the military has taken it over. At least, as chairman of the Schneller Orphanage Committee, I've been able to secure a temporary Schneller Orphanage for some of the boys in Nazareth; it's now called the Syrian Orphanage. But I also had to help place others; God knows if they'll be all right. Such a shame."

He stopped and sat back wistfully, thinking over some of the highlights of his life and career. Hilda and Flinders were accustomed to his long pauses, due to his tendency to stutter. After almost a minute, he continued. "I love to summer on Cyprus, but even that is doubtful." He paused again to tend to his drink. "I wish, however, that I could see my grandson back in Philadelphia. I received one of those cheap records from my daughter-in-law, and it has a recording of little Glenn wondering if his 'ganpa' is in there. But I can't see that happening anytime soon. At least my adopted son, David Tarazi Fisher, is doing well. He's teaching chemistry at Bishop Gobat School, and should be safe."

"That's nice, but it's a shame that you can't see your grandson," said Hilda.

"I'm surprised that the British haven't asked you to spy; they've given up on me," said Sir Flinders Petrie.

"Well, that's because you're, what, eighty-three?"

Hilda cut in, "He's eighty-seven and doing pretty well at that. But thank God, his spying days are over."

"Well, I had hoped mine were," said Clarence, pausing again. "And, at sixty-five, no one's asked me to do dangerous things like I did in the world war. My cover as an ambulance driver, although I did assist with bringing wounded from the Battle of Megiddo to Jerusalem, was valuable in helping both General Allenby and, especially, T. E. Lawrence against the Turks."

A waiter interrupted him, and he sat back and thought of some of the things he had accomplished in the war.

British general Edmund Allenby arrived in Jerusalem in June of 1917 to drive the Turks, who had aligned themselves with the Germans, out of Jerusalem and all of Palestine. Allenby quickly determined that he would need the help of Arabs who were willing to fight. It was suggested that he contact archaeologist Clarence Fisher, who was excavating at Beit She'an in Palestine, because Fisher was so well respected by the many Arabs he employed. Fisher hurried to Jerusalem and met with Allenby and a young British Army intelligence officer, T. E. Lawrence, who was later glorified as Lawrence of Arabia. Lawrence was a budding archaeologist working at Carchemish, in Syria, along with Leonard Woolley, an archaeologist from the University of Pennsylvania.

At the meeting with Allenby and Lawrence, Fisher agreed that he could help, via his contacts with many Arab leaders and his knowledge of a variety of areas throughout Palestine. Allenby suggested that Fisher could have a cover as an ambulance driver, and Fisher agreed to a commission as a captain in the Red Cross service in Jerusalem. During the war, Fisher worked closely with Lawrence and the Arab Bureau, and he provided regular updates to Allenby. He worked with Arab tribal leaders and assisted with organizing them into the fighting units led so well by Lawrence. Fisher later provided occasional assistance to Lawrence and British Oriental secretary Gertrude Bell, who were determining the post-war boundaries of the Middle East at the 1921 Cairo Conference.

The waiter left, but no one at the table noticed that the bartender continued to be within earshot of their table. Fisher continued, "I've had no more involvement in politics since that conference, until two years ago when I got a phone call from Jerusalem governor Keith-Roach. He said that British colonial secretary Malcolm MacDonald wanted me to immediately come to London to help try to ease tensions between Arabs and Jews at the Saint James Conference. MacDonald was trying to set a limit on the immigration of Jews to Palestine, and both sides were arguing. Ha! I got to London just as the conference angrily ended, with nothing resolved.

"Other than that, I've been involved with some Arab charities, including the Schneller Orphanage, which was run by Germans up until this past summer. So I was able to gather some information about Germany and also about the Zionist-Arab situation here in Jerusalem. I've been advising

Governor Keith-Roach whenever I learn anything, and he asks me questions all the time."

"Good work, Clarence," said Flinders. "Maybe someday, someone will write a book on the spying contributions of archaeologists!"

"Hear, hear," said Hilda, Flinders's wife of forty-three years. "No more spying, either of you, and may Britain—and Palestine—be safe! Long live the king!" She raised her glass of wine, clinking it against Flinders's and against Clarence's second full glass of whiskey.

"Say, Clarence, you ought to go easy on that."

"Ah, but Flinders, this afternoon I finished my last official day of work. Tonight I have fun; tomorrow I'll be sorry. And, after that, I will be working part time as acting director again, until Nelson Glueck arrives back from the States on August fifteenth. And I have my charities to attend to."

The Petries excused themselves, and Clarence got up, wished them a good night, and walked over to the bar, where their waiter was whispering with the bartender.

As he continued sipping, he thought of the differences between Flinders and himself. Flinders was much more famous. He had been knighted, written books, and given speeches all over the world. Clarence, partly because of his stuttering, did not like to speak publicly. He had written one major book on Egypt, *The Minor Cemetery at Giza*. It was more intended for use as a textbook and to showcase the Reisner-Fisher method of excavating wide areas so that buildings could be unearthed as they existed in the past. Although he had been meticulous about documenting his findings on index cards, Clarence did not like publishing his work; excavating and discovering were his passions.

Because of Petrie's insistence on excavating straight down in trenches, as opposed to Fisher's approach, and because, he had admitted to himself, he was jealous, Clarence did not get along with Flinders. However, in their years of living at the American School of Oriental Research, they both had mellowed, and both enjoyed telling one another stories of their many exploits as archaeologists.

Now Clarence asked for his third Balvenie whiskey, neat, as always. He knew that he had a drinking problem—had one for decades. But it usually didn't interfere with his work.

As he got more and more relaxed and, he realized, loose, he began to think of those times that his drinking had interfered with his dealing with his managers and employees. At the Penn Museum, he had argued with his employees and museum director George Gordon. In 1925, while softened by the effects of too much of his whiskey, he had sent a letter of resignation to Director Gordon, despite being awarded an honorary doctor's degree at the winter commencement in 1924. A similar problem followed at his most significant, most well-funded appointment as director of the University of Chicago's expedition at Megiddo, in Palestine, in 1925. That was to be his crowning achievement, funded by John D. Rockefeller himself, but drinking and health problems continued, leading to his dismissal in 1927.

The only one left at the bar at 10:00 p.m., Clarence began slurring his words to the bartender, Itzak Herz, as he was partway through his fourth drink. "You know, I was the world's best archaeologist. I excavated at the world's first pyramid and at a cemetery next to the big pyramids. Boy, were they huge!" He raised his arms in the shape of a pyramid and almost lost his balance. He paused to collect himself.

Another sip.

"And I found the palace where Moses pleaded to let his people go. I was famous. And then King Tut's tomb, and places in Egypt and Palestine. I was good; I told all those other archaeologists how to dig. And Howard Carter…Howard Carter. I told him where to dig for Tutankhamun, and we went in before anyone else, anyone else. And I found a document, an old papyrus, really old. It was in Tut's tomb, and no one but me and Howard knows what was in it. Nobody." He looked to his left and behind, where the tables had already been set for breakfast.

He finished his drink in one big swallow and leaned forward, whispering to the bartender, Herz. "It was proof that Moses—yes, Moses—was actually, no, really, the pharaoh Akhenaten. Really. Moses was Egyptian, an Egyptian! Not a Jew, not a Jew! But nobody knows that, only me and Carter. Ha! Carter even used it to threaten the British when they tried to kick him out of Egypt! Ha!"

His words were slurring as he said, "And I also know where there is a tomb with more treasures than Tut's; guy named Shishak. Filled with loot from under the dome, Solomon's temple, maybe the Ark of the Cov—"

Clarence then fell off his stool, almost collapsing. He lay there until the bartender helped him up. Staggering, he somehow made his way back to his small room.

• • •

Late that night, Itzak Herz left the ASOR and went to the home of his wife's cousin, Moshe Hakim, near the Edison Theater on Yeshayahu Street in the Zikhron Moshe section of Jerusalem.

"Moshe, Moshe. Wake up!"

"Itzak, what is so important that you have to wake me in the middle of the night? This better be important!"

"It is, it is!" Itzak could hardly contain himself. "There is an old man living at the ASOR, Clarence Fisher. He just retired today, and he got really drunk. The waiter, Nadal, overheard some of his conversation at dinner, and then Fisher started slurring—"

"Come on, come on!" Moshe insisted. "What did you learn?"

"That this man, Fisher, had proof that Moses was an Egyptian, not a Jew, and—"

"Hold on. What?"

"Fisher said he had discovered a papyrus in King Tut's tomb that said that Moses was some pharaoh, an Egyptian, and—"

"Wait. If true, that would really upset our movement."

"Yes, but there's more. The waiter found out that Fisher was a spy, at that German orphanage—"

"Schneller?"

"Yes, and that he has been advising Governor Keith-Roach on Arab-Jewish affairs. This Fisher seems to be very much involved with the Arabs and the British. Oh, and he also said he knew where there was a tomb with treasures in it."

"Okay, what time is it?" He looked at his watch. "It's three a.m. Okay, it's early, but this is important. But I'll get up and get the group together for a really early breakfast. Be sure to get Eliyahu for me."

CHAPTER 9

Friday, July 18, 1941
Nazareth, Palestine (Israel)

Clarence Fisher walked from the Azar mansion, near the market in the crowded Old City section of Nazareth, to his venerable 1932 Ford "woody" station wagon. Dusty and rusted in many places, the battered car still operated fairly reliably despite the extreme conditions year round in Palestine. Clarence's main concern was with tires; flats were common, and tires were almost impossible to get due to the war. A working spare was a necessity. He always parked the vehicle outside the Old City due to the crowded streets.

Clarence had been a guest of Fauzi Azar, a member of one of Nazareth's wealthiest families. Fisher had been in Nazareth for the last eight days assisting in the affairs of the relocated Syrian, formerly Schneller, Orphanage. Fauzi was a strong financial backer of the orphanage's move to Nazareth and always welcomed Clarence into his ornate three-story home.

Fisher reached the woody, started it, put it in gear, and proceeded along the bumpy but manageable road to Al-Hamma, a small town usually less than two hours from Nazareth.

• • •

"Quick, Eliyahu, run to my auto. Fisher is probably going to the hot springs again, only a little earlier than usual this morning. Run, you've got to get to the bakery well ahead of him. Don't forget—quit the mission if you have car trouble. And be sure you have the poison!"

"Yes, Moshe. I'll beat him out of town and get to the bakery. I'll prove my worth to you."

"Don't fail!" screamed Moshe Hakim at the receding nineteen-year-old boy, who was taller than any boy he had ever seen. "You must prove yourself to Avraham." Moshe was the leader in Nazareth of the Zionist underground group called Lehi. The Zionist underground traced its roots back to 1907, but now there were two lethal clandestine groups. Moshe had been a part of the Special Night Squad, which had been trained by the British captain Orde Wingate to perform acts of violence against the Arabs. But in August of 1940, a new paramilitary group called Lehi was founded by Avraham Stern. They were enraged that the Special Night Squad had joined with the British to fight any German plans to occupy Jerusalem. The Lehi, which were called the Stern Gang by the British, did not want the British controlling Palestine and wanted unrestricted immigration by Jews from all over Europe into Palestine. They even went so far as to reach out to Fascist Italy and Germany to try to get a settlement that stated that the Lehi would join them in fighting the British if the Axis would ensure a free Jewish state in Palestine with unrestricted immigration.

Moshe had learned from Itzak Herz that Fisher had gone to Nazareth on July 10 and that he would be there for two weeks. Moshe and Avraham Stern then decided that Fisher needed to be eliminated and that Nazareth was a very Zionist-friendly location for such an event.

Eliyahu's parents eagerly welcomed Moshe into their simple home outside Nazareth. Moshe had learned that Fisher was spending afternoons at the Syrian Orphanage and had assigned Eliyahu to follow him and learn what he could.

Eliyahu Czeny had begged Moshe to let him become a member of Lehi. Moshe was doubtful at first, due to his youth, but Eliyahu's strength, athleticism, and enthusiasm had convinced him. He was over six feet tall, with broad shoulders. His close-cropped hair gave him a boyish look; he had no facial hair. It was Eliyahu who followed Clarence and found that he started most days with a trip to the Hamma hot sulfur springs and the bakery. The three of them had come up with a plan to use potassium cyanide, a greenish paste that acts slowly and can be put in food, to kill Fisher. Today was the day.

• • •

Clarence Fisher pulled into the small parking area at the sulfur hot springs and told Shaker Ahmad Suleiman to leave his suitcase, bathing costume, and towel in the woody. Clarence had met him at the Al-Hamma railway station earlier. Shaker-Ahmad had arrived on the morning Jezreel Valley Line train from Haifa. He was a small, rotund man, with a round face, kind eyes behind round pince-nez glasses, and a small mustache. He was wearing a suit, like Fisher, but wore a fez on his head. Raised in Algiers, he had come to Jerusalem just before the Battle of Jerusalem in 1917. He had proved his value as a forward observer at the 1918 Battle of Megiddo, and had been a close confidant and advisor on Palestinian affairs ever since.

"Please, Dr. Fisher, tell me about the baths where we're going," said Shaker Ahmad, "I've never been to one." Shaker Ahmad was a close friend of Fisher's and served as a trusted manager and teacher at the Dar el-Awlad school in Jerusalem. More of an orphanage than a school, Fisher had organized it two years before for poor Arab orphans.

"You'll love the sulfur hot springs; they're so relaxing. All of the cares of the world seem to drift away in the soothing water. No concerns with Arabs and Zionists, with the British mandate and military, with the Nazis…" He trailed off.

"Anyway, you've probably had breakfast, but I'm taking you to a marvelous bakery near the springs. I particularly love their fresh bagels, with the most wonderful spread. I think you'll thank me for the bagels and the hot springs!"

Shaker Ahmad had come to spend time in Nazareth reviewing affairs related to both the Jerusalem and Nazareth orphanages that Fisher was so interested in. Fisher seemed to be spending much more time with his charities, which included the Jerusalem YMCA and the Jerusalem representation of the Lutheran Church in America. As permanent professor at the American School of Oriental Research in Jerusalem, he had been working on his *Corpus of Palestinian Pottery*, a massive project to catalog, photograph or draw, and date pottery shards from many biblical archaeological sites. He put in many long days working on this project so that he could have time to assist with his charities. Fisher had finally finished volume one of this massive project but had just retired to put all of his efforts into the charities. The remaining work on the *Corpus of Palestinian Pottery*— another three volumes—would have to wait for someone else.

Clarence and Shaker Ahmad walked the short distance from the parking lot at the hot springs to the Agadat Lehem Bakery. "They have a delicious hot cheese that they spread over the bagel. I love it! I wish that this bakery was here when I was excavating at Beit She'an; I would have wanted to drive up here every day. Ha! But I didn't have a motorcar then. The bakery, which opened in 1926, has a large brick-and-stone oven. It's known for its bagels, but then, that's just about all that's on the menu."

"I think I'll just have a plain bagel; I don't like cheese," said Shaker Ahmad.

They walked in, and Fisher gave his usual greeting to the owner. But this morning, the owner only mumbled hello, looked down at the floor, and appeared to Clarence to be either sad or frightened. Clarence also noticed a very tall, well-built boy standing near the counter. His apron was much too small for him. He somehow looked familiar to Fisher, but not from the bakery.

Clarence ordered tea and juice for both of them, a plain bagel for Shaker Ahmad, and a bagel with his favorite Akkawi cheese spread over it. "I like the combination of a cold bagel with the hot cheese spread over it. The baker tells me that the cheese will not spread until it is heated in the oven to just the right temperature. I love it!"

Shaker Ahmad was his usual quiet self, and this morning he just listened to Clarence. "The Hamma sulfur hot springs were discovered sometime around the reign of Roman emperor Hadrian in the second century AD. Before we go in, we'll look at the ruins from around that time that surround one of the springs."

Clarence was about to continue when he was interrupted by the young, serious-looking, and very tall boy bringing their food. Clarence didn't notice the boy's shaking hand as he put down the tea and bagels. He took a sip of hot tea and continued, "As I was saying, the springs have long been known for…" He paused to take a bite of the bagel, expectantly chewing it to savor its goodness. He stopped chewing.

"Hmm. This tastes vastly different today. It's kind of acrid, more like radishes. I can still taste the cheese, but it burns my tongue like spices. I guess it's okay." He continued chewing.

"Anyway, the springs are naturally at about one hundred and five degrees year round, and have about five percent sulfur in them; you'll notice the rotten egg smell. The water is kind of hard to get into, but you'll get adjusted to the temperature rather quickly."

He took another bite and then said, "I'm not sure about this. It's not bad, but it's very strong." He looked for the owner, but he must have been in the back. He did not see the boy either.

"There are many medicinal qualities of the water beyond just relaxing you. It's good for the joints, which I really need after all of my walking over the years, and my skin always feels better afterward. The only thing wrong is that it can make your heart rate go up."

He took another bite and then leaned into Shaker Ahmad and continued, "And it eases a hangover. I wish these springs were closer to Nazareth. Ha!"

He finished the bagel and made a face. "I'll never have that again! I need to find the owner. He'll need to explain, and I'll have to test it before I have another bagel here someday."

With that, he and Shaker Ahmad got up from the table. He still saw neither the owner nor the boy, so he left his money on the table. He walked over to the counter and called for the owner. He waited a minute and called again.

"Maybe he went for supplies," said Shaker Ahmad.

"I guess so. I'll give him the dickens when I see him again. Let's go."

They walked to the hot springs, where they went to the springhead from the Roman era. Clarence pointed out the ruins of an amphitheater and the walls of the ancient bathhouse surrounding the ancient, now dry, pool. Other pool areas had been open in more modern times, but they had fallen into disrepair and were overrun with vegetation. One of the areas had been rehabilitated, however, in 1936, and it was now a popular place.

They walked back to the modern entrance, and Clarence paid for them both. The pool was surrounded by well-kept changing tents, and a series of small huts was under construction. Clarence and Shaker Ahmad went into separate tents to change into their bathing costumes.

Clarence lowered himself slowly into the steaming water, but it was much more difficult for Shaker Ahmad, who stopped when he put his foot in. He was in as far as both knees when Clarence suddenly yelled and pulled himself from the water.

"Something is wrong with me! Help me, something is wrong!"

Shaker Ahmad quickly took his feet out of the water and reached to help Clarence, who was sitting up but breathing hard.

"Oh God, something is wrong, I've never felt like this before. My heart is racing, but that's not the problem. I feel like I have a temperature of a hundred and fifty degrees! Help me." He swooned and then lay on his side, fearful that he would pass out.

"Is there a doctor around?" yelled Shaker Ahmad. "Doctor! This man is very ill!" No one responded, so he ran to the entrance and asked where the nearest doctor was. He was told in Nazareth. He then made the decision to take Clarence back to Jerusalem where he knew he could get better care for him. "I'll get his belongings. Please, somebody, help me get him to the car!"

Shaker Ahmad ran into his tent and changed quickly, not even drying off his feet. He then gathered Clarence's things from the next tent. Only one man had responded to help; the others seemed to be preoccupied with their baths. Of course, there were no women allowed in the baths. The two of them supported Clarence as he walked feebly to the woody. Both men noticed how hot he was. "Dr. Fisher, you are so hot. Is it from the water?"

"No," Clarence mumbled. "I started feeling hot in the tent and thought nothing of it. I even hesitated before immersing myself, but went ahead, feeling it would pass. I wasn't in the water long enough, only seconds, and I kept feeling hotter. Someone, get me water!"

The other man ran to the entrance and came back quickly with a large jug. Clarence drank it all down before getting into the back seat of the motorcar, still in his bathing costume. However, just as he was about to get in the back of the woody, he vomited.

"Quick, get me somewhere," he said, and he passed out.

•　•　•

Shaker Ahmad got to the American School of Oriental Research just before dark. Fortunately, there were no incidents along the way. He quickly went inside and had them call for a doctor. Clarence was conscious, but just barely. The carried him to his bed, but he hadn't improved. The doctor arrived and took his temperature; it was 106 degrees. He had them remove all but his shorts, and he applied a cold compress to Clarence's head. "I don't know what's wrong, other than he has a high fever and he has edema in his lower extremities; look how dark his feet, ankles, and calves are. The only solution for his condition is to try to cool his body down. Use wet cloths, towels, anything to keep every part of his body cool. Try to keep this up all night, or I'm afraid we'll lose him."

"What's wrong with him?" asked Shaker Ahmad. "Is he going to get better?"

"I don't know. I don't know what's wrong; I haven't seen anything like it. Please try to cool him down. But if he doesn't improve, get him to the hospital."

At around 2:00 a.m., Clarence began a series of convulsions, and he was immediately transported to the British Section of the government hospital in Jerusalem. There, they continued trying to cool him down, and they gave him fluids intravenously. That seemed to stop his convulsions, but he remained unconscious.

At 4:00 p.m. the next day, Sunday, July 20, 1941, after more convulsions, Dr. Clarence Stanley Fisher died. He was sixty-five. His death was ruled to be by edema (swelling) and purpura (purple coloring beneath the skin) but no real cause was ever concluded.

Strangely, Fisher was given a full military funeral with a British flag over his coffin, but no reason was ever given for the presence of a British, not American, flag as his coffin proceeded from the hospital. Was it due to his service in World War I as a captain in the Red Cross? As an advisor to the British authorities on Arab affairs? Or was it because he had served as a spy for the British from the beginning of World War I and through the beginning of World War II?

His coffin was borne by an open British military truck through the streets of Jerusalem on its way to burial in the Protestant Cemetery on Mount Zion, overlooking Jerusalem and the Dome of the Rock. One year later, Sir Flinders Petrie was buried on the same row, directly across a narrow path from Clarence.

Fisher's widow, Florie Carswell Fisher, was surprised to learn of her husband's passing via a telegram from Secretary of State Sumner Welles. Months later, she received a sum of $3,281.28, seemingly from his savings. She received only a few of his personal effects, possibly because of the confusion of World War II.

PART TWO
CARSWELL BIBLE COLLEGE

CHAPTER 10

Friday, September 7, 2001
Carswell Bible College, Wrens, Georgia

"**N**ow what are you doing on your stupid computer? Every night, we come home from dinner to your computer. Every night, if we eat here, you jump right on your computer. Can't we have one night together?"

They had come home from dinner at Lil Jake's Bar-B-Q on Fenns Bridge Road at the railroad tracks, just a mile from their house in Wrens, Georgia. Anna had moved in with Lonnie in the middle of August.

Lonnie turned around to face Anna, "Half hour, tops. I just want to download the tool I was telling you about, LispWorks. Once I install it, I'll just start it up to make sure it's okay. I don't have any files to load into it yet."

"Okay, I'll just watch reruns." Anna sulked into the kitchen of their new, tan double-wide with green shutters set on a quarter-acre lot on Melody Lane. "It's amazingly cool out, so I'll open the windows."

Anna Hamed, twenty-two, had met Lonnie Jenkins, twenty-eight, in March at a lecture on Egypt and the Bible given by Greta Smithville, associate professor of anthropology at Pamplin College of Arts and Sciences at Augusta State University in Augusta, Georgia. Afterward, they had driven from Reese Library on the campus a few blocks to Sheerin's Irish Pub on Central Avenue. There, they both had fish and chips and started off just with iced tea. After finishing, they felt more and more comfortable with each other and ordered drinks; she a white wine and he a Corona with a lime.

Despite being raised in an upscale Muslim household in Cairo, Anna was trying as hard as she could to become Americanized. She had stopped the daily ritual prayers and had actually begun attending, on an occasional basis, Elm Baptist Church, just a few blocks from campus, on Sundays.

Anna's father was an Egyptian government official, and she had grown up in a high-rise condo on El-Nasr Road in Nasr City, across from the Mercedes dealer. Nasr City was the upscale district of Cairo, whereas metropolitan Cairo was populated by sixteen million people, mostly poor, including people who lived in the vast City of the Dead cemetery. Cairo was one of the most densely populated cities in the world. Housing in most of Cairo, and much of Egypt, consisted of buildings of one, two, or three stories with steel support beams reaching one or two stories higher. They looked more like buildings being demolished, yet they really reflected that subsequent generations of a family would be able to build higher residences on top of their parents' housing. By contrast, the Nasr City district included wide streets arranged in a grid pattern, high-rise residences and office buildings, and trendy shops and restaurants.

Anna had enrolled at the American University in Cairo in 1998 and became very interested in becoming an archaeologist. She had her first archaeology class in the fall of her sophomore year. From late August to early October, the nighttime class was taught by famed archaeologist Christopher Houser, who left at the start of the archaeology season to devote his time to the Theban Mapping Project, which was building 3-D computer models of ancient temples and tombs. The remainder of the course was taught by Professor of Egyptology Isabella Browne. Both had discovered in Anna a real talent and enthusiasm for archaeology, and both had urged her to transfer, if possible, to the University of Pennsylvania in the States to continue her studies, including graduate work leading to a PhD. She had applied unsuccessfully to Penn and other schools noted for archaeology, such as Harvard, the University of Chicago, and the Institute of Egyptian Art and Archaeology at the University of Memphis. As suggested by her counselors, she had applied to smaller schools as well. She was finally accepted by Augusta State University, which was trying to build a reputation in Egyptian archaeology.

While she had never worn a hijab, Anna had been raised in Islam. But on her long trip from Cairo to JFK airport in New York, to Hartsfield in Atlanta, and then to Augusta Regional, Anna began thinking about life in America. She began to believe that she might settle permanently in the United States. Though tormented and suffering through short periods of sleep on the long trip, she began to think about leaving her religion and trying to become a part of American culture. But she decided to wait to see how her new college life treated her.

Anna was amazed at how readily she had been accepted, especially since she was in a southern school. She found her roommate, who was from Hoover, Alabama, which is just southwest of Birmingham, to be very peppy and outgoing, friendly, and accepting. They hit it off right from the start by just sitting around talking about their many differences. As each hour went by on that first day, they found themselves growing closer and closer together. By the end of the night, they were close friends.

The other students on her dorm floor, including boys, to her surprise, were also very accepting. She joined with her roommate and two other girls in many off-campus activities, including drinking places and nearby malls. After several weeks, despite her religion, she found a taste for white wine but promised herself to never overindulge. She even learned about golf and the Masters, which was two and a half miles from campus. She even watched the last three hours of the Masters on TV at a bar and rooted for Tiger Woods, who earned his second green jacket.

Her dating, despite her pretty face, tan to dark skin, and attractive shape, was very sporadic. First, it was due to a lack of foreign students, whom she was more interested in. Later, in January of 2001, she decided to date anyone, but still was very selective.

Then she met Lonnie Jenkins at an evening lecture. She thought that her first dinner with him, at Sheerin's, went extremely well, and she sensed that he agreed. At the end of the night, he asked her out for Friday night, and she quickly, almost too enthusiastically, agreed. They exchanged e-mail addresses and phone numbers. At the time, Anna had a phone in her dorm room, while Lonnie had a Motorola StarTac, used mainly for work.

Lonnie, a tall and thin African American, was employed as the MVS/ESA mainframe systems programmer at Carswell Bible College, on Campground Road near Steilaville Junior High, east of Wrens, Georgia.

He had graduated in 1990 from Central Georgia Technical College in Macon with an associate's degree in computer science. Amazingly, he had gotten a job at nearby Mercer University's computer center, first as a mainframe computer operator, then programmer, and by 1997, he had advanced to the position of systems programmer on their IBM main-frame. In July 1999, he had taken a job in the fledgling computer center at Carswell Bible College in Wrens. He had jumped at the chance be-cause Carswell had just leased a huge, but used, IBM 3090 mainframe. It had required water cooling, delivered through pipes under the floor and chilled by a compressor on the roof of the building. It was way too much power, both electrically and computer-wise, but the E. Ruthven Carswell Trust was behind it, and the school wanted to delve further into the Dead Sea Scrolls. He was happy that he made the decision to jump, but it was hard work, because he had to support two programmers and also act as the college's PC specialist. But he loved the work. He assisted the technical people from the leasing company, all former IBM employees, with configuring the hardware and connections to the Internet. He had also gathered requirements for the MVS/ESA operating system and had created the "sysgen deck," which specified which pieces of the huge op-erating system needed to be installed by a computer process. The initial installation was successful, but, like most mainframes, the computer re-quired constant application of "fixes" by system programmers. Also, due to his competency, he was often called upon to help "debug" programs that the two programmers had written. He was an expert in drawing out of the programmers exactly what they were trying to do and what had gone wrong. Using this, and computer-generated traces, he was usually able to resolve issues quickly.

Lonnie soon was a favorite of Julia E. R. Carswell, the founder's great-granddaughter. In the mid-1970s, Julia had convinced her ailing father, E. R. Carswell III, to let her run the floundering school, and she had invested the foundation funds in high-tech companies. In 1996, with her stocks rid-ing high, she decided to get out of the market and invest the unusually high profits in the school. She decided to build the datacenter and hire Mark Hamilton, a former Baptist minister and Georgia state senator, to replace her as president. She wanted him to ensure the future of Carswell Bible College, both fiscally and academically. Julia retained her seat as board chairperson, spending much of her time on recruiting excellent students.

Through her urging and hard work, Julia was able to get Carswell Bible College accepted into a consortium of colleges, mostly on the West Coast, that banded together to significantly fund further research into the Dead Sea Scrolls. First discovered in a clay jar in 1946, these ancient texts number close to one thousand and date from as early as 385 BC to AD 82. Most scrolls are on parchment, and the earliest are on papyrus. Two scrolls, called the Copper Scrolls, are on copper and are said to contain the location of the treasures of King Solomon's temple. Despite much interest, however, nothing has been located. The scrolls have been excavated in eleven caves in the ancient settlement at Qumran, in the West Bank Palestinian territories.

Lonnie found, to his excitement, that he was to lead the development of a computer concordance of the Dead Sea Scrolls. The concordance would link each main word in the Dead Sea Scrolls to the passage in each scroll and the word in context in a sentence. The transcription of the Dead Sea Scrolls data into machine readable form on magnetic tape had been performed by the other schools in the consortium. Lonnie found that he was to be the system architect, system designer, project manager, and general guru for the entire, and major, undertaking. He was thrilled!

On his PC at home now, Lonnie finished the download, installation, and initial test of LispWorks, a programming system and language that allowed, after a somewhat steep learning curve, data residing in lists, such as in a concordance, to be manipulated in a number of ways. "Lisp" stood for list processor. It was ideal for what he had in mind to perform on his Gateway 2000 PC.

Shutting it down, he walked out on the small porch and took in a big breath of cool, fresh air. The sunset was a beautiful purple red, and he could see fireflies glowing and could hear birds chirping and insects buzzing as they all prepared for the night. A horn blared from a Norfolk-Southern locomotive crossing Fenns Bridge Road at Lil Jake's.

Lonnie paused to reflect on a discussion he had with Anna several weeks before. She had asked a reasonable question regarding the use of a concordance. He had answered that it would allow a researcher, or anyone, really, to find words from the Dead Sea Scrolls and find their use in context in all other places in the Dead Sea Scrolls. To demonstrate, he had found an online version of *Strong's Concordance of the Bible*. He typed in the word "Egypt," and the online program came back with 642 entries, each with the passage in the Bible where the word was found. He scrolled down and showed Exodus 3:11 to Anna:

And Moses said unto God, Who am I, that I should go unto Pharaoh, and that I should bring forth the children of Israel out of Egypt?

He then typed in "pharaoh" and found that there were 240 entries. He had scrolled through them all and found that none of the passages mentioned the name of a pharaoh. He tried "king of Egypt" and found forty-five entries. He scrolled through each of these and, to his surprise, found the name of Pharaoh Shishak in two passages. "Look, Anna. According to my searches, there's only one pharaoh named in the Bible: Shishak!" He then brought up the new online search tool, Google. He entered "Shishak" and found some entries regarding him. "It looks like Shishak was indeed a pharaoh, but he lived hundreds of years after Moses. So the Bible does not mention any name of the pharaoh of the Exodus. It's strange, because the Bible has so much about the pharaoh of the Exodus. I wonder why he wasn't mentioned? Strange."

Anna was fascinated and asked if there was a concordance of the Koran. Lonnie had replied that there was a printed version, but he could not find one online. She had then suggested that maybe Lonnie's work with the Dead Sea Scrolls would identify the pharaoh of the Exodus, and had mentioned that many Muslims thought that the pharaoh Akhenaten was the pharaoh who had decided to let the Hebrews go and that he, as Moses, had led them. Lonnie had been intrigued by the possibility, however distant, and had been working on it.

Anna joined him on the porch. "Are you done?"

"Yes, for the night. I want to do some more tomorrow morning, but I'm ready to relax now."

"Great," said Anna, as she hugged him and kissed him. "I'll open some wine and get you a beer and we can sit and you can tell me what you've been up to. You know I like to hear about things, as long as I can understand them."

Ten minutes later, they were on the porch as only the faint glow of twilight remained. "Hon, remember the suggestion that you made regarding discovering the pharaoh of the Exodus?"

"Um, I guess."

"Well, I've been acting on it. At Carswell, I've been working on the concordance data for the Dead Sea Scrolls as I'm supposed to, and I'm almost ready to produce a readable and searchable concordance. That's a big accomplishment, and I think it will bring a lot of attention to the college. Dr. Carswell will love it."

"That's great news," said Anna. "But what does that have to do with the pharaoh?"

"Well, I haven't told anyone yet, but I've created an assembler language program to quickly go through the concordance files and create a copy, for my own use later, that deletes most words and references. I'm only leaving behind words like 'king' and 'pharaoh,' and names of important people in the Old Testament. I'm including people like Moses, Aaron, Joseph, Jacob, even Pharaoh Shishak, but eliminating names of prophets and other people I recognize as not part of any search for pharaohs. I'll also include the word 'covenant,' since that may be a word that links two references. I then intend to do the same thing with an Old Testament concordance that we also have in computer format. Since the Dead Sea Scrolls only have references to the Old Testament, these two files will be much, much smaller.

"Tomorrow I'll use my 3278 emulator to have the mainframe combine them into one file. At work on Monday, I'll download the file to the PC using IND$FILE, then put the data on a 250-megabyte Zip drive cartridge and bring it home. I'll then use my PC and LispWorks to process the data on the cartridge. It may take days, since the data is big and the cartridge is slow. But as long as we don't have a power failure, it should run to completion."

Anna looked quizzically at Lonnie. "I didn't understand most of what you just said."

"You don't have to understand. I'm just going through the steps in my own mind."

"Okay. But I don't understand the word 'covenant.'"

"It's a contract, a legal document, even a lease. In biblical times, it could be a contract between two countries or between two people; a marriage contract. Or between God and the people. I'm looking for that word because it links two things."

Anna paused for a bit, then said, "Exodus, Moses, covenant; I know very little about your Bible. Can you tell me a little more about these things?"

"Well, I'm no Old Testament scholar. As a Christian, I don't know much about Jewish history, especially about their origins. I know that at the time of Moses, the Hebrews were enslaved in Egypt. The Bible says that Moses was abandoned as a tiny infant because Pharaoh was going to kill all newborn boys. He was found floating in the Nile by a woman of Egyptian royalty and was raised in the royal household. As an adult, he killed a slave master who was beating a slave to death and escaped across the Red Sea. There, God spoke to him in a burning bush and told him to return to Egypt to free the Hebrews.

"He returned and pleaded with Pharaoh to 'let my people go' but was turned down nine times. Each time, Moses provided a plague to try to force Pharaoh. After the tenth plague, Pharaoh agreed.

"On their Exodus from Egypt, they were chased by the Egyptian army, and Moses parted the Red Sea so that they could cross. Later God gave him two stone tablets containing the Ten Commandments. Later still, these tablets were carried in a box called the Ark of the Covenant and kept in Solomon's temple in Jerusalem.

"The ark, supposedly of gold and very beautiful, was kept below the temple in a room called the Holy of Holies, but it has never been found.

"Oh, there are some people who today think it has lightning bolts coming from it and has magical powers. The famous Indiana Jones movie had the Nazis stealing it so that they could win World War II, and Indiana Jones saved the world!"

"Wow, that's a lot to think about." She paused. "So what is your plan for all this work that you plan to do?"

"Next week I'll learn how to use the LispWorks for Windows program for doing list processing. With it, I should be able to compare the Dead Sea Scrolls to the Old Testament and find out any differences. Some may be apparent, while for other parts I may need Dr. Carswell to look at the original Hebrew and also look at microfilm we have of every part of the Dead Sea Scrolls. Maybe we'll find the pharaoh of the Exodus."

"Or maybe you'll find, as some of my Egyptian friends have suggested, that Moses was actually Akhenaten, and therefore Egyptian!"

CHAPTER 11

Saturday, September 29, 2001
Carswell Bible College

Lonnie Jenkins sat at his desk in his still mostly bare living room. There was a couch from his old apartment and a new coffee table that Anna had insisted upon. The couch faced a TV stand with a new TV on it. Below was a fifteen-year-old stereo set, passed down from Lonnie's older brother. It even had an eight-track player.

Lonnie picked up the one-foot-high stack of papers and computer manuals from his desk and put them on the floor, clearing a spot for the reference manuals that he had printed out for learning and using the LispWorks PC application. He was now ready to combine and compare the Dead Sea Scrolls to the Old Testament, work that he had hoped to complete weeks ago. It had taken longer than he thought; he had run into programming problems, and he had to make some extracts so that he could test the application against small files. He considered all this a worthwhile process, perhaps leading him to discover the pharaoh of the Exodus.

Lonnie was actually ready on Wednesday night, when he had finished programming LispWorks for Windows at home and had successfully run a series of tests. Thursday, however, he had a full day at the computer center planning for the work he had to do that midnight. He left work for home at 4:00 p.m., ate a nice dinner that Anna had prepared, and tried to sleep for several hours. He woke up at 10:30 p.m., took a quick shower, and drove back to the computer center.

The Carswell College computer center was the largest room on campus that was neither an auditorium nor a gym. It had a white raised floor, to allow room for a myriad of computer cables and the piping for the chilled water supply that cooled the behemoth mainframe, and high ceilings. There were multiple air-conditioning vents in both the ceiling and the antistatic raised floor. All of the IBM equipment in the room was about six feet high and four feet wide; only the lengths varied. The mammoth IBM 3090 processing unit, with its cabinets connected in an H pattern, took up most of the space in the room. Lonnie and Julia were both very proud of it, and it was a highlight of any campus tour for prospective students.

At midnight, Lonnie had disabled the unit that allowed external-user access and had begun to install a new release of the MVS/ESA operating system by doing a SYSGEN. Lonnie began the process by mounting a ten-and-a-half-inch magnetic tape reel on one of two tape drives. By 4:00 a.m., the process had completed, but he then had to repeat the process with a new tape reel to apply PTFs, or fixes. That process took another hour. He had begun testing at about 5:15 a.m., hoping to get the system in shape for the 7:00 a.m. up time that he had promised Julia. He missed that deadline, despite much time spent on the phone with IBM support, but had the system up by 9:30 a.m. He had then gone home exhausted.

He had slept most of yesterday afternoon, with only two phone calls about the new release, which he could handle on his cell phone.

By Saturday morning, he felt rested and alert as he inserted his Zip cartridge into his Zip drive. From both the Dead Sea Scrolls and the Old Testament, it now contained extracts of the Pentateuch, the first five books of the Old Testament, as well as both books of Kings and Chronicles. Over the last two weeks, Lonnie had reformatted the two extracts so that the data from both were in the same file in the same format. He had also sorted the data to speed up processing.

He now felt confident that his LispWorks program, using statements like MEMBER, MEMBER-IF, LDIFF, and TAILP, would produce a report, on his HP LaserJet 4L printer, showing those areas of the extract that were not in agreement. He pushed the enter key to start the process.

CHAPTER 12

Friday, October 5, 2001
Carswell Bible College

It was a beautiful, sunny fall day in Wrens, Georgia. The sky was clear, the humidity was low, the temperature was seventy-four degrees, and there was little wind. Lonnie Jenkins had wakened early and ate breakfast with Anna Hamed before she left for her classes at Augusta State. Lonnie set up a card table on the porch and then carried out the two 438-page print-outs, placing them on the card table. He was hoping that the wind would not pick up and disturb the printouts.

Yesterday, the processing on his Gateway 2000 was almost completed when Lonnie woke up at 6:00 a.m. to get ready for work. His HP printer had stopped, waiting for another ream of paper to be inserted. Lonnie had removed the output, pressed start, and then separated the few pages from the second report from the 438 pages of the first report. He had glanced at the first report and immediately determined that he had a lot of work to do. At work that morning, he had asked Julia Carswell if he could take a personal day on Friday, and she had agreed.

This morning, Lonnie took a sip of his coffee, sat back, and stared at the two stacks of paper. Each had the same data, but each was organized differently. The report on his left had two columns. The first column had every passage from his Old Testament extract, and the second column had lines from passages of the Dead Sea Scrolls that were adjacent or in close proximity to the Old Testament passages. Also, the printouts had words like "pharaoh," "king," "covenant," etc., printed in bold. The other printout was the same format, only in this report, the first column had every passage from his Dead Sea Scrolls extract, and the second column had lines from passages of the Old Testament that were near the Dead Sea Scrolls passages.

He began to quickly leaf through both stacks. He then began to scan the first stack, looking for areas that attracted his attention.

CHAPTER 13

Monday, October 8, 2001
Carswell Bible College

"**H**i, Momma."

"How are you, Anna? It's nice to hear from you."

"I'm fine. I—"

"We don't hear from you often enough."

"I know, Momma, but it costs so much, calling from a pay phone on campus. I'm calling before class. It's 8:30 a.m. here, so it must be 3:30 p.m. there." She paused. "Do I hear Daddy in the background? Who is he arguing with, and why is he home?"

"Your cousin Achmed Hamed is here arguing with your father. Your father stayed home today because Achmed was coming from Al-Minya. He said he had important, dangerous things to discuss with your father."

"What kind of things?"

"He said that there were horrible things going on in Mubarak's government; that Achmed's group had uncovered political and financial things that may hurt your father."

"Oh, praise Allah, will Daddy be okay?"

"Yes, but...What's that? Okay. Achmed wants to talk to you."

"Momma, I have to go, I—"

"Anna! My beautiful cousin Anna! You are a shining star in my eyes!"

"Thank you. But what about Daddy?"

"He should be all right, Anna." Achmed continued in anger, his voice rising with each sentence. "But our movement has uncovered financial and other misdeeds in the Mubarak government. And anyone who raises opposition is thrown in jail without a trial. He is cheating our people, abusing his position and power, and destroying any opposition! Mubarak must be stopped!"

"But, Achmed, what can Daddy do about it?"

Much calmer now, Achmed responded, "Only two things. Stay out of any trouble and report to me anything that we can use. I just need him to keep his eyes open and inform me of anything of value. Mubarak must be stopped.

"Our group, Al-Gama'a al-Islamiyya, is devoted to giving all Muslim Egyptians a better life. Our operation in Luxor proved our resolve, but we need to proceed with less violence."

"But please, Achmed," begged Anna. "Please keep our family safe. You owe that to the family."

"And you, Anna, who have left family behind, owe something to the family as well."

"What do you mean?"

"Not much. I just want you to keep your eyes and ears open. You are breaking our laws by living with a man who is not a Muslim. He happens to work at a college that is working with the Dead Sea Scrolls. These can hold secrets that are very important to all Islamic peoples everywhere. For your father's sake, let me know of anything that could help our movement."

"Are you threatening Daddy?"

"Of course not. But just remember that family is everything, family is everything. Everything. Here is your mother."

"Mommy, is all okay?"

"Yes, dear. We're just as concerned with Mubarak as Achmed."

"Okay, but try to stay clear of Achmed. He concerns me. I have to go now. Allahu Akbar."

"Good-bye to you. Please keep more in touch, Anna. Allahu Akbar."

CHAPTER 14

Tuesday, October 9, 2001
Carswell Bible College

L onnie Jenkins sat in a blue leather chair at Julia Carswell's desk. He had been told to go on in, as Julia would return shortly from a meeting. Julia's office was spacious and beautifully appointed. Her desk was as magnificent as could be imagined, with heavy mahogany panels, beautifully inlaid scrolling, and bright brass furnishings. Her desk was clear, except for a well-worn Bible in the corner nearest Lonnie. An IBM PS/2 PC sat on a credenza to the right of Julia's blue high-backed leather chair. Lonnie stared out the window behind her desk, but no one could be seen walking on Paul's Walk, which bisected the huge green, due to classes in session at this hour. The right wall of the office was one huge floor-to-ceiling bookcase, as was the area next to the door. On the left was a door that led to the boardroom and another door to a small bathroom. Between the two doors, picture frames sat on a low bookshelf beneath a large painting of her great-grandfather, Egenardus Ruthven Carswell II, the founder of Carswell Bible College.

The portrait was of a trim man, possibly in his thirties, with graying hair, dark mustache, and brown eyes. He was in a graduation gown and seated before a dark wall, possibly this office, with a diploma on it. Born in 1850, he had graduated from Mercer University, had studied law for a year, but then entered the ministry, preaching in churches in South Carolina and Georgia. In 1879 he, with significant financial assistance from his father, founded Carswell Bible College, with the purpose of providing a college education for Christians of faith. A multitalented, dedicated man, he wrote religious books, traveled around the country preaching the Gospel in hastily erected tents, and even got the first patent for a fitted bedsheet. In 1897, he founded two schools, one in Baltimore and the other in Philadelphia, that took in boarders who could spend their full time learning how to correct stuttering and stammering. He and his wife, Elvie, raised eight children, including Julia's father, E. R. Carswell III.

"Root" Carswell, as he was known to his friends, was very proud of his Scottish ancestry, as was most of the Carswell Clan in America. The name Ruthven was passed down through the centuries because of their direct ancestor, Lord Ruthven. He was part of a group that was not pleased with the Catholics that were influencing the young King James VI of Scotland. In the Raid of Ruthven, August of 1582, James was abducted and held in Ruthven (now Huntingtower) Castle, as well as other homes in Perth, for almost a year. Although Lord Ruthven was beheaded for treason in May of 1584, many Scots consider him a hero. James IV was the daughter of Mary, Queen of Scots, and in March of 1603 he became King James I of England. He later was a backer of William Shakespeare and sponsored the Bible translation known as the Authorized King James Version. Jamestown, Virginia, is named after him.

"Hi, Lonnie. What's on your mind?" said Julia, walking in from the boardroom.

Lonnie, wearing khakis and a blue shirt, stood and wished her a good morning.

"No, no, please sit."

"Thanks. Julia, I've been doing a little research on my own."

Julia's brown eyebrows went up. She was very petite, but very spry and active. Her shoulder-length hair accented her small horned-rimmed eyeglasses. At forty-eight, she looked both studious and attractive at once. "Research, how so?"

"After I finished making the Dead Sea Scroll Concordance—"

"A great effort that I thank you for."

"Thanks. And thanks for my pay increase. Anyway, I decided to try to use my skills and something called list processing to compare the Dead Sea Scrolls to the Old Testament." He paused.

"Okay..." said a very skeptical Julia. "And to what end? And how much did you do on the school's computer and on school time?"

"Almost nothing. I downloaded the two digital concordances to a Zip drive and did all the processing at home. I'm trying to see if I can use list processing to see what is missing between the Dead Sea Scrolls and the Old Testament. I thought that I could solve the question of who is the pharaoh of the Exodus."

"Okay, I guess that's a good goal, but how can you find what's missing?"

"Good question. Say I find a passage in the Dead Sea Scrolls that is missing from the Old Testament. The program that I wrote uses list processing instructions to look at other text surrounding both what is in the Dead Sea Scrolls and what surrounds the area that I expected in the Old Testament. I also had the program compare in the opposite direction."

"So did you find anything?"

"Well, no and yes. I could not find anything in the Pentateuch, or in either book of Kings or Chronicles, that would help with identifying who was the pharaoh of the Exodus. On the bright side, maybe I proved that the answer will never be known." He paused.

Julia frowned and said, "Well, that's interesting, but hardly newsworthy. Not even worthy of a research paper, despite all the effort you put into it."

"But I did find something interesting. 1 Kings 14:25 has a very interesting passage: 'In the fifth year of King Rehoboam, Shishak king of Egypt attacked Jerusalem. He carried off the treasures of the temple of the LORD and the treasures of the royal palace. He took everything, including all the gold shields Solomon had made.'

"Sunday night I did some research on this—"

"Lonnie, of course I'm familiar with this," Julia interrupted. "But go on."

"I went to our library and found that there are researchers who believe that the pharaoh of the Exodus was Akhenaten, all the way down to a pharaoh named Mereneptah. All of these are somewhere between 1400 BC and 1200 BC. However, there is a pharaoh named Shoshenq I who lived around 900 BC and conquered Jerusalem."

"Okay, maybe that validates the name Shishak. But—"

"Well, excuse me for interrupting, but I'm excited—"

"I see that."

"This is important because I found that there is nothing in the Dead Sea Scrolls matching 1 Kings 14:25–26 in the Old Testament. Same with 2 Chronicles 12:5, which also mentions Shishak. But in both places, I found multiple mentions in the Dead Sea Scrolls, surrounding the missing passages, of the word 'covenant.' It's as if there is more about a covenant than is generally known. At about 10:30 on Sunday night, I found that there was only one small fragment, named pap6QKgs, from 1 Kings found in all of the Dead Sea Scrolls. It was found in cave six and is on papyrus, which is the earliest Dead Sea Scrolls material found; later ones were on leather. I know that you can read ancient Hebrew and that—"

"Hold on. Slow down, take a deep breath." She paused. "Okay, you're thinking that I should take a closer look at this papyrus, you say is what?"

"Pap6QKgs."

"Okay, I should look at this to see if I can find something that no one else has about the word 'covenant' in it?"

"Well, yes, but I thought that maybe Dr. Feeney, who worked with Dr. Greg Bearman of NASA in 1994 to enhance the images of the Dead Sea Scrolls, could take a closer look. It may only take him an hour or so."

"Hmm. Let me see," said Julia. "I know Alex is always busy, but he may find this interesting. I'll talk to him. If he's interested, I'll ask him to talk to you. I'm too busy with business travel over the next six weeks, so I won't be able to help other than talking to Alex."

"Thank you so much!" said Lonnie, beaming. "I'm really excited, but I won't let it interfere with my computer work."

"Good." Julia began walking him to the door. "I did get feedback about that computer outage last week due to the new release."

"I'll stay on top of things, and thanks for your support. Bye now."

"Thanks to you, and good-bye as well," said Julia.

Lonnie shut the door and walked out with perhaps the biggest smile he ever had on his face.

CHAPTER 15

Thursday, November 15, 2001
Carswell Bible College

Lonnie Jenkins was seated with Dr. Alexander Feeney in the office of Mark Hamilton, president of Carswell Bible College. Both were dressed in their best suits. Dr. Feeney was a large man. He had suffered a career-ending concussion while playing fullback on the Georgia Tech football team, but it also brought him closer to God. He received his master's and doctor's degrees in religion from Princeton University and then worked as a researcher at Hebrew Union College in Cincinnati. There, he worked with a team that published previously unknown parts of the Dead Sea Scrolls. He was well known in the worldwide group of Dead Sea Scrolls researchers, but at Carswell Bible College, he had settled his family in Wrens and served as provost.

Julia Carswell continued to be tied up with traveling, and, knowing that Julia had briefed Mark, Dr. Feeney and Lonnie requested a meeting with him. They thought that what they had found was too important to put off.

Mark Hamilton came from a middle-class family. A high school wrestler, he was a runner up in the Georgia state high school championships two years in a row. He had straight As and was awarded a scholarship to Gettysburg College in Pennsylvania. While he had always participated in church activities and taught Sunday school, he decided in the middle of his sophomore year that he wanted to enter the ministry. After graduating from

Gettysburg, Mark enrolled in the Eastern Baptist Theological Seminary, outside Philadelphia. As part of his studies, his two summers were spent as an assistant pastor at Spruce Street Baptist Church, in nearby Newtown Square, Pennsylvania. There he met Brenda Brown, who was a Sunday school teacher and active as a soloist in the choir. After his graduation from Eastern, he and Brenda married and moved to Augusta, Georgia, where he first became an assistant and then was named the pastor of the Elm Street Baptist Church. He was well liked at Elm Street, but he became very disenchanted with the Vietnam War and the situation with civil rights, especially in the South. By then, his oratory skills were fine-tuned, and he became very vocal against the current government. In 1975, he decided to run for state senator and was elected easily. But after six terms in the Georgia State Senate, and with no further political plans, he decided to open himself up for other opportunities. The offer to become president of Carswell Bible College was too good to refuse.

Lonnie and Alex Feeney looked at each other. Both were nervous, with Lonnie constantly looking at his watch, and Alex checking his tie and suit coat sleeves. Despite their age difference—Alex was twenty years older—they had hit it off from the start. At the computer center, at Alex's modest campus office, at Lonnie's cubicle, and even at Sheerin's Irish Pub on Central Avenue in Augusta, they constantly researched, planned, and sometimes argued. They almost became obsessed with finding out more about the missing data from the translation of the papyrus of 1 Kings from the Dead Sea Scrolls. Dr. Feeney had indeed worked on the NASA images and had access to them. Lonnie had refined and rerun his computer program multiple times.

"Hello, gentlemen," said Mark as he opened the door. His office did not have an entrance to the boardroom and did not have a bathroom. Otherwise, it was similar to Julia's. "I apologize for not being able to get to you sooner. I've been busy, but I know that Julia won't be available until after Thanksgiving. I don't have much time. Please sit down and give me a quick update."

"Thanks," said Alex. "Lonnie and I have worked very well together and very hard on this, but mostly on our own time. I've reexamined, in much more detail, the NASA-enhanced Dead Sea Scroll papyrus from cave six. Lonnie has rerun his program multiple times—"

"And," interrupted Mark. "Please hurry."

"Okay. Our conclusion, our finding, is here in the text that's bolded in 1 Kings 14:25–26. It's shocking, but I'm confident in our work. We've been very thorough." He handed the typewritten, not computer-generated, paper to Mark. It read,

25 And it came to pass in the fifth year of King Rehoboam, that Shishak king of Egypt came up against Jerusalem, **proclaiming that pharaoh had granted only a one-hundred-year covenant to the Kingdom of Israel.** 26 And he took away the treasures of the house of the LORD, and the treasures of the king's house; he even took away all; and he took away all the shields of gold which Solomon had made.

The color in Mark's face drained as he sat back in his chair, clutching the paper. He seemed to be reading it over and over.

"Proof? Do you have proof?"

"Well, sir, I've been very thorough in comparing our concordance of the Dead Sea Scrolls to one of the Old Testament," said Lonnie. "That pointed me to a papyrus fragment, pap6QKgs, that has the only mention of 1 Kings."

"And I did further research, using photographic enhancements from NASA's involvement in the Dead Sea Scrolls," said Dr. Feeney. "I analyzed that papyrus closely and saw that part of that fragment was almost undecipherable. But I was able to transcribe the added clause above."

Mark Hamilton pondered this for almost a minute. He then turned his chair and stared out the window at the rain that was hitting the campus green. Students were scurrying across Paul's Walk, although others walked more slowly under their umbrellas. His mood quickly matched the gray, dreary day. Alex and Lonnie both knew not disturb him.

After several minutes, he turned back. "This could be the most important religious finding of the century—perhaps in history." Then he frowned and shook his head. "The Israelites were only given the right to their land for one hundred years? For one hundred years?"

He paused, but Alex and Lonnie looked at each other in agreement not to interrupt. "The world is in a terrible shape. In the early part of this century, the Zionists, Jews actually, and the Arabs fought with each other over Palestine. In 1948, the UN declared that Israel was a free state and a homeland for Jews from all over the world. That resulted in the first Arab-Israeli War. The Six-Day War, bombings—even tourist killings by Muslims in Egypt three years ago. There is terrible strife today all over the Middle East between Arabs and Jews, and for centuries, Arabs and Christians.

"Any way you look at this, it spells disaster. All of the Arab world could bind together with the goal of returning Israel to an Arab-controlled Palestine and deporting, or killing, God forgive, many or most Jews. The world would be thrown into chaos, and a massive war would break out.

"You've done good work; I applaud you for it. But this must end here!" He tore the paper into several pieces and threw it into the trash. "I will shred that when you leave." He leaned over his desk, with his fingertips supporting him. He looked down at the desktop and then raised his head. He looked first at Lonnie, staring deeply into his eyes. He turned his head to Alex, looked into his eyes, and then stood up, pursed his lips, and shook his head. In a loud, stern voice, he said, "I command you to securely get rid of everything on your computers, ours or those you may have at home. Destroy any papers you may have. This is dangerous stuff!" His face flushed. "I will not even mention this to Julia. I will tell her that we talked and that you found nothing. Nothing, do you hear, nothing," he said, his voice rising.

"Please go. I really commend you for what you've done. But I must warn you that you must never, ever speak of this again. Never! Forget that you ever worked on this. You should be proud of what you've done, but please erase all thoughts about it. And I repeat, never mention this to anyone." Mark dismissed them with a wave, and they exited into a hallway that was now filled with students hurrying to their next classes.

Later that night, Lonnie reviewed with Anna their conversation with Mark. He warned her of how devastating it could be and got her to agree that she would never mention it to anyone.

The next morning, on her way to class, Anna stopped to make a long-distance call from a pay phone. She asked the operator to reverse charges and called her cousin Achmed Hamed in Al Minya, Egypt. He answered on the first ring—it was 2:30 p.m. there—and he accepted the charges. After a few pleasantries, she said, "Cousin, I have something that I think is very important to tell you…"

CHAPTER 16

Thursday, August 15, 2002
Augusta, Georgia

"**M**ark, I really need your help. Thanks for meeting me. Please sit down," said Julia Carswell. Mark Hamilton had finally found Rae's Coastal Café not far from the Augusta National Golf Club, where the Masters golf tournament is held each year. "Did you have a hard time finding the place?"

"Actually, no," said Mark, "but only because I used my new GPS for the first time. I don't think I could have found this place without it. Down some narrow residential streets, then onto what, West Wimbledon Drive, which is only one lane wide. But I saw a lot of cars in the parking lot next to this almost shack. How did you ever find out about this place? It does look like a shack from the outside."

"I don't remember, really, but I've been eating here whenever I'm in North Augusta since, I guess, the early nineties. This evening I had to speak to a group at the Friendship Baptist Church near the Martinez Campus of Augusta University. Tomorrow, I have an early board of directors meeting for the Augusta Christian School at the Sheraton. So I'm staying overnight there. Oh, and what is a GPS?"

"It's a new device that links to satellites and can determine where you are anywhere on earth. On the tiny screen, I entered the address of Coastal Café, and it showed a map telling me how to get here. I understand that there are some GPS units that will even speak directions to you."

"I really didn't understand what you just said, but I guess it's some-thing new like my phone. Anyway, Mark, I want to talk to you about a project I want you to lead that may significantly help Carswell in the future. But let's order first."

As Mark turned to the menu, Julia continued, "There's not much to choose from, but I can vouch for everything."

Julia picked a bottle of red wine from the well-stocked but very plain bar and ordered Land and Sea, which was a filet with their signature coco-nut fried shrimp. Mark ordered the filet.

"We've had some successes, including the mainframe, which we start-ed using in 1999, and the concordance of the Dead Sea Scrolls last year. I thought those would help us, but…" She paused.

"We still have overall problems, problems that plague many schools. Applications continue to fall, enrollment is down, and most importantly, alumni contributions are down substantially. We need to turn those things around."

The server brought their entrees; Mark indicated that he was impressed.

Julia continued, "In mid-November, you told me, only after I grilled you, about the conclusions of Lonnie and Alex, a theory about Moses re-ceiving a one-hundred-year lease. You stressed how dangerous that could be. But it could be just what we need to raise the stature of Carswell Bible College, not just in the Christian community, but throughout the world."

Mark stayed silent, fearing what she might say.

"I want you to work with Lonnie and Professor Feeney to investigate this further."

"But—" he interjected.

"No, hear me out. I want you to spend at least half of your time on this; I'll lighten your load. I want you to learn all you can about what Lonnie Jenkins and Alexander Feeney have discovered. I want you to bring only a few others in on this, but only if necessary. Please don't make a blanket request to any of the consortium schools. Lord knows, I don't want general knowledge of this to get out." She paused, then continued, "I will even personally pay for any trips that you may need to make. Our reputation could be destroyed if this got out and it proved false. I'm afraid that if it's true, there could have been a conspiracy to conceal it."

Mark finally spoke up. "I don't think we should touch it at all. I agree with you on the consequences of it not being true. But if it is true, it literally could change the world—for the worse!"

"I know, but as an institution of higher learning, we have an obligation to uncover and publish truth."

"But—"

"But listen. I brought you in fourteen years ago to increase our stature among Christian schools. Stature meaning a growing number of high-quality applications, increased enrollment, and most importantly, increased alumni contributions. We've been going in the wrong direction, as you know. Now, I'm not blaming you for this; this has been as much my responsibility as yours. In fact, you have done a much better job with the academic side than I ever would have expected, which has freed me up for the other things. So don't get me wrong; I'm very pleased with you, and I'm glad you're here. But I need a boost, Carswell College needs a boost. We need to turn out more students devoted to Christ, with more turning to lead the youth of the church. And a new discovery such as a possible covenant would be that boost."

She saw Mark staring at the fish tank next to him. It was about three feet high and five feet long. It seemed so peaceful and serene to him. Bubbles at the left, rising to the top like tiny balloons and providing oxygen to the fish. A little village to the right, with two small fish going in and out of tiny openings. Mark didn't know anything about fish, but in the center was a larger fish, facing him and rhythmically almost kissing the glass.

Julia knew what Mark was thinking, so she let him look at the fish for almost a minute before saying, "Mark, I propose the following: One, you, Lonnie, and Alex learn everything there is about this covenant. This effort needs your organizational skills and, yes, your enthusiasm that I see you display in everything you do.

"Two, bring your conclusions to me, while making sure that all that you all are doing remains a secret. We'll of course drop it if it's false, but I want you to follow every lead.

"Three, if it's true, you, Alex, and I will spend a lot of time deciding what to do about it. We'll evaluate possible ways to announce it, and we'll then decide if we will announce it."

Julia noticed that Mark had stopped staring at the fish tank as soon as she had begun talking. His eyes had bored into hers, unblinking, forcing her to look away as she continued.

"Mark, I know this is hard for you. Please consider it."

Another pause. Mark then looked down at the table and said softly, "I guess that I can go through your first two steps. But I expect it will be impossible to talk me into releasing anything to the world."

With that, Mark gently put his fork and knife on his plate with his half-eaten steak. He took a sip of water and then pushed his chair back. "Julia, please excuse me. I love this steak, I love Carswell College, and, up to this point, I've loved working for you. I will do this, but only as an exercise in scientific discovery. I will learn as much as can, and I will lead the team. I will present you with a verbal report. But I cannot condone the publication of this.

"Now, I'm sorry, but if you'll excuse me, I've lost my appetite. Maybe we can return here another time. Good night." He got up from his chair and turned to leave.

Julia rose and called after him. "Mark, please believe me. I understand. I won't do anything reckless."

PART THREE

2001

CHAPTER 17

Saturday, September 1, 2001
Ocean City, New Jersey

I was now on my way, as Philadelphians say, "down the shore," to Ocean City, New Jersey. This was my annual, at least for the last seven years, one-week stay at an upstairs apartment that I rented from Nancy and Frank O'Connor. It was a block from the Ocean City boardwalk and beach.

"Down the shore" meant going from the Philadelphia area to any of the New Jersey beach communities. They are actually barrier islands that stretch sixty-one miles from Long Beach Island, seventy-five miles south of New York City, to Cape May, at the southernmost tip of New Jersey. I, and my older brother, Glenn, had grown up as "shoebies" since just after World War II. People who lived at the Jersey Shore or vacationed there for a week or more called people who came to the shore for one day shoebies, because the legend was that they came in their bathing suits and carried their lunches in a shoe box.

As I proceeded on Route 202 toward the Schuylkill Expressway, I put a CD into the player, searched for number four, and turned up the volume. The song was well-known in Philadelphia and South Jersey, but not elsewhere: "On the Way to Cape May," by Al Alberts, formerly the lead singer for the Four Aces, a group that was especially popular in the 1950s. The song, which is played every summertime Friday at 10:00 a.m. by a popular Philly oldies radio station, follows the pursuit of a spouse from Ocean City and through the beach towns south of Ocean City: Sea Isle, Avalon, Stone

Harbor, Wildwood, and Cape May, all connected by the beautiful Ocean Drive, which is a slow, island-hopping, leisurely drive.

Crossing the Walt Whitman Bridge, I glanced to my left at the dilapidated SS *United States*, once a majestic passenger liner. Built to US Navy standards, it could cross the Atlantic at an average speed of almost forty miles per hour. I looked ahead at the mostly flat New Jersey landscape. It was a wonderful view on a perfect day. Normally, Ocean City was two hours away, but I increased my speed to get there at least twenty minutes sooner.

Frank O'Connor was a friend of mine from my earlier days at IBM. The O'Connors owned a two-story home on Third Street, on the north end of Ocean City, an island that was seven miles long and, at its widest spot, one mile wide. The O'Connors lived on the ground floor all summer and rented out the second floor. I loved the upstairs apartment, with its three bedrooms, living room, dining room, bathroom, and kitchen. My favorite was the generous porch, where I could sit and read, and sleep and read, taking in the fresh air from the almost always present ocean breeze.

When we rented in 1993, Linda and I, as well as our daughter, son-in-law, and grandchildren, stayed for the week. Too soon, the oldest grandchild was old enough to be in grade school, so they stopped coming. And Linda decided a week was too long, so she and her friend Lenore would come down for just two nights. This was fine with me; I loved the time alone.

After coming off the bridge, I continued on Route 42 and then onto the Atlantic City Expressway. I continued past shopping centers and farms, past pine tree forests that were like cliffs lining both sides of the four-lane highway. After going through the Great Egg Harbor toll booth plaza, I pulled my Mustang convertible onto the side of the highway. Screeching to a stop, I replaced the CD, undid the latches on the convertible top, and pressed the top down button. As the top moved, I envisioned the car transforming itself from a somewhat noisy, cramped, rough-riding vehicle into a lean, mean racing machine. Well, not quite, but after five cars passed, on their way to Atlantic City or other Jersey Shore vacation resorts, I stomped on the gas.

As the tires squealed and the car quickly accelerated to seventy-five, I took a deep breath and started to relax. Once again, I was on my way to my dream vacation in Ocean City, New Jersey, the only shore town I really felt comfortable in. The car seemed to know the rest of the way by heart.

I eased the stock Mustang onto the Garden State Parkway south and stomped on the gas again to force my way into the steady stream of cars, most all on their way to take their weekend or weekly vacation rentals. It was the Saturday of Labor Day weekend, 2001, and I had reserved the second-floor apartment at the O'Connors' for the week. It was a beautiful day, and the week ahead promised more of the same. The traffic, mostly on its way to Ocean City or Wildwood, funneled off the parkway and onto the crowded two-lane street that connected the highway to the Somers Point traffic circle about a mile away. Easing into the circle, I punched up a Beach Boys CD and turned the four-hundred-watt stereo almost full on.

I passed the Circle Liquor Store on the right, always a booming business, due to Ocean City being a "dry" town. Turning right off the circle, I entered Route 52, the 2.1-mile Stainton Memorial Causeway that most people called the Ninth Street Bridge. I accelerated up the first drawbridge and looked left at the big bayside restaurant; below were the Somers Point docks. I backed off the gas as I entered the metal grating of the drawbridge and looked ahead at the outline of the bay side of Ocean City. Through the slight haze, I could see the Ferris wheel at Gillian's Fun Deck on the boardwalk at Sixth Street, and straight ahead, I could see the venerable Flanders Hotel, built in 1923. I smiled as I thought back to my early days at IBM, when my customer was Atlantic City's Boardwalk National Bank, which was headed by Elwood F. Kirkman. The Flanders Hotel was owned by Kirkman, and he had lived in the top-floor penthouse until his death at eighty-nine.

Moving down the drawbridge, I entered the flat part of the causeway. The tide was low, and I inhaled the pungent smell of the marsh gases, most likely caused by methane gas. I loved that smell, however offensive, because it clearly announced that I was at the shore. "Ahh," I said aloud, and turned the Beach Boys' "Surfin' USA" up louder. The metal grating on the second drawbridge made a buzzing sound like a swarm of bees as I looked at the condos on the right. They had replaced Hogate's Restaurant, where I had eaten as a child coming home on the one-day trips with my family.

I was now on Ninth Street and in Ocean City! I turned left, heading north on Bay Avenue, passing more condos and then the bay docks with their Sailfish and Jet Ski rentals. I turned right onto Fourth Street, proceeded through too many stop signs, and then turned left on Atlantic Boulevard. I turned right into a narrow alleyway and then turned left into the O'Connors' parking spot, next to their garage.

I knocked on the back door, and Frank came to the screened doorway. "I'm home!" I yelled; I had adopted that greeting after my first week at the O'Connors'.

Frank smiled and said, "Come on in. Nance," he called out to his wife, "Steve Fisher is here. How was your trip down?"

"Fine. Traffic was light, and I made it in record time." I pointed to my new Mustang.

"Wow, let me take a look at it," said Frank.

I showed him around the car and then said, "I'd like to move my stuff in and then go have my usual pizza at Mack and Manco's."

"Okay, then let me help you with your bags. Hey, I see you've brought lots of books."

"Yeah, I like to read almost as much as you. Let me use the bathroom, then I'll go right up to the boardwalk."

Frank said, "Fine. By the way, I think I saw a mention of your grandfather in a novel I just read. His name was Clarence, right?"

"Yes. What did you see it in?"

"Just a paperback mystery, written by a woman, about an Egyptologist who gets involved with a murder. It's only a sentence, so it's not a big deal, but I thought you'd be interested. I'll have it for you when you get back."

"Great!"

CHAPTER 18

Saturday, September 1, 2001
Ocean City, New Jersey

I exited the O'Connors' apartment and walked down Third Street, crossed Corinthian Avenue, and walked the short block to the boardwalk ramp, past the high-rise condo complex. On the boardwalk, I noticed the dark-suntanned college girl wearing a bikini and designer sunglasses. She was checking beach tags at the steps down to the beach. I looked out to the stone jetty that reached out into the ocean like the blade of an electric hedge trimmer and saw a lone fisherman. I saw a family with two children, one being carried, walking through the dunes carrying chairs and towels, and onto the burning hot sand. I looked across the wide beach, much wider than in my childhood due to almost constant wintertime beach re-plenishment, and at the black rock jetty, the waves gently kissing it like two women hugging hello. There was a cooling breeze coming from the relatively calm sea, and the sky was turning from white to a robin's-egg blue. I looked at my watch. It was 11:30 a.m., and the beach was already starting to get crowded on this perfect Labor Day weekend in Ocean City.

I turned right and headed down the boardwalk. At Fourth Street, I stopped at Oves Restaurant and checked when they opened. Good, 5:00 p.m.; I wanted to get there before it opened, to be sure of getting a seat that was open to the boardwalk. I'd get my usual fillet of flounder, cole slaw, and corn on the cob tonight. Walking farther, I passed the high school football field. It looked like there was going to be a football game there that night. I decided to check it out later.

I walked past Gillian's Wonderland Pier, which wasn't a pier at all; it had always been called Gillian's Fun Deck. It had a high Ferris wheel, a log flume ride, and a kiddie roller coaster. But mostly it had kiddie rides. The steel curtains at the front were partway up; Gillian's would open at noon.

I passed Seventh Street and walked up to Mack and Manco Pizza, the first of three on the boardwalk. I sat on the first seat inside the door and ordered two slices and a Coke. As I waited, I stared at two well-tanned and well-developed teenagers in bikinis. They were giggling and leaning over the counter that faced the boardwalk; they were flirting with the muscular twenty-something guy who was taking their order.

The pizza came, and I reflected on how, that night, there would be lines across the boardwalk with people waiting for Mack and Manco's, while pizza shops two doors away would have only a few customers. I relaxed, enjoyed my pizza, and issued an almost audible "Ahh."

• • •

Returning from my pizza on the boardwalk, I went up on the front porch, where Frank O'Connor was often found reading a book. Instead, Frank was at the side of their shore home watering the flowers. Frank loved taking care of the flowers, especially since Nancy was the daughter of a prominent suburban Philadelphia florist.

"Did you have a great pizza?"

"You bet, and I got to see some pretty girls!"

"Ha, good. Let me finish watering. I'll shout up to you, and you can come down and I'll show you that book."

I walked back to the rear steps that led up to the second floor. I entered through the kitchen and then began putting my things away. When I was done, I went out on the second-floor porch, sat in the chaise lounge, and sighed; I was happy to just sit there. I started to doze off.

"Steve, are you up there?"

"Yeah. Shall I come down now?"

"Sure. I'll get us Cokes."

I went back through the living room, dining room, and kitchen, down the stairs, and around the side to the front porch. I took a seat and waited for Frank to return with the Cokes.

Frank and I had known each other from working together on IBM's largest bank customer in Philadelphia in the mid-1970s. Frank was the almost-always well-dressed IBM salesman, and I was the not-so-well-dressed computer systems engineer, the techie guy who worked with client programmers. At work, both of us wore the IBM uniform: dark suit, white shirt, sincere tie, black socks, and wing tips.

Frank and I were, as we found out, born fifteen days apart; we were now fifty-eight. I graduated from the University of Pennsylvania, as did my older brother, Glenn; my father, Clarence Stanley Jr.; and my grandfather, archaeologist Clarence Stanley Fisher. Frank graduated from Brown and then got his MBA from Penn's famed Wharton School. Both of us left IBM during the early '90s, taking advantage of IBM's early retirement programs. I tried my hand at IT consulting, and Frank went to law school.

We were both of medium height, with Frank far thinner and in much better shape than me. I definitely had the middle-age paunch; a beer belly, but I didn't drink beer. My legs and arms were still slim, and I could still, from my diving days, easily put my palms on the floor without bending my knees.

Frank was a collector of Coca-Cola memorabilia; their home outside Philadelphia was lined with Coca-Cola framed advertisements and posters.

"Here," said Frank, handing the Coke to me. "It looks like a great week ahead. Do you have anything planned?"

"No, no plans, just seeing what happens. I like, for the few days when Linda's not here, to get up in the morning and wonder where I'm going to get some breakfast and what I'm going to do all day. Walk, read, sleep; I love it; no plans." I took quite a few gulps of Coke and gracefully let the carbonation out, avoiding a burp. I was very thirsty from the pizza and salt. "And tonight, I'll eat at Oves and maybe go to the Ocean City High football game."

"Sounds good, but take a jacket. It's supposed to be chilly tonight, even though it's perfect now. Let me show you this book."

A paperback, it was on the coffee table. Frank reached for it. He thumbed through it and found the marked page. "I was reading this mystery; it's actually one of a series of mysteries by Elizabeth Peters that all take place in Egypt from the early 1900s, I think, up through the 1920s. They each involve an archaeologist." Frank gulped his Coke as well, but was a little more discreet than me.

"Hmm, I've never heard of her," I said, "but that certainly doesn't mean anything. I don't go around looking for books about Egypt, despite my grandfather."

"Well, I was just reading along through this book, *He Shall Thunder in the Sky*, when a sentence jumped out at me. It was just one sentence in the whole book. Here it is, page two hundred: 'Clarence Fisher, who was about to begin work in the West Cemetery field, dropped by to have a look.' That's all there is." He closed the book and handed it to me. "I remember when IBM had a meeting at the Penn Museum, and you came and showed me the columns that your grandfather had unearthed. You were still teaching computer operating systems for IBM at the time, if I recall correctly, so it had to be about ten years ago. Does that sound right?"

"Frank, you have a good memory. I remember that your whole branch office was there for a sales kickoff meeting, and your branch manager, Jack Montgomery, even had me stand up, and he said a few words about my grandfather. I was pretty honored."

"Was your grandfather an archaeologist only in Egypt?"

"Egypt, and in Israel too. He started in Egypt and then pretty much left Egypt after Howard Carter found King Tut's tomb. He spent the rest of his life in Jerusalem and died there. My brother, who you remember is a minister, went on a biblical tour of Israel in the early eighties and took a picture of our grandfather's grave. He's buried alongside Flinders Petrie, who was way more famous as an archaeologist."

"Did you ever know your grandfather?"

"No, only my grandmother. Clarence died in 1941, when my brother was almost five. My mother, his daughter-in-law, often wrote to him, and we used to have one of those early records that you could make, with my brother saying, 'Ganpa, Ganpa, are you in there?'"

"Well, tell me more about him. Do you know much?"

"Some. In the days even before the Depression, my grandmother moved in with her sister and her husband, and my father and his cousin, Harriet, who we called Aunt Hoppy. They were all in the same house.

It seems to me that Clarence all but abandoned my father and grand-mother. But all Glenn and I heard was that he was married to his work and was always overseas. My grandmother once told me that Clarence had an actual gunfight with someone who was trying to steal objects they had unearthed. She also said that he was the second person into Tut's tomb."

"Wait a minute," said Frank. "I remember reading about the opening of the tomb. It said that Carter saw 'wondrous things' and that he and Carnarvon went into the tomb, followed by Carnarvon's daughter, I think."

"Well, I've read that too. But my father and grandmother both told me that Clarence was the second person into the tomb. In tenth-grade English class, we were supposed to write an autobiography, and I got permission from the teacher to write a biography of my grandfather. I interviewed my grandmother, and she repeated that he was the second person into the tomb.

"Frank, let me see that book again. I wonder why the author, um, Elizabeth Peters, would bother to add such a meaningless sentence." I read aloud, "'Clarence Fisher, who was about to begin work in the West Cemetery field, dropped by to have a look.'"

Unbeknownst to me then, I would be touring Egypt in thirteen months, an ordinary tourist whose trip would turn into a harrowing adventure.

CHAPTER 19

Tuesday, September 11, 2001
Philadelphia suburbs

After returning from a week at the O'Connors' in Ocean City, I was finally up to date on my work e-mails and some small items at work. I had come in the day before to find 173 e-mails in my inbox. I had spent most of yesterday, except for two thirty-minute meetings, going through and responding to e-mails. It was 8:25 a.m., and my next meeting wasn't until 9:00.

I sat back, took another sip of my usual twenty-ounce cup of Wawa coffee, and reflected on the past week at the shore. It had been a perfect week—highs eighty-five to ninety-five, lows in the seventies, low humidity, and sunny skies. And today, Tuesday, was another beautiful, cloudless day.

Last week, one morning when Lenore and Linda had gone shopping, I went to the modest Ocean City Public Library. There I paged through every single book by Elizabeth Peters that I could find. I found that Elizabeth Peters was a pseudonym for Barbara Mertz, who had a PhD in Egyptology from the University of Chicago. I knew that Clarence Fisher had been the first archaeologist in charge of the University of Chicago's excavation of Megiddo, also known as Armageddon, in Palestine, now Israel. I also found that Barbara Mertz had published other novels under another name, and that the name Elizabeth Peters was used for each of her Amelia Peabody murder mysteries, which involved archaeologists in Egypt from 1884 to 1923.

As I sat back and relaxed with my coffee, I thought back to what I had found at the library by going quickly through each page looking for "Fisher" to jump out. I had found another reference, but it mentioned Clarence's drinking champagne at a party, seemingly to excess. Despite that, I planned that when I got home that night I would write a letter to Barbara Mertz, explaining who I was and mentioning mysteries regarding Clarence Fisher. I knew that my grandfather died in Jerusalem in the summer of 1941. But I had also gotten a strange call from a newspaperman asking information about the archaeologist Clarence Fisher who had died in 1983. To my dismay, I was never able to account for this strange occurrence.

The phone rang. "Dad?" It was my son, Scott.

"Yeah."

"Did you hear about the plane crashing into the World Trade Center? They don't yet know if was an accident or intentional, but there were clear skies, and it was a big plane."

"Thanks. I'll turn on the radio."

PART FOUR

2002

CHAPTER 20

Saturday, January 19, 2002
Philadelphia suburbs

The wind continued to howl outside, and snow was blowing sideways, down and up, against the full-length glass of the storm door. The wind sounded like a low-flying jet airplane that was somehow hovering over the house. I was standing at the door, while Beasley, our yellow Lab dog, sat and watched the storm with me. It was a winter nor'easter, and it had already put down eight inches of snow. Beasley looked sad, with her always-present Frisbee clutched in her mouth like a precious treasure. All three major local TV channels had gone to full-time coverage, which consisted of weather forecasters predicting at least eight more inches, talking heads predicting that the governor was expected to restrict travel to essential-use only, and the typical, idiotic interviews with people at Wawa convenience stores, a Philadelphia favorite, saying that they were running out for milk, bread, and cigarettes.

I had already used my underpowered snow blower to remove what had already come down. I was wet, cold, and exhausted. As I looked out, I saw a township snowplow make a pass, adding to the pile already in front of the driveway, blocking us in until the next morning, at least.

I put my bright red parka into the closet with my ball cap, took off my boots, and went upstairs to change from my corduroys into my usual khaki pants. Yes, blue button-down shirt, khaki pants—Linda had said that I wore the same clothes ever since she met me in high school forty-three years ago. Returning downstairs, I grabbed a Pepsi from the refrigerator and made my way to my favorite chair in the family room, in front of the TV. At last, I could relax.

I couldn't relax, however, due to the pain from my chronic back problem, exacerbated by my struggling with the snow blower, which, of course, was better than using a snow shovel. Also, my mind wouldn't stop while I was fighting the snow, and it continued now.

My thoughts were on two things: the 9/11 attack on the World Trade Center, and my resolve to write to the mystery writer regarding my findings about my archaeologist grandfather, Dr. Clarence S. Fisher.

I had gotten over the anger that I usually felt whenever I remembered the terrorist attacks on the World Trade Center. I had much earlier worked at IBM with Bonnie Shihadeh Smithwick, who had died in Tower Two; her phone call to her husband, regarding her abandoning Tower One, had been abruptly cut off by the collapse.

I decided to finally write to author Barbara Mertz, who, as Elizabeth Peters, had written the novel that mentioned my grandfather. I had originally intended to write her after my vacation, in the evening of September 11, but with the horrific events of that day, I had dropped any thoughts of Clarence Fisher.

I walked upstairs to the den, which was more of a mess cave than a man cave. Justifiably, Linda had long ago refused responsibility for anything in it. I sat at my computer table and typed a letter to Ms. Mertz at her Maryland home:

Dear Ms. Mertz:

I hope that this does indeed get forwarded to you by MPM, because I have a true-life Egyptologist-Archaeologist mystery for you. On page 200 of the paperback version of "He Shall Thunder in the Sky," you (Elizabeth Peters) say, "Soon after we returned to work, other visitors came, whom it was impossible to drive away. Clarence Fisher, who was about to begin work in the West Cemetery field, dropped by to have a look."

The Clarence Fisher you refer to was my grandfather. Please let me state the mystery: Clarence Fisher died in Jerusalem on July 20th, 1941. In April of 1988, I was contacted by Eric Tobin, who is still the Reference Archivist, University of Pennsylvania Museum Archives. He was passing on a true mystery about my grandfather. He had been contacted by an obituary writer at the St. Louis Post Dispatch by the name of Lou Schucart. Mr. Schucart was calling to follow up on the death, in St. Louis in March of 1988, of Clarence Fisher, the noted Egyptologist who had been invited to the opening of King Tut's tomb. Mr. Tobin knew something of (the real) Clarence Fisher because of my earlier conversations with a Museum employee named Caroline Dosker, who had known my grandfather as a child. Mr. Tobin replied that Clarence Fisher had died in the early 1940s; surely Mr. Schucart had been mistaken about him dying in 1988.

Eventually, I contacted Mr. Schucart to try to find out more about his request. He stated that Clarence's son, Fred, had contacted the newspaper because he thought it would be appropriate for the newspaper to honor the distinguished career of his father, who had died in his 80s. He had stated that his father had participated at the opening of King Tut's tomb and had been a world-renowned archaeologist. He told Mr. Schucart that he had a picture of his father as a baby at the Pyramids. But he also mentioned that when he retired, his father had been the Chief Accountant at a company in St. Louis.

I then explained that in 1988, Clarence would have been 112 years old and that I knew of the photograph he was talking about; it was of my father, C. Stanley Fisher, Jr., taken at the Pyramids, the only time that my grandmother visited my grandfather in the field. I also asked, "You mean this world-famous archaeologist decided to change careers and become an accountant?" I requested that maybe Mr. Schucart could investigate this more and he agreed to talk to his editor. He later called me and stated that his editor had told him to forget about it.

So the mystery remains, and my brother and I, his closest living relatives, have ever since wondered if there was any way to find out more about it. Then I was introduced to your Amelia Peabody mysteries. Perhaps you could forge a mystery novel around the tale of the two Clarence Fishers? My guess is that someone obtained

Clarence's effects and assumed his identity. (He left some money to my grandmother, but very few of his effects from Jerusalem were returned to her.) I'm sure that there was plenty of that during World War II. But why would someone (a Nazi trying to establish a new life?) go so far as to tell his child about his former, but bogus, life as a world-famous archaeologist?

Ms. Mertz, I know that your time is very valuable, but I hope you've had a chance to read this. If you have any further interest, please don't hesitate to reach me. I have many materials about my grandfather, including a letter I sent to Mr. Schucart. And I would guess that Eric Tobin would also be willing to assist somewhat.

I also e-mailed a copy to Penn Museum archivist Eric Tobin, with hopes of finding if Eric knew anything more about the mystery. I copied my brother Glenn and then called him. I reminded Glenn about the sentence in the book that mentioned Clarence Fisher from last summer and that the events of September 11 had removed all thoughts about Clarence from my memory until now.

"So please read the e-mail with my letter to Barbara Mertz, since you're snowed in as well. I copied Eric Tobin, since he was the one who contacted me about the second Clarence Fisher. I don't know if it will solve the mystery, but it's worth trying."

"Sure," replied Glenn. "But I doubt if anything will come of it. It's been at least ten years since Eric told you about the reporter's inquiry."

"Fourteen, actually."

"Okay, but Eric has probably forgotten about it. Is he even still at Penn?"

"Yes, he's the chief archivist, and his e-mail address is the same."

"Probably nothing will happen."

"I agree, but it's fun to think about it. By the way, do you remember the map that you had on poster board; the one that Ganpa, I mean Clarence, made when he was in college at Penn?"

"Yes," said Glenn. "And I think I still have it. On the poster board was a street map of Philadelphia, and on the other side was the map you're talking about. Why?"

"Well, it would be neat to see it. If I remember correctly, the map was of a fictional city called Olympia, and from the very center of the city, the streets went out from the center like spokes in a wheel. And all the cross streets were perfect circles radiating out from the center."

"You have a good memory; I haven't thought about that map in almost fifty years. It's no longer on a poster board; it's folded. But I ran across it last week while looking for something else. I ignored it, but let me get it. Hang on." The phone was silent for two minutes.

"Here it is. Let me unfold it...It's like you remembered, laid out sort of like Paris, with streets that look like spokes and rings. There's a big train station near the center of the city, but the actual center is a park with two ponds in it. It shows business areas close to the center and more business areas around the outside perimeter. Houses closer to the center look like they're close together, while houses out further are larger and more widely spaced. There's no river shown, and the train tracks run from the lower right, pass through the train station, and then continue on to the upper right.

"The streets that are shown as rings are wide; there are five of them. All have names and are called drives; the outermost is North (or South) Outer Drive. The spokes also have names, and are all called avenues; one is called North (or South) College Avenue. And each of the avenues has trolley tracks in the middle. There are more streets within sections, each section bounded by two avenues and two drives. The streets are not named, but some sections have neighborhood names like Pepper and Harrison."

I asked, "So no secret map information? How about looking at the back? Anything there?"

"Nothing on the back...Wait a minute, I see indentations in a few areas that are unusual. Let me turn back to the front and see if I can match them up. Hmm."

"What? Did you find something?"

"I'm not sure. One of the indentations, when I turn to the front, looks like it is overlaying the name of a drive. Above the center, the drive is called North White Drive, but below the center it now says...in a very slightly different handwriting, it now says South Echna Drive. The change is very subtle."

"Can you look at it with a magnifying glass?"

"Sure, Steve." He returned after thirty seconds. "Okay, here it is. It looks like the word 'Echna' is indeed over top of another word that hasn't completely been erased. So maybe Ganpa—"

"Clarence," I interrupted.

"Yeah, Clarence, okay. Clarence may have changed the name sometime later, maybe years after he did the map as a college project. Hold on, here's another. The naming conventions hold for avenue names, which begin with North, South, East, or West, like East Franklin Avenue. But there's something strange. If I look closely at the map, I see another place where it's been very subtly changed. North Shewell Avenue is above the center, while now it's been changed to below the center to South Moise Avenue. If I follow those two roads, they meet at the intersection of South Moise Avenue and South Echna Drive. Does that mean anything to you?"

"Not a thing! Oh well, let me see the map sometime. Maybe we'll find that it will lead us to a secret treasure. Ha! Well, good luck with the snow."

"Thanks, same to you. Talk to you soon."

CHAPTER 21

Thursday, March 21, 2002
Philadelphia suburbs

"Hi, Glenn. It's your brother. How are you?"

"Okay. What's up, Steve?"

"Well, I have some pretty good news. Last night I got an interesting e-mail from Eric Tobin, the Penn Museum archivist. He apologized for not getting back to me sooner, and he said he didn't know anything more about the second Clarence, but he contacted another person who he thought may know something. Eric said that he knew that there was a young doctoral student in archaeology who was writing her thesis about Clarence Fisher. He said that Clarence had excavated more than half of the entire Penn Museum Egyptian Section's collection of Egyptian artifacts and that she was documenting many of these items for a thesis about Clarence! He also said that she knew who the second Clarence was, and she indicated that she would love to get together with us!"

"Wow, that's great!"

"Sure is."

"Eric also suggested I call Caroline Dosker, who's retired from the museum. He said that she knew Clarence as a teenager. I called her, and she said some interesting things. She's the one who came to our house on Alexander Avenue in the early sixties with Frances James and took away a box of Clarence material from our attic. Caroline told me that she was set to visit Clarence at his summer place in Cyprus when she was a teenager in the late thirties, but the impending war canceled those plans."

"Interesting."

"Get this. Her maiden name is Gordon, and her father, Richard, was the press secretary at the Penn Museum when Clarence was working there. Apparently, they were very close. She told me, 'My daddy always told me that your grandfather told Howard Carter where to dig for Tutankhamun's tomb.' And she repeated that multiple times.

"Anyway, I looked at the calendar and picked Saturday, April 13. I then e-mailed Tina Gilbert and asked if there was any way she could meet us for dinner, my treat, on the thirteenth at the Desmond Hotel, and she agreed; she lives in Radnor, so it's not far away. I told her that I would check with you and confirm back to her."

"Yes, that sounds really great. We can set the time later, but Sunny and I will be there. Maybe we'll find that the second Clarence was a Nazi spy like you suggested to Barbara Mertz."

CHAPTER 22

Saturday, April 13, 2002
Philadelphia suburbs

"Let me start by solving, hopefully to your satisfaction, the mystery about your second grandfather," said Penn doctoral candidate Tina Gilbert. She was seated at one of the round tables at the Desmond Hotel with Linda and me; our daughter, Cindy; and Glenn and his wife, Sunny. We had exchanged pleasantries and finished appetizers; several had ordered shrimp cocktails. We were waiting for our main courses in the hotel's nicely furnished and quiet Hunt Room. I had indicated that it was my treat and encouraged everyone to order whatever they wanted from the sumptuous menu.

I asked Tina to introduce herself. Tall and slender, but with wide shoulders typical of a competitive swimmer, Tina had been on the swim team at her high school in Medford, New Jersey, and at the University of Pennsylvania. Graduating from Penn with honors in 1998, she was quickly accepted into the Near Eastern Languages and Civilizations Archaeology master's program and had completed her PhD course requirements.

Tina was not what one expected in a PhD archaeologist. She was stunning, with high cheekbones, blue eyes, light brown eyebrows, and blond hair, which was fashioned into a studious bun. With her blue blazer and white blouse and pants, she looked like a college student, or a college recruiter, or a swimmer about to receive an award. But not an archaeologist.

"As part of my research on your grandfather, who made so many contributions to our Egyptian collection, I traveled to the University of Chicago last summer. I'd wanted to do some research on what he did for them at Megiddo. While going through his materials, I saw a picture of Clarence standing at the Pyramids with his nephew, also named Clarence Stanley Fisher, and not Junior, like your father. I also saw a picture of the two of them standing at the top of the Great Pyramid! The materials also included an address for the second Clarence in Saint Louis. Not knowing about his demise, like you did, I called hoping to speak with him.

"The phone was answered by Fred Fisher, his son. He told me that his father passed away in 1983. I only spoke with Fred briefly, but he said that his father was an accountant and that he worked as an accountant on several of Clarence's digs. I asked about the two Clarence Fishers, and Fred cleared things up. The archaeologist Clarence had a brother named Fred Fisher who named his child after Clarence. Go figure!"

"Wow!" I said. "That clears things up. So the second Clarence was not an imposter —ha—and not a Nazi. I guess the obituary writer back in 1983 got the two mixed up. The article did say that the Clarence who died was an archaeologist and then decided to be a chief accountant at some company—a very unlikely career change!"

"Tina," said Glenn. "Thanks so much. Now we know, but somehow I wish maybe that we didn't know. It was more fun thinking that someone, maybe a spy in the underground, had killed him—we always wondered about Clarence's death—and then assumed his identity. Or maybe an escaped Nazi officer or official assumed his identity rather than escaping to Brazil." He laughed.

Glenn was six years older than me, but due to his being at least an inch shorter, thirty pounds lighter, and with natural black hair, he looked much younger. A Penn graduate like me, he went on to earn his PhD in theology. As a Methodist minister, he had moved several times, all in eastern Pennsylvania.

"Sorry, no. Nothing exciting," Tina said with a smile.

Our meal came, and we all participated in small talk while we ate. I explained about my friend mentioning a line in an Elizabeth Peters book; Tina said that she had read them all.

"I was, I think, eleven when I read *Lion in the Valley*. It was one of the reasons I became interested in being an archaeologist, but I was only interested in Egypt. Also, around that time my father had taken me to several of Philadelphia's museums, including the Franklin Institute and the Penn Museum. But what captivated me was the Penn Museum, with its large columns excavated by your grandfather, and, of course, the mummies. That really sealed it for me. Unlike most of my friends, I knew what I wanted to do from that moment on."

I responded, "That's neat. My interest in my grandfather, who died before I was born, started with my grandmother, who lived in the next block from where Glenn and I grew up. Known to family as Pree, she allowed us to build a caravan in their living room. Chairs, a piano bench, and a card table were arranged in a row, and blankets were thrown over them. We were on a caravan going through the desert! Later, she would tell me things about my grandfather—he was always referred to as 'married to his work'—like how he had a gunfight with a robber, how she had cleaned excavated jewelry for the Harvard Museum, and that he had been the second person into King Tut's tomb."

Glenn spoke, "And I was almost five when he died. I know that our mother corresponded with him. I even made a record for him in a booth somewhere in Philadelphia. I guess we made two copies, with one sent to him. I remember saying something like, 'Hello, Ganpa. Hello, Ganpa. Is he in there?'"

Everyone laughed, and I continued, "In the first week of my tenth grade, our English teacher assigned us to write an autobiography. After class, I asked her if I could instead write a biography of my grandfather, and she agreed. I interviewed my grandmother for almost twenty minutes. I then wrote my paper, and the English teacher had me read it to the class. Gee, I wish I still had it. All I remember is what I've mentioned; about the gunfight and Tut's tomb. When I was in college, and also now and then, I've tried to find out if it was true about Clarence being the second person into the tomb. All I've ever found is that the first people were Howard Carter, Lord Carnarvon, and his daughter, Lady Evelyn; no Clarence."

"I've seen nothing more than that either," said Tina.

"I just remembered," I added. "I saw some newspaper clippings about Clarence. He was to help with the restoration of the Dome of the Rock in Jerusalem. Maybe he found the Ark of the Covenant just like Indiana Jones! I also saw that he made headlines, after getting sick, that said that he might have King Tut's curse. Wait, I can't believe that I'm remembering this. I remember that he made headlines when he quit Penn."

"Well, I can't help with the first two," Tina said. "But I can confirm that he had a stormy relationship later in his Penn career that resulted in him resigning."

After dinner and during dessert—most had ordered banana cream pie—Tina began about Clarence.

"Clarence Fisher was a very interesting, hardworking, dedicated, and talented man. He was wonderful at documenting what he found on index cards that are still at Penn. His organizational skills were excellent. There is an excavation technique called the Reisner-Fisher method that some think was really entirely due to Clarence's insistence on digging horizontally so that buildings could be seen as they existed; he was trained as an architect. Previous methods involved digging straight down in trenches, which was a quicker way of finding things. Clarence must have convinced his mentor at the time, George Reisner, that his method was better. And because of Reisner's name being on it, the technique was adopted.

"But Clarence was also a very complex man, I'm sorry to say; quick to argue and lose his temper, and also subject to illness. He quit Penn in 1925 over disputes with museum director Gordon. He was always asking for more salary, and he quit over the men that Gordon hired to work for him, and possibly to keep him under control.

"But he was amazing. He graduated from Penn in 1897 as an architect; he never had any formal training in either archaeology or Egyptian history. In today's world he would not be called an archaeologist or an Egyptologist. In 1898, he joined the museum's excavations at Nippur, in today's Iraq. I don't know what he did there. Was he an architect, a photographer, an artist? But he had to have been a quick study. In 1905 he had his first book published, *Excavations at Nippur*. He was twenty-eight!

"From there he worked with George Reisner, who was well respected, at Zawyet el'Aryan, the site of the third pyramid ever built. Clarence published an article about that for the Harvard Museum of Fine Arts, and he also wrote one on the jewelry that was found."

"Maybe that's what my grandmother cleaned," I interrupted.

"Probably. Anyway, Clarence became curator of the Egyptian Section of the Penn Museum in 1914 and performed fieldwork through 1925. He loved to dig and took meticulous notes, but he didn't like to publish, which has always been a requirement. What's the use of excavating if you can't let the world know?

"He also was very ambitious. He worked three sites at once: Memphis, which is south of Cairo; Dra Abu el Naga, which is across the Nile from Luxor; and Beth Shan, which is in today's Israel. One leg of that triangle is four hundred miles, another five hundred miles, and Luxor to Beth Shan is more than eight hundred miles. He did have use of a big boat on the Nile, the *Hapi*, which he used to travel between Luxor and Cairo. Those are tough trips today; just imagine in 1915! I don't know how he did it, but then again, he couldn't keep it up. His health got to him, including a bout of malaria, and the combination of exhaustion, health issues, frustration, and possibly drinking led him to resign from Penn in 1925. And possibly caused him problems at other sites as well.

"One nice thing: I brought a copy of a letter from an Arab man named Shaker Ahmad Suleiman who was with Clarence when he died and knew him well. It was originally sent to your grandmother, but I don't know how Penn got it."

I answered, "I do. A woman, Frances James, came with Caroline Dosker from Penn to my parents' house sometime in the late 1950s and took a box full of stuff about Clarence that was in our attic. I remember that it included those newspaper clippings."

"Okay. The letter says…Let me get it so I can quote it directly…Here it is: 'All the highly esteemed and honored faculties of humanity were embodied in him. May I assure you that what I have said and what I may say later comes straight from the bottom of my heart and feelings. One person I have ever known, honest, generous, sympathetic in all human race, that is Dr. Fisher.' There is more, but I'll let you read that later."

There was silence. Then Glenn replied for all with, "Wow! Thank you so much!"

"You're welcome. Look, I could go on and on, but why don't you just ask me questions?"

"I have one," I said. "Coming from a background at Penn, when you were in Chicago, did you find anything of interest about Clarence?"

"Well…I guess there were maybe two things. Unfortunately I did find more about why he was taken off the leadership of the Megiddo expedition. They said it was his health, but, and I'm sorry, it was really his drinking. And from an academic viewpoint, he found an interesting stele, which is inscribed in stone, called the Shishak or Shoshenq I Megiddo Stele. It's the only link so far to the name of a pharaoh in the Bible. That refers to a verse in the Bible where a pharaoh named Shishak raided Solomon's temple and took all the treasures in the temple."

"Including the Ark of the Covenant?" I was excited. "Maybe Clarence knew where all those treasures were buried. Maybe he knew where to find the Ark of the Covenant."

"Calm down," said Glenn. "Maybe he always intended to. If it was in Israel, Palestine, he probably could have persuaded someone to fund a search for the treasures."

"But if it was in Egypt, I know that he didn't want to return there until after all of the Tut controversies died down," said Tina. "But we'll never really know."

There was a pause while we all finished our desserts.

Sliding his chair back and wiping his chin, Glenn asked, "Okay, Tina, have you ever been to Egypt, seen the various sites?"

"No, but I've looked into what it would entail as a tourist, since Penn can't send me, at least not until I get my doctorate and, a big 'and,' they decide to hire me. As a potential tourist, I found that there's a travel agency in Chicago that's used almost exclusively by Penn. They can set up tours for small groups; they have contacts for all the great sites, excellent guides, and can put you on a great Nile cruise if you want. They handle everything."

"What about safety? Wasn't there an attack on tourists there fairly recently?" asked Sunny.

"Yes, in 1997 sixty-two tourists were killed at a popular site across the Nile from Luxor; actually very near Dra Abu el Naga, where your grandfather dug."

"So it wouldn't be safe to travel there now," stated Sunny.

"I wouldn't say that. Of course the travel agent would try to ease your mind, but they did tell me that Egypt has taken many steps to prevent further problems."

"Such as?" interrupted Glenn.

"Such as three levels of security: one you can see, one you may see, and one you can't see. I've been told by my colleagues that you can see police, you may see someone in a polo shirt and jeans but notice that he's hiding a gun, and, at the sites themselves, it may be possible to spot an Egyptian in one of their long white robes, with something long hidden under it, possibly a Kalashnikov. And I understand that they've cut back most cruise trips all the way from Cairo to Aswan, since the cruise would go past Minya, which is the hotbed of the terrorists. The cruises now go just from Luxor to Aswan; you fly to Luxor from Cairo. I hear that there are a few ships that make the whole cruise from Cairo to Luxor, but they now have mounted machine guns."

"Oh my," said Sunny.

"Why do you ask; are you planning to go?"

"No!" shouted both wives simultaneously.

Cindy said, "Go for it!"

Glenn and I were silent.

CHAPTER 23

Saturday, August 31, 2002
Ocean City, New Jersey

"Hey, Frank, I'm home!" I yelled.

Once again I had come down on the Saturday of Labor Day weekend, cruising comfortably in my Mustang convertible. The weather was perfect, and, as I made my way over the causeway linking Ocean City to Somers Point, my mind went over the many times I had made this same trip. First was a flash of a picture waiting to board a train to return from OCNJ when I was only six years old. Then, more flashes, of preteen one-day shoebie trips with my mother, aunt, two cousins, and brother all piled into an old Chevy. Thankfully, my mind settled on the good parts, the trips I made during high school and college, when I was able to make the trip in my yellow-and-green 1954 Chevy Bel Air. Yes, "Let's go down the shore!" was the cry. The guys, girls, making out, surf and sand, water skiing, the boardwalk, Mack and Manco's pizza—great memories. Another memory, of posing on the end of a diving board in the Middle Atlantic diving championships, watching the Ferris wheel at the amusement park next to the Flanders Hotel pool. And a more recent one, of standing at the water's edge as my three grandsons splashed with joy in the surf.

Frank O'Connor came to the screened back door.

"Ha, it looks like a nice week ahead, good for your Mustang convertible, which I see you still have. Let me help you take your things in."

"Thanks, and thanks to you for our Egypt trip," I said.

"All I did was point out one sentence in a book."

"Yeah, but it started a chain of events that ends with our sixteen-day trip to Egypt in October!"

"But why isn't Linda going?"

"Well, she wasn't that interested, but the main reason is that her high school reunion is the Friday night after we return, and she's in charge of everything.

"But we're all set. My brother and I and a Penn doctoral candidate, Tina Gilbert, leave October 18 for sixteen days. We're being helped by Zahi Hawass, who you may have seen on television. He's the head of all expeditions at the site of the Pyramids, and he's opening doors for us because he actually studied my grandfather's book when he was getting his doctor's degree at Penn. So we'll see sites that other people don't get to see. We're trying to follow in the footsteps of my grandfather, but we'll just be normal tourists. We'll stay at the Mena House for six nights by the Pyramids. We'll then fly to Luxor and stay four nights in the Winter Palace, where I'm sure my grandfather stayed occasionally. We hope to see King Tut's tomb. Then we take a four-night cruise to Aswan. These are all the touristy kinds of things. But I'll tell you more when I get back from having my Mack and Manco pizza!"

● ● ●

Frank, Nancy, and I were seated on the O'Connors' porch, enjoying Cokes. I placed the large folded map on a table.

"Steve, tell us about how all this came about," Frank said.

"Frank, it all started with you. I searched through some more of Elizabeth Peters's books in the library here, and then decided I'd write to the author, who is actually Barbara Mertz. I found out that she's actually a PhD Egyptologist who writes novels, including those under another name, that aren't about Egypt.

"Anyway, I planned to write her on the day after I returned to work. But that turned out to be 9/11. I actually knew someone who worked at the World Trade Center; she tried to reach her husband, got his secretary, and then she was cut off."

"How horrible," said Nancy, "Did you know her well?"

"No. I've had no contact with her for almost twenty years. But a strange coincidence: although she was about nine years younger than me, she somehow knew of me from my days as a diver. Anyway, I forgot all about it until January. One night I wrote to Barbara Mertz, and she responded several months later. She was nice, said that she certainly knew about my grandfather, but she couldn't help with my mystery."

"Mystery?" asked Nancy.

"Yeah. I guess I never told you about the second Clarence Fisher?"

"Huh?"

"It's crazy. In 1988 I got a call from the archivist at Penn. He had gotten a call from a newspaperman, an obit writer, I guess, about the death of the famous archaeologist Clarence Fisher in Saint Louis in 1988. But my grandfather died in 1941! We thought that maybe someone assumed his name to come into the country, maybe a former Nazi! Anyway, long story short—and I'm getting ahead of myself—the Penn archaeology student who's going with us on our trip solved it. There was indeed a second Clarence Fisher who was on several of my grandfather's digs as an accountant. She said the second Clarence Stanley Fisher was my grandfather's nephew, which I later confirmed in some of my father's papers. So no big deal.

"Okay, I had copied the Penn archivist, who's really been great with us, on my letter to Barbara Mertz. He responded that Tina Gilbert, who's working on her doctorate and doing a thesis on my grandfather, had the answer. He suggested that maybe she would agree to meet with us. So I reached out to her and invited her to dinner at the Desmond Hotel.

"At dinner, she solved the mystery and told us stuff about Clarence. Glenn asked her if she had ever been to Egypt, and she said no; it was mostly a matter of money since Penn wouldn't pay for a student's trip.

"I then did more thinking, went online, and visited Penn to go through the archives for things about Clarence. My brother and I talked quite a bit, I talked with Tina many times, and I talked to a travel agent who specializes in Egypt trips. My brother and I finally decided to take our inheritance from our aunt Hoppy, actually my father's cousin, to pay for our trip and to pay for Tina's portion of the trip, airfare and hotels."

"Wow, that's certainly generous of you," said Nancy.

"Well, no. It's the only way we would go. We needed someone who knew about Egypt and my grandfather. We just had to adjust to her schedule, and she had to work it out with Penn. She's only writing her doctoral thesis now; her classwork is done. But in my research, I talked to a woman who retired from the Penn Museum and actually remembered my grandfather well from when she was a teenager."

"Wow, you're really into this."

"Obviously. There are a lot of mysteries about my grandfather."

"Such as?"

"Many. The retired woman, who I talked to in person, said that her father, who worked at Penn and was a friend of Clarence's, told her many times that Clarence told Howard Carter where to dig for King Tut's tomb."

"Interesting."

"Both my father and grandmother told me that Clarence was the second person into Tut's tomb."

"Really?" said Frank.

"I thought I told you that last year."

"Probably. Go on."

"I have no proof, and there's nothing in his papers and nothing anywhere, and I've done a lot of research, that indicates he was there. I did find, in one book, a theory that Carter and Carnarvon went in early and used a basket to cover up a hole that they made. Maybe it wasn't Carnarvon. Maybe it was Carter and Fisher. Who knows, but it's fun to think about."

"Wow. Anything more?"

"Ha, only about five more mysteries."

"Go on. This is exciting, isn't it, Nance?"

"Yes, fascinating!"

"Okay, you're going to get the whole list. Many archaeologists have been spies during wars; they are well known by native workers, often engage with officials, and know the geography and history. We know that Clarence was an ambulance driver during World War I. But was he a spy? I don't know, but I've seen a picture of when he died in Jerusalem in 1941. His coffin was covered by a British flag! He was a US citizen; why the British flag? I know that he was an advisor to the British on Arab affairs both before and after the war, but who knows?

"Another mystery is his death. I have a letter that a man who was with him sent to my grandmother when he died. From what he describes, it could be that Clarence was poisoned. I did some research on poisons, and something like cyanide could have killed him and, back then, not be detected."

"Are you kidding me?" asked Frank. "Who would want to do that?"

"I know that he was very charitable toward Arab orphans; he even started a school for orphans, and he formally adopted one. He also faced danger from Zionists who were fighting the Arabs in Jerusalem before World War II."

"Huh?"

"Another. I have newspaper articles that say that he was selected as the architect/archaeologist consultant on the restoration of the Dome of the Rock."

"Is that the golden dome you see in pictures of Jerusalem?" asked Nancy.

"Yes. But it wasn't golden back then. It's supposedly the site of the Ark of the Covenant. Remember, from *Indiana Jones*?"

"It sounds like your grandfather was Indiana Jones."

"That's been suggested, but only as having a career like the fictional Indiana Jones. My grandmother told me that Clarence once had a gun-fight with someone who was trying to steal things that he had excavated."

"I remember you telling me that."

"But maybe Clarence knew where the Ark of the Covenant actually is."

"Hmmm…Just think about that. Are you going to look for that? I think you'll be famous if you find it," Frank said with a smile.

"And rich! And I do have a map…"

"What, a treasure map?" said Frank, growing more and more cynical. "Next, you'll tell me that you're going to find a pot of gold!" He laughed.

"No, but Clarence did brag to a newspaper that he knew where there was a site with more treasures than King Tut.

"Get this…My brother found two spots on the map that had the names changed. Clarence drew a very detailed map of a theoretical city when he was in college studying to be an architect. But we always had this map and thought nothing of it. But my brother found where changes had been made, probably years later. One has been changed to Echna, and the other is Moise. Must be pointing to a tomb with lots of gold!"

"Unbelievable! Incredible! Any more?" asked Frank.

"That's it!"

"That's enough!" said Nancy.

"Here, can I look at the map?" asked Frank.

"Sure." I unfolded the map on the table and showed the two places where the street names had changed.

Frank spotted the changes as I pointed them out. "Can you turn the map over?"

"Sure, why?" I turned the map over and spread it out.

"I thought so. See, you can see the indentations from the pen on the back of these two streets."

I looked closer. "Geez, we didn't think to look there."

Frank looked closer. "Here are two more places. And look, that looks like a dot has been added." He turned the map over.

I looked more closely. "True. One's north, and the other's east. And the dot looks like it's marking a spot on a graph."

Frank and I continued looking at the map for almost a minute, both thinking.

"Doesn't tell me anything. But it could possibly mean a spot on another map. I'll have to ask Tina on our trip."

"Means nothing to me either." Frank paused. "So you're going on this trip with all these mysteries. Do you think you'll solve any of them?"

"No. We're just ordinary tourists."

"Well, be careful. There are terrorists over there; it looks like we're getting prepared for a full-scale attack on Iraq. And maybe the Mossad will be after you because you have a map that shows you where to find the Ark of the Covenant!"

We all laughed.

CHAPTER 24

Friday, October 18, 2002
John F. Kennedy International Airport,
New York

Our flight to Cairo was scheduled to leave JFK Airport in New York at 11:00 p.m., but I insisted that we allow plenty of time for dinner, for check-in, and for any possible traffic delays. We left our house at 3:10 p.m. Driving my SUV was my son, Scott. I was up front, and Glenn and Tina Gilbert were behind. The rear area was loaded to the top with our luggage.

• • •

As we crossed into New Jersey, I said, "I've been trying to decide whether I should tell everybody this, but I guess I'll tell you so you can have a good laugh. I am superorganized and really prepared for this trip. Last night I packed my suitcase with enough clothes so that I only need to have laundry done once at the Mena House and once at the Winter Palace. I also packed in a voltage converter, two extension cords, and cables to charge all of my gadgets. I need the chargers for these things…" I began counting on my fingers. "Video camera, digital camera, iPod, Palm Treo cellphone, my electric razor, and an HP portable picture printer. I'll be able to take pictures during the day and make copies in the evening. I'm going to wear my Scott eVest the whole time, with Treo phone, digital camera, cash, passport, wallet, and water bottles in it. So I may be a nerd, but I am organized!

"But here's the thing. How did I pack all this, including a sports jacket, sweater, jacket, dress shoes, and walking shoes? I bought some kind of plastic bag from QVC that you fill up with clothing and things and then attach a vacuum cleaner and suck all the air out of it. So there I was last night, all ready to use the vacuum cleaner. But then I realized that I may not be able to get access to a vacuum cleaner on the trip. Oh, no!" The others snickered but did not laugh.

"But then I had a thought. I closed up the bag with all of my stuff in it, and then I got on the floor and laid right on top of it with my belly on it. I then rocked back and forth, up and down, and I squeezed all of the air out. I should have had a video: a big beached whale! But I got it closed." Now the others laughed as they pictured the ugly sight.

"I'll have to do that four more times: when we leave the Mena House in Giza, the Winter Palace in Luxor, the cruise boat in Aswan, and the Cairo Hilton on our last night. And I may have to do it again for customs both ways! Oh, and one other thing." I turned to Tina in the back seat. "I'm really a picky eater. I'm a hamburger, fries, and pizza guy. From what I've learned, I'll be eating a lot of rice in Egypt."

As we crossed over the Verrazano-Narrows Bridge, Scott remarked about the missing Twin Towers of the World Trade Center. "At least it's a nice view of Lower Manhattan, but what a tragedy! I hope you guys will be okay."

I answered, "Well, the travel agency said that things have been quiet and very safe in Egypt. And there are a number of safeguards in place. We can expect inspections, metal detectors, at almost all of the places we visit."

Tina added, "Penn Museum had a small team there this summer. They were quite safe. Headed by David Carpenter, the curator of the Egyptian Section, the purpose was to take measurements at the site of Mereneptah's palace, which your grandfather excavated. They are trying to put together a proposal to have the floor of the Upper Egyptian Room strengthened to hold the columns and reconstruct a part of Mereneptah's palace."

"You mean they'd move all those columns up there?" asked Glenn.

"Yes, and more. They'd restore the columns to their original height, bring up the door frames and anything else from the excavation; there's much more in the basement. They'd also appealed to Zahi Hawass, the head of all expeditions at the Pyramids. He got his master's and doctor's degrees from Penn, and he knows much about your grandfather. As we all have, he had to use your grandfather's book *The Minor Cemetery at Giza* in one of his courses."

I cut in, "I have that book, and we're supposed to visit the Minor Cemetery."

"Yes, but there's more," said Tina. "I found out that the museum's Upper Egyptian Room was built to specifically house the Throne Room of Mereneptah's Palace. The plan was that people would be able to walk into the Throne Room, which would be reconstructed to its actual dimensions. You've probably noticed how high the Upper Egyptian Room is. It was built to house the full height of the columns."

"So what happened? You mean the columns everyone sees are cut off?" asked Glenn.

"Yes, if you look closely, you can see where each column has been cut, with the middle section taken out to fit. You see, after the Eckley Coxe Jr. wing was built, with its Upper and Lower Egyptian Rooms, and fortunately before any movement was attempted, a major engineering mistake was found. Wait till you hear this." Tina paused. "The specifications called for the upper floor to be built to hold some number of pounds per square inch. But it was built to handle that number of pounds per square foot! Thus it is impossible to hold the Throne Room in the Upper Egyptian Room.

"Curator Carpenter's plan is to put the measurements, the weight of items that we have, and the weight of items that we could get back from Egypt, into a proposal to fund an engineering study to determine the cost of strengthening the floor. I don't know how long all this will take; there are many unknowns."

"When I win a multimillion-dollar lottery, I'll fund it," I said. We all laughed. "Or maybe I should say if!"

• • •

Because we encountered no traffic, we pulled into Terminal Four at JFK Airport at 6:10 p.m. Scott helped unload the bags and carry or roll them into the terminal, and then drove away.

Inside, we immediately checked our bags but found that we'd have to wait until 7:30 p.m. to go through check-in and security for an 11:00 p.m. flight. We decided to get dinner. I found a pizza site, and Glenn and Tina went off to search for healthier food. By 8:00 p.m. we were through security and had walked up to the EgyptAir lounge. Since we were so early for our flight, we had to wait for the host, who then checked our tickets and allowed us in, since we had business-class tickets.

"Enjoy your sodas! Remember, there's only bottled water the next two weeks," said Tina. We were seated at a table, and there appeared to be no one else in the lounge. Tina seemed to be acting as a guide, since she had so much knowledge of Egypt. "How about I talk about our Cairo schedule?" Glenn and I nodded in agreement.

"Tomorrow we'll get to Cairo about two fifteen p.m. their time. Our guide and driver will take us in a Pyramid Valley Tours van to the Mena House Hotel, which is located next to the Pyramids. We'll have dinner with our guide, Hatim Selai, our driver, and possibly the head of the tour company. It's a grand old hotel, with newer sections, but you'll love looking at the Pyramids. Sunday we'll first tour the Egyptian Museum and then have lunch with Dr. Chris Houser, who's a well-known archaeologist. In the afternoon we'll visit some of the non-Islamic sites, including a Coptic church, the church where the holy family stayed. They escaped to Egypt due to Herod killing all firstborn males. We'll also visit a Jewish synagogue.

"On Monday morning, we'll visit the Layer Pyramid at Zawyet el'Aryan, where your grandfather and George Reisner excavated, and—"

I cut her off, "My grandmother cleaned jewelry from there, and we believe our father was there as a little boy."

"Yes. It's taken special permission to get in there. No one's asked to go there for over fifteen years! We'll have lunch at the Saqqarah Country Club, and then go to Memphis, where Clarence Fisher excavated the columns you see in the Lower Egyptian Room.

"On Tuesday, we'll view the Pyramids and, again by special permission, we'll go into the Minor Cemetery, as in your grandfather's book. My understanding is that no one has asked to go there for fifty years! Later I hope that Zahi Hawass will be able to see us. After lunch by the hotel pool, we'll go to the Sphinx. Wednesday is a free day, and then on Thursday we'll see some of the Islamic sites. Then we fly to Luxor.

"Oh, and one thing I should mention to you. I've been told that our guide will insist on taking us shopping, both in Cairo and Luxor. Apparently guides have deals with places like jewelry stores, papyrus stores, and rug factories. They get a kickback. I'm also told that we'll be hounded by children selling pens or asking for candy or money. We should give no more than a dollar to anyone."

"This is all so exciting, I doubt if I'll be able to sleep tonight," I said. "I always have trouble sleeping on an airplane anyway." Glenn and Tina nodded in agreement.

Tina continued, "At each of the sites that we'll visit, our travel agent has arranged that we'll have the necessary inspectors available to take us to those sites that the public cannot visit; at the Pyramids, the Layer Pyramid, and the Minor Cemetery. While in Luxor, we will need an inspector to visit Dra Abu el Naga, where your grandfather also excavated."

Glenn asked, "I wonder if we could take a trip to Amarna on our free day? I've been interested in Pharaoh Akhenaten being the first pharaoh to adopt monotheism, the worship of only one god. He built a whole city, Amarna, to worship the one god, Aten, and moved the capital there."

"The pharaoh you're referring to was actually Amenhotep IV. He changed his name to Akhenaten, and the city was called Akhetaten; now it's called el Amarna." She paused. "Actually, I'd like to go there too. We can ask our guide tomorrow whether they'd be willing to do it and, of course, how much it would cost."

We sat thinking about all this, and then I reached into my large camera bag and pulled out a large, faded, folded piece of heavy paper. As I carefully unfolded it, I said with a smile, "Let me show you my treasure map." Little did I know at the time what trouble this would get me into. "I have two copies of it, but this is the original." I paused to open it further, spread it on the table, and said with a smile, "Well, anyway, it's a map that Clarence created in an architecture class at Penn." As I spread out the map on our table, none of us noticed that other passengers had come into to the lounge, some within earshot.

Glenn added, "We've known nothing about the map except that it was dated when he was in college. I just know that I've had it since I was a child. Do you want to turn it over?"

"In a minute."

"Tina, this is a map of, we guess, a fictitious city. He called it Olympia. Its streets, as you can see, are laid out in a circle, with streets coming out from a central railroad station. The circular streets are named drives, and the streets coming out from the center like spokes are called avenues."

Tina leaned in to study it closer. "It's kinda neat. It looks like shops are in a ring close to the railroad station. There's a residential area in the northwest and another in the northeast; it looks like houses, and maybe apartments, are closer together in the northeast than in the northwest. In the southwest there's an office building complex, and another industrial area is in the southeast."

"Yes," I said. "You can't tell how wide the drives and avenues are, but this map looks like the city is designed for travel by streetcar. The northwest section, maybe for the upper class, is close to the office complex, while the northeast quadrant, maybe for laborers, is closer to the industrial section. Multiple streetcar lines go between each quadrant and into the center shopping area. The railroad runs from the central railroad station north and through the blue-collar section, if you will, and also south and through the industrial section, which makes sense. All quadrants have centrally located schools and parks. Note that the white-collar section has pools, with tennis courts—even a golf course—while the blue-collar section has baseball fields and a ballpark."

Tina commented, "While it's quite a city layout, it definitely looks like it's dividing people into two classes. But I guess in the late 1890s, that was common thinking, at least by the upper class!"

"Agreed," said Glenn and I simultaneously.

I added, "Maybe this is the world's first city master plan."

"So this is a nice map, created when Clarence was in college. How could there be any treasure?"

Glenn answered, "The best way to look is to turn it over, although you can see it from the front. Here, let me turn it over." He then held it up to the light and showed Tina where it looked like something had been erased from the other side and indentations from a pen had been made on top of the erasure. Glenn then turned it back and pointed. One passenger in particular seemed to have great interest in us and did his best to try to follow our conversation, but I ignored it. "Earlier, I said that all of the circles are called drives and all the streets coming out from the center are called avenues. But there are also streets running north and south, and they are all named streets.

"I found this almost by accident by looking at the front of the map, then I confirmed it when I looked at the back. Two names have been changed: there is now an Echna Street and a Moise Avenue. And the two cross here. It must be some kind of clue, but we don't know what."

"Hmm," said Tina. "I can tell you two other names for those streets. How about Akhenaten Street and Moses Avenue? The pharaoh Akhenaten has also been called Echnaton and, in many languages, Moses is called Moise. But I don't know why he would change the street names."

"Well, the two streets meet. Could that mean something?" I asked.

"Maybe he's trying to say that Moses and Akhenaten are one and the same?" said Glenn. "There are scholars, not many, who say that Moses was Akhenaten. One of the first, apparently, was Sigmund Freud. After some years in Amarna, Akhenaten was removed from power, and I don't think much is known from that point onward. So maybe he became Moses and…" Glenn's mind drifted away in thought.

"Well, I certainly can't confirm that," said Tina. "But why on earth would your grandfather change the map for that? What could he possibly know about Moses and Akhenaten? There's certainly nothing in the material I've investigated that would indicate that Fisher had anything to do with that. Or with Akhenaten. And I can't possibly imagine that any treasure could be associated with that. Very strange!"

"Another mystery about Clarence," I said. "But there are four other changes on the map. They're harder to see. They look like they may be newer than the other two. And there's a very small dot at the intersection of two of the streets. Here, look."

I held up the map again. "There is now an intersection at Beck Avenue and Lincoln Highway, which is the only highway on the map. And there's a dot where two other streets with changed names meet: At the corner of First Avenue and Stack Drive. To me, it looks like the dot is marking a spot on a grid. Here, look."

Using a pad and pencil placed on our table, I drew a vertical line and a horizontal one. I then drew a third line up from the horizontal line and a fourth line out from the vertical line. I now had what looked like a mathematical graph.

"The engineer in me sees an *x-y* graph that has as its zero point at Beck Avenue and Lincoln Highway. The dot at the intersection of First Avenue and Stack Drive could be the point where there's a treasure. What do you think?"

Tina said, "Fascinating, and perhaps possible. But I'll have to think about those names. Lincoln Highway, Beck, First, Stack—strange. Especially Stack. I don't know."

With that, I put the map away. We continued discussing the map, both the thoroughness of the city layout and the possible meanings of the changes, all the way to the aircraft gate.

• • •

When the group with the strange map left, one of the passengers checked the sign-in sheet and then made an overseas call. "Achmed Hamed, please; it's Hisham." A pause of thirty seconds. "Achmed, a passenger here in the lounge for my flight to Cairo tonight just held an old map to the light, and the two others he was with all seemed really interested in it. One of them drew a graph of some kind, almost as if they've found something important. They also mentioned Moses and Akhenaten, and going to el Amarna. I'll keep my eye on them. It looks like two are brothers, Glenn and Steven Fisher, from Philadelphia. The other is named Tina Gilbert, and she's with the Penn Museum. Our flight arrives at three thirty p.m. I'll try to see what travel agency they're using."

"See what you can find. I'll have to work immediately to replace their guide with one of ours."

Achmed hung up, then called his cousin Anna back in Wrens, Georgia, to see if she knew anything about the Fisher brothers.

CHAPTER 25

Saturday, October 19, 2002, 8:30 a.m.
Herzliya, Israel

"Hello?"

"Director Czeny?"

"Yes. Who is it, and why are you calling me so early?"

"Director Czeny, my name is David Banai from the Technology Department. I have information from our computer that protocol says I should contact you immediately. I know you're retired and that this is not a secure line, but the computer-generated e-mail says that I'm to tell you that someone is coming regarding your first assignment."

"Hmm…" Eliyahu Czeny paused, thinking back to his first assignment as a new member of Lehi, the Zionist organization active just before and during World War II. At eighty, it was hard for him to remember things, but he was never able to erase his first killing assignment, at age nineteen. No, he never forgot poisoning that archaeologist. And it had been easy.

"I'll be there in less than two hours."

Czeny retrieved his car from the Carmel Beach Hotel garage and headed south, first onto Highway 4 and then onto Highway 2, the Coastal Highway. Eliyahu Czeny had retired from the Mossad as an assistant director in the Collections Department in 1997. He moved shortly after into a state-supported suite on the seventeenth floor of the beachfront hotel southwest of Haifa.

Czeny was happy in his retirement and was happy not to have had to participate in any work for the Mossad for the last five years. He was angry at having been summoned this morning, but he was also curious. He wondered what could possibly be connected to his murder of archaeologist Clarence Fisher in 1941.

His successful execution of that task, with no suspicion of his or any Lehi involvement, allowed him to enter into an inner circle in the organization. After carrying out other "tasks," Czeny was chosen to lead the Cairo assassination of Lord Moyne, the hated British minister for the Middle East, in November of 1944. The two Lehi members who assassinated both Lord Moyne and his driver were captured and were later hung without revealing Eliyahu Czeny's name.

Eliyahu joined Mossad in early 1950, shortly after it was formed. He rose quickly in that organization, and in 1962, he led Operation Damocles against former Nazi rocket scientists, but it mostly failed. Despite that, he eventually became a Mossad assistant director, responsible for intelligence operations and analysis.

After driving forty-eight miles on the Coastal Highway, he turned off at the Glilot Ma'arav Interchange onto Yunitsman Road and proceeded into the headquarters of the Mossad in Herzliya, north of Tel Aviv. Since he had turned in all Mossad identification when he retired, it took him twenty minutes to finally be admitted to the office of the director of research, David Solot. With light, sandy hair, blue eyes, and a fair complexion, Solot looked unlike most Jews, almost Aryan. The two had known each other from previous assignments, and after pleasantries, David called in David Banai.

"Hi, David," said Director Solot. "This is Eliyahu Czeny, who was, and is, one of the unknown heroes from our great struggle." Despite his stooped posture, Eliyahu towered over the other two. Eliyahu's face was wrinkled and showed scars of years of dedication to, and fighting for, the young nation of Israel.

"Nice to meet you, sir. I hope I didn't wake you this morning."

"No, no, I was up already," said Eliyahu. He looked at Banai, who was the opposite of Solot: short, medium build, but with very black hair and a very low forehead. His dark, thick beard hung over his chest. "I was just surprised to get a call on a Saturday; I have no children, and it's been, thankfully, a long time since I've heard from anyone in the Mossad. But your call certainly interests me. What's going on?"

Director Solot answered, "We have had an intercept on a call from the EgyptAir lounge in New York to a known, dangerous terrorist, Achmed Hamed, in Cairo. David, why don't you read the entire message?"

"Sure. It starts with, 'Achmed Hamed please; it's Hisham.' Then there was a pause, I guess while he came to the phone. The caller, this Hisham, then said, 'Achmed, a passenger here in the lounge for my flight to Cairo tonight just held an old map to the light, and the two others he was with all seemed really interested in it. One of them drew a graph of some kind, almost as if they've found something important. They also mentioned Moses and Akhenaten and going to el Amarna. I'll keep my eye on them. It looks like two are brothers, Glenn and Steven Fisher, from Philadelphia. The other is named Tina Gilbert, and she's with the Penn Museum. Our flight arrives at three thirty p.m., and I'll try to see what travel agency they're using. See what you can find.' He then hung up."

Director Solot continued, "We don't know anything about your first mission, and there doesn't seem to be any trace of it. And we have no idea why the database would trigger the need for a call to you, but there you have it."

"Well," said Eliyahu, "I can explain, but first I'll tell you that it means we need to follow them closely. If it was just people coming from the University of Pennsylvania, or archaeologists from there, it would be nothing. But put together the name of the Penn Museum and the name Fisher; that's why I got called.

"I obviously have no idea what they're up to, but I'm suspicious. My first mission concerned a man named Clarence Fisher; you never forget your first. He was indeed an archaeologist, but he was also a spy, an organizer of the Arabs fighting against Germany in World War I, and a man who was very pro-Arab and anti-Zionist. In 1941, while drunk, he started bragging about what he had accomplished. He said that he and Howard Carter had discovered that our Moses was actually an Egyptian pharaoh. He said that they were the only two who had seen proof of this. Howard Carter, who discovered King Tut's tomb, died in 1939, so it was decided by my leaders in Lehi that Fisher should be eliminated. Can you imagine if it had gotten out, even if not true, that Moses was Egyptian? There would have been chaos, and our State of Israel would probably not exist today."

"Oh no!" said the director. "So why are those people here, and why do we care about them?"

"We've got to find out why they're here. It's not so much that they think that they may have a treasure map. Lots of people go to Egypt with that in mind.

"No, the concern is that the two brothers could be descendants of Clarence Fisher, but put them together with a Penn archaeologist accompanying them. Add that together with their mentioning Moses, Akhenaten, and Amarna, and we could have a problem. You see, Fisher believed that Moses was the pharaoh Akhenaten. And Amarna is the city that Akhenaten built to worship one god. He built the city from scratch and moved the priests and the government there. The city was abandoned after Akhenaten died. Ha, or became Moses!

"This could all be nothing, but we shouldn't take any chances. There's really nothing I can do to help, but please keep me informed. There's much that I haven't told you, so please don't hesitate to call."

"We will, and thanks for your help," said Director Solot. "I'll call security right now. Please stop there and pick up a secure phone so that we don't have to talk in person. And nice work, David."

"Thank you, Director," Banai answered. "And, Director Czeny, it was my honor to meet you."

"Thank you both. We'll get this all sorted out."

When they left, Director Solot picked up his phone and called Bob Weintraub in New York. The phone was answered after twelve rings.

"Hello?"

"I need to speak to Bob Ebel. That's E-b-e-l."

"This is Bob, uh, Ebel. It's what…four seventeen a.m. here. It must be important."

"It is. I need you in Cairo as soon as possible. As always, I'll explain later, but I need you to get to Teterboro Airport as soon as you can. My secretary will make the arrangements, but I want you on one of our jets in two hours."

"Okay. Will I be seeing you?"

"No, but we'll probably talk quite a bit."

"Okay. I'll get moving."

"Thanks, Bob. Good luck."

Mena House Hotel, Cairo, 6:30 p.m.

Tina, Glenn, and I were seated at a table in the Khan Khalili dining room at the Mena House Oberoi Hotel in Giza, thirteen miles southwest of downtown Cairo. With us were Anok Badawi, our guide for the entire sixteen-day trip, and Bassam Farag, the president of Pyramid Valley Tours. From our table, we could see the top of the Great Pyramid through the palm trees.

Our flight had arrived early at 3:06 p.m. As we descended the high steps onto the tarmac from our EgyptAir Boeing 767, we were immediately hit by the high heat and humidity. When we left Philadelphia the day before, it was a balmy, low-humidity seventy degrees. Now, we instantly found the heat oppressive. After a short walk on the tarmac to the terminal, we easily went through customs, but I was surprised that we had to give up our passports, which we would receive later at our hotel. We were met by a new guide, Anok Badawi, who held up a sign as we exited customs. We noticed that he had been talking with a man we recognized from the EgyptAir lounge the night before. Anok told us that the guide originally planned for our trip, Hatim Selai, had to suddenly leave to take care of his mother. He described his background and assured us that he was a very experienced guide who would take good care of us. At the time, we thought nothing about the change in guides.

Anok was thin, about six feet tall. His skin was brown, his hair was black and closely, neatly cropped, and he had a full black mustache. He wore wire-rimmed glasses and was dressed nicely in a clean long-sleeve shirt and pants. He seemed to have a good command of English, but his heavy accent made it hard for me to understand him.

Anok helped carry our bags out into the heat, and we made our winding way to their Pyramid Valley Tours van. As we were about to pull out, with Anok in the front passenger street, the driver, Tarek El Shamma, turned to me and said, "Just yesterday, Sophia, the queen of Spain, sat in your seat. She chose Pyramid Valley Tours to be her escort to the sites."

Our trip from the airport on El-Nasr Road took us past the City of the Dead, Cairo's huge cemetery. There, we saw the squalor of people living out in the open or in horrible shanties. As Anok pointed out, it was among the worst, most-populated slums in the world, especially the section of the cemetery called Manshiyat Naser, also known as Garbage City. We then proceeded across Rhoda Island in the Nile and onto Al-Ahram Street, which ended at the Mena House Hotel.

As we exited the van at the hotel, we could see the top of a pyramid. "See the cut-off top of the pyramid? That indicates that it's the Great Pyramid, the largest," advised Anok.

We entered the spacious lobby, with its tiled ceiling with wood beams arranged in intricate patterns. After check-in, Anok said that he and Pyramid Valley Tours president Bassam Farag would like to join us for dinner at the hotel. He asked if we could all meet in one hour, and we all agreed. Our individual rooms were in the two-hundred-room garden wing, constructed in 1978. Still, we were happy that we could each see the Great Pyramid from our balconies.

As we ate, Anok explained the background of the Mena House Hotel, which he stated was one of the world's grand hotels. "The original section was built as a hunting lodge for Egypt's king in 1869. It was sold and later opened as a hotel in 1886. Its highlight, of course, is the views of the Pyramids, especially from the original rooms. Many famous people have stayed here, including Queen Mary, Winston Churchill, and even Frank Sinatra."

"What time do we start out tomorrow?" asked Glenn.

"We'll pick you up at eight a.m. to get an early start at the Egyptian Museum. We'll have lunch at the Arabesque Restaurant in the Khan El Khalili in downtown Cairo, and we'll be joined for lunch by archaeologist Christopher Houser. After that, we'll visit a Coptic church, El Muallaqa, which is built over a Roman fortress. We'll go into the grotto in the Coptic Saints Sergius and Bacchus Church, where the holy family stayed while escaping King Herod. And finally, we'll visit the Ben Ezra Synagogue, which was built on the site where baby Moses was found. A full day."

"Well, we're starting out strong," I said.

"I'm wondering about Amarna. We have a free day on Wednesday, and I wonder if we can go there," said Glenn. "I'm interested in Amarna because of Pharaoh Akhenaten, who was the first pharaoh to worship one god. As a retired minister, I've been researching some of the alternate views of early Christianity, the Dead Sea Scrolls, and the relationship of Akhenaten to Moses."

Bassam Farag, who was short and portly but was dressed similarly to Anok, spoke up, "I can arrange that. It's about four and a half hours away; we'll pick you up at five thirty a.m. It will cost an extra six hundred dollars. It's something we've done in the past."

Glenn looked at us, and I said to Tina, who looked doubtful, "Tina, Glenn and I can cover this." I looked at Glenn, and he signaled his approval. "Tina, okay?"

"Sure, and thanks."

We finished eating and then began to return to our rooms. In the hallway, Glenn said, "Boy, how about that driving on the way here. I was scared to death!"

"Me too," I said. "There were no traffic lights anywhere. They seemed to drive using their horns constantly, and they seemed to be flicking their headlights on and off. Awful!"

Tina responded, "I was warned by my colleagues about that. They said there is some kind of code about using their headlights. There is only one traffic light, and it's in downtown Cairo, and they drive at night with their lights off. They also said that when we're on some roads that are little more than two lanes wide, there will be four lanes of traffic. Nearest the edge may be a boy on a water buffalo. The next lane may be a bus, the next may be a truck, and the fourth lane may be a speeding car. All going one direction. And facing the same thing coming the other way. They tell me that somehow it all works out!"

Glenn and I looked at each other and sighed.

•　•　•

On his way back from the hotel, Anok placed a call on his mobile phone and waited for Achmed Hamed, whose cousin Anna was living with Lonnie

Jenkins at Carswell Bible College in Georgia, to answer. "Hello, Achmed. It's Anok. It's confirmed. We're taking them to Amarna on Wednesday, and they're really interested in Akhenaten and Moses. It's really good that you had me assigned to them this morning. In my college thesis, I argued that Akhenaten and Moses were one and the same. I'll keep you informed every step of the way."

CHAPTER 26

Sunday, October 20, 2002
Kahn El Khalili Bazaar, Cairo

The next day, as planned, we ate breakfast at the Greenery Restaurant on the first floor of the newer wing of the Mena House and met our new guide, Anok, in the lobby. We entered the van and started on our first day of sightseeing. We retraced last night's path over Al Ahram Street, then went north to the Qasr al-Nil Bridge. Crossing two branches of the Nile and Al Gazira Island, the van driver, Tarek, then joined the impossible traffic circling the roundabout at Tahrir Square. We held our breath as Tarek steered, repeatedly accelerated and braked, and, with his horn blowing and headlights flashing, somehow made it out. Anok and Tarek were relaxed throughout. Glenn and I looked at each other and mouthed, "Wow!"

We proceeded two blocks north to the Egyptian Museum, a large red-brick building opened in 1902. At the museum, we were amazed that Anok was able to have us all bypass the long entrance line. We immediately went to the Tutankhamun Room on the second floor and, like everyone else, we were amazed.

We first entered a room that had an artist's drawing of Tutankhamun's tomb showing, in color, how the tomb was laid out when Howard Carter and Lord Carnarvon first entered. It was helpful to get a perspective of the tomb. We were able to get up close to one of the huge ivory-and-gold statues of Nubian guards, of course behind glass. We saw Tut's beautiful golden throne, with its inlaid images of Tut and a woman who was his consort and, possibly, his half sister and cousin. We saw his canopic chest, beautifully carved out of ivory, which held, as Anok explained, his internal organs. We also saw the three chambers from the burial room; the innermost originally held Tut's sarcophagus.

But the highlight, of course, was Tut's burial mask. Made of solid gold, it was brightly painted to show beautiful eyes, a blue-and-gold headdress, and a long, braided beard. It has to be one of the most recognizable objects in the world!

We also entered a dark room where the beautiful jewelry from the tomb was exhibited under narrow-beam spotlights, and the Mummy Room, the only part of the museum that was air conditioned.

Finally we explored a gallery that featured items from the Amarna Period. There we saw a huge statue of Pharaoh Akhenaten. While his face looked reasonable, his body was exaggerated to look like a woman: a curvy waist, with large, rounded hips. Could he really have been that weird looking?

After three hours in the museum, we drove to a crowded bazaar. We exited the van and, with Anok guiding us, entered the narrow alleyway called Khan El Khalili in downtown Cairo. It was crowded, mostly with tourists; we all but had to push our way through the crowd. Between trying to follow Anok and keep from hitting people, we had little chance to glance at the narrow storefronts or inspect the many wares on the many tables blocking our way. Mostly selling things for tourists, the shops offered brass hookahs, loads of King Tut souvenirs, ornate lamps and hanging globes, and tapestry. One word could describe it all: colorful.

We finally made it into the narrow but deep Arabesque Restaurant. We first encountered an area where men were sitting and sharing hookahs, called "shishas" in Egypt. Anok explained that these water pipes burn charcoal to heat the air that is sucked in. The hot air passes through the tobacco, vaporizing it. The vaporized tobacco is then passed through water, losing heat. The result is cooled, vaporized tobacco smoke being drawn into the lungs through a hose. We actually stopped to watch three men using three hoses on one shisha and another shisha with two men sharing the same hose.

We were taken into a room at the back and to a table next to an intricate tapestry that reached almost to the wooden ceiling. Seated at the table was famed archaeologist and occasional TV documentary host Dr. Christopher Houser. He was wearing an unusual tan shirt with many pockets. He seemed of medium height and build, his sandy hair was receding, and he wore horn-rimmed glasses. He looked like someone ready to go on a dig. Dr. Houser stood, introduced himself, and began explaining his mission in Egypt for the American University in Cairo.

"We started the Theban Mapping Project in 1978 with the goal of creating an atlas containing maps and survey information of every tomb and temple on the west bank of the Nile in Luxor, called Thebes in ancient days. We've gotten more sophisticated with our technology over the years, with lasers and ground-penetrating radar.

"Your grandfather excavated the temple of Pharaoh Amenhotep I." He held out his right hand, palm up, and curved his fingers upward like a claw. "His drawings matched our computer-generated drawings"—he did the same with his left hand and then moved it over his other palm so that the fingers touched—"almost exactly! Amenhotep I was the first pharaoh to separate his tomb from his temple, but his tomb has never been found."

I interrupted, "My grandmother told me that Clarence once said that he knew where there was a tomb with more riches in it than King Tut's." Dr. Houser looked down at his food and made no comment. I, however, noticed that Anok quickly sat up straighter and looked deeply interested in what I had said.

Seeing that Dr. Houser had no more comment, and not wishing to bring up anything about Clarence's map, I turned to Glenn and said, "Why don't you show Dr. Houser the ring?"

"Sure." As he reached into his pocket for the ring, I again noticed Anok's keen interest. "We found this ring in our aunt Hoppy's things. She's actually Clarence's niece, our great-aunt. We're not sure if it was given by my grandfather to my grandmother or to Hoppy, or maybe it was worn by Clarence. There were a few, very few, effects returned to my grandmother from Jerusalem after he died, so it could have been one of those. See, it looks like there's a scarab underneath with some hieroglyphics."

I handed it to Dr. Houser, who took off his glasses for a better look. He stared at the ring intently for almost a minute, with everyone wondering if it was of any importance or value. Houser immediately seemed to recognize it as being ancient, but proceeded to study it more.

Houser finally said, "Well, the gold looks like it's sixteen karat, which is not common in the USA. That's probably from Egypt, from the early twentieth century. But the scarab…" He looked at it some more. "My wife, Beth, would know better; she knows more about scarabs than I do." I noticed that he gave a nervous laugh and his voice seemed to quiver as he continued, "I'd say that it's from around 700 BC and from the Phoenician coast of what is now Lebanon."

With that, he handed the ring back. "I suggest that you not show that to Egyptian officials or when you're getting on the plane home."

Shortly after that, Anok excused himself and made a phone call.

CHAPTER 27

Tuesday, October 22, 2002
Al-Minya, Egypt, 7:30 a.m.

"**H**ave a seat. I just finished talking with Anok. He keeps me posted on every activity that they do. He says that the three Americans will be leaving the Mena House at five forty a.m. tomorrow to go to El Amarna and should be leaving there around three p.m. I asked him to call me from the police station in Deir Mawas to report if anything unusual happened."

Achmed Hamed and Abu Ayyub al-Khawi were seated outdoors at a small bakery on Sharia al-Hussaini Street, near El Saaha Square in Al-Minya.

Achmed continued, "I will station myself south of Minya, probably near Haret Sina, and call you when they go by. I want you to be stationed north of Minya, maybe just north of the university football stadium. I want their van to be in an area where cars will be going at least fifty kph. I want you to pull off the road as if you've had car trouble and then hide by some trees near an irrigation ditch. When I call, it will mean that they will probably go by a half hour later, after going through Minya.

"Abu Ayyub, I know how good you are with a rifle, as you have proved many times, especially at Deir el-Bahri. It is extremely important that this incident looks like a tire problem. You take one shot at the front tire of the van, and then get back in the car and return to Minya. Do not look around, do not hesitate; just drive back to Minya as if you had already gone past the 'accident.' If there is some sort of trouble, maybe you'll have to lose yourself in the university."

"But even if I have a perfect shot, how will that guarantee that they will be killed?"

"It won't. I see three things possible. One, you miss—unlikely, I know—then you get back, and we try something else later. Two, there's a bad accident, and they get hurt enough that it will take most of their time in Egypt to recover. They're here for thirteen more days, so we may have to try something else. And three, they are killed or very seriously injured so that they cannot continue their trip at all. We know that they're up to no good in Egypt, so I want them dead or not able to continue their trip."

"But what about Anok and the driver, Tarek?"

Achmed replied sternly, "If they are hurt, we will take care of them. They do not and cannot have any idea of what we're planning. And if they die, then, well, remember your colleagues at Deir el-Bahri. They committed suicide rather than being captured. You were the only one who escaped because from eleven hundred meters you shot the security guard who was outside the temple."

In what was known as the Luxor Massacre, in 1997, six gunmen, plus Abu Ayyub, attacked a crowd of tourists at the popular Temple of Hatshepsut in Deir el-Bahri, which is near the Valley of the Kings across from Luxor. Sixty-two people were mutilated and killed, including a five-year-old-boy. Achmed Hamed was one of the leaders of the Al-Gama'a al-Islamiyya terrorist group, and Achmed directed the raid.

"I will carry out your instructions without fail, Achmed."

Cairo, 1:00 p.m.

"I'll bet you're Isabella Browne; your niece Jeanne showed your picture to me," I said.

"Yes. Are you Glenn or Steve?"

"I'm Steve, this is Glenn, and this is Tina Gilbert, a doctoral candidate in archaeology from Penn. It's so nice to meet you, and it's an incredible coincidence that's brought us together."

"It sure is. I haven't seen Jeanne or Frank in, I don't know, fifteen years. And they live near you?"

"They're really just two houses up from us, across the street. My wife and I were at a neighborhood picnic in early September, and I mentioned about our trip. Jeanne spoke up and told us about your connection to her. Amazing."

"Let's sit at that table over there," said Glenn.

We were eating at the Nile Hilton Hotel, along the Nile Corniche near the Egyptian Museum.

When we were seated, Tina asked, "Pardon me for asking, but since I'm about to become an archaeologist researching and, hopefully, excavating somewhere in Egypt, I'd love to hear about your background and how you've ended up here."

"Sure. I was born in Ambler, PA, which is outside of Philadelphia, one of four daughters." She looked at Steve. "So Jeanne's mother and I are sisters…but I'm the youngest by ten years." She smiled.

Turning back to Tina, she said, "I graduated from Villanova, got my master's in Oriental studies from Princeton, and my doctorate in Near Eastern history, also from Princeton. I think Penn turns out the archaeologists, and Princeton turns out Egyptologists."

"What's the difference?" interrupted Glenn.

"Oh, Princeton is a much better school!"

"Huh!" said Tina, Glenn, and I simultaneously.

"I'm just kidding. Glenn, I knew what you were asking. As you're aware, an archaeologist finds and excavates ancient ruins. In Egypt, their focus is on Pharaonic Egypt; tombs, mummies, pyramids. Egyptologists don't dirty their hands—kidding again. No, Egyptologists are more interested in the history of Egypt—its arts, languages, religion, architecture. Again, most Egyptologists are interested in Pharaonic Egypt, but I study, and teach, Islamic history. And I really love my students."

She looked at me, "I know about your grandfather, who is still well regarded by many archaeologists in Egypt. May I ask why you are all here?"

"Well, the short story is that a friend showed me a novel that included a sentence about Clarence and the western cemetery—"

"An Amanda Peabody book?"

"Yes."

"Did you know that those books were written by an Egyptologist named Barbara Mertz, who has a PhD in Egyptology from the University of Chicago?"

Tina answered with a smile, "I didn't know that. Maybe if I switch to Egyptology, I can become a best-selling author!"

"Anyway, I'm sorry for interrupting. Steve, please go on."

"After that, I wrote to the Penn archivist, Eric Tobin, about one of the mysteries surrounding my grandfather. He said that Tina had been researching Clarence Fisher, and the result is that we're here for a full sixteen-day trip. But in addition to the usual sites, we want to focus on things that Clarence did."

Tina spoke up. "And Zahi Hawass has granted us access to Fisher's and other sites that are not open to the public. We meet with Zahi, who's the head of all activity at the Pyramids, on Thursday, mostly to say thanks."

"That's great. You'll like Zahi. Being from Penn…" She turned to Glenn and me. "I know that Clarence went there, and Tina's there now. Do you two have Penn connections?"

"Yes," said Glenn. "We both graduated from Penn. And my daughter did also. Our father went there as well, so it's four generations of Penn alumni!"

"Wow. Zahi will really enjoy speaking with you! But you mentioned mysteries surrounding your grandfather. Can you tell me?"

I looked at Glenn and then spoke. "Well, both my father and grand-mother, Clarence's wife, told me that Clarence was the second person into King Tut's tomb. There have been theories that Howard Carter and Lord Carnarvon both went into the tomb and covered it up."

"Ah, the 'basket lid covering the hole' theory." She explained that she was referring to a theory that was based on a photograph that showed a basket lid oddly placed against a wall in the tomb. Some scholars hold that Carter and Carnarvon went into the tomb before any authorities and made a small hole to look into the burial chamber and then covered it with the basket lid.

I continued, "I think it might be possible that Carter and Fisher sneaked in instead of Carter and Carnarvon. I also talked to a woman who retired from the Penn Museum, Caroline Dosker. She told me that her father said that Clarence told Carter where to dig. We know that he found jars with papyrus in them at Dra Abu el Naga, so maybe—"

"So maybe Fisher found something in the jars that told Carter where to dig, and he and Carter got into the tomb before Carter's benefactor, Lord Carnarvon, arrived? Sounds possible but not likely," said Isabella. "Especially after all this time—eighty years."

I added, "Clarence also told my grandmother that he knew where there was a tomb with far more treasures in it than Tut's. Maybe that's at Dra Abu as well, although we're not going treasure hunting."

"Don't you dare!" said Isabella. "It's way too dangerous—and illegal! You don't want to complicate things while on your trip," said Isabella. "Anok, you've been quiet, but as their guide, you have to make sure they don't try anything stupid."

Anok nodded. "Of course. Their well-being is my job."

"Here's another mystery that I'm interested in," added Glenn. "As a retired minister, I wish I could follow the mystery of whether Moses and Akhenaten are one and the same."

"Is that all?" asked Isabella with a smile. She paused. "I can't help with any of those, but I can add to the list." We leaned in closer, especially Anok.

"I'm very fond of my students, and I'm very close to many of them. I've been hearing a rumor for the last year or so that some people believe that when Pharaoh gave the Promised Land to Moses, he gave him only a one-hundred-year lease, or covenant, to it. Think about it. If that were true, then Moses can't be Akhenaten, because he wouldn't give himself a lease. If it's not true, then we're back to the argument that some people believe that Akhenaten became Moses. There's just no proof."

"Please tell me more," I asked. "This is fascinating."

"I don't know any more, other than they're calling it the Carswell Covenant."

"What does that mean?"

"Sorry, but I have no idea where that name came from. It means nothing to me. But it seems to refer to a one-hundred-year lease for the Holy Land. And I'm almost afraid to ask about it; I just keep my ears open."

Mena House, 6:30 p.m.

"This is crazy! This is dangerous! We should turn back before something happens to the three of us," screamed Glenn above the roar. "This is nuts, Steve—turn back!"

"No, we're almost there. I can see the pyramid on our right still, and I'm sure we're almost there. At least, we're more than halfway there, so there's no sense in turning back."

We were all frightened at this point, even me. Twenty minutes ago we had met in the lobby of the Mena House Hotel, and I had persuaded Tina and Glenn to go back to the Pizza Hut near the Sphinx. When we were there earlier, I had pointed out the Pizza Hut on the cul-de-sac directly across from the entrance to the Sphinx. As we exited the gates of the Mena House to go to dinner, I had turned to Tina and Glenn and was able to convince them that we could walk to the Pizza Hut. I argued that I had watched on our return to our hotel in the van and found that the van just made two lefts, out of the cul-de-sac and onto the street with the Mena House. I had convinced them that we would be good because we could spot the pyramid along the way.

"Steve, look, the sidewalk has ended; we have to cross over!" yelled Glenn.

The traffic was intense, both directions, and there seemed to be no openings. Even I was frantic now, as we individually darted through the crazy, nonstopping, horn-honking, lights-flashing traffic, like a death-defying game of dodgeball. Two blocks later we finally spotted the Pizza Hut and somehow made our way back across the street. What we hadn't realized was that we had effectively walked the length of the two longest sides of the Mena House Golf Course, the full width of the Great Pyramid and its parking area, and the full width of each of the other two pyramids.

"We should have listened to the cabbies at the hotel. They said it was too far to walk," said Glenn.

"Yeah," I said. "But we got to play a real-life game of Frogger." Tina laughed, but Glenn looked at me quizzically.

Tina said, "But we sorta proved that Egypt was safe."

We all had a great "American" meal at Pizza Hut, but afterward we took a cab back to the hotel.

CHAPTER 28

Wednesday, October 23, 2002
El Amarna, Egypt

"Okay," said Anok. "As I said, we're almost there. On the left ahead is the police station at Deir Mawas. We'll stop there. We can use the facilities, and I'll have to check in. Then we take a ferry across the Nile to the village of el-Hagg Qandil and drive about ten minutes to the first site, east of the village of el-Till. There are actually three places we'll go. First will be the tombs, up on the top of those cliffs you see across the river. Then we'll drive to the Boundary Stela to see just one of the huge inscribed boulders marking the outer corners of Amarna. Finally, we'll drive to another spot where you can see the ruins of the temple, in the village of el-Hagg Qandil.

"At the foot of the cliffs, there's a small place where you can buy water and soft drinks, if you like. We'll eat our box lunches there first. But the only facilities are at the police station."

We had left the Mena House at 6:00 a.m., after having an early breakfast. We bought water bottles and box lunches from the Greenery Restaurant. We headed south on the only highway connecting Cairo, Luxor, and Aswan: the Cairo-Aswan Agricultural Road. We went through three security checkpoints about fifteen minutes apart, and then we pulled over behind a battered blue pickup truck. There was a metal roof over half of the pickup bed. The enclosure had a bench in it, but it was not high enough to allow standing. Two policeman were sitting under the roof.

Both carried what I assumed to be Kalashnikov assault rifles. They faced rearward, and in front of them was a mounted machine gun. There was a blue emergency light on the truck cab's roof. Up front were a driver and a police colonel. The crew of four would escort us from this point forward.

"This shows how seriously we take protection of tourists after the Luxor Massacre," Anok had said. "Most of the Nile cruises from Cairo to Aswan have been stopped; they only operate from Luxor to Aswan, as we'll be doing. The few that go the entire distance have been outfitted with mounted machine guns."

Anok added, "You'll also see security people on the cruise with us. And, unlike Cairo, you'll have to go through metal detectors almost everywhere we go in Luxor."

As we traveled south on the Cairo-Aswan Agricultural Road, we mostly followed the Ibrahimiyah Canal, which we could see to our left. Anok told us that this large irrigation ditch was built in 1873 and runs beside the Nile for 217 miles.

We passed quickly and without incident through the city of Al-Minya. Isabella Browne had warned us the day before that it was a hotbed of terrorist activity. She thought, however, that we would be safe with the usual police escort.

At one point on our way to Amarna, I thought that we would make a good target for terrorists. Our police escort was followed by our van, which was boldly marked Pyramid Valley Tours in both English and Arabic. Ha, or maybe the Arabic said Aim Here. I assumed nothing would happen on the way down, but I wondered about our return, when terrorists would know we were coming back. But I dismissed the thought, knowing that the driver and guide were both Egyptian. I thought that there would be no attack with the two of them in the van.

"Look to the left, there's a big barge coming down the river," said Glenn. "I hope it doesn't hit us when we we're out there," he said with a smile. We were at water's edge, the ferry landing point, about one hundred feet down the Nile bank and to the right from the police station.

"We'll be fine," said Anok. "And just to set your bearings, we're on the west bank of the Nile, and Cairo is on our left, about 250 miles away. Unlike American rivers, the Nile flows south to north. So the barge is going south, toward Luxor, against the current."

After about ten minutes, the ferry landed. Our "convoy" had to wait for three pickup trucks to come off the ferry and go up the hill toward the police station and road. The ferry looked like it could hold six cars or small trucks on its flat bed. There were similar ramps on both ends of the ferry, outfitted with pulleys that would lift the ramps up at a small angle to serve as bows.

We proceeded across the wide river and looked back at the barge, which passed behind us. It was actually three vessels: a tug in the middle and barges lashed to both sides. The barges looked empty, and it looked like the crew was eating lunch as they proceeded.

"I can't believe that I'm actually going across the Nile River in a small ferry," said Glenn.

We passed through the village of el-Till, avoiding the women and children hawking small trinkets, and entered a straight dirt road crossing the desert plain. The cliffs seemed close, but as we drove, they didn't seem to get any closer. Finally, we stopped at a small building for lunch. Inside was a counter where some souvenirs were sold and electric coolers for the drinks. Power came from a generator in the rear.

We exited the air-conditioned building into the 105-degree heat and began our climb, through sand, up paths and steps, almost to the top of the ridge. Glenn and I sat on a stone bench near the top to catch our breath, but Tina and Anok were eager to move to the first tomb. I looked at the building and our van far below. Through the haze, I could barely see the Nile in the distance, but I could see the village and the areas of green vegetation. The desert that stretched out from the irrigated areas to the foot of the cliff below was crisscrossed with dirt roads, seemingly going nowhere. Clearly marked, however, was the straight dirt road that we had come across. From our bench, it looked like a landing strip for small airplanes.

We resumed our climb. Near the top, I noticed a man standing in a galabia that reached his feet. I noticed that his robe seemed to be covering something long and straight. I figured that I had gotten my first glance at the third level of security; I was sure that the item under the man's galabia was some type of rifle.

We visited all three sites that Anok had suggested and did more walking and climbing in the hot, humid air than I would have liked. Tina was extremely pleased with our time at Amarna, but Glenn and I were disappointed. We had entered the tombs, and some actually had high ceilings supported by decorated columns. But most traces of Akhenaten, the reason that we had come to see where he had founded his city, were destroyed. We saw beautifully colored and inscribed walls, many of which showed the sun god Aten's rays beaming down. In all cases, the sun had been gouged out, as was Akhenaten's face. When Akhenaten was deposed and the capital moved back to Thebes, all traces of Akhenaten were destroyed. Glenn found nothing that could link Moses to Akhenaten.

Recrossing the Nile, we again stopped at the police station to use the facilities. I noticed that Anok had once again separated from us and was using his mobile phone.

• • •

Achmed Hamed had stationed himself at the bridge over the canal at Maqusah, just south of Minya. He had waited there for more than two hours, just to make sure that the van would not turn off to bypass the city on the El-Cornish Road and in case Anok hadn't called. When he took Anok's call, he knew that it would be about forty-five minutes before the convoy reached him. Achmed would then called Abu Ayyub al-Khawi to update him and verify that he was in position.

The convoy went by as expected, and Achmed called Abu Ayyub and told him to expect the van in no more than a half hour.

• • •

Anok used his mobile to call to the police escort. Both vehicles pulled in to the Al Garage, just past the gasoline depot, and filled up. After using the clean facilities there and getting a snack, we then continued through Minya.

Due to traffic, we slowed after passing the Talla Road Bridge. As we veered left just before the Bade El Zaman Bridge, we came almost to a complete stop; there was a mass of people ahead. Two trains, one from Cairo and one from Luxor, had pulled in almost simultaneously at the train station across the short bridge. Many people were crossing the canal bridge and into the intersection just ahead of the van. Also at the intersection were workers just getting off their shift at the huge railway maintenance facility ahead and to the left of the van. We moved slowly through the crowd, which barely gave way to us. The police escort had almost disappeared in the throng ahead.

Thump! The van stopped quickly, and Anok and the driver jumped out of the van simultaneously, leaving us unattended.

"What was that?" yelled Glenn. "Did we hit something?"

"I think we hit a girl. Her head came right against my window," said Tina. She looked back. "She's on the ground, and I can see that her head is bleeding and Anok is tending to her." She paused. "Now they're helping her up and taking her somewhere into the crowd. And now they're out of sight."

With that, the crowd that had been surrounding us started knocking on the windows on both sides of the van. Glenn shouted, "What should we do?"

I solemnly said, "I don't know." The banging continued. I looked out the front and saw that the police escort was completely out of sight. I said worriedly, "On the way down, I thought that we would make a great target for terrorists, but maybe not until we would have been on our way back. But then I thought that terrorists wouldn't do anything with our two Egyptians up front. Now I can't even see the police truck."

The banging on the windows continued, but the people, most of them women, weren't yet rocking the van. Tina said, "Pull down the window shades. It's the only thing I can think of to do."

"That may make it worse," I said.

"Let's do it," said Glenn, and he proceeded to pull down the shade at his window. I pulled down my shade, and Tina pulled down the shades on both sides of the van; she was in the back seat.

We sat in stunned silence. I assume that Glenn prayed, but I somehow thought only about possible headlines announcing our deaths. Tina seemed to be the calmest of us, probably thinking that no harm would come.

Tina was right. After twenty-five minutes, the crowd had disbursed, the police escort had backed up, and Anok and Tarek returned to the van.

Our convoy then continued, with Anok and Tarek both silent about the incident.

The three of us sighed with relief, but we didn't share our thoughts.

•   •   •

"Where are they? Why are they so late? Did they go another way?" Abu Ayyub had called Achmed after waiting almost an hour. Achmed was slow to pick up since he was driving home. "Oh no, here they…"

Abu Ayyub dropped the phone and grabbed his rifle quickly. He figured he only had time to squat rather than get down to his preferred prone shooting position. He had to twist around as the van went by. He took the shot.

•   •   •

Crack! The sound came from just in front of the van. In the opposite lane, I saw a small panel truck crash onto its left side like a ten pin hitting the seven in a seven-ten split. It careened past us, slipping and sliding into our lane less than fifty feet behind us.

"Oh no!" I exclaimed. "That truck almost hit us! A split second sooner, it would have been a head-on collision. Anok, shouldn't you stop?"

"No, I think they may have had a flat tire; they were going very fast. That's very common in Egypt. Someone will be along to help them."

Once again we looked at each other but kept our thoughts to ourselves. But I thought that it sounded like a rifle shot rather than a blown-out tire. At home I live near a police shooting range, and I felt that I knew a rifle shot when I heard one. But why would someone shoot out a tire? Could they have been aiming for us and missed?

Cairo, 11:00 p.m.

"At dinner my brother insisted that the two incidents were related." I took another sip of my Scotch, neat, and Tina sipped her red wine. "But I'm not so sure. They seemed to be so random: hitting a girl in a mob, and then almost being hit by a truck with a flat tire. But to me, I think it was a rifle shot."

"I'm not convinced either way," said Tina.

Tina and I were having drinks together for the first time. Glenn, Tina, and I had returned to the Mena House at 9:30, and we immediately had a quick dinner in the Greenery Restaurant. We were all tired and on edge, and Glenn decided to go to bed. I had asked Tina if she needed a drink as much as I did.

We were at a table for two in the Khan El Khalili Restaurant, where we had eaten on Saturday night. The Great Pyramid lights were off at this late hour, but thankfully there were two other couples having drinks to prod the staff into keeping the restaurant open.

"If there was no coincidence," said Tina, "can we explain what happened? Let's see if we can figure out any reason for anyone to come after us. Let's start at the beginning of the trip. Who knew that we were coming, and who knows that we're here?"

"Well," I said, "there's our travel agent, who you said Penn archaeologists had used before."

"No problem with them."

"Then there's basically Anok and the two other people from Pyramid Valley Tours...and Christopher Houser and Isabella Browne."

"I think we can eliminate Dr. Houser and Dr. Browne, but maybe they mentioned it to someone associated with them. But it could be Pyramid Valley Tours. But why would anyone want to harm us?"

"Wait a minute. I just thought of someone. When we got off the plane, one of the passengers kept looking at us as we walked across the tarmac and again inside the terminal. I think I saw him talking discreetly to Anok, and I believe I recognized him from the EgyptAir lounge. And then I saw him again in the parking lot as we were getting into the van."

"But why?" said Tina. "Unless...unless he overheard us in the lounge."

"I seem to remember that he was sitting pretty far away. Maybe he could read lips."

"Or maybe he saw you holding up the map." She paused, thinking. "And I seem to remember you getting pretty excited talking about a treasure."

"Could be. Also, maybe someone overheard us at lunch with Dr. Browne. We talked about the map, and she warned us against searching for treasure. Maybe someone overheard us there. And, of course, Anok was there."

Tina paused and then said, "You don't have any secrets, do you, Steve?"

"No. Only that I think my grandfather may have had a drinking problem, and maybe he was gay. I need another drink. You?"

"Sure…But, if I may ask, why do you think that?"

"I've seen references to his drinking in Amelia Peabody novels—"

"But those are only novels," interrupted Tina.

"Yes, but those books were written by a PhD Egyptologist. Why would Barbara Mertz make up something like that about one of the extremely minor characters? He quit Penn, had health problems that could really be a cover-up for his drinking problems, and he was let go from his biggest excavation, Megiddo, for Rockefeller and the University of Chicago. As for his being gay, it's just something I've wondered about. He basically abandoned my grandmother, we have photographs of him with young men who don't seem to be archaeologists, and we know that he spent at least one summer at the somewhat radical Arden Art Colony, outside Wilmington, Delaware, not far from his wife and son. And he adopted a young Arab boy, David Tarazi Fisher."

"But it sure seems that you have no real proof of any of this."

"You're right, but I have spent many years wondering about things like this, mostly because of the way he treated my grandmother."

We continued talking for another half hour. We seemed to be warming up to each other, probably because our drinks warmed us up. And, I was glad that Tina didn't follow up when I mentioned the rifle shot. She had probably dismissed that thought from her mind; it was too hard to believe.

CHAPTER 29

Friday, October 25, 2002
Luxor, Egypt

Our flight from Cairo arrived in Luxor late Friday afternoon. That morning, we had packed our bags for our flight to Luxor. We had no trouble with security at the airport, and I insisted on getting myself a Sbarro pizza in the food court, even though lunch would be served on board.

During the flight, I could not stop replaying in my mind our ascent yesterday into the Great Pyramid and our walk between the paws of the Sphinx. When booking the flight, I had requested to be able to go into the Queen's Chamber. I had learned that there was much scientific interest in two shafts in the Queen's Chamber that were oriented toward the constellation Orion. In fact, a small robot had recently gone into one of the shafts, only to back out after hitting an obstruction.

The plan was that we would be escorted by an inspector into the pyramid and the Queen's Chamber. After a twenty-minute wait, Anok told us to start up the outside of the pyramid. We climbed the outside steps, which was a harrowing journey, to twenty feet above the entrance, then descended to the opening. We waited again as one group was led in ahead of us. Finally, since our inspector had still not arrived, we were told to proceed into the pyramid. As we were about to proceed up a steep ramp, a group was descending. We were told to wait in a small cubbyhole.

We crawled into the cramped quarters. Glenn and Tina were okay, but my claustrophobia came on in full force. It was hot and humid, my back hurt from bending over in the small space, and the walls seemed to be creeping in. I was in trouble, but I also wanted to go up into the pyramid. I started to feel better after the last of the group finished their descent.

We were now ready. Ahead was the Ascending Passage. About three and a half feet wide, it was maybe four feet high. It rose at a very steep angle. We could get traction on a series of wooden strips placed about eighteen inches apart, and the railing helped as well. It was like climbing a ladder without actually climbing a ladder!

We reached the bottom of the Grand Gallery, which is twenty-six feet high, deep inside the enormous structure. To our left was the passageway to the Queen's Chamber. We could see into the Queen's Chamber, but to get there, we would have had to crawl at least twenty-five feet. I'm not sure that I could have even fit into the small passageway. No thanks!

Fortunately, the Grand Gallery was not very steep; we could easily climb. Oh no! We now had to get on our hands and knees to crawl into the King's Chamber. Fighting claustrophobia again, I crawled through the two dark, cramped passageways into the King's Chamber. Finally we were there.

I gasped as I realized I was in a chamber built 4,500 years ago. I was interested in the alignment of the slabs making up the room. The accuracy was amazing; the rows of the giant granite slabs and the joints were perfectly aligned. I looked up at the giant slabs above, which were also aligned perfectly. I had earlier read that each was eighteen feet long and weighed as much as forty tons. I could not imagine how that chamber, and of course the entire pyramid, could have been built. To think that I almost backed out due to my claustrophobia!

The walk between the paws of the Sphinx was much easier. Granted access by Zahi Hawass, whom we met with for less than five minutes at his office by the Great Pyramid, we were able to walk around the entire base of the Sphinx and completely between his paws. I took delight in looking up his nostrils! But maybe the best part was looking at the tourists looking down at us from the visitors' areas. Yes, I felt very special!

As our EgyptAir flight approached Luxor, I looked out the window and thought that I could make out the Valley of the Kings. As we descended, I could see hills with white paths that I assumed could be the paths between the tombs.

At the Luxor airport, we were met by a new Pyramid Valley Tours van and driver, which took the four of us, Tina, Glenn, Anok, and me, into Luxor proper. From the airport, we had traveled the nine miles in to Luxor, mostly on the Al Matar. Turning left onto the Corniche el Nile, we traveled south, passing Luxor Temple on our left. I was very surprised to see the many Nile cruise ships anchored to each other, extending into the river as many as four ships deep. I guessed that there may be as many as thirty cruise ships in port. We would be embarking for Aswan on one of them on Wednesday afternoon.

Traffic was much lighter and more organized than in Cairo, so we made our way quickly to the Winter Palace Hotel. This grand hotel, opened in 1886, is on the Corniche el Nile along the east bank of the Nile. Among many famous long-term guests were Agatha Christie and Lord Carnarvon. Howard Carter's excavations in Luxor were sponsored by Carnarvon, even after Carnarvon's death in Cairo in 1923, which was popularly, but incorrectly, attributed to the "mummy's curse."

The van pulled into the semicircle in front of the Winter Palace, and we unloaded our luggage and proceeded into the street-level baggage area. We took the elevator to the lobby floor and were told to go through a metal detector as soon as we got off the elevator.

I was the first to complete registration, once again reluctantly surrendering my passport. A porter waited to take my bags to my room on the second floor. As I waited for the others to check in, I glanced to my right and at the revolving door leading out to the curved front patio and curved steps leading down to street level. Turning to my left, I admired the square supporting columns, with their tops intricately carved in a Greco-Roman style rather than looking like ancient Egyptian columns. Above was an elegant chandelier. Farther in was the beautifully furnished lobby sitting area, with a grand piano surrounded on two sides with tapestries hanging on the walls. Steps began on the right wall of the room, went across the far wall, and then up the left wall to the second floor, where they met the hallway and the entrance to what appeared to be the palace suite. I could see that this pattern repeated up to the third floor, with each floor being at least twenty-five feet high.

Opening my room door, I could see a patio through the sheer curtains at the window. I immediately walked over, opened the door to the patio, and stepped out. To my right, I could see the palace suite, with its large awning-covered patio. Ahead, I saw three cruise ships lashed abreast, leading out into the Nile like shoes on the floor of a closet. There were people in bathing suits or sun outfits on the top decks of all three ships, even though sundown was quickly approaching. I could barely make out what looked like a ferry dock on the other side of the Nile. Beyond were the hills and cliffs that I assumed were the sites we would visit over the next few days.

We weren't meeting for dinner for another hour, so I decided to relax and just take in the view. I grabbed my camera and last remaining bottle of water, took off my shoes and socks, and sat at the small deck table. I discerned movement at the back of the outer cruise ship and then watched as the back of the ship headed out into the Nile, looking like a slowly opening door. It stopped at a forty-five-degree angle, followed by the front of the boat heading out to point the boat south toward Aswan. As it motored out of view, I grabbed my camera to take pictures of the setting sun; the best shot included a felucca framed between palm trees, with the sun disappearing behind the Valley of the Kings.

●　　●　　●

The three of us (Anok mostly ate by himself) ate dinner in the cheapest, most American restaurant in the Winter Palace complex. The Spartan restaurant was located in the New Winter Garden Hotel, which was connected to the Winter Palace by a hallway. We decided that we would eat breakfast there each morning. We were all tired, so there was little talk except raving about the Winter Palace. After dinner, Glenn returned to his room, but I asked Tina if she would like to join me for a drink. She readily agreed.

We entered the Royal Bar, with its deep red walls and elegant wooden bar. The bartender spoke very much like a Britisher, which matched the ambiance of the bar.

"I have an idea," I said. "What do you think of getting up early tomorrow morning and trying to find Ed Harer at the Luxor temple? Remember that as we were leaving the Hilton, Isabella Browne told us that he was excavating there, that he knew about Clarence, and that he got in very early in the morning."

Dr. Edwin Harer was excavating at Luxor Temple under the sponsorship of the University of Chicago. From October to April, he resided at the university's Chicago House, which was north of Luxor Temple on the Corniche el Nile. Fully staffed, the Chicago House is home each season to twenty to thirty researchers from the university and from around the world.

"Hey, that sounds good to me. Will you tell Anok?"

"No. It would be nice to do something without him around. But I will tell Glenn in case we are late."

After deciding on our plans to eat breakfast and try to find Dr. Harer, Tina asked me to tell her about myself. "I know about your finding the sentence in an Amelia Peabody book, but how did you get so involved with this?"

I thought for a moment. "What really started it was the newspaper article that Penn archivist Eric Tobin sent me. It said that archaeologist/accountant Clarence Fisher had just died. Boy, did that get me going! But you solved that!

"And, I remember as a kid in grade school hearing about King Tut's tomb. There seemed to be a fad where everyone was buying a little plastic coffin, a magic trick maybe two inches long, with a blue King Tut inside. There was a magnet in both the mummy and in the base of the little coffin. You slid the magnet on the bottom of the coffin away from Tut's head, and he stayed in. You showed someone how you could take it in and out. After taking Tut out and surreptitiously sliding the magnet to the top of the coffin, you handed it to someone. They, of course, couldn't put Tut back in because the magnets then repelled, so it was impossible to keep his head in. Did you have one of those?"

"Oh my God, no. But I'd love to have one to add to my Egyptian collection! I love to collect cheap, garish, gaudy, glitzy souvenirs of Egypt things. My fiancé barely tolerates them, especially my Egyptian cuckoo clock. You should see it. It's about twenty inches high, the cuckoo at the top is Nefertiti, and there are two lions with Tut heads. The clock is surrounded—I tell these details to everyone—by two cats, and the base has a very pointy pyramid. Two Egyptian women and two soldiers rotate around the pyramid on the hour, and it plays music! I love it, but unlike almost everything else, it wasn't cheap."

"Ha! It sounds neat. Anyway, I was so proud to tell my classmates that my grandfather was an archaeologist; I couldn't spell it at the time. I asked my grandmother about King Tut, and that's the first time that she told me that my grandfather was the second person into Tut's tomb. I believed that through my college years because both my grandmother and my father repeated it multiple times. But sometime after I graduated, I saw somewhere that the first three into the tomb were Carter, Carnarvon, and Lady Evelyn Carnarvon, Lord Carnarvon's daughter. So I really doubted it, until Caroline Dosker from the museum—did you know her?—told me that Clarence told Carter where to look. So now I don't know what to believe."

"Well, I didn't know Mrs. Dosker, but I can tell you how I got interested in being an archaeologist. I saw *Raiders of the Lost Ark* when I was nine or ten, and that hooked me. I was always a good reader, so I started reading what real archaeologists do, not the Indiana Jones stuff, but the research, the planning, the fighting for funding, the amassing and directing of a workforce; that's what I wanted to do."

"Yeah, but maybe we're finding that Clarence was more like Indiana Jones than we knew. Did I tell you that my grandmother told me that he once had a gunfight with someone who was trying to rob one of his expeditions?"

"No. Tell me more."

"That's it. I only found out when I was in high school, and when I asked her for more details, she said that's all that she remembered."

"Too much." Tina laughed. "Maybe you and I will be Harrison Ford and Karen Allen."

"Well, you're much better looking—and younger—than Karen Allen when she made that movie. And I, um, who would play me in the movie? Richard Dreyfuss?"

We both had a good laugh at that and ordered another drink.

CHAPTER 30

Saturday, October 26, 2002
Luxor, Egypt

I met Tina for breakfast at 6:00 a.m. in the restaurant in the new section of the Winter Palace.

After ordering, I looked at the restaurant. "This place sure doesn't look like the rest of the Winter Palace. Yeah, it's got some plants and curtains at the windows, but basically it looks like a high school cafeteria."

"I agree," said Tina. "My room isn't much, but it's definitely cheaper, like the rest of this new wing."

"It looks like a nice day out. There's a clear blue sky with none of the smog haze like we saw last week in Cairo and at the Pyramids."

"I'll bet that it'll be over a hundred degrees when we go to the Valley of the Kings."

We finished breakfast, bought bottled water, and returned briefly to our rooms. I walked down the around-the-walls steps to meet Tina in the lobby. We walked out through the revolving door and down the curved steps leading to the street. Then we turned right and proceeded up the two blocks to Luxor Temple.

After paying admission, we walked to the front of the temple, where we stopped to take pictures with our cameras. Mine was digital, while Tina had a film camera.

"Here, take a look at this; I think I got a good one."

Shielding the camera from the sun with her hand, Tina looked at my camera and laughed. "You got a great picture of a water closet sign!"

"Huh?" I looked at the dim image on my camera. "Oh yeah, a big WC sign. I can't be the only one who included that in a picture. Oh well, the rest of the picture is good."

We entered the main portion of Luxor Temple, in search of Dr. Edwin Harer. We walked past an obelisk on the left, and then a statue on each side. Next was a court, followed by the Hypostyle Hall, with its thirty-two ornate columns. We saw what might be an excavation as we looked between one pair of columns. Turning left, we walked over to the site. Low scaffolding had been set up around an area no more than twenty-five by twenty-five feet. There were two Egyptian workers on the ground within the scaffolding. One had a small shovel, the other was stooping and dusting part of the ground with a small brush. Between both was a square box made of two-by-fours, two feet on a side. The bottom was a screen, and the top was open. A small amount of sand was gently shoveled in, the sand falling through. This time, even when sifted back and forth, only small stones were left behind. To the side and on the scaffolding was a thin man with a dark goatee, sunglasses, and wearing a typical archaeologist's hat, which was a cross between a fedora and a cowboy hat.

"Dr. Harer?"

"Yes?"

I extended my hand. "I'm Steve Fisher, the grandson of archaeologist Clarence Fisher. And this is Tina Gilbert, a doctoral candidate in archaeology at the University of Pennsylvania."

"Nice to meet you both. I believe that we're expecting you for dinner at the Chicago House on Tuesday."

"We're looking forward to it," said Tina. "I wonder if we can spend some time in your library before or after dinner. I'd like to do some research."

"Of course. I'm not certain what time dinner is—usually seven o'clock. So plan on arriving at six, and stay as long as you'd like after dinner."

"We've been told that dinner is at seven." I looked at Tina, who returned an acknowledging glance. "So we'll certainly be there by six. I'd... we'd like to look through whatever you have regarding Fisher's work."

"Certainly. I'll have the materials retrieved by our staff. Here, let me show you around." He walked us on the narrow scaffolding closer to where the two Egyptians were working.

"Archaeology is a painstaking process, as I'm sure you're learning." He turned to Tina. "Very painstaking. Here you see them with a shovel and dust broom. The sifter is now between them. The challenge is that you want to dig quickly, but that could break or hide something. But you can't just sit there and dust and sift; you'll never get anywhere that way. So digging must be done very carefully."

"Oh, I know," said Tina. "In the summer of 1998, I was an intern under Henry Carstairs at Penn's Copan excavation in Honduras."

"So you know." He paused. "Would you like to see the other work I'm doing?"

"Sure," I said.

Dr. Harer then led us to a relatively clear area beyond the dig. There, we saw a small wall surrounded by assorted stones. "These blocks are from some houses here in Luxor that have been rebuilt. Look here." He pointed to two blocks, one on top of the other. "The houses were built with blocks from some ancient temple. We've found that through the ages, people have taken blocks from archaeological treasures and used them for building their dwellings. But look closely at the engravings."

Tina and I moved closer. Though it was faint, we could see that the bottom stone contained the lower part of the side of a face, below the eye and ear. The carving extended down to the neck and shoulders. The stone on top of it was matched to the face. We could see the eye, ear, and head. It was clear that these stones had been matched in antiquity.

"Did you find them this way?" I asked.

"Oh, no. I've been working trying to find matches. It's not easy."

Tina responded, "Wow. It's like a giant puzzle." She turned to look at an older Egyptian who was approaching. He was in a galabia, with a short turban on his head. He was tall and thin, with extremely weathered skin and a wide white mustache.

"Ah, that's my inspector," said Dr. Harer. He walked over to him and then indicated that he should join the group. He spoke to the inspector in Arabic; the only word that I could understand was "Fisher."

At that, the inspector, who looked to be in his seventies, said in English, "Ah, Amenhotep I." He then continued in Arabic and bowed slightly to Tina and me. Dr. Harer responded and seemed to dismiss him. The inspector walked away.

"There is a lot of interest in finding the tomb of Amenhotep I. Your grandfather is well known to many for excavating Amenhotep's temple. In fact, there is a team from Poland who is excavating on the hill at Dra Abu el Naga, which you can see from this side of the Nile. They are excavating to try to locate the tomb of Amenhotep I."

I interrupted, "Also, we're supposed to meet Donald Hughes tomorrow. He excavated at Dra Abu for Penn in 1968."

"Yes," said Dr. Harer. "But he's here trying to get interest and donors to support him in a new concession at Dra Abu. So far, I understand, he's having no luck; the Poles have the concession." He paused and smiled. "It's been nice talking with you, but I really should get back to work. I'll see you again on Tuesday night. We can talk more then."

"Thank you!" we both said simultaneously.

We turned and left Luxor Temple; we were to meet Glenn and Anok next. Our day ahead included the Luxor Museum in the morning and back to Luxor Temple that night. And, Anok insisted on taking us on a shopping trip in the afternoon.

As we walked back, I said, "I'm confused. In Cairo, Chris Houser said that Amenhotep I was the only pharaoh whose tomb has not been found. Now, the inspector immediately linked my grandfather's name with Amenhotep I. It would seem that Clarence was referring to Amenhotep when he told my grandmother that he knew where there was a tomb with more treasures than Tutankhamun. But the map doesn't seem to have any clue to that. There's no Amen Drive or Hotel Street."

"I agree. Let's look at the map more closely tonight."

CHAPTER 31

Sunday, October 27, 2002
Dra Abu el Naga, Egypt

We met Anok at 9:00 that morning. Tina, Glenn, and I went to the Valley of the Kings and gained entrance to the typical tourists' tombs.

I could see why kings would be buried here. It reminded me of the City of the Dead in Cairo, only with huge cliffs almost completely surrounding the valley. The entrance was just about a hundred feet wide. My Casio thermometer watch told me that it was 105 degrees. The valley floor seemed to moderately rise in front of us, but the cliffs were steep, with paths going up to rectangular entrances to tombs. Our first goal was King Tut's tomb, which was on the valley floor.

We had paid extra to visit Tutankhamun's tomb, but we were not impressed. Compared to other tombs in the valley, it was very small. We had to walk down only thirteen steps and then across a slightly sloped passageway to the A. While we didn't expect to see any of the contents, the room we were in had no wall decorations. Likewise, when we stooped to see into the annex, it was barren. To our right was a waist-high wooden barricade with a closed gate guarding the entrance to the burial chamber. Beyond, however, the walls surrounding the tomb were colorful, though very dull. Since Anok had stayed at the entrance of the tomb, the three of us, along with an inspector, were the only ones in the tomb. We did not realize that Tut's body was under the glass on his tomb, so we did not ask the inspector if we could enter. Disappointed with Tutankhamun's tomb, we exited after less than ten minutes.

We toured several other tombs; ones that did not have lines to get in. Some were not very exciting, but I took pictures inside several others. We climbed to one tomb that was almost at the top of one of the cliffs. It was an exhausting climb, but it turned out to be the best that we had seen. It was the tomb of Tuthmosis IV, whoever that was. Looking down with my back to the tomb entrance was spectacular. The tourists on the valley floor looked like ants, and the cliffs around were more grayish than sand-colored, as they looked from below. Most interesting, to me anyway, were the white paths running throughout the cliffs, leading to other tombs.

Returning to the valley floor, we exited the site on the tramway vehicles that took us back to the parking lot and our van.

Leaving the Valley of the Kings, we next toured the outdoor Ramesseum. Anok told us that it was the mortuary temple of Pharaoh Rameses II. He said that Rameses built statues of himself and his queen, Nefertari, all over Egypt. On the final part of our trip, he told us, we would fly from Aswan to Abu Simbel, where we would see huge monuments to the two of them.

The Ramesseum was all ruins, mostly toppled. But there were several large columns that looked like those in the Penn Museum. I looked up at the top of one of the columns. The fluting around the top was painted underneath. I guessed that they were protected after three thousand years by being on the underside. Through the zoom lens on my camera, I could see multiple golden cartouches, each separated by three blue horns. On one cartouche, I could see a red circle, possibly the sun god Aten. The colors looked spectacular against the bright blue sky.

We then went to the Marsam Hotel, which was close by, for lunch. Located on a dirt alleyway, the Marsam Hotel was not at all promising. The outside was stucco, drab, and mostly windowless, and it was clear that the outside was mostly unattended to. Inside, we found the ceilings high and the walls plain, but we were quickly greeted by a woman with a strong Australian accent.

"Welcome to Marsam. My name is Helen Mears. This building has an interesting history," she began without pausing. "It is the oldest dig house in Luxor and home of the Chicago House from 1920 to 1939. Now it is a modest but clean hotel. I think you'll enjoy our lunch, which is served out on our patio. Please follow me."

We walked out through a door that looked like it was always open and onto a shaded terrace overlooking a farm. We looked at what seemed to be miles of fertile, green farmland. Tina remarked, "This is sure in sharp contrast to the front of the Marsam. That looks out on the start of the desert hills, the hills we could see from the Winter Palace. Here, it looks like farmland in America." Seated at a table shaded by a tree, we saw a sandy-haired, red-faced man, who stood immediately. "Hi. I'm Donald Hughes."

We exchanged greetings and sat down. There was a slight breeze, and despite a temperature approaching one hundred degrees, it felt cool. After climbing through the Valley of the Kings, I was happy to sit back and relax.

After introducing ourselves, Hughes began, "In 1968, I excavated at Dra Abu el Naga for the University of Pennsylvania. The notes and diagrams left by Clarence Fisher were extremely helpful. Dra Abu is the burial place mostly for pharaonic officials. Some of the tombs have sloped entrances, while others require descending through vertical shafts.

"In the remains of one of the dwellings occupied by Coptic Christians over one hundred years ago, your grandfather found two bullet-shaped clay jars, with the tops bound closed with ropes. Inside, he found multiple ancient pieces of papyrus, written mostly in demotic. They held mostly bookkeeping types of information. Boring stuff, like marriage and divorce papers and items related to land acquisition.

"Interestingly, before World War II, the Egyptians demanded that the jar contents be returned from Penn; why, I don't know. The war intervened, but in 1950 Penn's Henry Fischer, I think no relation to your grandfather, returned about half of them to Egypt. And it's believed that some are missing. I certainly don't know what the fuss was about."

"Hmm." I paused for a moment. "Boy, does this make me think. Both our grandmother and father told me that Clarence was the second person into Tut's tomb. Also, do you remember Caroline Dosker?"

"Yes, she was not a professional, though. She worked a number of jobs at the Penn Museum. A wonderful lady."

Hughes's eyebrows narrowed as if he was contemplating the implications.

"Yes," I said. "But her father was Richard Gordon, not museum director George Gordon. Her father was the museum's press secretary and was a good friend of Clarence's. Anyway, Caroline said that her father told her multiple times that Clarence told Carter where to dig. Is this crazy? Could my grandfather have told Carter where to dig, and that resulted in Carnarvon funding one more season, and Fisher and Carter got into the tomb first?"

Hughes did not respond for thirty seconds, but then his face turned to one of skepticism, as if he had found a way out of his concerns. Smiling, he said, "Ha. Next, you'll tell me that he found the location from the missing papyrus."

"Yeah, well?"

Seemingly now relieved, Hughes casually said, "I can't imagine it. All of these events have been looked at, studied, investigated by many over the years. People are always finding new theories to write about."

"Okay, I give up," I said. And the subject was dropped. But Tina and I shared a glance.

The rest of our meal was spent telling Donald about last week and our plans for this week. Donald suggested that he stop with us at the Polish House, which was nearby, to see if Daniel Polz was there. He explained that Polz was the leader of the Polish expedition at Dra Abu.

After finishing lunch and driving a short distance, we walked into the headquarters for the Polish team. Luckily, Polz was on his way out. Hughes stopped him and introduced us, but Polz cut us short, saying he was running late.

"Well, that was a surprise," said Hughes. "I hope he was really in a hurry, although he knows that I also want to dig there."

"Or maybe he got spooked because we said we were Fisher's grandsons, wanting to see Dra Abu."

"I don't know. We'll go to Dra Abu, but unless there's an inspector, I won't be able to take you up the hill. I was hoping he'd invite you."

From the Polish House, our van turned onto Wadi Al Melok Road. At an intersection, Donald Hughes told us that straight ahead was the entrance to the Valley of the Kings. We turned left. A man in a white galabia rode by on a donkey, controlling the donkey with a small stick. Donald pointed out the crumbling pink house on the left after we made the turn. "That's the former dig house of the University of Pennsylvania, where Clarence Fisher lived when he was in Dra Abu el Naga. It's occupied by squatters now, I'm told, but it was nice many years ago. And up ahead, we'll park on the left opposite the alabaster factory."

We exited the van and started across the street. A dirt parking area, with several baby goats wandering around, was in front of some kind of structure. The facade was a freshly painted mural, about fifteen feet high and more than sixty feet wide. To our left was a similar facade with Nile Valley Alabaster Factory on it. It had a nice wooden entranceway and door. I wondered aloud if the wider facade covered the actual factory, while the other building was the store. No one was interested in finding out.

Beyond, but still on the flat area, were a number of one- and two-story buildings. Partway up the hill were more two-story houses in various stages of decay. Many appeared to be abandoned and boarded up. There was one old man in a galabia making his way slowly up the hill—a pretty dismal sight. Between two structures was a narrow dirt road leading up to a mud-brick building. There were electric poles lining the road. Other than these few signs of civilization, the hillside was dotted with scattered and crumbling small stone walls. Dotting the hillside, however, were numerous openings. Some were almost circular; others were arched. Several had rectangular openings, probably built by archaeologists.

Glenn paid attention while both Donald Hughes and Anok pointed out features of the hillside and some of its history. But my thoughts were elsewhere. I was trying to figure out if Clarence's map, with its coded points, could possibly be of any use in finding a new tomb.

As we walked back to the van, Tina leaned close to me and whispered, "Did you see the look on Donald's face when you first mentioned Clarence, Dosker, and Gordon? To me, he clearly showed that it was possible, despite his scoffing at the thought. Having seen that the hill is not so daunting, when we get back, I'm going to call back to my fiancé at Penn and ask if he can find and fax me a map of the Dra Abu tombs."

"Yeah, hopefully he can get it to you by the time we're done dinner. Glenn is interested, but he's way too cautious on all this. How about if we discuss this afterward at the bar?"

For dinner that night at the Winter Place, we decided to eat at the elegant 1886 Restaurant at the hotel. We knew that the meal would be expensive, but we decided to go ahead and treat ourselves. The next day,

Monday, we were slated to tour the sites at Dendereh, where Fisher had also excavated, and also Abydos. We were told that the ride would take about an hour each way and that all of the tourist buses and vans would go in a police-led convoy.

After a leisurely but overpriced meal, we retired to our rooms.

But a half hour later, Tina and I met again in the Royal Bar. I had been there for about ten minutes when Tina entered and sat down. "No luck on a map so far. I was able to leave a message for my fiancé, but I remembered that he had a public lecture at the museum until four p.m. eastern time today. Anyway, I reached him just now. He wanted to know why I wanted to get a map of the tombs at Dra Abu el Naga, and I told him a little about the changes to Clarence's map. Ha—he told me to be careful and not do anything stupid like looking for treasure, and I said that it's just a curiosity. He then said that he knew of no such map, but he would ask Eric, the archivist, first thing tomorrow morning.

"But I have a little news. I mentioned some of the names from Clarence's map. He agreed that two of them referred to Moses and Akhenaten, and he said that he could not figure out what Stack Drive and First Avenue might refer to. But he thought that Beck Avenue and Lincoln Highway might be a code referring to two tombs at Dra Abu: Bakenkhons, who he thought was a priest, and Huy, who he knew was a priest for Amenhotep I."

"So if we locate on a map the tomb of, who, Bakenkhons, and the tomb of Huy, then we have two of the three points?"

"Yes. I now feel that your grandfather was indeed pointing to two spots on the Dra Abu hillside," said Tina. "Whatever Stack and First mean may very well point to another tomb. That spot could be another known tomb, or it could point to an unknown tomb. If it was a known tomb, why on earth would he bother to come up with a coded map and get it out of his hands and into your grandmother's?"

"Good question. But I'll bet we're onto something. Maybe we can get a map of the Dra Abu tombs when we go to the Chicago House on Tuesday night…And find out what First and Stack mean. I suggest we be very cautious about mentioning any of this at Chicago House. Maybe you can just ask casually for a map of the Dra Abu tombs—say that you'd like it for your research."

"Agreed."

CHAPTER 32

Tuesday, October 29, 2002
Luxor

Tuesday's agenda was packed. We were scheduled to travel back to the Valley of the Kings to visit the tomb of Pharaoh Seti I, check in to the *Sonesta Moon Goddess* for our cruise from Luxor to Aswan, revisit Dra Abu el Naga, and have dinner at the Chicago House. We would stay on the cruise ship overnight; the departure for Aswan was set for 11:15 a.m. on Wednesday, October 30.

Anok had informed us that we could check in to the *Sonesta Moon Goddess* early in the morning, so we decided to do that right after breakfast, leaving the rest of our day free for touring.

We completed our checkout from the Winter Palace and check-in to the *Sonesta Moon Goddess* with no complications other than giving up our passports to the ship's purser. After moving our bags into our rooms, we met again in the ship's magnificent three-story lobby; we were anxious to get to the Valley of the Kings.

We exited the *Moon Goddess*, which was parked nearest the shore, entered our van, and went south to the Luxor Bridge. Anok explained that the bridge was built in 1998; previously, the only way to get to the sites was by taking a ferry across the Nile.

After crossing the bridge, we turned right at the first highway and traveled through the towns of Ad Dabiyyah and Al Aqaltah until we turned left onto Al Tmalyn. This led us past the Colossus of Memnon and onto several roads leading us through a valley and on to the site of the Valley of the Queens.

After we toured several tombs, we entered the tomb of Queen Nefertari, the wife of Pharaoh Rameses II, also known as Rameses the Great. This tomb was on two levels. The first level, the antechamber, had beautiful wall paintings based on the Book of the Dead, an Egyptian burial text used for more than 1,500 years in guiding the deceased to the after-life. The second level, the similarly decorated burial chamber, included the sarcophagus, which was surrounded by four rectangular pillars. Above both rooms were celestial ceilings, consisting of gold stars on a dark blue background. We agreed that it was the most beautiful site yet.

Emerging, we reentered the van and returned for a second tour of the Valley of the Kings. The van passed the sharp corner with the Pink House on our right, proceeded north for a quarter of a mile, then turned left onto Kings Valley Road. Like we had on Sunday, we went through the entrance booth, parked with the other cars and vans, and rode a motor tram up the path. Exiting, we were escorted up the hillside to the tomb of Seti I. We had been given special permission to visit the VIP-only tomb by Zahi Hawass, the supreme head of antiquities, during our short visit with him on Thursday.

Anok said to us, "We're going into the tomb of Seti I, who was the father of Rameses II and the grandfather of Mereneptah, whose palace your grandfather excavated."

The inspector unlocked the heavy, iron-barred gate, and we proceed-ed down a steep flight of modern wooden steps, with railings on both sides and in the middle. The railings were definitely needed for assistance both descending and ascending this first steep set of stairs. Continuing down more steps and ramped passageways, we finally entered the first pillared hall, which was similar to Nefertari's. After proceeding through a total of five sets of steps and corridors, we reached the burial chamber. Anok explained that we were 152 feet deep, having traversed 328 feet horizontally to get to this point.

Anok led the way into the crypt, which was beyond the burial cham-ber. He turned around and merely pointed up. We were amazed to see the ceiling of this chamber. Anok pointed out that it was twenty feet high and that it represented the constellations and calendars. The ceiling curved at the edges. The depictions were white on blue. At the far end, and just below the ceiling, was a magnificent eagle with green wings.

I said, "This is easily the most beautiful thing we've seen. To be so far underground and see that three thousand years ago they cut a room this big, and this deep, out of solid rock. To see the incredible painted ceiling looking so good after all these years. It's incredible!"

"This is why I wanted to become an archaeologist. Maybe there's nothing more to be found in Egypt but—"

Glenn interrupted Tina, "Amenhotep I, according to Chris Houser at lunch last week."

"Okay, I was going to say that maybe there isn't much left to be found here, but certainly other places around the world…" Tina drifted off, thinking of the possibilities ahead of her.

We turned and began our long climb back to the entrance, stopping occasionally to view the wall paintings, most of which were intact. Our main purpose in stopping was to catch our breath. Finally, we used the railings to help us up the steep part leading to the entrance.

Dra Abu el Naga, 11:30 a.m.

Entering our van, we rode to the Marsam Hotel, passing the Pink House on our left and Dra Abu on our right. Like yesterday, Helen Mears greeted us in the lobby and took us to the outside terrace. Anok excused himself to make a phone call. Helen took his place at the table.

"Please tell me why you have traveled to Luxor. Just sightseeing?" she asked.

I started with my standard answer, "Well, our grandfather," and I pointed to Glenn, "was an archaeologist named Clarence Fisher, and we're—"

Helen interrupted me, "Amenhotep I?"

"Huh? Yes. He's been dead for sixty years, and now you're the second person to immediately link Clarence to Amenhotep."

"Steve, the West Bank is a very small place. My hotel and one other that is closer to the Valley of the Queens are the only two places where archaeologists, other than Egyptians, stay. Other than, of course, the Polish House and, across the river, the Chicago House. So I know most always what is going on. And right now, there is a lot of talk regarding finding the tomb of Amenhotep I. There are the Poles who have the concession now…Funny that they are led by Daniel Polz. Anyway, Donald Hughes, who you had lunch with yesterday, is trying to get support for a concession, and there are at least two others who are looking at other nearby areas beyond the Dra Abu concession. Everybody is looking for Amenhotep I's tomb, and, since your grandfather excavated Dra Abu and Amenhotep's temple, his name is well known…as if he might have had a clue to the location."

"Hmm," I said, as Anok returned to the table. Helen got up, and I looked at Glenn and Tina and shook my head, hoping to signal them to not talk about the map. They seemed to understand. Helen stayed on her feet as Anok sat down. "We're just following our grandfather's footsteps, seeing the places he excavated. The rest of the time, we're just normal tourists."

"Sounds wonderful. I hope you have a great trip! And, please, let me know if there's any way I can help you."

Helen departed just as our lunch was served. Our discussion during lunch revolved around the two beautiful tombs that we had entered, especially Seti I's.

"I've been fascinated with the building accuracy of the ancient Egyptians," I said. "I read in *The Complete Pyramids* that the granite blocks in the ceiling of the King's Chamber in the Great Pyramid weigh forty tons. There are theories on how the Pyramids were built, but moving forty-ton blocks is beyond belief. When Tina and I went into the King's Chamber, and I looked at the seams in the walls and ceiling…Perfect! While I didn't think to look when we were in the tombs today, I'll bet that those are all perfect as well."

Anok responded, "The Great Pyramid was constructed about 4,500 years ago, while the tomb of Seti I was built almost 3,300 years ago. The ancient Egyptians were excellent builders, as you have seen."

Tina replied, "There are a number of studies looking at tombs of the ordinary workmen, to try to gain clues into how they could build so accurately. Of course, some kooks have written books saying that it was aliens from outer space who did it. I know that there are excavations of the workers' areas in Giza, and I think there may be some around here."

"Yes," said Anok.

I said, "I was disappointed that we couldn't go up the hillside at Dra Abu yesterday. Before going back to the *Moon Goddess*, I'd like to revisit Dra Abu and take more pictures."

"So would I," said Tina. "I'd like to walk the whole distance, from the road of course, and take pictures to use back at Penn."

Anok started to object, strangely, but then hesitated, before reluctantly agreeing.

Fifteen minutes later, we insisted that the van driver not make a U-turn at the Pink House but continue straight north, for we could still see tombs on the Dra Abu hillside. We continued up to Kings Valley Road, where I had the driver make a U-turn and proceed south. I had the driver stop when Tina first saw tomb openings on the hillside ahead and to the right.

"This is good," said Tina. "I want to take pictures to take back to Penn from this point on. We'll walk past the alabaster factory we saw yesterday until we see that there are no more tombs."

All four of us exited the van, but Anok walked ahead. When he was out of hearing, I said, "I'll take overlapping pictures with my digital camera as well. Tonight, we can see how they fit together."

"Why are you doing that?" asked Glenn.

"I think that there's a reason that they wouldn't let us go up there. Maybe the overlapping pictures will help reveal something about them, something in relation to our map."

"But you still only have two possible points on the map, which may be nothing at all. And besides, I hope you're not thinking of doing something stupid."

"Of course not," answered Tina. "As far as I'm concerned, we're just collecting possible scientific information at a site that may never have had this kind of a look."

"Well, we just all need to stay safe!" said Glenn. "Who knows what was going on with our ride back from Amarna?"

"Of course," I agreed. "We won't do anything stupid."

We walked on, Tina and I agreeing on the best tomb or hillside feature to use as a point to take the first photo.

•　　•　　•

Meanwhile, about fifty yards up ahead, Anok made a phone call. He looked at his watch and noted that it was 1:30 p.m. "Achmed? It's Anok."

"Where are you?"

"Yesterday we went to Dra Abu, and nothing happened; they were just tourists. Today they insisted that we go back."

"Why did you let them do that?"

"I really had no choice…without seeming obvious. Anyway, I'm calling because they are up to something."

"What? Something important?"

"Maybe. That's why I'm calling. They made us stop the van at Kings Valley Road, near the Carter House. They got out and are taking pictures, on foot from the street, of all of the Dra Abu hillside. They look like they're walking along taking pictures every few yards, as if they're taking overlapping pictures. The girl, Tina, said it is for Penn, but Steve Fisher is also taking pictures, and he has a digital camera. I don't know what they're up to, but I don't like it."

"Neither do I. Is tonight your last night in Luxor?"

"Yes, we're on the boat already, but tonight they go to the Chicago House for dinner. Tomorrow, we'll go to Karnak Temple early, but then the boat leaves at eleven fifteen."

"Hmm. Okay. I'll put a tail on them when they leave the boat tonight."

"I'm not sure that's enough."

"Why?"

"Based on other nights, Glenn will go back to the boat after dinner. But Steve and Tina will probably go for drinks at the Winter Palace. It's across the street from the boat, but it seems to me that it would be good to cover there too."

"Okay. Anything else?"

"No, but I'm never sure of what Steve and Tina are up to. They really seem to be getting along well together, but he's old enough to be her grandfather. So beyond that, I just have a feeling that they know something or that they're planning something."

CHAPTER 33

Luxor, 3:00 p.m.

We returned to the *Moon Goddess* at 3:00 p.m. Glenn decided to go to his room and meet us at 4:45 p.m. in the ship's lobby. Tina and I agreed to meet at the open-air bar on the top deck in fifteen minutes.

I walked up the curving staircase to my room on the second level of the *Moon Goddess*. I entered the room, walked to the window, and opened the balcony door. The balcony was maybe four feet wide, with just a padded settee on it. I decided to sit out there and not bother to freshen up, despite having soaked through my shirt. I needed to unwind.

As I sat there, I reflected on the trip. My thoughts, however, were not on the tourist parts of the trip. Instead, they were on the things that revolved around the mysteries of my grandfather. These thoughts did not calm me, as I had hoped. Instead, I jumped up and reentered the room after closing the balcony door. I decided to change into nicer clothes for our dinner—a blue Penn embroidered polo shirt and clean khaki pants. I tried to brush the sand and grime from my sneakers as best I could. I grabbed one copy of the map and then headed straight to the top-deck bar.

There were already people on the deck, sunning themselves or swimming in the small, shallow pool at the front. There was a small bar about halfway back, with a light brown awning over it. Almost the entire rest of the back of the boat was covered with another brown awning. At the very back were items that looked like they were ready for use with a cookout.

I went to the bar and ordered a screwdriver. I then sat at a table near the back and waited for Tina. Once the vodka hit my stomach, I relaxed and sat back in my chair. I took out my Treo phone and called home, mostly because I could. There was a strong signal practically everywhere along the Nile, and I found it fascinating that I could call home from Egypt and talk so clearly to Linda. After discussing what was new with Linda, the kids, the grandkids, and her reunion planning, I described the visit to the tomb of Seti I. I went on and on, but then stopped as I realized how much the call was costing. I ended the call, saying that I would call the next day from somewhere on the Nile.

Tina arrived twenty minutes later than we had agreed. I greeted her, "Wow! You look fantastic...Oops, I guess I'm not allowed to say things like that!"

"Oh, that's okay. I decided to clean up and put on some poolside clothes." She was wearing a white short-sleeve shirt with a buttoned-down collar and the Penn emblem embroidered on it. The red-and-blue emblem pays tribute to William Penn, the founder of Pennsylvania, and Benjamin Franklin, the founder of the university, by incorporating parts of their family shields. Tina was wearing a pair of blue short-shorts—that's what I called them anyway. She had on clean white sneakers. And for the first time, I saw Tina with her hair down, stylishly accenting her narrow face. She had on more makeup than I had ever seen. She looked beautiful. I kept staring.

"Yeah, I can let my hair down. Hey, your screwdriver looks really re-freshing," she said, pointing to distract my attention.

"Here, can you put this in your pocketbook?" I asked. I handed her the map copy. "I'll get you a screwdriver. Have a seat. Or should we go out by the pool, since you're dressed for it?"

"No, let's just sit here under the awning; I've had, we've both had, plenty of sun."

I returned. "I went out on my patio to try to relax. But I couldn't stop thinking about all that we've done and how we still don't have any an-swers. Can I go over this now?"

"Sure," said Tina, "but we need to make time to just sit here and un-wind. Promise?"

"Okay." I paused to collect my thoughts. "We know nothing more about Clarence and Carter getting into Tut's tomb ahead of the others, although I didn't expect to learn anything about that anyway. We think we have points on Clarence's map pointing to the tombs of two priests, Bakenkhons and Huy. We have another point on the map that may have something to do with a tomb, if we can figure out the connection between First Avenue and Stack Street."

"Don't forget," added Tina, "that Isabella Browne said that there was a rumor that whoever was the pharaoh of the Exodus, he gave to Moses a one-hundred-year lease, er, covenant, for the Holy Land. What, she called it the Carswell Covenant?"

"Yeah, but that can't possibly involve us."

"Remember, too, that your grandfather excavated the palace of Pharaoh Mereneptah, and at the time, it was thought that he was the pharaoh of the Exodus." She paused. "Why don't we think back to the good things on our trip? How about starting where Chris Houser said that your grandmother's ring was 2,700 years old?"

"Yes, that's pretty neat. I don't know what good it will do us, unless we want to sell it, which I don't. But let's see…Tut's tomb was neat, and it was awesome to climb into the King's Chamber of the Great Pyramid. The trip to Amarna—remember how scary the return was—was bad, but seeing Ed Harer at an actual, working site was good. And of course, the tomb of Seti I was absolutely fantastic. As far as following in the footsteps of my grandfather, we did see the places he excavated, but I've really been disappointed with what we were allowed to see at Dra Abu. I keep feeling that they're keeping us away from it."

"Me, too. But as a new archaeologist, I really liked going to the aboveground sites, especially walking through the Western Cemetery at Giza and, like you said, talking with Dr. Harer. But I really wish we could find out more about your map and how it relates to Dra Abu."

"Suppose tonight we are not able to find out what First Avenue and Stack Street mean. Suppose we find out that there is no tomb of 'First Stack' or whatever. What could we do with two tombs and a point on a map?"

I finished my drink, took out my pen, and began to write on a napkin. "I've been thinking about this. Let me put the three points on this napkin in the same relative position as on the map. Here, does this look about right?"

Tina looked at it. "It's close enough…for a secret map to a huge trea-sure on a napkin!" She laughed.

"Well, if we were to find the two tombs and drew lines down and across, like this." I put the pen on the leftmost dot, which was also the highest, and drew a straight line down from it. I then put my pen on the rightmost dot and drew a line back to the left until it reached the first line.

"Now we have a graph. The highest dot is on the y axis, the rightmost is on the x axis. Now we draw a line down from the third dot, and also to the left from the dot. It looks to me like the third dot is halfway to the right and two-thirds up. If one of us were to walk up and the other walk over, then we would find the place where the unknown tomb is. The one that holds the greatest treasures the world has ever seen!"

Tina laughed. "Ta-da! Actually," she said as she studied the napkin, "I think it could work! All we need is to find out what we can about that third dot."

"Here's a suggestion. Tonight, why don't I look through whatever of Clarence's material the Chicago House has set aside for me. Meanwhile, maybe you can find a map showing the tombs of Bakenkhons and Huy. Perhaps Ed Harer will help with that."

"Sounds like a plan," said Tina. "Now let's relax for an hour." With that, she got up, walked out from under the awning, and leaned back in a lounge chair, baking in the strong sunshine. I decided to sit next to her despite the sun.

"I thought you'd had enough sun."

"And I've changed my mind on a lot of things," she said coyly.

"What do you mean?"

"I mean that I really want to return to Dra Abu tonight. With or without a map, I want to walk around on that hillside."

"Count me in. But I'll take my camera to the Chicago House tonight. I don't plan to take pictures, but if we get a map of the two tombs, we can try to locate them from the overlapping pictures. If we think it's worth it, I don't see why we couldn't take a taxi over and have him wait for us. But I see no need to tell Glenn. He's always been the older one who always thinks of caution. Ha—my whole life! He'd try to talk us out of it."

Tina changed the subject. "Let's talk about something else. We both graduated from Penn, years apart. Tell me about Penn back when you graduated."

"You mean about thirty-eight years ago? I guess the most fun thing is to tell you about my fraternity, Sigma Alpha Epsilon, SAE. The nicest thing to tell you about was that we won the award for being the best fraternity on campus my senior year. My freshman year, I lived in the dorms. Then I lived in the fraternity house sophomore year, but junior year I lived in an off-campus apartment. And senior year, I commuted from my home in Upper Darby. So I knew all about the Penn experience."

"What was the best?"

"They each had their pluses, but I guess living in the fraternity house was best; at least it was the most fun. We paid a cook who made us excellent breakfasts, lunches, and dinners. And boy, did we party. Every home football game, we had a party with drinks for anyone, no age checking, and with live bands. We actually wore suits to the football game, and our dates had to dress up. Then we changed, usually into Bermudas, to dance to the twist, the frug, and other early sixties dances like the Bristol stomp. These parties were crazy, and at least two of the live bands released records. During the winter and spring, we had the same kind of parties at least once a month. I didn't drink, and I drove home from campus and loaded up my car with senior girls I knew from my high school. They then hooked up with fraternity brothers, and then I drove them home; often they were drunk. Oh, and I married one of them!"

"Linda?"

"Yes. With all that, we still didn't allow girls above the first floor, to where our rooms were. Funny, as I think back, we allowed underage drinking but no sex."

"Ha—that sounds wild, just like from some movie. Are you sure you weren't at Penn State?"

"No. In fact, I went to several SAE fraternity parties at Penn State. Being in the middle of the state, they had no access to live bands. Their parties had a record player going, and the dates were all undergrads. Totally different!"

"Geez, my Penn experience was nothing like that. I commuted from my home in Springfield only freshman year. I lived in the dorms the rest of the time. I went to some dances, called mixers, and I had a date take me to several fraternity parties. No bands, but a lot of drinking.

"I was in several clubs and did some volunteering, but mostly I studied. I was determined to make it all the way through to my PhD. I'm almost there. And my fiancé was an instructor in one of my classes. We really hit it off after class; I first ran into him at a food truck. He's smart, he's fun loving, and he's extremely excited about archaeology in Egypt. My dream is that someday we will author some books and lead a Penn expedition to Egypt and find a lost pharaoh. And maybe…Maybe someday have a son or daughter and have him or her go with us."

Tina trailed off in thought, and I kept quiet. She then looked at her watch. "Uh-oh. I need some time. Can we meet in the lobby here in twenty-five minutes?"

I looked at my Casio. "Yes. See you soon." We got up and walked to the stairway to return to our rooms.

CHAPTER 34

Luxor, 5:00 p.m.

The Chicago House, which opened for the University of Chicago's Oriental Institute in 1924 with funding from John D. Rockefeller Jr., faced the Nile and a row of cruise ships. Our taxi ride up the Corniche el Nile took only five minutes. Tina and I exited the taxi. Glenn had declined to come; he was having the stomach problems that so typically affect tourists. We walked through the entrance that was guarded with an iron gate and onto the grounds lined with palm trees. Entering the concrete structure, we were greeted by Ed Harer, who had just arrived from his dig site.

After pleasantries, Ed said, "We will eat at seven p.m., but I hope they've set out some of your grandfather's books in the library. Here, I'll show you. If you need anything, let us know. All who work here know of your grandfather, and we're delighted to have you dine with us."

Tina spoke up. "I'm wondering if you happen to have a map of the tombs at Dra Abu el Naga. From some writing of Fisher's," she lied, "I'm particularly interested in Bakenkhons and Huy, although I'll be happy with anything you might have."

We walked to the left, from the Spartan building lobby, and into the library. Rectangular, it contained two large tables with seats around them, and two walls were lined with bookcases. The other two walls contained the arched windows that could be seen from the street.

Ed said, "I see that they've put out some books and documents for you. Steve, if you'd like, you can sit down, and I'll take Tina with me to see the librarian."

Tina said, "Wait for just a second. Steve, I recognize that book. We used it as a textbook in one of my classes. Reprints, of course." She pointed to the big book that was separate from the stack of books on the table. "It's an incredible book."

"Yes, I have that book at home," I said. Sitting down nearest to the stack of books, I immediately recognized the large book as *The Minor Cemetery at Giza*, written by my grandfather in 1924 for the University of Pennsylvania.

As Tina and Ed departed, I glanced through the book again. Consisting of over three hundred pages, the book included three foldout watercolor pages, three intricate foldout plan diagrams drawn by Clarence Fisher, fifty-two plates (pages of pictures), and one chapter on inscriptions and sculpture written by Dr. Alan Rowe. My favorite picture from the book as a child was of a mummy whose head was just a skull.

I then turned to the stack of books. On top was a book, written by my grandfather, called *The Excavation of Armageddon*. Published in 1924 by the University of Chicago Press, it was only seventy-eight pages long. Called Armageddon by many, the area is actually known as Megiddo and is in Israel. As I scanned through the book, I saw that it contained many photographs and drawings. Thumbing through it from the back, I stopped after glancing at a drawing of two hieroglyphs. I looked closer at the one on the right, because it reminded me of the inscription in the scarab on my grandmother's ring. Too bad the ring was back in Glenn's room on the ship.

Since it was short, seven pages, I decided to read the foreword, written by the famous archaeologist Dr. James Henry Breasted. About halfway through it, I stopped and reread one paragraph over and over. In it, Dr. Breasted stated that on his first day at Fisher's excavation at Megiddo, Fisher showed him a fragment of a stela that he thought had the hieroglyph of Pharaoh Shishak I on it. Much more versed in hieroglyphics, Breasted confirmed that it was, indeed, Shishak I, also known as Shoshenq I or Sheshonk I. Breasted followed this with a quote from 1 Kings 14:24–26, wherein Shishak conquered Jerusalem and took away all of the treasures from King Solomon's Temple.

I sat back and started thinking of the implications of this. Clarence had discovered a piece of a stela with Shishak's mark on it. I had a ring that may also have that same mark in the scarab. I thought, "But wait, the ring was from one thousand to nine hundred BC, according to Chris Houser. When was Shishak in Israel?" I scanned through the book more intently and found on page 16 that Solomon had fortified Megiddo in 970 BC, and I found that Megiddo was conquered by Shishak in 932 BC. Could my ring really be from Shishak I?

A thought hit me like a speeding train. "Could it be," I mumbled to myself, "that First Avenue…let me reverse it…that Stack Street and First Avenue refer to Shishak I? Could it be that Clarence's map pinpoints where he thought the tomb of Shishak I is? Oh my God, oh my God!" I got up from the chair and began pacing around the table and looking out the windows, my mind going fifty miles an hour. Still pacing, I thought, "But has Shishak's tomb been found already? I'll have to ask at the dinner table."

Finally, I stopped my pacing and sat down and started looking through the other books. But I continually would stop reading and lift my head up to think. Finally, from a sudden fatigue, I put my head down on the table and fell asleep.

I awoke with my shoulder being shaken by Tina. "Wake up, old man." She laughed. "Wake up—it's time for dinner!"

I woke up with a start. "Huh? What time is it?"

"It's six thirty, but we have lots to talk about." She sat down next to me. "I know you're exhausted, as am I, but I have a map and some info about the tombs."

"That's great," I said. "But listen to this first."

Tina looked at me quizzically.

"I know what the third dot means! I figured it out. I—"

"Okay, okay. But please slow down."

"Yes, yes. Let me start from the beginning. The first book on the pile of my grandfather's work is about excavating Armageddon, um, Megiddo, in Israel. There, Clarence found a stela with the cartouche of Pharaoh Shishak I on it. I think that cartouche matches my grandmother's ring."

"Okay…That's why you're so excited?"

"Partly, but mostly I think I've broken the code. I think that the map's Stack Street and First Avenue refer to Pharaoh Shishak I. Get it? Stack is Shishak, and First Avenue makes it Shishak I."

"I think you may be right. Oh my God! So we now have names for all three dots: Bakenkhons, Huy, and Shishak?"

"Yes. So, did you get a map?"

"I did! The librarian, Lucille Noble, was very nice. It took her a while to find a map of Dra Abu, but she was successful and made two copies. She also said that Bakenkhons's tomb should be easy to find. She said it was two-thirds of the way up the hill, behind the alabaster factory. It has rectangular columns on both sides, is marked as TT35, for Theban Tomb 35, and has an iron gate with rocks piled in front of half of it. Unfortunately, she was not familiar with Huy, so she said it might be a rectangular opening or more likely just a rough hole. It should have the marking TT14 and would either have an iron gate or rocks, or both. Looking at the map, it appears to be down and to the right of Bakenkhons's."

With that, it was time for dinner, which was held in a room that mimicked the library. There were fourteen people seated around the table. Dinner talk was the usual conversation about our trip. Also, some of the others reported on their activities that day, but I could only understand Dr. Harer's references. While we were having after-dinner coffee, I explained that I had found references to Shishak I in one of Fisher's books. "Has the tomb of Shishak I been found?"

While several started to answer, Ed Harer took over. "No, the tomb of Shoshenq I has never been found. And everyone here knows the biblical story of him taking the treasures from Solomon's Temple. So there is speculation that those treasures may be in Egypt, but I believe they would still be in Israel. Most Egyptian archaeologists, who may be biased, believe that he may be buried in Tanis or Bubastis, which are northeast of Cairo, or Memphis, now Mit Rahina, which is just south of Cairo.

"Did your grandfather find anything about Shoshenq I at Memphis?"

"I don't know. Tonight was the first time I've seen any reference to Shishak, and it was in my grandfather's book *The Excavation of Armageddon.*"

"Shishak I lived during the Third Intermediate Period. Pharaohs of the period were mostly buried in Memphis or Tanis. One thing I'm sure of," said Harer, "as a pharaoh, Shoshenq I would not be buried among the officials at Dra Abu el Naga. And I seriously doubt that he would be in the Valley of the Kings." He paused. "It's interesting, I think, that you don't hear of people trying to find the treasures from Solomon's Temple, like in *Indiana Jones.*"

"Yeah, I guess not," I said. "If anyone was Indiana Jones, I'm beginning to think, it was Clarence Fisher. Unfortunately, he didn't find any treasure!"

With that, we made our good-byes, and Tina and I walked out onto the Corniche el Nile. Fortunately, we were quickly able to hail a passing taxi. "How about if we go one last time to the Winter Palace and compare my pictures to the map?" I asked. Tina agreed, and we sat in silence the rest of the short taxi ride. All I could think of was returning to Dra Abu and hoping that Tina would want to go.

At the Royal Bar, we ordered our usual drinks and sat near the back of the room. I pulled out my Nikon point-and-shoot camera, which had a great night capability and an amazing two megapixels of resolution. "Let me quickly scroll backward to find the alabaster factory."

I quickly found the image and proceeded to push the camera's zoom control to zoom in. Using the navigation buttons, I found what I thought was the tomb of Bakenkhons, and I showed it to Tina.

"Looks like it to me," she replied. "It certainly has the rectangular entrance described by Lucille Noble, with columns outlining the entrance. It's not facing us on the street—more, probably, facing southeast. But I think that's it. But I don't know how we can find Huy's tomb."

"Let me have the map you got tonight and my grandfather's map. I hope you have it in your bag." Tina took both out and gave them to me. I brought out a pencil, compared both maps, and said, "I think that the two maps match regarding the tombs of Bakenkhons and Huy." I then pointed at a spot on the new map. "It looks like this might be where Shishak's tomb might be. Agree?"

"Yes, that looks good, but we only know about one spot, the tomb of Bakenkhons."

"Yes, but let me try this." I drew a line straight down from the tomb of Bakenkhons. I then located Huy's tomb and drew a line to the left to meet the line from Bakenkhons. "Now let's try to see if we can look at the proportion of the distance from Bakenkhons to Huy as it relates to the overall map that you have." The distance was the width of my little finger. "I think that it's pretty close off to the right."

I then scrolled one picture forward on my camera. I could make out the tomb of Bakenkhons at the far left, and I tried to imagine where Huy's might be. I found a location of a large but uneven opening behind three buildings with blue facades. The three buildings were lined up one behind another, and the tomb entrance seemed straight up from their right edge. I then looked from the picture and back to both maps.

"Uh-oh."

"What?"

"The good news is that I'm confident that we have now found the tombs of both Bakenkhons and Huy."

"Yeah…What's the bad news?"

"This puts the spot for Shishak up in the air."

"Let me see." Tina compared the image to the map and thought for a moment. "No problem. I think that Shishak's tomb is just over the top of the ridge. I wish you could mark the spot on your image, but zoom as much as you can up to the top where it looks like there are two paths. I think that the tomb is just over the top of the hill near the path to the right."

I looked closer and then agreed with her assessment. "But if that's a path, then maybe someone has already located it. Then again, there seem to be more paths than we saw at the Valley of the Kings. So it looks like we would have to verify the location of the two tombs, Bakenkhons and Huy, then just walk up to the path on the right and look for an opening partway down the other side of the ridge, judging how far down from Clarence's map."

I turned serious and looked at Tina. She was looking serious, lost in thought, as well. "How about if I get another round of drinks?" I asked.

"Please do."

As I got up, I realized that I had failed to notice that another person, an Egyptian of medium height, thin, and with a wiry build, had come into the bar. He sat closer to our table than I would have liked, but I gave him only a quick glance.

• • •

Achmed Hamed, whose cousin Anne was living with a Carswell Bible College IT guy, Lonnie Jenkins, had taken the call from Anok at 1:30 p.m., as Tina and Steve were photographing Dra Abu. He immediately called Abu Ayyub al-Khawi, whom he had already stationed in Luxor. "They are up to something," he told Abu Ayyub. "I don't know what, but if they're going to do something, like going back to Dra Abu, it would have to be tonight, since their ship sails tomorrow morning. Make sure that you follow them and keep me up to date. From Anok, it sounds like one of the Fisher brothers and the girl have had drinks each night at the Winter Palace. I'm going to leave now and probably go right to the Winter Palace." He hung up, collected his Glock Model 23 and Kalashnikov, and left for the 280-mile trip from al Minya to Luxor. He hoped, with traffic, to get there in less than six hours, which would get him there by 8:00 p.m.

• • •

I returned with drinks, but this time switched to Macallan Twelve neat. "It's to calm me down."

I sat down and handed Tina her glass of wine. "Let's stop and think about where we go from here." I paused. "As the old man here, the more responsible one, I think that we should take this information back to Penn, not telling anyone, even my brother, and let Penn set up a mission, maybe with you in charge, to return."

"We could do that," said Tina. "Or this immature but gutsy person says that we should buy two flashlights at one of the booths outside, go to Dra Abu, pay to have the taxi driver wait for us, and try to locate Shishak's treasure."

"Well, as the more mature one, I have to say…" I paused. "Let's do it!" I watched Tina's beaming face and then said, "Drink up. I know that I'll need some extra courage."

We got up quickly, downing our drinks as we rose. We turned left out of the Royal Bar, walked down the corridor to the lobby, and exited. We walked down the curving outdoor stairway of the Winter Palace and turned right. We quickly found a store, more a booth, that sold us two flashlights and two bottles of water. Since we both were wearing comfortable shoes, we decided not to return to our rooms on the *Moon Goddess*, in case we would not be allowed back off. We hailed one of the always-waiting taxis and departed for Dra Abu, a drive that took us south of Luxor, over the Nile Bridge, and north to Dra Abu el Naga.

CHAPTER 35

Dra Abu, 10:45 p.m.

We had the taxi driver pull into the parking lot at the alabaster factory. I asked him the amount of the fare and paid that to him in Egyptian pounds. I then took out three twenty-dollar bills and said, "I want you to wait here. When I return, I will pay you the same amount I just paid you. But now, I will give you twenty American dollars. When we return I will give you forty more."

The driver took the money, smiled wryly at me, and then gave a lurid wink to Tina.

We had decided to first locate the tomb of Bakenkhons. As we walked up the path between the alabaster store and the alabaster factory, I said, "Did you see the look he gave us? He thinks we're going up there to have an affair, although I don't know why anyone would. This is not a romantic place. But he probably thinks that we're immoral infidels!" With that, we heard the taxi start up and watched it drive away.

"Oh, that's just great! Now what?" Tina asked.

"I'll just take out my gun and try to shoot out his tires."

"You have a gun?"

"No, of course not. But I wish I had one."

"This is serious. What do we do?"

"When we're done, we can walk to the Marsam Hotel and call for a taxi from there. I'd guess it's about two miles away, just down the road to our right. We've passed it several times." We were partway up the hillside when I said this, and I could see only a few lights in the distance. There were no lights at the Pink House across the street; we had been told by Donald Hughes that it was lived in by squatters.

• • •

Achmed and Abu Ayyub had followed the taxi in Achmed's car. They drove by the taxi as it was discharging Tina and Steve, then quickly turned around, parking behind the Pink House. They peered around the house and saw Tina and Steve making their way up the hillside. They carefully followed them up the hill.

• • •

So far, due to the lighting from the half moon, we had not needed our flashlights. It was actually a chillier night than we expected, and despite the climb, Tina had goosebumps on her arms and her highly exposed legs. "I have goosebumps, but I'm not sure if it's from the cold or from fear."

"I would bet that most archaeologists have had the same feeling."

Tina gave a nervous laugh.

We easily made our way up to the tomb of Bakenkhons just by following the dirt road, which even had electric poles along it, leading to an unlighted shack.

Before we continued, Tina said sheepishly, "I have to pee. I should have gone back at the hotel."

"Me too. There's nothing around, so go behind that shack; then I'll follow."

Continuing, we quickly identified the tomb by the rusted iron marker that read TT35. We then walked down to the bottom of the hill, over to the first building with a blue facade, and up the path that led to the right and to the back of the third building. From there it was tough going. There was no path, the ground consisted of sand and rocks mixed in with pebbles. Some of the rocks were large, not boulders, and there were ruts and holes. We both aimed our flashlights at our feet.

We finally got to the opening that we hoped would be Huy's tomb, TT14. The opening was indeed rough, and we did not immediately see a marker. I decided to try to use my hands to scrape off some of the dirt and sand that covered both sides of the opening. I finally found a very sand-encrusted TT14 marker.

"I don't believe that we found these so easily," said Tina. "Let's hurry up to the top where the path is and see what we can find on the other side. Or, we could just go have an affair." We both laughed, but our laughs were nervous laughs.

"God, my heart is racing. Partly from the climb, but mostly it's out of nervousness and anxiety."

Tina agreed and then said, "Look up near the top. What looked like paths from down below look more like they could be gullies. My understanding is that the Aswan High Dam, which the Russians constructed in the 1960s, has changed the weather. Not only has the dam stopped the annual flooding of the Nile, but I understand that it rains more often, caused by moisture forming over the huge Lake Nasser behind the dam."

"You could be right. I doubt that these gullies would have been here in the early 1920s." Winded, I said, "Please let's stop. I'm breathing hard, and I'm now sweating to death!" When I collected my breath, I asked, "I wonder if we can see the Valley of the Kings from the top, even in this light?"

"I don't think so. There are more hills before the Valley of the Kings. I don't know what's on the other side, but I'm pretty sure we're far from the valley. The road to the Valley of the Kings is just up the road to our right. Remember how long it took us to get there?"

"Yeah, I guess you're right." We continued on.

We reached the top of the ridge and looked down the other side. From above, we could see only the same mixture of rocks, sand, and pebbles as on the way up. We shined our flashlights, but to no avail. "Let's go lower and then look up," I suggested.

We climbed down about as far as we thought Shishak's tomb would be, and then twenty feet more. Looking up, we didn't see anything different, until Tina saw something off to her right. It was another gully, but it was very faint. "Look over there," she said, as she shined her flashlight on a pile of rocks about four feet wide by four feet high. "Could they have been washed together like that by rains for the last thirty years?"

I went over to investigate and started pulling at the rocks. "Help me pull these away."

We both worked quickly for about five minutes, when Tina suddenly pointed out that there was a rough opening. I joined her, and we quickly exposed an oval opening three feet wide by a maximum of three feet high. I got on my stomach and shined my flashlight into the opening. "The opening gets wider and higher about fifteen feet in. I can wiggle in and then stand or at least crouch."

"No, don't! It's too dangerous. There could be snakes, scorpions, bats. We've gotten what we came for."

"No we haven't." I shined my flashlight in all directions in the entrance. "We've uncovered a concealed hole and a passageway beyond. It's very rough cut. It could be used for trash, since I don't see any markings. Then again, I don't see any trash either." I said all that with an air of confidence. But I was just putting it on for Tina's sake. I was scared to death. I planned to back out at the first sign of anything creepy.

I started crawling in, with Tina pleading with me to stop. After crawling about twenty feet, I was able to get up to a crouching position; the passageway was less than five feet high. Oh boy, this was going to kill my back.

I shined my flashlight around, revealing that the passageway moved slightly down. It ended about twenty-five feet in, but I could see that there was another passageway to the left. I proceeded in, with my back knotting up in pain, to the end of the passageway and then shouted to Tina, "It goes off to another passageway to the left." I got no response but thought nothing of it; I was too involved in my search. I didn't even feel claustrophobic; it didn't even cross my mind.

I squatted to take the strain off my back. I tried to decide if I should crawl, duck walk, or just walk hunched over. Still bending so that my head would not hit the ceiling, I continued down another slight incline for what seemed like thirty feet. I still saw no signs of wall paintings or other markings. I thought, "With no markings and no trash, maybe this is a treasure store." I continued on. After my initial left turn, I had alternately taken four more right and left turns, each passageway about twenty feet long, going lower but only at a slight angle. "Maybe they were bringing in something very heavy," I mumbled.

After one more right turn, I came to a vertical shaft that was as wide as the passageway but six feet across. I was sure glad that I had proceeded carefully. As I looked down, I saw that it was maybe fifteen feet deep. I looked up again and saw markings crudely scratched on the opposite wall. "I'm no expert, and my recall is not very good," I thought. "But that looks like it could be Shishak's cartouche. Strange how crude it is, as if a worker had quickly scratched it into the rock."

I decided to sit down and collect my breath and my thoughts. I didn't know how far or deep I had come into the passageway, but here was a shaft that would require a ladder. I decided to sit once again and reflect upon my crazy adventure. I was dead tired, my back was killing me, and the confidence-building buzz from my scotch had worn off, replaced by a splitting headache. I was ready to get out of here. My old enemy, claustrophobia, was creeping toward me, an unwanted stranger in the night. I thought that maybe I should go back and report finding a big shaft.

I looked again into the shaft. I knew that there was no way for me to get down there and then climb back out, so I decided to see how far I could lean down from the edge to shine my flashlight.

Getting down on my belly, I extended my arm into the shaft. My flashlight illuminated an opening, possibly into a room, the top of which was about six feet down. "No way I can get to that." As I looked, I could see some sort of glow, some sort of reflection from the opening, possibly a golden color.

I frantically needed to try to get farther into the shaft. With my flashlight in my right hand, I inched my way farther out. I braced myself against the left wall with my left arm, inched out, and bent down farther. I could now see deeper into the passageway, or maybe it was a chamber at the bottom of the hole.

I dared to inch just a little more, precariously, but what I saw took my breath away. It was the end of a chest. It was gold, all gold! I could only see the end of it, but it looked to be about three feet wide. The chest was maybe two feet high, and above it was what looked like the back of a small golden figure with wings, also two feet high. There were two rings on the outside where the figure met the chest; these appeared to be where poles were inserted for two or four men to carry the chest, depending on its weight.

On the floor to the left of the chest was a gold necklace, composed of rows of gold beads. Attached was a golden medallion of some sort. I could also see what looked like the bottom of an engraved stone, maybe ten inches on its bottom, propped on its side against the left wall.

I shivered as I realized that maybe I had found the Ark of the Covenant! But that shiver was enough to make me feel like I was falling in. I tightened my arm against the left wall and reached out forcefully with my right arm. When it contacted the right wall, it forced me to drop my flashlight. It landed with a clang but stayed on. Oh no!

I quickly recovered, pressing both arms against the walls. I grabbed several breaths, realizing the precarious position I was in. Slowly I wiggled back, away from the opening. I crawled back several feet and then stood up slowly. I was safe! I looked at the opening, and it still had a very faint golden glow, probably from the flashlight shining on the golden chest. I decided not to approach the edge but to make my way back and out of the tomb. Or was it a storeroom? Or treasure trove? I had no trouble walking to the end of the passageway and turning left, but then I discovered what darkness really was. Looking back, I could only see the faintest light, but ahead was total darkness.

I moved ahead slowly and carefully, until my outstretched arm and hand reached a wall. Remembering, I turned left and proceeded. Now everywhere I looked was total black, dark as a coal mine. Another turn and claustrophobia started to creep its unnerving way in. The walls seemed to be closing in, although I could see nothing. I started getting dizzy, and suddenly, I saw flashes of light, even with my eyes closed. I felt dizzy, and I had broken out in a cold sweat. I was nauseous and shaking, almost violently. I wanted to scream, but I broke out in somber sighs.

I decided to sit down and catch my breath. After a minute, I stood up, but too quickly. My high blood pressure medicine has always made me dizzy if I stand up quickly. Usually no problem, but now I got disoriented from the experience. "Oh my God, what if I'm going the wrong way?" I paused.

Finally, I came to my senses and continued on. I lost track of how many turns I had made, but I realized, when I reached the last wall, that there was only a turn to the right. I walked ahead a few feet and then thought that I should crawl because the way narrowed and got lower ahead. I felt that I was now in the last crawlway, and I could finally see dim moonlight ahead. As I started to come out of the entrance, I excitedly yelled, "Hey, Tina, I think I found…What the hell?"

"We're the police. You are under arrest. Hands up!"

CHAPTER 36

Wednesday, October 30, 2002
Dra Abu, 1:40 a.m.

"**O**fficer, what's this all about? We've done nothing wrong!" I looked over at Tina, who was being held by a bearded man in a galabia. "You're under arrest for trespassing and committing crimes against our sacred treasures!"

I noticed for the first time that the rifle held on me had a handle like a pistol and a gun clip that arced forward like a quarter moon. Was it a Kalashnikov?

"You're holding a gun like that on me? A machine gun? Let me see your creden—"

"They're not police!" screamed Tina. "They're—" Her voiced was muzzled by the man in the galabia.

"Tina Gilbert, you're a pretty one. Achmed, I hope she keeps struggling!"

"Don't be so rough, Abu Ayyub," said Achmed, the man with the rifle. "Only if we have to. You, Fisher, start up the hill. We'll then go down the other side behind one of the buildings."

"How do you know my name? What do you want?"

"In time. Now keep quiet!"

We crested the hill and then started down the path or gulley on the right. "Over there," said Achmed, who was clearly the leader. "Behind that building." We moved down and over behind a mud-brick building.

Achmed used the butt of his Kalashnikov to try to break through the wooden door. Muttering what I assumed to be Arabic curses, Achmed was successful after ten hard hits with his rifle. "In there!" he commanded. We both were shoved into the two-story mud-brick building, which was abandoned and totally empty. The front door and all the windows were boarded up as strongly as the back door had been. On the left side at the front of the building was a narrow, crumbling set of steps to the second floor; the railing did not look sturdy at all.

We were roughly pushed into the middle of the room. Abu Ayyub reached into his shoulder bag, pulled out a candle, lit it, and put it on the floor away from the entrance.

"What is this about? What could you possibly want from us? We're just tourists."

"Shut up!" Achmed said. "See your girlfriend, Tina, over there." I looked and was almost knocked over by the slamming of the heavy rifle into my upper left arm. Despite the pain, I tried to move my arm, but it wouldn't cooperate. "There's more where that came from. Now, tell me why you are here!" He shoved me into the left corner.

"She's a student in archaeology, and I'm just a tourist."

"I see...Abu Ayyub, why don't you see how pretty Miss Tina feels."

With that, Abu Ayyub moved instantly behind Tina, thrust his arms through her armpits, and cupped both breasts. "She feels good to me!" he said with a big grin. Tina shrieked and struggled, and he let her go, still in the middle of the room.

"Now, let's talk," said Achmed. "Why are you here?"

"Okay. I'll tell you everything." I glanced at Tina, who nodded. "First, I recognize you from the Winter Palace tonight. Tina is indeed a student in archaeology at the University of Pennsylvania. My grandfather, Clarence Fisher—"

"Ah, Amenhotep I," interrupted Abu Ayyub.

"Yes, that Clarence Fisher. He died before I was born, but Tina accompanied my brother and me on this trip to Egypt to follow in his footsteps. So we've been to a number of places that my grandfather excavated, including here at Dra Abu el Naga. We've even been granted access to certain special places by Zahi Hawass. You know of Zahi Hawass? He used a textbook written by my grandfather when he was a graduate student at the University of Pennsylvania in Philadelphia. So we just came over here to look around where he had dug before. That's all." Achmed nodded to Abu Ayyub, who quickly moved into his former position with his hands on Tina's breasts.

As Tina screamed, I looked at her, and Achmed delivered a crippling blow to my stomach with the butt of his Kalashnikov. I doubled over in the worst pain of my life, unable to breathe. I was on the verge of passing out. I slowly recovered, crawled a couple of feet, looked over at Tina, and saw that she had stopped struggling against Abu Ayyub's intrusive hands. "Tell him!" she gasped.

"Okay, okay. Just release her." I stood up. Achmed nodded, and Abu Ayyub removed his hands. It looked like this team had gone through this act many times before.

"Okay, my grandfather once said that he knew where there was a tomb with many treasures in it. My brother and I found a map that had strange clues on it. We solved those puzzles and used a map provided by the Chicago House to come here. We should have waited, but we thought that nothing could happen to us." I paused. "How long have you been following us?"

"Since you left New York," Achmed said. "But you have more to tell us!" he demanded, holding the rifle up as if to hit me again with the butt.

"Okay, okay! We went over the hill and found a pile of rocks. We removed those rocks, and they showed a narrow entranceway. I crawled in and then found that I could almost stand up. I walked ahead and found a passage to the left. I found another passage after that, and one more. I gave up after that."

"Why?"

"Because we originally thought that it might be the undiscovered tomb of a pharaoh named Shishak. But there were no markings on the walls, and it was all roughly cut out, which is not at all the pattern of normal ancient Egyptian tombs; they all have smooth walls and at least some wall paintings. As I started to come out, my flashlight died, and I panicked. It was very claustrophobic."

"But when you came out, you shouted, 'Tina, I have found...' What did you find?" He glanced again at his comrade, who then started kissing Tina on her neck and telling her what he wanted to do to her.

"I was trying to say that I found that I could conquer my claustrophobia by just stopping for a couple of minutes. It was very dark in there; it was horrible without a flashlight. I felt that the walls were moving in on me. It was horrible, horrible." Just then I thought of an inconsistency in my story: I had said that my flashlight died, but it was at the bottom of the shaft, probably still shining on the ark. If the flashlight died, why didn't I carry the dead flashlight out? Thankfully, Achmed didn't seem to catch it.

"Abu Ayyub, you can now go to the next step," Achmed said.

With that, Abu Ayyub reached around and slowly unbuttoned Tina's blouse. Next, he undid her bra strap, as Tina started to cry. Moving around to her front, he pulled her short-shorts and panties down to her knees. Abu Ayyub then moved behind her again. Achmed said, "The next step is for my friend to bend her over and give her a good but rough time. She may like it; Abu Ayyub is very good, aren't you?" He glanced again at Abu Ayyub, who nodded yes and smiled lasciviously.

Turning back to me, Achmed screamed at me, spitting in my face, "Now! Do you want to watch my friend have a date with your girlfriend? Or do you want to tell me about the covenant?" He made another motion with his rifle, and I flinched.

"Covenant? What covenant? I, we, we know nothing about a covenant."

"The Carswell Covenant. The proof that Pharaoh gave Moses only a one-hundred-year covenant to the land that the Jews have taken from all mankind. It will show the world that your holy land belongs to us! Israel will no longer exist, and Palestine will once again be returned to its rightful glory, with no Jews. No Jews."

Achmed noticed the look of horror on my face.

"Tina," I yelled. "Give him the map; the map we've been following." She reached into her bag and extracted just the map from the Chicago House. She held back the map from Clarence.

I continued, "Yes, I crawled into the hole, and like I said, the walls were very rough cut, and there were no paintings on it. It's not a tomb. But it may hold treasure. If it's treasure you're after, let her go, and go see for yourself.

"But I have never heard of a Carswell Covenant. Why would a covenant, like you said from Moses's time, have the name Carswell? The only thing I know about a covenant, and I can't tell you anything I don't know, is that we met last week with an Egyptology professor at the American University in Cairo. She said that she had heard about some rumors among some of her Egyptian students from Asyut and Al-Minya. The rumors say that there may have been a one-hundred-year covenant or lease. But, please believe me, please, I know nothing about any covenant or any Carswell Covenant. Honest, you now know everything! Please believe me. You've got to believe me! Oh my God, help me!" I started to sob, overcome with fear, joining Tina. I began to collapse against the corner wall.

Achmed looked at the map, walked outside. I could see him holding it up against the Dra Abu hillside, and then he returned. "Abu Ayyub, let her go. We're done here." He folded and tucked the map into his pocket as Tina started to get dressed.

"Tina, join your lover in the corner and stay there until we have a chance to leave." As she joined me, I felt a little relieved. "Get down, and lean against the wall. That's it." Achmed Hamed left first. But as Abu Ayyub al-Khawi left, he turned around with an evil smile on his face and a bottle in his hand that he had taken from his shoulder bag. He removed the cork and replaced it with a rag. Using it as a wick, he pushed it into the bottle to let it soak. He lit the wick with a lighter—it looked like a Zippo— and stepped outside. He then threw the bottle in the air so that it landed just inside the door and broke. The flames quickly ignited, turning almost instantly into an inferno. Our only way out was completely blocked!

●　　●　　●

"Get down, get down!" I yelled to Tina. "On your belly. I was trained as a firefighter! I know what to do. Listen to me!"

Tina did as I said. "Oh my God, oh my God," she kept repeating. I was afraid that she might freeze up with fear.

"Stay calm; I've been in a fire just like this before. There's no real fuel, and the flames will start billowing at the ceiling and then will probably go out the door; a flashover. Down here will be the coolest, and there will be air. So stay low; lick the ground, as they used to tell us in training." The smoke was already down to about two feet off the floor, but we had no trouble breathing.

"We'll let it burn for maybe thirty more seconds, then crawl over to those steps in the other corner. I don't think the windows on the second floor will be boarded up."

With that, Tina started to stand up to get to the steps. She screamed and immediately dropped to her stomach due to the intense heat. "Oh no, oh no," she said, sobbing.

"Please stay still, and flat, until I tell you to move." I waited about thirty seconds, but even I had trouble tolerating the intense heat that was fueled by gasoline as an accelerant.

"Okay, now crawl over to the bottom of the steps, like a turtle, and stay there until I tell you." I followed her, thankful that, as I had said, the flames were rolling out the rear door. There was no problem with the air at this low level, but the last time I was in a situation like this, I was thirty-six years old and wearing a heavily insulated fire coat and pants.

"When I say go, I want you to take a deep breath and leap up from the floor and run up those steps as fast you can. Don't take a breath going up the steps, and try to ignore the heat. When you reach the top, dive to the left and onto your belly again. I'll then come up. The hardest part will be the heat. You will feel like it's killing you, but you have to keep on climbing. Take the steps two at a time.

"Deep breath! Go!"

Tina did as she was told and, fortunately, she did not stop. She dove to the floor at the top and then rolled over and rolled again onto her stomach. I followed and did the same maneuver. After a second, I saw that I was lying with my left arm and shoulder over her. It didn't seem at all awkward.

"Let me slowly get up to see how hot it is." I crouched and then said, "Okay duck walk as quickly as you can to the window in the far corner." She had no problem getting there, despite the smoke cascading up the stairs, twisting her way around some wooden chairs. I took another path, around a bed frame and an old, partially stuffed chair, but my foot broke through a spot in the middle of the room. I quickly pulled my foot out, almost losing my sneaker. Looking out the open window, I said, "We'll go out here. It's about fifteen feet high. No problem!"

Tina started to balk. "I can't do it! I can't do it! It's too high!"

"No, you'll be fine. I'll go first and help break your fall. I want you to land with your knees bent. Don't try to stand, just land on your feet with your knees bent and then immediately fall forward, breaking your fall with bent knees and arms. And I will certainly help break your fall. Okay?"

"Yes, but I'm scared."

"It's okay. I'm scared, too!"

I jumped but twisted my ankle. As the pain shot through me, I asked myself why I didn't follow my own instructions. "Some macho man I am," I uttered.

Tina jumped, but she did follow my instructions. Her bent knees helped break her fall, and her arms and hands assisted as well. As her head was about to hit the ground, I pulled her up by grabbing under her arms. "There, nothing to it," I said with a big smile.

"You were right! Now I know how to jump off a burning building." She laughed. Then she began to sob, leaning into my arms. I held her tight, both of us breathing very heavily. Her sobs turned into almost hysterical crying. I understood and held her tight, as if I was calming a crying child. Somehow, this calmed me as well.

Sobbing, she broke from my embrace and said, "I never knew fire was so hot."

"That's what every firefighter says the first time."

"I was close to giving them your grandfather's map. If that prick had tried to do anything else to me, I..." She continued with heavy crying again, and finally said, "I would have given your grandfather's map to him."

"You could have the first time, since I have the other map of Dra Abu, and I have another of my grandfather's. And I don't think it would have mattered. They were after the Carswell Covenant, whatever that is! Do you know what it is?"

"Absolutely not," she said while beginning to wipe her tears away.

We had moved farther back behind the burning building. Below I could see a battered gray Toyota pickup driving away. I believed that it was our two assailants, but I couldn't be sure.

Tina finally recovered, and I said, "We need to wait here for a couple of more minutes and then sneak behind those buildings to our left."

After five minutes, I looked out from behind the building. There were no nearby lights, just a few from beyond the farms near the Nile. Luxor, in the distance, was painted with light, even at this hour.

"Okay, but then what will we do? I'm exhausted, we won't be able to find a taxi, and I can't walk back to Luxor."

"Tina, we knew that our taxi left before all this happened. As I said earlier, we can walk to the Marsam Hotel; it's not too far. Hopefully, we can raise someone. Let's go. Crouch down, and follow me over to the back of that building." We started, but Tina noticed that I was limping. When we got behind the other building, she said, "You're limping. How did you do that?"

"It's okay. I tried to be macho and tried to stand when I landed; I didn't do what I told you to do."

"Why don't we just go into this building and wait until morning? Maybe you can walk better then, and we can get a taxi."

"Um…We have a ship to catch!"

"Of course. Lead the way to the hotel."

The hardest part for me was the trip down the hill. Once on the street, my ankle seemed better.

"I don't think anything's broken. Maybe not even a sprain. Here, let's go right and follow the road back to the Marsam." I paused. "Ha. I sure never thought that I'd be in Egypt at age fifty-nine, limping near my grandfather's house in the middle of the night and being held up by a beautiful woman less than half my age. I feel so old!" We both laughed and said, simultaneously, "It only hurts when I laugh."

We walked on in silence. Then I tried to lighten things. "You know, I'm really upset."

"Gee, what could you possibly be upset about?"

"We missed tonight's disco party on board the *Moon Goddess*!"

Tina finally cracked a little bit of a smile.

A pause. "Well, Indiana Jones I'm not," I said.

"Huh?"

"From the first hit, I had tears in my eyes. When I crouched on the hillside, I tried not to show that I was starting to cry. And when they had us in the corner in that building, I almost—"

"Enough. You got us out of the building."

We walked on, but after five minutes, Tina said, "Hey, you said that you were a firefighter? Really?"

"Really. At age thirty-five, and at the urging of a neighbor my age, I joined a volunteer fire company. I wasn't a young kid looking for some kicks. One reason I did it was that, as an engineering graduate, I didn't serve during the Vietnam War. So I felt that being a volunteer firefighter would be a way of giving back.

"I really learned a lot in training, which was weekly. I looked forward to those Monday nights, despite my job at IBM. I was also the fire company treasurer, then, after seven years, I stopped being an active firefighter and became a board member and, eventually, board chairman. It was very rewarding."

"Did you ever get hurt?"

"Not really. I was in a few scary situations, and I got a small burn during a training session, when a hot cinder dropped on the back of my neck. That hurt, but the worst was a funny one."

"Funny?"

"I had a fire company portable pager with me at all times, except when I was at work. It went off one Sunday afternoon when I was working on paying fire company bills. It was a fire at the home of an assistant chief, Danny Rubino, who was a guy I really respected and like to this day. Anyway, I went running down the steps from upstairs and quickly slid both feet into my fire boots and pulled up the attached pants, snapping the suspenders over my shoulders."

"Really?"

"Yes, my fire coat and helmet were kept at the firehouse, but my yellow pants with, get this, red suspenders, were at the bottom of the steps in our foyer. That was so I could quickly jump into my boots and pants and bolt out the door and run to my red Ford Maverick with a flashing blue light on the roof. All this to make the quick two-minute race to the firehouse.

"Anyway, I threw open the storm door and raced out, only to find that my wedding ring got caught in part of the door handle. The door held, but I was almost pulled off my feet. It hurt like hell, but I quickly pulled my ring off. My finger swelled up, but that only lasted about week. And it was just a stove fire, with no damage, so I wasn't even needed."

We walked on, with my limp working itself out.

"Another question. What were you really trying to say when you came out of the tomb?"

"Okay, stop. Let me catch my breath." I paused. "Are you ready for this? I think I found the Ark of the Covenant!"

The Ark of the Covenant is described in the Old Testament as containing the two tablets inscribed with the Ten Commandments that Moses received from God. It was carried in advance of the Exodus of the Israelites. When King Solomon's Temple was built, the ark was placed underneath the temple in a room known as the Holy of Holies. There are many theories regarding the current location of the ark and its supposed mythical powers.

"What? Are you kidding me? Really—no, really?" questioned Tina.

"Yeah, I think so. I'm not really sure, but it reminded me of some paintings, all imaginary, of it that I've seen. But what I saw was smaller than what I would have expected; not the size depicted in *Indiana Jones*. Let me explain what really happened."

I then went on to explain everything that happened to me in the tomb. "But I'm really not sure that I saw the Ark of the Covenant. It certainly didn't have electric bolts shooting out of it. It didn't have any glow; although, when I dropped the flashlight and it shined on the object, it gave a reflection that was a golden color. And as I moved away from the shaft, the only light was from the flashlight in the shaft, and what I saw was a golden glow. But that must have been the expected reflection of a flashlight shining on something a golden color."

"Holy—"

"Ha. Yes, holy may be right. So is it Shishak's storehouse of treasures? The only marking I saw anywhere was on the wall directly across in the shaft, about a foot down. It was a hieroglyph. And it sure looked like the one of Shishak that I saw in my grandfather's book at the Chicago House."

"Wow! Wow, wow, wow! This could indeed be a discovery with more treasures in it than Tut's, as your grandfather said."

"At the Chicago House, I read that Shishak lived hundreds of years after the tombs in the Valley of the Kings and here at Dra Abu were built. So he might have planned this site to build his treasure storehouse, holding what he took from King Solomon's temple."

"You may be right." Tina paused. "I sure hope that the terrorists, or whoever they are, don't bother to go back to Dra Abu using our map. They did, however, seem more interested in the, what, the Carswell Covenant, whatever that is."

"Hopefully. While they have the map of Dra Abu we got from the Chicago House, the map only has the dot where the tomb might be, with no particular reference to the tombs of Bakenkhons and Huy. And I really do know nothing about a Carswell Covenant. Funny, though…that's my grandmother's maiden name, but I don't know. Maybe there's a college with that name."

Tina paused before we continued walking. "I think that we should keep totally quiet about this until we get back to Penn."

"I totally agree. I won't even tell my brother. But we have to make up a story about what happened tonight. Hey, why don't we make up a story that we were having an affair, since I've seen some people look at us that way. That terrorist called you my girlfriend." I had a smile on my face, but Tina couldn't see it in the darkness.

"I don't think so! That's awful—creepy even! Besides, who would believe that anyone would go to, take a taxi to, that creepy hillside? Absolutely not!"

"Okay…sorry. I was kidding. How about we say that we went there after a few too many drinks, since we never had the chance to get up close to real tombs. And that we were accosted by two men who wanted our money?"

"Sounds good to me," said Tina.

We continued to walk. The building on the hillside behind us continued to burn; the second story was fully engulfed in flame. No fire engines were evident.

"So tell me more about your fraternity days; that maybe will brighten me up."

I thought for a minute. "Well, rent the movie *Animal House* sometime. That will tell you a lot about our house. Our rec/party room in the basement had a bar, there were names on the ceiling written in the soot from candles, and someone had a stolen highway sign pointing into our chapter meeting room, where couples at parties could go for some privacy and darkness. The sign was stolen from a real town in Lancaster County,

Pennsylvania: Intercourse! For our toga party, all of our bed mattresses were taken into the chapter meeting room. The lights were out, there was a candle at the front of the room, and a keg was in the middle of the floor. The rest of the floor was covered with mattresses.

"Oh, and at one party we had a band called the Carroll Brothers, who later went on to record an album. We had two other fraternities go in with us to help pay for the band. At one point, the music and crowd were at a frenzy. All of a sudden, a couple jumped up on our mantelpiece, turned around, and mooned the crowd. At that, someone pulled them down, and the band took a break."

"Ha. Now you've made me laugh. I did see that movie, and you're right, you were like *Animal House*."

"But outside of that, we were a good fraternity. Each year, we had many brothers elected to the senior honor societies: Sphinx, Friars, and Hexagon. I was even a member of Hexagon, which was for engineers. You must know of them."

"Yes. Are we almost there?"

"We go left just ahead."

As we turned off the road and walked down the alleyway leading to the Marsam, we noticed the dome on the roof for the first time. "That's right," I said. "Didn't Helen Mears say that it used to be the Chicago House?" With only two small windows facing the street, the Marsam was totally dark. I knocked on the door. It took about three minutes of alternately knocking and waiting for the door to open. Finally, it was opened by a very tired-looking and annoyed Helen Mears. She was wearing a robe, and her hair was straggled almost like seaweed.

"What are you two doing here at this hour?" She looked at us suspiciously. "Up to no good? Then she looked at our clothes, especially Tina's. "Oh my God, girl, did he try to do something to you?"

"Good God, no! Steve and I were attacked searching for tombs at Dra Abu!"

"What? Oh my God, come on in. Let me get you something to drink, then we'll go out on the patio; it's cooler there, and you look hot. And tired."

We followed her in and sat on a wicker settee. "What can I get you?"

I looked at Tina and said, "How about two cold bottles of water, if you have it." Tina nodded in agreement.

When she returned, Helen said, "I have a suggestion. Rather than going out on the patio and having me ask a bunch of questions that are none of my business, I think you two should get some sleep. Sorry, but I only have one room left, and it only has one twin bed; it's very Spartan. Why don't you sleep there and get a good rest? Whenever you get up, I'll make breakfast, or maybe lunch. Then I'll get you a taxi."

"Well, that would be nice," offered Tina, "but our ship leaves at eleven fifteen a.m."

"Oh, okay. Hmm. How about this? You two get some sleep, I'll wake you at six fifteen, I'll have breakfast at six forty-five, and I'll have a taxi here by seven. It will be impossible to get a taxi here before that. I get up around five each day, anyway, so I'll wake you and have a taxi here by seven. Come, let me show you to your room."

Helen then noticed a glow in the distance, above and beyond the building across the alleyway. "Is that a fire up the hill? Is that why you smell of smoke?"

I responded, "Yes. We walked by it."

Helen was skeptical but kept quiet.

Tina and I each took another gulp of the cold bottled water and followed Helen up the steps. She pointed to the bathroom at the end of the hall and opened the door to our room. The room number was one, and it matched the room: one window, one nightstand, one table, one lamp, one chair, one bed. At least it looked clean.

When we were alone, I smiled and tried to make light of our situation. "This is the first time in my life that I've slept with another woman. And to think, we're both dead tired and I don't have any Viagra!"

Thankfully, Tina laughed, rather than being offended, and took another swig of her water. I gulped down the rest of mine. "Why don't you use the bathroom first?"

"Thanks," said Tina. As she left, I walked over to the window. I looked out on the patio and the farm beyond. In the distance, I could see the glow from the lights of Luxor, much dimmer at this late hour. I sighed, longing for some sleep.

Tina returned. "Your turn. I may be asleep when you return."

The shower was great, and I wanted to stay in it for hours. But I was so exhausted, I basically used it to rinse off.

When I returned, I found her asleep on the bed, which had not been turned down, with only her shoes off, on her side facing away from me. I realized that I was in a predicament. Sleep on the floor, sleep in the wicker chair? Ignoring chivalry, I took off my shoes and socks and got onto the bed in the only way possible: facing her in a spoonlike position. There was barely room, and because of my gut, I knew that I had to have my butt off the edge of the bed. But she didn't stir as I adjusted myself carefully onto the bed. I took one deep breath, let the air out, and quickly fell asleep despite all of the events of the last ten hours flying around in my mind.

• • •

I was awakened by a knock on the door. I got up, opened it, and Helen barged in. I looked at my watch. "Oh no! You let us oversleep. It's eight forty-five. We'll never make the boat."

"Relax, please. Relax," said Helen. "I called my regular, and extremely reliable, taxi driver, and he said that he couldn't make it at seven a.m., but he could be here by nine fifteen. That will give you two hours to get there. Please wake Tina up, and be down for breakfast on the patio at nine o'clock."

Helen left, and I woke Tina. "Huh?" she asked. "What time is it?"

"It's ten of nine." She quickly sat up and almost jumped out of bed. "We'll never make the boat!"

"Relax. Everything's okay. Helen's driver is coming at nine fifteen. That gives us two hours. She has a very reliable driver, but he couldn't be here until nine fifteen; I don't know why. I suggest you wash up and try to be on the patio in nine minutes for a quick breakfast. I'll use the bathroom downstairs."

It was 9:05 by the time we were both together on the patio. Before us were scrambled eggs, toast, and coffee. I addressed Helen, saying, "Thanks, but we won't have much time before the taxi gets here."

"Don't worry. You take your time, and I'll keep my eye out for him."

She returned. "My driver just called and said he will be here at nine forty-five, due to traffic and construction. So you still have plenty of time to finish."

"Okay," said Tina. "I hope we'll be all right."

The driver arrived as expected, and Tina and I said our good-byes and offered Helen money for the room and the food. She refused, but I realized she had caught us in a lie: If we had been robbed, how come we offered her money?

Perplexed, she still just said to the driver, "Please get them back by eleven. Their ship leaves at eleven fifteen." She didn't ask if we had money for the taxi.

Once underway, I nervously kept looking at my watch, especially when we encountered construction leading to the Luxor Bridge and again on the road south of Luxor.

Tina quietly asked, "What happened last night? Where did you sleep?"

I responded with a smile, "I slept in the chair. You were on your side, curled up, and taking up most of the bed."

"Oh, I'm so sorry. Did you sleep?"

"Actually I lied. I curled up next to you; we were spooning. Only I fell asleep instantly."

"Good!" And she turned away from me.

I knew that looking at my watch wouldn't make us arrive at the ship any faster, but I couldn't stop looking at it at least three times a minute.

We finally arrived at 10:50, paid the driver handsomely, and quickly walked through the entrances of three ships before we reached the *Moon Goddess*, which was now the farthest out into the Nile.

The purser was at the lobby desk and gave us a dirty look. "Let me see your passports and photo IDs."

Happy to realize that we could easily have had our wallets, money, and passports taken, we eagerly complied.

"This is highly unusual. You weren't at dinner last night, you didn't sleep in your cabins, and"—he looked at me—"your brother has been worried about you; he's in the bathroom over there. Please go get cleaned up. We expect you at lunch, and I expect that I won't have to be concerned about you again. I could have refused you entry onto the boat."

"We apologize," said Tina, glancing at me. "You won't have to even think about us again."

With that, Glenn came out of the bathroom. "Where have you been? I've been worried sick! You both look terrible!"

As we walked away from the desk, I said, "We're both okay. We've had a bad night, but all is well now. It's a long story, but we'll see you at lunch and explain. Right now, we both need to change and clean up. Really, we're okay."

"But you smell like smoke. What happened? Tell me, now!" he insisted.

"I can't, it would take too long."

• • •

The *Moon Goddess*, despite our "adventure," moved out into the Nile on time. The ship was 232 feet long, but its width of 46 feet was dictated by the Nile River locks that we would pass through on our way upstream to Aswan.

Despite desperately needing to shower and clean up, I wanted to watch our departure from Luxor. I sat on the small deck outside my room, watching the process of moving the back end out and then the front end. I watched as the ship started forward up the Nile toward Aswan. I could see the Winter Palace behind me, then another hotel, and then more ships lining the east bank of the Nile. When the *Moon Goddess* passed under the Luxor Bridge, I showered and got dressed. I then moved to the dining room, the lowest of the four decks—the windows were just inches above the waterline—for the buffet lunch.

Glenn was already seated at the table with Tina and another man when I came down the winding steps to the dining room. Unlike me, Tina had taken time to improve her appearance. She looked very attractive in her Penn Museum cotton tee and Bermudas. When I sat down, Bob Ebel introduced himself to me.

"Nice to meet you, Steve. I'm Bob Ebel. I'm a publisher from Chicago." Bob was of medium height but seemed very muscular. He had salt-and-pepper hair, a rugged complexion, and steely black eyes that seemed to see right through you. Even in a starched white shirt and black slacks, he looked very intimidating. His handshake almost crushed my hand.

"My wife took ill just before we were to leave for Egypt, but she insisted that I come anyway." He turned to Tina. "I understand from Glenn, who I had dinner with last night, that you are an archaeologist?"

"Yes, but not just yet. I hope to be able to finish my PhD thesis when I get back. I did fieldwork one summer in Honduras, but this is my first time in Egypt. I'm grateful to Glenn and Steve for making this all possible." She waved a hand of inclusion and looked directly at me. "We've had quite a time, so far!"

"You went to Chicago House last night?" asked Bob.

"Yes," said Tina. "They were really nice with us and we had a nice meal."

Bob asked, "I know that Glenn was here this morning. Where did you two go, if I may ask?"

I spoke up. I looked at Glenn and tried to look sheepish, like I was embarrassed to admit that I had done something stupid. "After dinner, Tina and I had drinks at the Winter Palace. Since it was our last night in such a wonderful place, Tina and I ended up having too much to drink.

"As we walked down the steps to return to the ship, we passed a booth that had flashlights for sale. We bought them, saying that it would be fun to tell people that we went back to Dra Abu and climbed into tombs. Then, I guess, the booze got to me. I told Tina that we really should go back to Dra Abu el Naga. We had gone there twice, where my grandfather had excavated, but each time, we were not allowed up the hill. I was mostly kidding, but Tina, to my surprise, agreed. We were both curious why there was no inspector to let us up there.

"We talked a little more, standing outside the Winter Palace, and then we both stupidly agreed to go. We easily hailed a taxi, paid him in advance to go over the bridge to Dra Abu and back. When we got there, I paid him twenty dollars to wait for us and promised him forty more when we came back down. As soon as we started up the hill, he drove away.

"At first, we thought it was funny, then we got serious. We decided to just go up the hill and use our flashlights to look into some tombs. We saw tombs that were gated and barred, and in some we could even see wall paintings. I crawled into one on my hands and knees, and Tina crawled into another. We did it so that we could tell people that we went into tombs by ourselves. We came out with our clothes pretty dirty and disheveled.

"We then wondered how we could get back. It was later than we thought, so I suggested that we walk to the Marsam Hotel. On our way there, we saw an old wooden building going up in flames." He turned to Glenn. "You know me, I just had to stay and watch until the fire engines got there. After fifteen minutes, they hadn't come, so we walked on. I guess that's why my clothes smelled like smoke.

"We got to the Marsam. Helen Mears—remember her?—let us in. She told us that we would not get a taxi that late, that she'd get one in the morning for us, and offered each of us a room. The taxi was way late in coming for us, and we were delayed by road construction in getting here. We arrived with, what, twenty minutes to spare."

Glenn spoke up. "But when you went up the—"

I cut him off. "Look, we'll talk later today." I looked at Tina. "I, at least, didn't sleep well on my bed at the Marsam Hotel. It was more like a cot. I'm dead tired." Tina nodded in agreement. "So let's discuss this later today. Let's eat, and then I'm going to take a nap."

We got up to join the line at the buffet.

●   ●   ●

After lunch, Bob Ebel excused himself and went up to the top deck. There, he moved to the rear of the cruise ship and made a call on his secure mobile phone to Mossad headquarters in Herzliya, north of Tel Aviv.

Bob Ebel was muscular, with broad shoulders. A handsome guy at forty-five years old, he maintained his fitness for his job as a Mossad agent based in the United States. He had been born Bob Weintraub in Brooklyn in 1957. His paternal grandparents had been refugees from Turkey to Palestine during World War I and had moved to New York in 1927 to live with relatives in Brooklyn. His father had been born in 1932 and married Sarah Elliott in 1954. Bob was raised in a Conservative Jewish home but drifted away from formal participation in his faith. At age twenty-four, he became passionate about the survival of the State of Israel. This was triggered by the Israeli destruction of Iran's nuclear reactor in 1981 and solidified by attacks of the Palestine Liberation Organization in 1982.

In 1982, Bob went to Israel to enlist in the Israeli army. He easily completed basic training and excelled as a soldier. Following a 1987 crackdown on Shin Bet's use of excessive force, Bob was recruited into Shin Bet, the intelligence unit of the Israeli army. A short time later, he was promoted into Yamas, the special operations unit. He was a part of the team assigned to Prime Minister Yitzhak Rabin. After Rabin's assassination in 1995, Bob was transferred to Israel's foreign intelligence service, Mossad. He was then transferred back to the United States, on call anywhere in the world. Now, his task was to find out more about the Fishers' trip and learn whether there was any proof that Moses was indeed the pharaoh Akhenaten.

After identifying himself and giving a password and two code words, he was put through to Director David Solot.

"Hi, David. It's Bob Weintraub, er, Bob Ebel."

"Hi, Bob Ebel!" Director Solot said with emphasis. "What's up? Are you, Bob Ebel, Bob Ebel, on the cruise ship?"

"Yes, and I want you to know that something is up with our friends. Steve Fisher and the girl went, rather secretly, to the Valley of the Kings last night. They had been to the same place, they call it Dra Abu, twice on their trip, but went back last night by themselves."

"What did they do? Why did they go?"

"I don't know. They claim they wanted to be able to say that they went into a tomb, but I don't believe it."

"Neither do I. Bob, you must find out what they're up to. If they're trying to uncover something that would link Moses with a pharaoh, Akhenaten, then we're in trouble. The world would be in trouble. Think of the turmoil it would cause if there was proof that Moses was actually an Egyptian pharaoh. It would be—"

"I know, a world crisis! David, look, I will find out more about this, I promise. But I will need to maneuver, get to know them better, get them to trust me."

"Good, Bob. I don't care how you get it, but find out what they're really up to. So long, Bob." Director Solot ended the call.

•   •   •

Although Tina and I were exhausted from our ordeal, we were too hungry to forego the luncheon buffet. Following our lunch with Glenn and Bob Ebel, where we were able to avoid more discussion of the night before, we each retired to our rooms. As planned, Tina and I joined Glenn on the top deck at 5:30 p.m. I had taken a long shower and then a long nap.

We had just started to tell Glenn more about our escapade when we saw Bob Ebel approaching.

"Glenn, quick, don't say anything to Bob or ask me about last night. Tina and I will tell you everything later, but I'm not sure about Bob."

"Can I join you?" Bob asked.

"Sure," I said.

"It seems there are things that you're not telling me about last night," said Bob. "Surely, you can supply more details?"

"We've told you everything," I said excitedly. "We had too much to drink, and we stupidly went to Dra Abu just to say that we crawled into a real tomb. We were really stupid to think that the taxi driver wouldn't take off with our money and leave us stranded."

"Wait a minute," said Bob. "Pardon me for asking...I'm just curious." He paused. "Glenn told me that your grandfather was an archaeologist and that he excavated, among other places, on the hillside at Dra Abu el Naga. You tried twice to see it as part of your tour. And now you tell me that you went back to Dra Abu late at night just to be able to say that you went into a tomb? There has to be more than that!"

I replied, "No, Bob! That's it. We're just tourists—"

Tina interrupted, "No, Glenn and Steve are tourists. But I'm a doctoral candidate in archaeology at the University of Pennsylvania. I'm research-ing Clarence Fisher; they're not. We're here for different purposes. Them, to follow in their grandfather's footsteps, and me, to learn if I want to concentrate on Egypt.

"I'm the one that pushed to go back to Dra Abu a second time and, last night, a third time. I'm the one who wanted to go into a tomb, and Dra Abu seemed like the only place where I could really just go up to a tomb. Our drinking last night helped us get up the courage to do this."

Thankfully, Bob was cordial at dinner that night, but we all declined his invitation to join him later at the Nubian party on the *Moon Goddess*.

CHAPTER 37

Thursday, October 31, 2002
Moon Goddess, Aswan, Egypt

On Thursday morning, the three of us met at breakfast with Bob Ebel. Late the night before, the *Moon Goddess* had docked at Edfu, which is about a third of the way to Aswan. This morning, we disembarked with Anok and took a carriage ride to the Temple of Horus at Edfu. The temple, which is nearly intact, was built in 237 BC, Anok told us. It is one of the best-preserved temples in Egypt.

But I was getting tired of seeing temples in Egypt; one seemed to blend into another. On our carriage ride back to the street, I saw a dirt alley with many merchants in booths, mostly hawking multicolor dresses and rugs hung from horizontal poles. What amazed me was that at the start of the one-block alley, there was a sign advertising an Internet café; the sign also depicted a telephone. Quite a contrast.

That afternoon, the ship continued on to Kom Ombo, where Tina Gilbert, Glenn, and Anok departed to see the temple. I stayed on board, burned out from seeing so many sites and from our "adventure." I watched as the ship maneuvered to allow another ship to dock. I had just settled down with a screwdriver in the sun on the upper deck by the pool, when Bob Ebel joined me again.

"Please tell me more about your grandfather. Did you really come all this way just to follow in his footsteps?"

I paused. "Bob...I don't mean to be rude, but yes, I came to Egypt out of curiosity about my grandfather. That's it. But my interest in anything to do with Egypt and my grandfather was over when we left Luxor. I insisted on taking this cruise just so I could relax and get some sun. I've seen enough Egypt sites; now I want to have some peace and quiet. Can't we talk again later?"

Bob agreed and left, but he appeared to be very angry. I could not understand why, but I resolved that neither Tina, Glenn, nor I would describe anything more about Clarence to him. Bob was quiet at dinner that night, before we docked in Aswan, and didn't show up that night for the galabia party, which occurred, coincidentally, on Halloween.

Friday, November 1, 2002
Moon Goddess, Aswan, Egypt

"Hands up, Fisher!"

"What the..."

"Shut up," said Bob Ebel. "And do what I say!" Chicago publisher Bob Ebel and I were alone on the top deck of the *Moon Goddess*. This was our last night on board the Nile cruise ship, and I was enjoying the beautiful night. The galabia party had ended two hours earlier. Tina and I ditched our rented galabias and stayed afterward to have drinks on board for the final time. Tina had left, quite tipsy, ten minutes ago, and I had walked unsteadily over to the side of the docked ship to look across at the west bank at Aswan, dimly lit by the thin crescent of the waning moon.

Earlier that day, Tina, Glenn, and I had gotten off the ship, which had docked in Aswan the night before, and had taken the short motorboat ride to Philae Temple. The weather continued to be hot but beautiful, and the breeze coming in my face was quite refreshing. I was able to get several beautiful pictures of the temple against a bright blue, cloudless sky. Anok told us that Philae Island was flooded by the completion of the Aswan Low Dam in 1906, and all of the structures were moved to the present location on Agilkia Island in the 1960s, when the Aswan High Dam was built.

The trip by motorboat was very relaxing, and Tina and I were happy to celebrate two entire days without any incidents. Even Bob had seemed less pesky.

But now I was in trouble again. After Tina left, I was sure that I was alone on the deck; the bar had closed, and even the bartender had cleaned up and departed. I had been standing at the railing for less than five minutes when I heard footsteps. I had turned and saw Bob Ebel approaching with a smile, or was it a smirk, on his face. Annoyed that Bob was back again, I had turned back to face the wide Nile and said, "Ahh, what a night," as Bob got closer.

Bob now pressed the gun firmly into my back, pushing me hard against the railing. I raised my hands.

"Turn around. Now move to your left, toward the back of the boat," insisted Bob. I complied. "Okay, now put your hands down, but don't make any moves."

"Bob, what's this all about? What the hell? Our last night on the cruise, and you have a gun on me? What do you want? I'm just a tourist!"

"Be quiet. I need information from you. I think you've been lying, holding back information. I believe that you're after something, some-thing on that hillside. You two can't possibly be lovers, look at you, and no one would go up there by themselves at night just to say that they were in a tomb."

"But—"

"But nothing. Talk, now!"

"But—"

"There's that 'but' again. Talk!"

"B...I don't know what you want me to talk about."

Ebel suddenly brought his gun up directly into my face. The clicking sound that I heard breaking the silence of the still night I assumed to be the gun's safety mechanism.

I decided to tell him everything that I told the terrorists three nights before. "My grandfather had a map—"

"Let me see it," interrupted Bob.

"It's in my room."

"Okay, keep talking."

"It was a map he drew while he was a college student in architecture. We noticed that he had changed the names of some streets years after he drew the map. We decoded them and found that they were locations of three tombs. Two were tombs my grandfather had excavated, and the other was unknown. We were able to figure out from the map where the third tomb might be. That's what we went to look for."

"Okay. See how easy this is? Keep going."

"Well, I crawled in and went through multiple turns. As I got further in, I found a shaft. I tried to lean down to see if I could see anything with my flashlight. I was so excited that maybe I had found great treasure that I almost fell into the shaft. To save myself, I accidentally dropped the flashlight. It broke and I panicked; I'm claustrophobic."

"So what did you find?"

"Maybe a new tomb. But it had no markings on it. The shaft went about fifteen feet down, but from the top, I only saw an opening. I tried to shine the flashlight into the opening, but I dropped it."

"Then what?"

"When I finally came back out, I saw that Tina was being held by two terrorists. They said they were police, but of course they weren't. They took us down to a wooden building, punched me, and almost raped Tina. It was awful."

"What were they after?"

"They said that they weren't after any treasure; they were after something called the Carswell Covenant."

"The what?"

"That's what I said. I know nothing about any Carswell Covenant. I did tell them what happened at lunch back in Cairo."

"What's that?"

"An archaeologist mentioned a rumor among her students that someone at a college in the States found a reference that said that a pharaoh named Shishak had stated that Moses had received only a one-hundred-year covenant, or lease, to the Holy Land. Shishak conquered Jerusalem and maybe stored the treasures somewhere. I would love to find the treasures, but the terrorists only wanted proof that there was a covenant.

"After hurting us and scaring us to death, they must have realized by the frightened look on our faces that we knew nothing. It was probably the same look that I have now; I'm scared to death and have no more information. Anyway, it seemed that they were going to let us go, when all of a sudden, one of them threw a Molotov cocktail in on us. But we were able to escape; that's why you smelled smoke on us."

"Fisher, I don't care about the treasure."

"What? Neither you, whoever you really are, nor the terrorists care about the possibility of treasure? Do you care about this Carswell Covenant?"

"No. I don't know what that is. I care about what you are hiding from me!"

My mouth dropped open, and I began shaking from an adrenaline rush. "I'm not hiding anything from you. I've told you everything that I know!"

"Steve, Steve...I know all about your grandfather. A spy. Anti-Zionist. Pro-Arab. Advisor to the British for Palestinian affairs. An enemy of today's Israel."

"Are you with the Mossad?"

Bob ignored me. "I believe that your grandfather found proof that Moses was actually the pharaoh Akhenaten. That proof would tear the world apart. All Arabs—yes, all—would come together to push Jews out of their rightful place. Do you hear me, Fisher? You have information that could destroy Israel. We have information that in 1940 your grandfather, while drunk, bragged that he had a document that said Moses was actually Pharaoh Akhenaten."

I couldn't believe it. They, whoever they were, somehow knew that Clarence Fisher was my grandfather and that I was coming to Egypt.

Bob kept on interrogating me, "I need to get that proof from you, even if I have to shoot you in the kneecap!" He lowered his Glock and aimed at my knee.

"But I have no information about Moses being Akhenaten. Really! Honest! You've got to believe me! I'm just a fat, old guy trying to find out more about my grandfather, who died before I was born. Yes, we went to Amarna because my brother, Glenn, the minister, was interested. And so was Tina. I had no interest there or about Akhenaten. As far as I know, my grandfather was never in Amarna; he certainly didn't dig there. Please..." My voice was quivering, and I started to shake.

"I mean it, Fisher! Tell me the truth. What did your grandfather—"

I suddenly looked over Bob's right shoulder and yelled, "Glenn, get help!"

CHAPTER 38

Saturday, November 2, 2002
Moon Goddess, Aswan, Egypt

With his gun still down, pointed at my knee, Bob turned to his left to look for Glenn, and I instantly pushed his chest with my right hand, turned left, and dove over the railing. My knees hit the railing, causing me to flip over. Instinctively, I tucked in my knees to further complete the somersault. I heard a gunshot and a splash in the water. After flipping, I looked for the water and entered it not in a dive but in a piked "poof" position so that I wouldn't go deep. I had no idea how deep the water was, so I bent at my waist and entered the water with a big splash.

Worried that more bullets would follow at any second, I swam downward but found that the water was only about eight feet deep. Using my breaststroke skills from my competition as a teenager, I quickly turned left and swam away from shore, hoping that Ebel would think that I would head to shore. I heard the swoosh of something heavy hitting the water a few feet behind me; it may have been Ebel.

Despite my knees occasionally hitting the rocky bottom, I swam until I could no longer fight my screaming lungs, almost thirty seconds. I surfaced, not looking back, just enough to catch a deep breath, dove down again, and continued out into the Nile. I surfaced again and took a deep breath and, as I submerged again, had a quick vision of a newspaper headline: Former Swim Champ Drowns in Nile River!

My next thoughts were about crocodiles. Was I going to encounter one in the Nile? Was I going to encounter one as I approached land? Or on land? I didn't know at the time that Nile crocodiles, one of the most aggressive of crocodile species, were only found south of the two Aswan dams. I was safe, but I didn't know it.

I surfaced again. This time, I paused to look around, catching my breath. No sign of Ebel. Was he underwater? Had he swum after me? Had he given up and swum to shore? Or, could he have dived straight in and hit the rocky bottom, which could have broken his neck?

The *Moon Goddess* was well behind me, as the current had carried me at least a half mile downstream, toward Luxor and Cairo. Treading water, which was extremely easy for me, I kicked off my sneakers, which were weighing me down, and considered my next move. I struck out for shore using freestyle. In college, I competed in the 440-yard freestyle event, so I knew that I could eventually reach shore.

I tried to keep on a straight course for land, but the current kept pushing me downstream and away from shore. The *Moon Goddess* had docked near the Helnan Aswan Hotel, and just downstream, the land jutted out into the Nile. Unfortunately, the current pushed me too far out to reach it. I kept swimming.

After swimming for almost a half hour, I exhaustedly reached shore about one hundred yards before three darkened cruise ships that were docked next to each other. I wanted to collapse on the shore, but I was still concerned with the possibility of encountering crocodiles. I staggered up to the road that I hoped would lead me south and back to the *Moon Goddess*. I sat down to rest, thinking about my swim in the Nile, which had to be severely polluted.

After five minutes, I checked the time and temperature on my waterproof Casio watch. The temperature was seventy-six, and I was happy that the Nile had seemed warm. The time was now 2:30 a.m., and I had no idea how long it would take to get back to the boat. I started walking.

As I walked, my tired mind thought back to the incident, and I laughed out loud. "I don't believe he fell for that old TV trick. I remembered that from a cowboy movie I saw in grade school. Ha!" I was referring to the trick that diverted attention by calling to someone who wasn't there. I always thought that that worked only in movies. It was a split-second decision to try it, and I luckily got away with it.

I also wondered why I only heard one bullet; maybe Bob Ebel only intended to scare me with the gun. Or maybe I couldn't hear more bullets since I was underwater. Or was the splash I heard Bob Ebel diving in? I also worried about what would happen when I got back on board the ship. Would Bob still be after me, threaten me again? Or was the fear on my face enough to convince Ebel that I knew nothing about Moses being Akhenaten?

But maybe I did. I suddenly remembered my grandfather's map. In our race to find the possible treasure tombs, Tina and I had glossed over the intersection of the two streets that we decoded as Akhenaten and Moses. Maybe that was Clarence's way of signaling that Moses was, based on what he may have found, the pharaoh Akhenaten.

"Oh well!" I said aloud.

Five minutes later, as I shakily walked barefooted, I thought, "I don't believe I did a poof!" That brought up pleasant memories of aquacades and water shows from my youth. As long as I could remember, I'd longed to be in the summertime events. And at age thirteen, I was old enough and good enough to be a participant. These shows were popular at swim clubs, pools, and country clubs during the '50s and '60s. These typically included synchronized swimming, swimming demonstrations, and fancy diving. But the water shows always concluded with a clown diving act put on by the divers. Dressed in crazy clown outfits, the divers came running out and went off the diving boards with a variety of crazy stunts, usually ending in a belly flop. The idea was to get the audience to go "Ooh" or "Ouch" to the impending pain-inflicting belly flop. But divers had a way of avoiding the pain of landing on their bellies: they often finished their entry into the water by doing a poof. They would approach the water totally flat, but then, at the last second, they would pike, or bend at the waist, in order to prevent the pain of landing flat. I had done a poof in order to avoid smashing into the bottom of the Nile, in case it was shallow. It was a good thing that I did this, because I later found out that the draft of the *Moon Goddess* was only about five feet, and the water was just three feet deeper than the ship's keel.

"Ha! Al Walton!" I exclaimed as I continued staggering along on the Al Khatar Aswan, which had now turned into Corniche el Nile. When I was a summertime lifeguard in college, Al Walton and I had been brought in as the clown divers at the Men's US National Swimming and Diving Championships, held at Philadelphia's Kelly Pool. While I had done some easy, nonhurting clown dives, like the mother-in-law dive (riding a broom into the water yelling "the old witch"), Al Walton did tricks never seen before.

On one dive, Al pretended, in his clown costume, to be cleaning the top of the diving board with a broom. When he reached the end of the board over the water, he put down the broom, lay on the board, bent at the waist over the end of the board, flipped over, and hung by his hands. He then lifted his feet and hung by his toes. While hanging, he grabbed the broom and began sweeping the bottom of the board.

On another, he went out to the end of the board and turned around. But instead of standing at the end of the board like an Olympic diver doing a backward dive, he made another quarter turn, so that he was at the end but standing on the side of the board. He lifted his arms and stood like a real Olympic diver. He then bounced up into a swan dive position, but he was over the diving board. He landed on his chest on the board, which then flipped him back in the air, forcing his legs harshly up under the board. His shins hit the edge of the board, and he then did a perfect back flop. At the time, I laughed so hard that I almost couldn't continue. Afterward, Lou Vitucci, who two years later dove in the 1964 Tokyo Olympics, praised us as the best clown divers he had ever seen.

"Ha," I said, trying to continue my walk to the ship in my now sore bare feet. "My highest diving praise ever!"

I had to keep thinking of nice things as I trudged on in the darkness on a road with no traffic. I thought back to the summer before my senior year of high school, when I dated a girl named Nancy. She taught me a valuable lesson, and it was comforting to think of it now.

She insisted that people are funny and they do funny things. She said never be afraid to do something that may be funny or be afraid to laugh at something you've done.

I then reflected on the story I told her at her father's funeral. Two years before, I was assigned to do the opening for the last class that I was teaching at IBM. All of my peer instructors were in attendance as I began very animatedly going through some introductory board work. I covered a major part of the whiteboard with multiple colors of dry-erase markers. As I confidently and proudly finished the introduction, I picked up a paper towel and squirt bottle to erase the board.

I turned back to the board and used the squirt bottle. Suddenly, I realized something was wrong. My face was wet and stinging; I had held the bottle the wrong way when I squirted!

Fearing that I had a face full of acetone solution, I went running to the restroom, to the laughter of all the students. My peers gave the loudest laughs, and they kept it up even when I returned.

Yes, I've played that over many times in my mind. The experienced instructor making a fool of himself! However, it always somehow had a comforting effect on me.

It was thoughts like this that kept me going. I was scared, I was getting cold, and my feet were getting bloody. And my head was hammered by a headache from my hangover. But now I had new energy to continue. And I had to keep one thing in mind. We had to disembark from the ship by 11:15 a.m.

Finally, up ahead I saw the Chicago House on the left and, after what seemed like an eternity, I reached the *Moon Goddess*. I had correctly guessed that there would be a guard at the entrance to the boat. I also knew that I had only a wet driver's license; my passport was back in my room. So I took out a wet twenty-dollar bill.

As I walked across the gangplank, the guard stopped me and demanded my passport. I showed him my US picture driver's license and tried to explain that I had been drunk after the galabia party and had fallen overboard. I offered him the twenty-dollar bill and said, "I know I had too much to drink, but I'm sorry; I need to get on board." The guard let me pass, seemingly pleased with his twenty dollars' baksheesh.

However, I next ran into the same purser as two days before. "Ah, Mr. Fisher. I see that you have had more trouble. You have been a very troublesome passenger. Please explain."

"Bob Ebel and I got drunk last night, and I fell overboard. I was lucky to live; I got carried far downstream. Now I need a shower. Oh, by the way, have you seen Bob Ebel since late last night?"

"I haven't seen him, and he hasn't come down for breakfast. He's probably still in his room after his episode with you, Mr. Fisher. Please understand me. You have been an embarrassment to our fine ship. You will never be welcomed aboard this ship again. Never. I'm glad that this is checkout day. I will be glad to see you leave. Now go!"

I returned to my room and took a long, hot shower and dried off. Then I took another shower. I hoped that I had gotten everything from the disgusting Nile off of me.

CHAPTER 39

Tuesday, November 5, 2002
UPenn Museum, Philadelphia, 6:15 p.m.

Tina Gilbert and I were nervously seated in the beautifully paneled office of the director of the UPenn Museum, E. Wells Newsome, PhD. His office was on the first floor of the original building, which was built in 1889.

A few feet in front of Dr. Newsome's ancient and beautiful rolltop desk, which was cluttered with books and papers, was an irregularly shaped but mostly oval conference table. The table was a solid piece, probably cut in the early 1900s from a large redwood tree. The table was set such that Dr. Newsome could turn from his desk, roll several feet in his chair, and be at the head of the conference table. I looked at the table and then at the office door. There was no way, I surmised, that the table top could have come in through the current doorway; the office configuration had to have been built around the table.

Joining Tina and me around the conference table were David Carpenter, PhD, Egyptian Section curator; Timothy Barnes, PhD, associate curator/field director and Tina's fiancé; and Eric Tobin, museum archivist. Dr. Newsome's executive secretary, Bill Marshman, had let us into the office and mentioned that Dr. Newsome was running late. All were silent following introductions and a few pleasantries. Once again, I mentally practiced what I would say to the group. Then I reflected on how we had come to this point so quickly.

On the return flight from Egypt, Tina and I had decided to keep our adventures a secret. I would only tell my wife, Linda, and Tina would only tell her fiancé, Timothy Barnes. We had agreed that Timothy was the key to taking the next step: discussing my find with Penn Museum management to persuade them to fund an expedition to Dra Abu el Naga.

Dr. Newsome arrived fifteen minutes late. He was of medium height, with a high forehead, thinning dark hair combed back, and a full, dark mustache. With his wire-framed glasses, dark brown suit, button-down collar, and light tie, he reminded me of a photograph of my grandfather. He shook hands with me and said to the group, "Okay. This meeting was mysteriously called to discuss what? Dr. Carpenter?"

"I'm as in the dark as you are. Dr. Barnes pleaded with me to arrange this meeting, and I trusted his judgment. He only told me that it was about an important find in Egypt. The find was apparently made by Tina Gilbert and Mr. Fisher on their trip to Egypt; they arrived back on Sunday."

"So what is this important find? Let's not waste time here. I'm sure we'd all like to go home."

"Dr. Newsome," said Timothy Barnes, "I suggest that we let Mr. Fisher take over. He's well versed in this, and, as you probably know, his grandfather excavated the columns in the Lower Egyptian Hall, and more than half of the objects in our Egyptian collection were excavated by him."

"Okay, go ahead. But please be brief."

"Thank you, Dr. Newsome, and I appreciate all of you arranging this meeting so quickly."

I paused, looking at Tina, who returned a small smile. "Before I reveal the find, Ms. Gilbert and I agreed that I should describe my background to try to give you some comfort that I'm not a complete nut."

Dr. Carpenter laughed. "What? Did you find the Ark of the Covenant?" Only Dr. Newsome and archivist Eric Tobin joined him in laughing. I ignored the comment.

"Again, my name is Steve Fisher, and I am the grandson of Clarence Fisher. I assume you all have some familiarity with him, if only from the columns in the Lower Egyptian room. I graduated with a BSEE degree from the Moore School of Electrical Engineering here at Penn in 1964. My brother, Rev. Dr. Glenn J. Fisher, graduated with honors from the college in 1958, and his daughter also graduated from Penn. Our father attended Penn as well, although he did not graduate. Immediately upon graduating, I joined IBM in Philadelphia, where I worked with the major Philadelphia banks. During my twenty-seven years with IBM, I taught computer science at Saint Joseph's Evening College for six years and taught full time for IBM for another six years. I took an early retirement package from IBM in 1991, and I've worked since then for a company that makes lending software for the largest banks. I have two children and three grandchildren, with another on the way. Please believe me; I am not a nut."

Before continuing, I first made eye contact with Dr. Newsome, then looked at Dr. Carpenter, who was looking down, and then made eye contact with Tina, who smiled and nodded.

"Yes, Dr. Carpenter..." I looked directly at him and waited. When Dr. Carpenter looked up, I said, "Yes, Dr. Carpenter, I found the Ark of the Covenant and at least one tablet in a storehouse of Pharaoh Shishak I at Dra Abu el Naga."

I paused for effect. Tina and her fiancé, Dr. Barnes, looked at each other with broad smiles on their faces. Dr. Carpenter had a very surprised look on his face, but Dr. Newsome frowned. "That's preposterous!" Dr. Newsome exclaimed. He turned to Dr. Carpenter. "Why are you wasting my time with this nonsense?"

"Please hear him out," said Dr. Barnes. "I know the whole story, and I firmly believe it's true."

"Okay. Go on. Go on."

"Thank you. I'll give the short story. My brother, Glenn, and I decided to go on a sixteen-day trip to Egypt, hopefully following in Clarence Fisher's footsteps; we returned two days ago. Ms. Gilbert accompanied us—at our expense, not the university's. We took with us a map that my grandfather had coded, and we were able to solve the clues he left. They pointed to two known tombs that he had excavated at Dra Abu: those of Bakenkhons and Huy. We were able to pinpoint those two tombs using a map from the Chicago House and photos we had taken of Dra Abu. At the Chicago House, I quickly skimmed through Clarence Fisher's book *The Excavation of Armageddon*. After leaving Penn in 1925 for the University of Chicago, Dr. Fisher excavated a stele of Pharaoh Shishak I, or Shoshenq, at Megiddo. I discovered that the stele contained Shishak's cartouche and that it matched the engraved scarab in a ring we had from Clarence. At that point, I made the connection on the map: Clarence had changed two street names on his map to First Avenue and Stack Street. I solved the puzzle; Stack Street meant Shishak, and First Avenue meant one—Shishak I!

"We then compared the positions of three points on Fisher's map, tombs of Bakenkhons, Huy, and Shishak, to the map of the tombs given us by Chicago House. This put Shishak's tomb over the hill, near a path leading to the top of the hill.

"Tina and I then agreed"—I paused to look at Tina, who nodded— "that we had discovered the location of Shishak's tomb, one that's never been located. By triangulation, it was on the other side of the hill at Dra Abu el Naga, probably beyond Fisher's concession. At that point, Tina suggested that we pass all of this information on to Penn, as I'm doing now. We walked back to our Nile cruise boat, which was leaving the next day, and Tina returned to her cabin.

"However, I decided to leave the boat and go across the street to the bar at the Winter Palace for a nightcap. After several drinks, I crazily decided to hire a cab to go to Dra Abu to see if I could find anything. I located the tombs of Bakenkhons and Huy and then went up to the top of the hill where the path began. Only it wasn't a path; it was a gully formed by the increased rains that possibly followed the building of the Aswan High Dam. The gully went down the other side. I followed it down and saw rocks that seemed to be washed against a small entrance. I cleared the rocks and crawled through that small opening, only to find what was definitely a tomb.

"So yes, I believed that I had found the tomb of Shishak I. Now think of this…Here's what the Bible says of Shishak—I've memorized it: 'So Shishak king of Egypt came up against Jerusalem, and took away the treasures of the house of the Lord, and the treasures of the king's house; he took all: he carried away also the shields of gold which Solomon had made.' That's from 2 Chronicles 12:9. So finding the tomb of Shishak would probably be really important.

"Fool that I am…" I paused and looked again at Tina. "I went further into the tomb. I had to crouch in the passageway, which was very rough cut and undecorated. The passageway descended and took several turns, finally reaching a shaft about six by eight feet wide. I did not immediately approach the opening. Instead, I shined my flashlight around the walls surrounding the opening. Like the rest of the passageway, there were no decorations. Nothing. Except opposite the opening. There was only one marking, a scratching of the cartouche of Shishak I that matched my ring. I was now convinced that I had found the tomb of Shishak I, but I wondered why there were no markings as in other tombs.

"I carefully approached the shaft. It appeared to be about fifteen feet deep. As I pointed the flashlight down at the shaft, I could see that there was a horizontal shaft leading away from the opening. And I saw gold!

"I then got on my belly, leaned over as far as I safely could, and tried to look into the new shaft. I could only see the bottom of the opening, but what I saw made my heart leap! The end of a golden chest! I could see that there were decorations in the gold, and I saw the beginnings of what could be some sort of statue on top. Next to it was a medallion of some sort, and just beyond that was the bottom of a stone tablet that seemed to be laid on its side.

"I couldn't believe my eyes! I then tried to look in further, and I almost lost my balance. In trying to keep from falling in, I somehow dropped my flashlight. There was nothing more I could do, so I found my way back to the surface in complete darkness, a darkness like I had never seen before. Luckily, my cabbie was still there, and I returned safely to our Nile cruise boat.

"I know there must be questions…"

"I still say this is ridiculous," said Dr. Newsome. "You want me to fund a new expedition based on this crazy story? Dr. Carpenter?"

"I'm as skeptical as you are. But I've always trusted in Dr. Barnes. Timothy, what are your thoughts?"

"I agree that it sounds crazy, but I'm sure you're all aware that Tina is my fiancée. She's told me this in depth, and I believe her."

"But this is the word of one person. His being the grandson of Clarence Fisher does not lend him any credibility in my eyes," said Dr. Newsome.

"In fact, I suggest we end this meeting, go home, and have a stiff glass of reality. I—"

"Let me speak," Tina interrupted. "You must believe Mr. Fisher. He's trying to protect me and my professional reputation. Go ahead, Timothy, describe what really happened."

Dr. Barnes began but decided to not tell the part about the terrorists. "Tina actually was there. She had a drink with Mr. Fisher, rode in the taxi with him. She accompanied him up the hill, followed the gully, found the rocks, and helped Mr. Fisher move the rocks until they found an opening.

"She argued that they should return and refused to go into the tomb, which we now believe was not a tomb but rather a storehouse for Shishak's treasures. She—"

"I was there when Mr. Fisher went into the opening and when he crawled out," Tina interrupted. "I saw his face, his body, when he emerged without his flashlight. He was shaken, trembling, excited, smiling, happy, all at once. He told me what happened and what he found. I totally believe him. He has made the find of the century! Please believe him… believe me…believe Timothy! And please don't hold my bad choice to accompany Mr. Fisher against me in my doctoral quest. Thank you."

I quickly added, "Ms. Gilbert is telling the truth. I wanted to protect her. She was there, but she did not enter the storehouse."

Tina added, "I've done a lot of thinking about this, and I had a chance yesterday to do more research on Shishak. On why there's no indication that he went into Jerusalem. On why he would build a storehouse at Dra Abu el Naga. On why the treasures would be so visible. I think that I have answers, so please hear me out.

"The Bible mentions Shishak, who is thought to be the pharaoh Shosheng I, looting the temple, but there is no archaeological mention of this. I believe that Shishak believed that his treasures were so important that he wanted to leave no record of his being in Jerusalem.

"Also, there is a tomb DB320, at Deir el-Bahri, that contains the mummies of eleven pharaohs and at least thirty-nine other royals and officials. These mummies range from the Seventeenth to the Twenty-First Dynasties. During the reigns of Shishak I and his predecessor, Psusennes II, the bodies of the pharaohs were moved from their original tombs to a common tomb at Deir el-Bahri. In this time, the mummies from former dynasties were vulnerable to grave robbery and were moved there to protect the mummies of these royal personages.

"Shishak's tomb has not been found, but some believe that it may be in Tanis. Or it could be at Dra Abu. Maybe we didn't find Shishak's storehouse; maybe we found his tomb. It may be possible that there are more rooms at this site, either off the treasure room or off the passageway Mr. Fisher was in.

"Finally, why were these treasures so easily found? These treasures, possibly the Ark of the Covenant and the tablets of Moses, would surely be well hidden. But if this was the tomb of Shishak, then maybe these treasures, which really meant nothing to Shishak, were meant to satisfy any robbers so that Shishak's tomb would remain intact."

With that I exclaimed, "Wow! That's a lot to think about. Ms. Gilbert did not tell me her findings. Perhaps Dr. Barnes can discuss this further with you all. Ms. Gilbert and I can leave the room." I thought it best to remove myself from the room at that point, and I wanted to take Tina with me to take any pressure off the PhDs in the room.

"Good idea," said Dr. Newsome.

With that, Tina and I exited, walked through Mr. Marshman's office, and sat on a wooden bench in the hallway. We discussed the meeting and tried to guess the outcome. Then, Tina changed the subject. "You know, I've been doing a lot of thinking about what both the terrorists and Bob Ebel were looking for. Bob Ebel was looking for proof that Moses was actually the pharaoh Akhenaten, while the terrorists were looking for proof about Moses and a one-hundred-year lease.

"If Moses was actually a pharaoh, why would he give a one-hundred-year covenant to himself? There seems to be only one way that Akhenaten became Moses: another pharaoh set Akhenaten-Moses and the other Israelites free. That one way is that all three of these points have to be true:

"One. Moses really was Pharaoh Akhenaten. We found that Freud was the first to suggest this, in 1939, but there's never been any proof of it, and most biblical scholars dismiss it. Could it be that the name of the pharaoh is not in the Bible because Moses didn't want to name himself?

"Two. Pharaoh Akhenaten was removed in a coup, possibly by priests and led by a soldier named Ay. Akhenaten had moved the government to

Amarna, the place we unfortunately visited, and tried to force a religion of one god, Aten, on the people.

"Three. The body in Akhenaten's tomb is not Akhenaten. If there was a coup, and Akhenaten became Moses, then maybe someone else was buried so that people would think that Akhenaten had died and not led the Israelites from Egypt.

"If all these were true, which I think I doubt, then the pharaoh of the Exodus could be his little-known successor, Smenkhkare. And there could have been a covenant granting the land for one hundred years."

"Let me understand what you're saying," I said. "Pharaoh Akhenaten was removed in a coup, he became associated with the Jews, changed his name to Moses, and was granted a one-hundred-year lease by the pharaoh who succeeded him, Smenkhkare. Oh, and another man is in Akhenaten's tomb. Is that right?"

"I don't know if it's right or true. But it seems to me to be the only way that both the terrorists and Bob Ebel would have reason to come after us. This whole thing is scary. We need to keep this quiet. Treasure, yes; Akhenaten-Moses, no; one-hundred-year covenant, no."

With that, the office door opened, and Bill Marshman showed us both back into Dr. Newsome's office. We took our seats. Dr. Newsome was at his rolltop desk, making some notes, it appeared. He rolled over to the table, turned, rose, and greeted us.

"Well, it looks like there may be some merit to what you've said. Have a seat."

Tina sat next to Dr. Barnes, and I sat next to her.

"Here's what I'll do: I'll contact the board and call an emergency meeting to discuss possible ways to fund such an expedition. Dr. Carpenter and Dr. Barnes, and of course Ms. Gilbert"—he paused and looked at Tina—"will work together to come up with a projected cost of such an expedition. Dr. Carpenter will contact Zahi Hawass to see if he and the Egyptian government could back us for such an expedition."

He looked at Dr. Carpenter. "David, be careful with Zahi. Tell him what he needs to hear so that he'll back us for a concession. But don't tell him too much, or he'll want to take it all for himself!"

He turned and looked directly at me. "And Mr. Fisher. Thank you for your passion about your grandfather and your courage in entering that tomb, er, storehouse, as you call it. But do not, I repeat, do not tell anyone about your find or about this meeting!"

He turned now to the group and, with a sweep of his hand, said, "In fact, this goes for all of us. We must keep this all quiet. All of us!"

He turned to Tina and then back to me. "Ms. Gilbert and Mr. Fisher, I thank you for your crazy but hopefully very productive trip. You may indeed have made the find of the century."

He looked at Dr. Carpenter. "David, I expect a report on the cost of this expedition on Friday. And an update on Zahi. I expect that such an expedition would include Ms. Gilbert. And Mr. Fisher could be there for at least part of it.

"Thank you all. And again, I cannot overstress the need for secrecy and security. It seems to me that we should move quickly on this. Others, such as your cabbie, may be wondering what you were doing over the hill. Hopefully," he said, smiling for the first time, "he'll have thought that it was a strange place for a lovers' tryst!"

He looked first at me, and I raised both hands, palms up, in surprise, shaking my head. He then looked at Tina, who grabbed Timothy's hand, violently shaking her head in disgust. "Okay, let's end the meeting on that. I meant no offense. I wish us all good luck. Thanks."

After we got into the hallway, Tina said, "I don't believe he said that. A very important meeting, and he ended it by making a remark like that?"

David said, "I know Wells pretty well. He likes to end meetings on a humorous note. But he went overboard on this one. Please, just try to ignore it. And think about what was accomplished tonight. We may indeed get funding to find the Ark of the Covenant!"

I said, "Now that's how he should have ended the meeting! Oh, and one more thing," I said to Tina as I turned to leave. "I've been thinking about this for the last two days. After we went through customs in New York, I thought I saw a man outside customs who made me think of Bob Ebel. Could he have flown back ahead of us?"

Tina's mouth dropped, but I continued, "He had blond hair and wore horn-rimmed glasses, but his eyebrows were black. But maybe it wasn't him."

CHAPTER 40

Friday, November 8, 2002
Upper NetherCrest High School 40th
reunion

"Hi, Steve. Remember me?"

"Of course, Brenda. I've known you since grade school, but I don't think you've come to any of your high school class reunions."

Five hectic days after I returned from my trip—days that were busy with work and deadened by jet lag—Linda and I were at her fortieth high school reunion, which was held at the Desmond Hotel. My fortieth Upper NetherCrest High reunion had been held two years earlier.

The room was nicely decorated with purple and gold streamers, our school colors. Each table had either a purple or gold flower arrangement. Linda had organized the whole thing, and I assisted by setting up a computer so that she could enter returned questionnaires. Linda's class had almost seven hundred students, and she had contacted almost all of them, so it was a huge effort. I had then used my computer to prepare a file for printing and binding into a reunion booklet.

"No, this is our first. And this is my husband, Mark Hamilton."

"Nice to meet you, Mark, and this is my wife, Linda. I've followed your career, Mark, since Brenda has responded to Linda's reunion questionnaires every ten years. You've been a Baptist minister, a Georgia state senator from Jefferson County, and you're now the head of Carswell Bible College."

"Wow," interrupted Mark. "How do you know so much?"

"Well, based on responses to this year's questionnaires. I've worked with Linda to put together the booklets for each reunion, both mine and hers. So I really know something about many of the attendees. But you're special."

Mark looked at me quizzically. "What do you mean? Brenda knows I'm special," he said and turned to her with a smile. "But how about you?"

"There are two coincidences, one interesting and the other pretty big. The first is that my brother, Glenn, retired three years ago as a Methodist minister. He taught Brenda in Sunday school, and I thought maybe she had mentioned something about Glenn to you."

"Yes, I think she did, but I'd forgotten that."

"The big coincidence is that my great-grandfather, I found out just yesterday, was the Egenardus Ruthven Carswell who founded Carswell Bible College."

"Wow! Then you know my boss, Julia Carswell?"

"No, no. My grandmother's brother was ER III, who I think ran the college at one time. He was my father's uncle. I met him once when I was little; he was called Uncle Root, I guess for Ruthven."

"Yes, I'm the president of the college, but for big things, I report to Julia. I understand that she's the fourth generation of Carswells. Do you know much about the school?"

"No. I know a little about the founder, my grandmother's father. I know that he was a minister, and that he founded Carswell College, but it looks like he was a kind of an entrepreneur. My father said that he did other things, including starting a school for stutterers and stammerers. My grandmother taught there; that's where she met my grandfather, archae-ologist Clarence Fisher."

"Your grandfather was an archaeologist? Where?"

"He started in Egypt and then went to Palestine, er, Israel, to do bib-lical archaeology. He excavated Megiddo, you know, Armageddon. He lived in Jerusalem, pretty much abandoning my grandmother and father. He died in Jerusalem before I was born."

"Brenda will tell you that I'm really interested in archaeology—"

I interrupted him. "Well, just quick…My brother and I just got back this past Sunday afternoon from a sixteen-day Egypt trip. It was fascinating, to say the least. Thanks to Zahi Hawass, who you may have seen on TV, we were able to follow in Clarence's footsteps and also see sites normally closed to tourists. One site was very interesting. At Memphis, we looked down at some water that had a cutoff column in it, about five feet in diameter. The remaining columns were excavated by my grandfather, and you can see them at the Penn Museum. They were part of Pharaoh Mereneptah's palace, where my grandfather believed—it made headlines all over the world—that Moses pleaded with Pharaoh to 'let my people go.'

"But let me ask you something. While in Egypt, I heard rumors of a Carswell—"

"Wait, let me speak," Mark interrupted. His body seemed to tense, and he leaned over. He started to continue but then paused for an almost embarrassing period of time. He looked into Linda's eyes and then in mine. He paused again before finally saying, "Suppose, just suppose now, just suppose…" He paused again. I leaned in to hear him as Mark began to whisper, "Suppose, suppose now, suppose that Pharaoh gave Moses, just suppose, a one-hundred-year lease, a one-hundred-year covenant to the Holy Land. Just suppose." He looked at me.

I was shocked but tried to remain calm. I wanted to say something about the Carswell Covenant, but I thought of my vow to remain silent regarding the two controversies that caused us so much trouble on our trip. I then said, "Well, if that was true, it would certainly upset the world situation. Let's hope it's not true. In fact, I abso—"

I was cut off by another classmate who interrupted to have me quickly go over to the DJ's table. I shouted back to Mark, "Let's talk some more!" Linda and I went to the DJ table and met other classmates after that. By the time I was able to look again for Mark and Brenda, they had left.

I never talked to Mark again.

PART FIVE

2003

CHAPTER 41

Saturday, August 30, 2003
Ocean City, New Jersey

"Hey, Frank, I'm home!" I yelled.

Once again I was starting my vacation at the O'Connors' in Ocean City. It seemed that the year had passed by so quickly, but the past twelve months had been the strangest ever for me.

As I drove north on US Route 202, I couldn't help but think about my, ha, "fun-filled" Egypt trip. I tried to think of the beautiful and wonderful parts. The view of the Great Pyramid from my hotel room, inside the King's Chamber of that pyramid, walking between the paws of the Sphinx—yes, Zahi Hawass had given us access to that—inside the beautiful tomb of Seti I, the joy of finally being home; these flashed in my mind, but not long enough.

Soon, I was reflecting on the scary parts. Our van hitting the girl, the shot, and the truck careening into our lane, the terrorists and the fire at Dra Abu, Bob Ebel pulling a gun and shooting at me; I dwelled way too long on these.

But then, as usual, my thoughts turned to the open questions. Why were the terrorists after me? The Mossad? Was there really an attempt on us while we were returning from our trip to Amarna? Did my grandfather know anything about Moses being the pharaoh Akhenaten? Was Moses really a pharaoh? What is the Carswell Covenant? Was Moses really given a lease? I felt that I would never have answers to these questions.

My thoughts then turned to the University of Pennsylvania. Would they ever get funding and a commission to excavate what I believed to be Shishak's treasure, including the Ark of the Covenant? Or would terrorists, the Mossad, or even Zahi Hawass get there first? Would Tina Gilbert, now Dr. Tina Gilbert Barnes, lead an expedition? Would I be invited to go along? Why would I want to?

As I finally turned onto the Garden State Parkway, my thoughts turned to my hopefully relaxing week ahead and to Ocean City itself. I thought about how different Ocean City was from other beach towns; it was a dry town. Founded as a retreat for Methodist ministers in 1879, Ocean City has maintained its ban on bars and alcoholic drinks served at restaurants through multiple referenda. Accordingly, it has won accolades as one of the best family vacation spots in America. Of course, private drinking is allowed, and bars and takeout stores are only a mile over a bridge at Thirty-Fourth Street or 2.1 miles over the Ninth Street Bridge to Somers Point.

As I exited the Garden State Parkway, I smiled, thinking about Somers Point, on the mainland across from Ocean City, and its drinking spots, fueled by summer crowds of almost all ages coming from the much larger Ocean City. I remembered the 1983 cult-classic movie *Eddie and the Cruisers*, which was set in 1964 and shot in Somers Point. Many rock-and-roll music scenes were filmed inside Tony Mart's, a Somers Point bar popular with the eighteen-to-twenty-eight crowd before it closed for good shortly after the filming was completed. This led me to reflect on my fraternity days at the University of Pennsylvania, where I'd graduated in 1964. While Penn had never been known as a party school, two or three nights a month, my fraternity had parties with live rock bands, including Dicky Doo & the Don'ts, whose "Click Clack" was a minor hit in the late '50s.

Frank came to the back door. "Ha! Here, let me help you carry things in. I see you brought your Mustang again."

"Yep, third year in a row down here in it. I'm in heaven!"

"I can't wait to hear more details about your trip."

"Sure, but do you have about three hours?"

"Of course—you know I'd love to hear all about it."

"Sure, let me get this stuff in, then I'll go have my Mack and Manco's pizza, then I'll grab you before I even unpack."

I wasted no time taking my luggage up the steps to the apartment. I then walked quickly to the boardwalk and to Mack and Manco's. I had my normal two slices of pizza and a Coke and watched the people on the boardwalk; it was early for lunch. After downing the slices, I hurried back to the O'Connors', where I found Frank on the porch reading a book. It was a slightly hazy day, with higher humidity than other years. Still, it was worth sitting out on the porch.

"Can I get you a Coke?"

"Not yet. I wasn't kidding about the time it will take to tell you everything. Is the coast clear?" I walked over to the edge of the porch and dramatically looked around.

"Ha! What are you doing? Are there spies?" Frank said laughingly.

I sat down with a smile on my face. "Maybe. You'll be looking, too, after I finish!"

"Come now, that's crazy…So tell me about it. You told me a lot about it in your e-mail after you got back. I want to hear more details, but I can't imagine what you're talking about looking for spies."

"Well, before I get into the crazy part, and it was crazy, let me give you some more detail about the normal part of the trip. First the food; you know the limited range I like to eat: steak and potatoes. Well, my three best meals all sixteen days were at Pizza Hut by the Sphinx, Sbarro at the Cairo airport, and MacDonald's in Luxor."

"Ha," Frank interrupted. "But give me a clue. You weren't in any trouble?"

"Ah, actually, yes. Three times."

"What? Please tell me!"

"Just wait, please." I paused. "Remember the map I showed you last year? My brother pointed out two places where it looked like the map was changed, and you pointed out three more places."

"Yes, but what…Did you find a treasure?"

"Maybe, but please, just wait. You know me," I said, "I insisted on getting to Kennedy way early, in case there were traffic problems. After we went through security, checked our bags, and ate, we went to the EgyptAir first/business class lounge."

"Okay."

"We were extremely early, getting there just after the lounge opened for our eleven thirty p.m. flight. There was no one there but the host. We sat at a table pretty far from the host, so I opened up the map for Tina Gilbert, the Penn doctoral candidate that we paid—her expenses, that is—to accompany us. I told her that we had found places where the map seems to have been changed. Remember, the map was from when my grandfather was in college, but it had been changed, we think, many years later.

"Anyway, Tina looked at the street name changes and quickly came up with two of them. She said that Moise, for Moise Avenue, could mean Moses. She said that in some languages, Moises means Moses."

"Wow. And…"

"And she said that Echna, for Echna Drive, could stand for Echnaton, which is another name for the pharaoh Akhenaten. She said that he was the first pharaoh to worship one god, the sun god Aten. She told us that he moved the capital of Egypt to a place now called Amarna. So, for some reason, maybe Clarence made a connection between Akhenaten and Moses. No, please hold on, Frank," I said, raising my palm.

"My brother, Glenn, the minister, said that he was interested in Akhenaten and suggested that we could maybe change our trip to include going to Akhenaten's ill-fated city. We ended up going there on Wednesday."

"Did anything happen there?"

"Sort of, but I'll get to it."

"You keep me hanging on." Frank laughed.

"Bear with me. So we had a nice flight, landed in Cairo, where it was very hot, as expected, and we checked into the Mena House Hotel. Frank, I could see the big pyramid from the balcony of my room; it seemed about a quarter mile away! That night, at dinner with our guide, we asked about going to Amarna. He said it was four hours away, and Glenn and I decided to pay the extra charge.

"The next day, we went to the Egyptian Museum, where I took pictures of King Tut. I'll show you and Nancy my pictures sometime this week. That day, we had lunch with archaeologist Chris Houser, who's been on TV, and we showed him my aunt's ring. It had a scarab in it that Houser said dated from possibly seven hundred BC. But I later found out that it was from around nine hundred BC! It contained the cartouche of a pharaoh named Shishak; more about Shishak later…Anyway, Dr. Houser also said that he's doing a radar/computer survey of different sites, and that my grandfather's drawing of the temple of Amenhotep I almost exactly matched the computer-generated one."

"Okay, go on."

"We left at six a.m. Wednesday for our four-hour trip to Amarna. Stupid tourists; it was six hours each way, and when we got there, it was pretty boring. We had a police escort in a pickup truck. Up front was a driver and a colonel. Riding in the back were two soldiers with a machine gun."

"What? Where were you going?"

"It turns out that we had to go through Minya, which is a hotbed of terrorist activity. On the way down, I thought that we could be a sure target on the way back, what with our well-marked tourist van and our police escort. But I took some comfort that our Egyptian driver and guide were up front. Amarna was very boring; I couldn't wait to get back to our hotel. On our way back through Minya, the streets were crowded with people, and our van hit a teenage girl."

"Was she hurt badly?"

"No, but our driver and guide both got out of our van, and our police escort, not knowing what was happening, disappeared around a bend. Then people started banging on the van windows!"

"Yikes! Were you frightened?"

"Oh yes, but there wasn't anything we could do. Finally the two Egyptians came back, saying they had handled the situation. We took off and caught up with our escort.

"But get this, once we cleared most of the city and were on open road doing about fifty, I heard a bang like a rifle shot and saw a truck coming the opposite way lose control, turn over, and come into our lane behind us. It just missed us."

"This is getting interesting."

"Yes, but I'll try to speed it up. We flew to Luxor and stayed in the marvelous old Winter Palace Hotel. I'll bet that Clarence must have stayed there. We saw the sights in the Valley of the Kings, etcetera, including touring the absolutely amazing tomb of Seti I. I have great pictures of that. But King Tut's tomb was boring.

"We stayed in Luxor four nights, where I stupidly did something that turned out more dangerous than you could ever imagine. Well, we lived through that, then got on our Nile cruise ship, where there was another life-threatening incident."

"Life threatening? Two life-threatening incidents? What in the world are you getting at?"

"Let's take a break, Frank. I need to go upstairs, and you can get another Coke. But don't get me one; I'll need to bring down a scotch to continue."

When I returned, both Frank and Nancy were out on the porch. Frank began, "I told Nance some of what you told me, and maybe you can say more when you show us your pictures. Nance, he said that his life was threatened. And twice!" He turned to me. "Is that right?"

"No, maybe three times. I can't believe it myself," I said, taking a sip of my Dewar's on the rocks. Frank frowned, like he wasn't going to believe anything I was going to say.

"Remember I mentioned earlier about the map and the Penn grad student, Tina? She's in her twenties and very pretty, and we got along really well and had a lot of fun together. Especially at the bars in the two hotels and even on the cruise. No, don't look at me that way. She just married an archaeologist assistant professor at Penn; they were engaged then. I was even invited to their wedding. I really like her and think of her more like my daughter.

"Anyway, one night at the Winter Palace in Luxor, we both had a little too much to drink. We were alone in the paneled, very British-looking bar, and we looked at the map again, at the three places you had pointed out. Without going into detail, I can tell you that we thought that the streets referenced two tombs on a hill across the Nile, where Clarence had excavated. And she said that the other dot you found could indicate where another tomb might be, in relation to the two tombs.

"In Luxor, we had dinner one night at the Chicago House. It is supported by the University of Chicago, has about fifteen archaeologists in residence in season, and has a large library. Before dinner, I discovered in one of my grandfather's books that that dot pointed to the tomb of Pharaoh Shishak I, and that the hieroglyph on my grandmother's ring matched that. Tina mentioned that Shishak is mentioned in the Bible as conquering Jerusalem and taking all of the treasures from King Solomon's temple!"

"Wait a minute, Indiana Jones," scoffed Frank. "You're saying that your grandfather might have known where the treasures of King Solomon are?"

"Well, maybe he knew where there was a tomb where he suspected that the treasure might be."

"Next you'll tell me that he knew where the Ark of the Covenant is. Ha!"

"Well, hang on…Based on a map given us by the Chicago House, we were able to spot the two tombs from my grandfather's map and figure out where Shishak's tomb may be. So after more discussion and planning over drinks in the Winter Palace Hotel, Tina and I foolishly decided to hunt for it. Yes, we went treasure hunting!"

"Unbelievable! Go on, go on!"

"We took a cab over the Nile to Dra Abu el Naga, a small village where my grandfather excavated. We walked up the hill in the darkness and found what we thought were the two tombs from the map. Holding the map up, we walked up the hill at the angle of the dot. I saw some rocks, removed them, and climbed into a slightly sloped passageway—"

"Are you kidding me? Are you nuts?"

"No and yes, Frank, but I guess I had too much bravado, or maybe too much scotch; I really thought that I was on to something. Treasure, Frank, treasure!" I took a sip of my scotch.

"Believe it or not, I crawled deeper into what I thought was a pharaoh's tomb. But it was strange, because the walls were all rough and there were no wall paintings. Even minor officials' tombs have paintings. But I continued on, around multiple turns, each leading slightly downward."

"Come on, Steve, you're kidding me! What the—"

Nancy interrupted, "Let him continue, Frank. This is exciting!"

"Yeah, but—"

"Ha. No, I'm not kidding. This really happened, and the rest that I'll tell you is not made up either.

"After I went around multiple turns, I reached a shaft. It was as wide as the path, about six feet across, and about fifteen feet deep. When I stood up and shined the light in, I could only see an opening to a chamber, but I saw one roughly scratched marking on the opposite wall. It was, it turned out, the hieroglyph of Shishak I, matching my ring. But then, I got on my belly, inched out so that I could bend, and reached down with my flashlight—"

"Did you see anything?"

"Only gold!"

"What?"

"I saw the end of one object, totally gold. The bottom part was a chest, and on top was the bottom of some sort of figure. I later found out the figure could have been a cherubim."

"The Ark of the Covenant!" said Nancy.

"Could very well be. There have been many depictions of the ark, including some like in *Indiana Jones*. Several almost looked like the end of what I saw. However, I was so excited, I dropped my flashlight. I can tell you that there were no lightning bolts coming out of whatever it was. Believe me, it was very claustrophobic coming back out."

"Wow!" said Frank.

"Yes, but now the fun begins. When I crawled back out, the police were there. They said we were trespassing. But they weren't the police— probably terrorists. They marched us down to an abandoned building."

"What the—"

"Once inside, they threatened us, punched me in the stomach, hit me with the butt of their Kalashnikov, and then threatened that they would begin touching Tina, and worse, if I didn't tell them about the covenant."

"Were you hurt?" asked Nancy.

"Yes. I've never been punched like that, and I almost threw up. And the Kalashnikov blow to my arm left me unable to move it for a while. But I was more scared to death than hurt. I was also angry. Also, they started molesting Tina, with a threatening routine they've probably used before. She gave them, and I don't blame her, the map from the Chicago House that showed the location of the tombs. But then they almost undressed Tina and made her bend over. The guy spat in my face and demanded I tell him about the covenant."

"What covenant?" asked Frank.

"They called it the Carswell Covenant, whatever that is. They claimed that Pharaoh gave Moses only a one-hundred-year covenant to the Holy Land."

"That's absurd."

"Well, maybe not. I forgot to tell you that we had dinner in Cairo with a professor at the American University who, coincidentally, was an aunt of a neighbor of ours. One of the things she said was that there were rumors, she didn't know from where, among Egyptians to that effect. Also, just this spring, I've found out that Carswell Bible College, which my great-great-grandfather founded in Georgia, is among the leaders in Dead Sea Scrolls research. My grandmother's maiden name was Carswell!"

"Well, I still think that's crazy. So were you hurt badly?" said Frank.

"It hurt at the time, and I had bruises, but I didn't need to see a doctor. But it was hard to tell them what they wanted to hear when I knew nothing. I quickly mentioned what the professor said about the rumor. I had Tina give them the map and told them again that I thought there might be treasure. After they molested Tina but didn't rape her, they finally seemed to believe that we knew nothing about the Carswell Covenant."

"Obviously they let you go."

"Not quite."

"Huh!"

"They had us sit in the corner of a shack and started to leave. We relaxed some. But then they tossed in a Molotov cocktail, blocking our only exit."

"Oh my God!" said Nancy.

"I was able to use what I learned as a volunteer firefighter, and we made it up some rickety stairs to the second floor, where we jumped out a window."

"Totally unbelievable," said Frank. "Did you go to the police?"

"No. We made it back the next morning to the cruise ship barely in time for its departure."

"Is that all that happened? All...Why did I say 'all'?"

"That's all that happened about our search for treasure at Dra Abu." I laughed. "But wait, there's more!"

"What did you do about the treasure, the Ark of the Covenant?" said Frank.

"We decided not to tell anyone until Tina got back to Penn and we could make a presentation to the head of the museum. All this time—almost ten months—and they still haven't been able to get a concession, which is really difficult. And Penn really can't say what the find is and how they found out about it. Tina and I were trespassing. I hope they get the concession soon, and I just hope that they have Tina lead it!"

"Good God, Steve. You said there's more?" asked Nancy.

"Yes. We set out on our cruise, hoping that all would go well for the rest of the trip, since we were satisfied that they were terrorists—yes, terrorists—not police.

"So here comes the next part. It turns out that the cruise was very strict about the seating arrangements at meals. We were seated with a somewhat pushy man named Bob Ebel, from Chicago. He was traveling alone and seemed very interested in our trip. The three of us sort of hung with him on our cruise to Aswan. I didn't mention any details about the map or the ark, but I did mention the incident at Dra Abu. Sounds like a movie title, doesn't it? *Incident at Dra Abu!*

"Anyway, get this! The last night on board, as we docked by the side of three other boats at Aswan, there was a galabia party. As others did, I rented a galabia, which is the long, traditional Arab covering. Tina and I sat there drinking and talking long after all the people left the party; it was our last night. At one point, she left, and I drunkenly got up and walked over to the river side of the ship and looked out at the black, very polluted Nile. When we first arrived in Egypt, we had been warned to stay away from it because the water was loaded with bacteria from animal and human waste."

"Yuck," said Nancy.

"As I stood there, Bob Ebel walked up behind me, and I felt something poking into my back." I saw the looks on the faces of Nancy and Frank. "Yes, no kidding, it was a gun!"

"Oh my God," said Frank.

"I turned around to talk with him, and he started asking questions about Moses actually being the pharaoh Akhenaten. Once again, I was being threatened by someone over something I knew nothing about. I told him I didn't know anything, and he then aimed the gun at my knee. He told me that they had information that in 1940 my grandfather, while drunk, bragged that he had a document that said Moses was actually Pharaoh Akhenaten. They somehow knew that he was my grandfather and that I was coming to Egypt. He didn't punch me or hurt me, but he kept threatening me with the gun. I kept pleading with him, but he started to get really serious, really threatening and pushing. I asked if he was Mossad, but he didn't answer. Desperate, the only thought I had was the old TV cowboy movie trick. I looked over his shoulder and yelled, 'Glenn, get help!' He turned, and I dove over the side, expecting to be shot at any time. I guess I startled him when I dove, so he took a shot and missed just as I entered the water. At that point, I wasn't taking any chances. I held my breath as long as I could, swimming underwater breaststroke as far out into the Nile as I could, thinking he would expect me to swim to shore. I took a quick breath and swam away underwater some more. Finally, I made it back to shore and was able to get back to the boat the next morning. And I never saw that Bob Ebel again."

Frank was stunned. "I'm speechless; I don't know what to say. I keep expecting you to say that you're kidding, but I know you're not. I feel like I'm talking to Indiana Jones!"

"Yeah, some Indiana Jones I am! Old, fat, stupid..."

"My God, are you okay? Are you depressed or anything, unable to sleep?"

"Well, Frank, I've had my nights, and there are times when I get a little paranoid, but I was kidding when I looked around here before talking to you."

Frank said, "But let me see if I can understand all this. First, you were kidnapped by terrorists who thought that you had proof that Moses was—"

"No, no!" I interrupted. "I know it's confusing. The terrorists were after us because they thought I somehow had proof that there was a one-hundred-year lease."

"Okay. So you were kidnapped by terrorists about the lease?"

"Yes, but after all that happened, I also think that maybe the sound, maybe a rifle, that we heard as we came back from Amarna, was aimed at us by terrorists. But I'm not sure about that."

"Okay, so please hear me out. So then a guy from the Mossad—"

"We think that, but maybe he wasn't from the Mossad," I interrupted.

"But he pulled a gun on you because he thought you had proof that Moses was actually the pharaoh...What was his name?"

"Akhenaten."

"Whatever. Okay, Pharaoh Aka-something only gave a one-hundred-year covenant to Moses for the Holy Land?"

"No. This Bob Ebel guy was after me because he thought I had proof that Moses was actually Pharaoh Akhenaten. The terrorists were after me because they thought I had proof that Moses was given a one-hundred-year lease. Two different things."

"Steve, this is unbelievable," said Nancy.

"Of course it is! But I'd sure like to know why my life was in jeopardy on our trip. I firmly believe, but I can't prove, that my grandfather and Howard Carter got into Tut's tomb before Lord Carnarvon arrived. But that's all. I really know nothing more than that. And as for the one-hundred-year covenant, it sounds absolutely ridiculous."

"Agreed," said Nancy and Frank simultaneously.

I paused for a minute, but signaled that I had more to say.

"Okay, okay. Are you ready for this? I've only told my brother about this. There's one more thing."

"Oh no," said Nancy. "How can there be? You've had an adventure of a lifetime. What all does this mean? Who came after you?"

"Obviously, Tina, my brother, and I have talked quite a bit about this, on the trip home and at other times. We decided to not go to the police after the water incident in Luxor. The only thing I can think of is that two different groups were after us. I think, but I have no proof, that Bob Ebel was Mossad. When he held the gun on me, he told me that they have information that in 1940 my grandfather, while drunk, bragged that he had a document that said Moses was actually Pharaoh Akhenaten. They somehow knew that he was my grandfather and that I was coming to Egypt."

"But wait, Steve, I don't think that there was a Mossad in 1940," said Frank.

"You're right, but I've since discovered that there was a strong Zionist underground called Lehi even before 1940, and maybe they kept good records. And, some of those that served in that underground in World War II later became members of Mossad when it was formed."

"Maybe. But seriously, I can just imagine what would happen if this were true. It would be a worldwide disaster!"

"I agree completely, Frank. But here's the other part. If there was a one-hundred-year lease, or covenant, then it also would have serious complications in today's world. And it seems that the only way the Mossad could know I was coming and had a map was either the host in the EgyptAir lounge or maybe a bug. I could see that the terrorists could have found out about us from our guide or driver. But a member of the Mossad as the host in the EgyptAir lounge? This whole trip was crazy."

"Boy, my lips are sealed. I could see why this can be very dangerous. I almost wish that you hadn't told us."

"But, Frank, you know I had to go to Egypt; you're the one that pointed out, two years ago, that one sentence in a novel that mentioned my grandfather." I paused. "Let me end by telling you the other thing that I've only told my brother about. About two big coincidences at Linda's fortieth high school reunion."

"At Upper NetherCrest High? That always sounds like you made up that name. Sorry, go on," said Frank.

"I met up with a girl at the reunion who was in Linda's class. I've known her since grade school and from church, but she's never come to a reunion. She married a guy named Mark Hamilton, who is a Baptist minister, a former Georgia state senator, and who is now the president of Carswell Bible College in Georgia. And, get this, Carswell College was founded by my great-grandfather, Clarence's father-in-law! And it's big, I found out, in doing research into the Dead Sea Scrolls."

"Hard to believe, but go on."

"Sure, sure. I'll tell you more this week, but just quick. At the reunion, Mark Hamilton and I somehow got into a discussion about my trip, and I mentioned that some things happened on our trip based on many mysteries surrounding my grandfather. I elaborated a little, but Mark quickly took me aside and said, 'Suppose, just suppose, that Pharaoh gave Moses a one-hundred-year lease to the Holy Land. Just suppose. Just suppose.' Before I could respond, a classmate interrupted us."

"But what does that mean?"

"Well, as I mentioned, Mark's the president of Carswell College, which is big in research into the Dead Sea Scrolls. When we were in Egypt, one of the archaeologists said that there was a rumor among her Egyptian students that Moses was given a one-hundred-year lease to the Holy Land. The students called it the Carswell Covenant."

"So, with all you've been through on your trip," said Frank, "you're now saying that Moses, or Aka-whoever, was given only a one-hundred-year lease. If this became general knowledge, it would change the world, even cause a third world war. And along the way, you just happened to find the Ark of the Covenant and maybe King Solomon's treasures!"

Frank paused as I nodded my head in agreement.

"Steve…you are Indiana Jones!"

CHAPTER 42

Saturday, September 6, 2003
Ocean City, New Jersey

I was up early on Saturday morning. For the first time in many weeks spent at Ocean City over many years, it was raining. Since I was leaving that morning, I didn't care about the rain.

I finished most of my packing and tidied up the apartment. I walked down the outdoor steps and around to the street. Since Labor Day was four days in the past, I was able to park on the street each night. I then headed out to the Fourth Street Wawa to get twenty ounces of take-out coffee. For the first time in over a week, I picked up a copy of the *Philadelphia Inquirer*. I then parked on Asbury Avenue, directly in front of Ward's Bakery. I bought two boxes of their delicious butter cake to take home.

Back at the O'Connors', I took two slices of the cake, which seemed to be made of just sugar, icing, and butter. I began eating my cake and reading the paper. After turning to page three, I jumped up, grabbed the front section of the paper, and ran down the steps to the O'Connors' apartment below. Fortunately, Frank and Nancy were in their kitchen eating breakfast.

"Can I come in?"

"Sure, come on in," said Frank. "How are you?"

"Okay. Hi, Nancy. Frank, you've got to read this," I said hurriedly. "Oh my God, oh my God!" I handed the paper to Frank.

GA COLLEGE PRESIDENT DEAD
HOMICIDE SUSPECTED
HAS LOCAL TIES

Augusta, GA: Carswell Bible College president and former Jefferson County state senator Mark Rudrauff Hamilton died Thursday, September 4, 2003, at University Hospital, Augusta, at age 60. According to Wrens Police Chief Clarence R. Jordan, Hamilton became sick in the hot tub at the North Jefferson Family Y on Highway 17 in Wrens on Wednesday, September 3.

Said Chief Jordan, "We are treating this as a possible homicide. We have interviewed several colleagues at Carswell who were with Mr. Hamilton just hours before the incident. They all said that he was in excellent shape and in his normal good humor. Additionally, we have interviewed one of his IT staff employees, Lonnie Jenkins, who also said he was in excellent condition. Mr. Jenkins said that he arrived at the gym shortly before Senator Hamilton arrived, at his normal time, around 18:00 hours. Senator Hamilton had stopped at a bakery on his way, as he often did. As they had many times, after their workout they entered the hot tub. But after only about 30 seconds, Mr. Jenkins stated, Senator Hamilton quickly exited the tub and vomited. Apparently, the Senator was breathing normally, but felt very hot to the touch. The Senator suggested to Mr. Jenkins that maybe his condition was due to a bagel he had eaten. Senator Hamilton apparently complained that the bagel tasted acrid, like radishes, and burned his tongue like spices.

"Again according to Mr. Jenkins, the Senator insisted on dressing himself, but agreed to let Mr. Jenkins take him to the Wrens Medical Center. There, his temperature was a high 104 degrees. They gave him medicine for the fever—I don't know what they gave him—and released him to his wife, Brenda, telling her to apply cold compresses.

"At 02:04 on Thursday morning, Mrs. Hamilton called 911, stating that his temperature had risen to 106 and that he had two convulsions. He was transported to University Hospital, arriving at 03:11. There, he was given additional medicines and infusions, and was placed in an ice bath."

"My understanding is that he did not improve, and he passed away at approximately 16:00 that same day.

"We are leaving open the possibility that this is a homicide due to his unusually excellent condition; I understand that he had a complete physical just last week. Of course, we are awaiting the full results from the medical examiner and a toxicology screen.

"I can also announce that we have detained a person of interest for questioning. She is Anna Hamed, a college student with family ties to a known Egyptian terrorist leader, Achmed Hamed. She has denied any involvement.

"My understanding is that Mark Hamilton has made a very positive impact at Carswell College and was well liked by both faculty and students. Professor Julia Carswell told me that Senator Hamilton had recently been working on a monograph entitled 'Kings: A new look at an ancient Dead Sea Scrolls papyrus.'"

"I'd like to make a personal statement, if I may. I consider Mark Hamilton a friend; he was a very gentle, caring man. I met with him multiple times, at Carswell and elsewhere, and my wife and I have had dinner multiple times with him and his gracious wife, Brenda. My heart goes out to Brenda, their grown children, Robert, David, and Andrew, and their three grandchildren. May God be with them. Thank you."

Brenda Brown Hamilton was born in Media and is a graduate of Upper NetherCrest High School and Bryn Mawr College.

EPILOGUE

October 2, 2013
Ferrell's Travel Blog, WordPress.com

Vandalism in Protestant Cemetery on Mount Zion

At some point on Sunday, not sure exactly when, vandals said to be associated with a Price Tag group entered the cemetery (not hard to do from the back/side) and smashed multiple tombstones which were bearing crosses. They also damaged at least one tombstone with Arabic writing. I checked all the graves which you have written about on the blog (at least what I could find on the blog). The only grave with damage seemed to be Clarence Fisher. After talking with Dr. Wright, he says this tombstone was actually damaged in a similar attack about six months ago (photo attached). The stone has been set back somewhat upright on the grave.

https://ferrelljenkins.wordpress.com/2013/10/03/vandalism-in-protestant-cemetery-on-mount-zion/

AUTHOR'S NOTE

I firmly believe, but can't prove, that my grandfather and Howard Carter entered Tut's tomb eighteen days before Lord Carnarvon arrived. But that's all. I know nothing more than that. I know nothing about Moses being Akhenaten or about any one-hundred-year covenant. These two plot lines are based solely on my imagination.

But much of this is true. For example: my brother, Glenn; his wife, Sunny; and I, along with a researcher, Barbara Keller, took a sixteen-day trip to Egypt in the footsteps of my grandfather in 2002. We did indeed meet with a number of archaeologists, thanks to Zahi Hawass, but I've changed their names and added some things that they did not say. The incidents along the road returning from Amarna—hitting the young girl, people pounding on our van, and a sound like a backfire or blowout and a truck overturning and sliding into our lane behind us—actually occurred.

We saw the sites as described, went on the cruise, stayed at the two hotels mentioned, ate at the Chicago House with "Edwin Harer," and visited the sites described. We did not go up the hill at Dra Abu.

Much of what I've written about my grandfather is true. He did make two entries in his journal describing Lord Carnarvon's invitation and his tour of Tut's tomb. He did discover two jars at Dra Abu el Naga. Caroline Dosker's father told her that Clarence told Carter where to dig for Tut's tomb. Clarence did not find a papyrus in Tut's tomb, nor does the hieroglyph on my grandmother's scarab ring match Shishak's, but Fisher was selected to inspect the Dome of the Rock. Whether he actually did that is unknown. During World War I, many archaeologists were spies. Fisher drove an ambulance, and when he died in 1921, his coffin was covered by a British, not American, flag. Why, I do not know. But I have no proof that he was a spy. According to my grandmother and father, he was "the second person into Tut's tomb." My grandmother told me that he did have a gunfight at some point; whether he shot anyone is unknown.

Most of the other background information on Dr. Clarence S. Fisher is true, although I have no proof that he was poisoned. His death certificate reads, "Generalized oedema, purpura haemorrhagica." My research has indicated that both of these can be symptoms of cyanide poisoning, but it would be hard to expect that doctors in Jerusalem in 1941 would have suspected poisoning. The circumstances of the events leading up to his death after being in the baths at Al-Hamma are from the condolence letter his friend Shaker Ahmad Suleiman sent to my grandmother.

My grandmother taught and was the principal, as I discovered in my research, at the Carswell School for Stutterers and Stammerers in Philadelphia, and her father, E. R. Carswell, founded it. Other than knowing that she traveled to Jerusalem in 1928, I have no idea what she and Clarence discussed there. But I'll bet that what I've written is close to it.

Egenardus Ruthven Carswell, her father, was indeed an interesting person. He was a minister and a traveling evangelist, he founded a school for stammerers and stutters (that's how my grandmother met my grandfather), and he indeed invented the first fitted mattress sheet. (Google E. R. Carswell, and you can find a number of fitted sheet patents that include him as the first.)

I have a 570-page Carswell genealogy book going back to AD 1100; you can visit Huntingtower Castle outside of Perth, Scotland, where my ancestor, Lord Ruthven, held King James hostage in 1582. The ancestry data for Glenn and me is from that book.

My grandmother's grandfather, the first E. R. Carswell, founded Carswell Institute in 1876 at Antreville, South Carolina. However, it was more a church or church school. It eventually became a public school.

I did a lot of research for this book, including reading many books about Akhenaten, Tutankhamun, and the Dead Sea Scrolls. Most scholars will dismiss my theories, but others may believe that they could be plausible.

One final note: Since the modern timeframe (1998–2003) of this novel, DNA testing has proved that Akhenaten, the mummy in grave KV55, was indeed the father of Tut. Check that: the testing has shown that the mummy in grave KV55 is definitely Tut's father. The reverse logic has been that the mummy in KV55 must therefore be Akhenaten. But direct evidence has not been found that Amenhotep III, the father of Akhenaten, is the father of the mummy in KV55. Hmmm.

Acknowledgments

My first thanks go to Jennifer Houser Wegner, whose passion for all things ancient Egypt inspired me greatly. My grandfather would have been fascinated by you and your husband. Please note that Jen has in no way contributed to this novel; she would, famed archaeologist that she is, probably find it all silly.

Thanks also to Penn graduate Barbara Keller. Doing research on Clarence Fisher, she solved the real mystery of the "second" Clarence Fisher. She was the real "Tina" who accompanied us on our trip. We would not have gone to Egypt without her.

I thank both Google and *Wikipedia* for their assistance, but many of my descriptions were from photographs taken by my sister-in-law, Sunny Fisher, and me. Thanks, too, to Sarah, my editor at CreateSpace.com. Her attention to detail really helped.

I also thank Sunny for the marvelous album she assembled; it helped me reconstruct our trip. And I thank my brother, Reverend Doctor Glenn J. Fisher, who, though six years older, was my biggest coach and supporter throughout my life. His suggestions for this book, as well as his biblical knowledge, have been invaluable. My daughter, Cindy, assisted by proofreading and making many valuable suggestions.

My thanks, also, to the McKeaneys; they started me on this amazing journey.

My thanks to the following who reviewed this book in its early stages and made excellent suggestions: Frank McKeaney; Kim Campbell; John

Mott; Barry Joseph; Diane Campbell; John Gimbel; Glenn Fisher; my wife, Linda Fisher; and my daughter, Cindy Christine.

Thanks also to the following archaeologists and Egyptologists whom we did meet on our trip: Zahi Hawass, George Scanlon, Kent Weeks, Ray Johnson, and Lonnie Bell. Thanks for the knowledge you imparted!

Thanks also to Penn Museum senior archivist Alessandro Pezzati, who provided much archival information about my grandfather. He also accompanied Barbara Keller and me when we interviewed Caroline Dosker, who said, "My daddy often told me that your grandfather told Howard Carter where to dig for Tut's tomb."

Finally, my thanks to my wife, Linda, for putting up with me throughout this long project.

All mistakes, even though this is fiction, are my own.

Steven R. Fisher, June 2016
www.eightpointfive.net
carswellcovenant@gmail.com

About the Author

Steve Fisher is a retired IT professional who received a degree in electrical engineering from the University of Pennsylvania in 1964. He is also a former diving champion who once held state and national swimming records for his age group.

Steve traveled to Egypt in 2002. Although he traveled to the country as a tourist, he hoped to discover more about his grandfather and the mysteries surrounding his life and death. Learn more about Fisher's trip, his grandfather, and the exciting facts behind The Carswell Covenant on his website, EightPointFive.net.

Fisher lives in a Philadelphia suburb with his wife, Linda. The couple has two children and four grandchildren.

Made in the USA
Middletown, DE
21 March 2023

27295056R00170